DIRTY
FRACKING
BUSINESS

Peter Ralph

M
MELBOURNE BOOKS

Published by Melbourne Books
Level 9, 100 Collins Street,
Melbourne, VIC, 3000
Australia

www.melbournebooks.com.au
info@melbournebooks.com.au

National Library of Australia Cataloguing-in-Publication entry:
AUTHOR: Ralph, Peter.
TITLE: Dirty Fracking Business
ISBN: 9781877096228 (pbk.)
DEWEY NUMBER: A823.4

Cover illustration: Ning Xue.

Foreword

Most of us would like to think that Australia's mines are situated in the deserts, on barren mountains or on infertile, useless land.

Fifteen months ago I read a paper by Dalby Lawyer, Peter Shannon, which basically said that Queensland landowners were virtually without rights if a coal seam gas miner, armed with an exploration licence, wanted to sink wells on their properties. I had to pinch myself when I read that farmers and graziers who had put years into developing their properties could be forced to let coal seam gas miners access their properties. It was then that I discovered that the landowners only owned the 'above the surface' part of their properties and that the crown, in Australia's case the State, owned what was below the surface and this is what enabled exploration licences to be issued. I was staggered by the inequity of this and thought and still think that it's 'un-Australian'.

I then started communicating with Debra Anderson, the producer/director of the superb US documentary, the aptly titled *Split Estate*. Debra gave freely of her time and I bought her DVD so that I could learn more about land rights, which I did, but I learnt far more about the horrors of coal seam gas. Around this time, *Gasland* was released at the Nova Cinema in Melbourne, and I was the total audience at the first showing. This documentary is a graphic portrayal of the damage that coal seam gas miners have wreaked in the USA. To further my knowledge I read Tara Meixsell's detailed exposé, *Collateral Damage,* which added to and reinforced what I had learnt from *Split Estate* and *Gasland*.

I had visited the beautiful Hunter Valley in NSW many times and was shocked to find that coal seam gas mining was taking place there. After spending a little time on the Net I was lucky enough to find the CEO of

The Hunter Valley Protection Alliance, John Thomson, who has been an enormous help to me. I suggested to John that I visit him but he said, before doing so, I should go to the Darling Downs and meet Drew Hutton of *Lock the Gate* and Dayne Prazky, aka *the Frackman*.

As it turned out, I met John and Drew at a meeting of the Greens in Sydney to protest the granting of exploration licences in St Peters and the eastern suburbs of Sydney. I later travelled around the Darling Downs, in Queensland, with Drew, whose assistance was invaluable, looking at gas wells and meeting farmers. I interviewed Dayne Prazky at length and was amazed by some of his revelations. I then visited the Hunter Valley and saw the onset of the gas wells and spoke to a number of locals, including shopkeepers, who were unanimously opposed to coal seam gas.

This story is fictional and many of the events have not taken place in Australia, but similar events *have* occurred in the USA.

Land rights and the unfair treatment of landowners remains a huge issue in Australia, while the mining of coal seam gas puts at risk our air, water and food security. This issue transcends politics, and Greens, farmers and graziers, and those to the right, like Alan Jones, find themselves unlikely allies in the fight against coal seam gas.

Peter Ralph
Melbourne
January, 2012

Chapter 1

It was a rainy, dark Friday. The solemn ringing of church bells echoed around the near-deserted streets of the small New South Wales country town of Paisley. Many of the townsfolk braved the bleak conditions to attend the funeral of Charles Willis Paxton Junior, who had succumbed to cancer before his seventh birthday. Those who could not be there stayed at home as a mark of respect.

Four pallbearers carried the tiny white coffin down the steps as white-haired Father Michael O'Rourke, stood ram-rod straight, consoling mourners as they left St Stephen's Church. At the bottom of the steps, the organist, a plump, pleasant woman, was passing out long-stemmed red roses. A large, ruddy-faced man, eyes red with tears, hunched over in the manner of one far older, lurched from the chapel, supported by a petite, auburn-haired woman wearing a black hat and veil. Her mouth was drawn in a thin line as she fought to hold her composure. Father Michael took the man's arm. 'Charles, his suffering is over and he's with God in heav...'

Charles Paxton momentarily straightened up and shoved the priest's arm away with a huge, calloused hand. 'Don't talk to me about God, Father. If there were a God he would've never made poor little Charlie suffer in the way he did.' Tears streamed down his anger-contorted face.

'Now, now, Darling.' Faye Paxton sniffled, squeezing her husband's arm. 'Father Michael is only trying to help. It's not his fault.'

'We all know whose fault it is and they're going to pay in blood,' he snarled, pulling away from her and stumbling down the slippery steps.

'I know the pain you're feeling, Faye, but God can help ease your burden. Please don't forsake the church.'

'I won't, Father.' She sobbed and hurried down the steps to catch up with her husband.

Paisley cemetery was at the southern end of town, perched on a grassy hill and surrounded by a small white picket fence. There were about two hundred graves and fresh flowers adorned many tombstones. Charlie would be buried in a plot next to his paternal grandparents and his dad's brother, Uncle Joe, who had been killed in a tractor accident two years earlier. Charles Paxton had cursed God then, as he did again now and, being deeply religious, he wondered whether his cursing may have been responsible for Charlie's death. He didn't dwell on this thought for long – he knew who the guilty parties were.

Charles Paxton was the owner of a medium-sized dairy farm, where the family lived, and the largest privately owned vineyard and winery in the valley, which together employed many of the townsfolk. A third generation owner, he had worked tirelessly to improve the properties but, still childless as he approached his forties, he had despaired of ever having the son he so desperately wanted. He started to ponder the meaning of life and the sacrifices he was making and wondered what the point was if he had no-one to leave his legacy to. And then, after years of IVF, the terrible discomfort for Faye, the inconvenience, the travel and cost, she fell pregnant. Suddenly everything they had endured was made worthwhile. When a healthy little Charlie came into the world in the early hours of a perfect spring morning, all Charles's prayers were answered. He was overjoyed.

Charlie had flaming red hair, freckles, the lightest of light blue eyes and a perpetual smile. He was a curious young kid who had to have his nose in everything. His father bought him a black German Shepherd pup, Cosmos, just after his second birthday and the two became inseparable, exploring the wonders of the family farm. By the time he was three he could swim and float well enough to save himself, and he could ride a horse, milk a cow and shout instructions at the Border Collies which kept the herds in check. He would follow his father around the farm, wearing cut-down overalls and oversized gumboots. Sometimes, when in a mischievous mood, he would chase the hens around the pen and the family would go without eggs for a few days. Unlike most toddlers, Charlie had never wanted or needed an afternoon sleep and he and Cosmos were on the run from dawn to dusk. Shortly after he turned four, this changed and he started taking afternoon naps. Charles and Faye thought this natural and paid little heed to it. As the year progressed, however, Charlie became more listless, his throat became sore, his nose ran incessantly and red welts appeared on his chest and back.

When their son's symptoms showed no sign of improvement, they took him to the local doctor, George Bingham, expecting him to prescribe a tonic that would soon fix Charlie. They were surprised when the doctor was circumspect about what was ailing Charlie and became more concerned when he took blood samples and sent them to Sydney for analysis. Ten days later they received a phone call from Dr George asking them to come to his surgery, instantly knowing by his tone that the news wasn't going to be good. What they had never anticipated was cancer and, when they plied the doctor with questions, he gently explained that he wasn't qualified to answer them. He had, however, made urgent appointments for them with specialists and oncologists. For the next two weeks they trudged around Sydney, where Charlie was prodded and poked, had more blood tests, x-rays and numerous scans. When the tests were over the specialists delivered their dreadful verdict – Charlie had aggressive tumours attacking his kidneys and liver which had progressed to the extent that treatment was pointless. Charles, while shocked, was dismissive of the specialists' advice; Faye clung to hope, the strength of her husband and her prayers.

Charles and Faye took Charlie to the best specialists in New York and, when that met without success, took him to Harley Street and, after that failed, to the quacks in Thailand and India. By the time they returned to Australia, Charlie's condition had severely deteriorated and the cancer, radiotherapy, chemo, drugs and other concoctions had all but destroyed his immune system. Desperate, his father turned to the internet and the secret elixirs and powders that fast-buck merchants flogged as hope to those facing death. Charlie's final months were a living hell, as he was forced to eat and drink potions extracted from frogs, powders made from diluted snake venom and other vile remedies concocted by heartless quacks. As the cancer devastated the last of his bodily functions he could not eat anything solid and the weight fell from his frail body. His eyes were sunken and his ribs protruded from his tiny body; this tore at the heartstrings of his doting parents. Finally there was no choice but to admit him to Paisley Memorial

Hospital where, with tubes poking into every part of his body and with the aid of morphine and other drugs, his life was unnecessarily prolonged. Faye tenderly cleansed his transparent skin and weeping red welts. 'I … I … I'm going to die aren't I Mum?' he rasped, his throat red raw.

Faye looked at her husband, unable to answer. 'No,' Charles lied, fighting back the tears. They were the last words they would hear little Charlie utter. Still praying for a miracle, Charles insisted that a bed be made up next to his son's and he didn't leave his side during the final sixteen gut-wrenching days. When Faye wasn't at the hospital she was at St Stephens praying with Father Michael.

The rain went from drizzly to pouring during the burial. The hundred or so black umbrellas that went up around Charlie's grave reminded his father of an evil shroud, as blind hate replaced the feelings of loss and sorrow that had devastated him for the past three days. Father Michael sensed the anger emanating from the mourners and knew better than to draw the burial out with extended prayers. After a few kind and carefully considered words, he nodded to the undertaker and the coffin was lowered into the grave. After the internment the rain stopped and weak rays of sunlight fought their way through the clouds. The smell of incense hung in the air as mourners filed past the grave, dropping their roses on top of the casket.

Tom Morgan was a small self-made man who had made a fortune out of retailing, before buying a run-down stud on two hundred and fifty acres of prime land some thirty kilometres from Paisley, and restoring it to its former glory. He restocked it with some of the finest stallions from the northern hemisphere and now owned the largest stable of thoroughbreds in Australasia. Paxton had raced many horses, the best being the brilliant Cox Plate-winning mare, Gentle Lady, who was in foal to the mighty stallion, Achilles, at Morgan's stud. The two friends agreed to race and own her progeny in partnership. Morgan was a hard man and some said that he was stingy and still had the first dollar that he'd made, but this was unfair as he generously supported many worthy charities. However, he always demanded complete anonymity – anxious not to be seen as a soft touch.

Charles and Faye Paxton were thanking and farewelling mourners as Morgan approached. His rapidly receding fair hair was soaked and water ran down his craggy face. 'A black day my friends and I cannot adequately express my sorrow, but if there is anything I can do you need only ask.' He placed one hand on Faye's arm while with the other he reached up and grasped Charles' shoulder.

'They killed him Tom, as sure as if they'd shot him, and I'm going to make sure the bastards pay.'

'I know they did Charles, but you're not going to help anyone by taking the law into your own hands. We can bring these heartless mongrels down but we won't do it by being violent. God, I know how you feel.'

'You're a good man and a good friend Tom, but don't tell me you know how I feel. You haven't just lost your only son – you haven't just lost your best mate – you haven't just lost the most fantastic little boy who was ever born.' Paxton closed his eyes and ran his hands up his weather-beaten face past his bushy eyebrows and through his wet, dark brown hair.

'I'm sorry Charles. What I said was inappropriate. Take care Faye and remember, if there's anything I can do ...' Morgan sheepishly took his leave.

A tall, skinny, dark-haired, young man had been standing just behind the Paxtons and had heard every word of their exchange with Tom Morgan. Steve Forrest was a reporter with the *Paisley Chronicle*, the only reporter; he was also the editor, accountant, distribution manager and the son of the retired owner. After completing a commerce degree he had joined one of the four big accounting firms but, after three years, the only high point was being sent to Harvard to undertake an advanced management course. Suffering from acute boredom, he returned home to spend a few days with his mates only to find that the family's newspaper business was in diabolical trouble and that his elderly parents had mortgaged everything they owned to save it. The *Chronicle* was a Monday to Friday tabloid and, if the obituaries, engagements, marriages and a few paid advertisements were removed, it amounted to about four pages of gossip, recipes and the fortunes of the Paisley Football Club. Circulation had fallen to less than a thousand copies per week and advertising revenue and subscriptions no longer covered costs. Steve, with little objection from his father, Len, took control of the newspaper. He got rid of the old equipment, created a website, reformatted the layout, removed the gossip column, *Heard Around Town*, increased the coverage to the whole of the Fisher Valley and replaced the old homilies with current affairs and exciting news stories. The circulation increased tenfold. Len Forrest was well-liked and the community had wanted to support him but, as he had aged, the standard of the paper had slipped from average to abysmal and the valley had welcomed his son's return and supported a vastly improved *Chronicle*. The increased advertising revenue more than covered costs and Steve managed to pay off half of his parents' debts and, on his projections, they would again own their home within five years.

'I'm so sorry about Charlie, Mr and Mrs Paxton.' Steve awkwardly scratched his large crooked nose, the result of a football injury.

'Thank you Steven.' Faye was weeping, glad they were not holding a wake and wishing the dreadful day was over.

'Steve, you know they killed Charlie. Are you going to expose those scumbags?'

'It … it's not tha … that easy Sir but we … we're doing our research, build … building our story bu … but we have … have to be careful,' Steve responded, anxious not to upset him.

'Dammit! Didn't you hear me? They murdered my son. That's all you need to damn-well print.'

'I … I can't, Sir. Our lawyers won't let me. I'm sorry.'

'Everyone's sorry but no-one's doing anything. Well, I'm going to fix that. Write that in your rag, Steve. Tell your readers that I'm going to exterminate the blight that's destroying our beautiful valley. Tell 'em that Steve. Tell 'em!' Paxton shouted, as Faye grasped his arm.

'Let's go home, Darling.'

'We don't have a home.' He choked. 'All we have is a bloody empty house.'

Steve watched as they shuffled down the cemetery path and his heart went out to them. He didn't know if what Paxton had said was true; without scientific evidence he could not run the story. Charlie was the only young child to die in the town for years and it wasn't as if there was a cancer epidemic running through the community. Maybe little Charlie had just been plain unlucky. He waited a few minutes before following in the Paxtons' footsteps, anxious not to catch up to them and receive another rebuke.

As he reached the gate, Steve heard angry voices coming from across the street. He looked up to see Tom Morgan jabbing his finger into the chest of Andrew Brown, the local branch manager of the Federal Bank of Australia, who was strenuously trying to push him away, while furiously shaking his head. Simon Breckenridge, one of the town's more eminent lawyers, got between them and seemed to be pleading with Morgan to stop. Never one to miss a story, Steve headed straight for them but, when they looked up and saw him coming, they broke apart, taking off in different directions. Glancing behind him he saw Dr George stooped over and dragging his feet along the path. He was prematurely grey, with deep creases in his forehead and sunken jowls that belied his thirty-three years.

'It's a terrible day, George.'

The doctor had been deep in thought and looked up in surprise. His face was kind and gentle but his eyes were red and there were still tears on his cheeks. 'That it is, Steven.'

'I'm sorry; it must have been terrible for you. Charles is certain it was the poisons being pumped into the ground that killed Charlie.' Steve paused to let his words sink in. 'I guess you'd know better than anyone whether that's true or not.'

'Steven,' Dr George said, giving the younger man a wan smile, 'when have you ever known me to gossip or to disclose any information about my patients?'

'I … I di … didn't think …'

'You didn't think it applied after a patient had passed away? Well it does. You're going to have to wait for the coroner to deliver his findings. And, Steven, today is not the day to be hunting up a story.'

'Sorry George. I didn't mean to overstep the mark. Don't forget we've got the final of the indoor cricket on Tuesday night.' Steve was anxious to change the subject.

'I'll be there.' The doctor looked down at his watch. 'I have to get back to the surgery.'

Charles and Faye Paxton had made the agonising decision to donate Charlie's organs, after being told that those not affected by cancer could save the lives of other little children. There was a rider, though: Paxton's insistence that a full autopsy be carried out and that the doctors give the pathologist a letter from him in which he outlined his suspicions. This was a most unusual request but the medicos were desperate to harvest Charlie's organs and saw no ethical impediments.

There were other towns in the Fisher Valley but Paisley was its unofficial capital and boasted the largest pub, a three-person police station and the only courthouse in the valley. Its population was not quite twenty thousand but it also housed the auction yards; farmers, graziers and racehorse owners came from all over Australia for the cattle and thoroughbred auctions. It was a peaceful town in the geographic centre of the valley, which was surrounded by mountains to the north, east and west and by lush rolling hills and a koala-inhabited eucalypt forest to the south. A small river with numerous tributaries wound its way down the mountains and meandered through the valley's lush pastures, paddocks and vineyards. The only blemish on this beautiful landscape was the coalfields, but they were on the outskirts of the valley and did not deter the millions of tourists looking for peace, harmony, fresh crisp country air, fine food, great restaurants and, of course, tastings of the superb local wines.

In early 2002 the NSW Government granted an exploratory mining licence to a subsidiary of a large public company, which sought to find gas on crown land at the extreme northern perimeter of the valley. The locals paid little attention when an enormous drilling rig seemed to grow day by day at the mine site and many hoped the discovery of gas would bring them new wealth. A short time later, Clean Energy & Gas Limited made an announcement to the Australian Stock Exchange that it had discovered a potentially huge reserve of coal seam gas. Life in Paisley and the Fisher Valley changed forever that day.

The tragic death of little Charlie Paxton in 2010 symbolised that change.

Chapter 2

Donny Drayton was a thirty-year-old former dreamer. After completing a business studies degree, he had joined Energy & Gas Limited as a junior management executive. EGL was the largest user of fossil fuels in Australia but, in an attempt to improve its tarnished image, it made some small investments in wind and solar power and added 'Clean' to its name. It then launched a major advertising campaign espousing its green credentials and young Donny, who was looking to save the world, decided that this was just the type of company he wanted to carve out a career with. He wasn't half as smart as he thought he was but he had outstanding qualities that CEGL shrewdly detected: everyone liked him, he was personable, gregarious and one of those rare people who instantly captured the trust of others. CEGL was quick to move him out of management and into customer relations, where he was charged with pacifying disgruntled customers, a job he handled admirably but which provided him with little satisfaction and made no contribution to saving the planet. When an opportunity arose to play a role in developing clean gas he had jumped at it and accepted an appointment as a land access consultant. This involved convincing landowners that it would be beneficial to let CEGL explore for coal seam gas on their properties.

Before commencing his new job, Donny was put through an intensive training course covering the legalities of entering landowners' properties, the obtaining of licences, the actual drilling process, the reinstatement of the property and, of course, the documentation. He was then instructed on how to present to landowners in such a way that the information he provided was nebulous and that full disclosure was only made when it benefited the company. He was told that providing too much information would unnecessarily confuse landowners, so he should aim to make his presentations as simple as possible. It was stressed that the representations he made were largely unimportant so long as the documentation, which had been prepared by a leading firm of lawyers, was properly executed by landowners. By the time Donny phoned to make an appointment to see his first grazier, he knew more about the relevant law than most lawyers.

CEGL and the other gas companies, after identifying prospective tracts of land, applied to the government for easily-obtainable exploration licences. After the exploration licences were granted, CEGL still had to negotiate with landowners, farmers, graziers and viticulturists before it could enter their properties and drill bore holes to test the gas flow. Failing this, CEGL had to make application to the Planning Minister under Section 3A of the *Planning Act,* which usually resulted in an arbitrated access agreement, but this was time-consuming and costly.

Donny's job was simple: he just had to convince landowners to sign access agreements that would allow CEGL to come onto their properties and sink exploration wells. The first step was a phone call to arrange a no-obligation chat to explain how CEGL could assist. He had parameters within which he had to work and usually offered $1500 a year rental per well but could go as high as $5000. He could sweeten this by offering to replace and rebuild roads, tracks and fences on the landowner's property. These offers were usually made with verbal undertakings that there would be minimal disruption and that, even if commercial quantities of gas were found, it would not necessarily result in the sinking of production wells.

Land access consultants were instructed to negotiate with landowners separately and the offers made to obtain access agreements were often markedly different from neighbour to neighbour. An executed access agreement was nearly always accompanied by a CEGL-prepared confidentiality agreement that precluded the landowner from discussing the terms of the agreement with any other party. Donny informed the landowners that the confidentiality agreements were to protect them.

Donny never really understood his popularity, mistakenly putting it down to what he saw as his quick-wittedness and intelligence. He wasn't handsome but his face was sensitive, delicately boned and, in a way, pleasant and he was blessed with a smile that could light up a room. But what made him so well liked was his sincerity, that he was unthreatening, hardly ever raised his voice and persuaded rather than argued.

Donny was far more successful than his colleagues and had negotiated countless access agreements on the Spurling Downs in Queensland. However, the landowners of the Fisher Valley were proving far harder to crack, having banded together to form a Protective Alliance, whose sole purpose was to make sure the gas companies did not get a toehold in the valley.

This morning, his bitch of a boss, Moira Raymond, had put a rocket under him and the other land access consultants, telling them in her charming way, 'You'd better pull your fingers out and get some access agreements signed or you'll be drawing unemployment benefits next month.' He was still pondering her threat as he got out of his car and opened the gate to old Artie Cleever's property. He was determined that Artie, whom he had been working on for months, would finally sign an access agreement today.

Donny had believed in CEGL and, even after he suspected that he was telling lies, the company assured him that they weren't harmful and were to protect landowners. He didn't know how it had occurred, but over the years the little lies had become big lies and the morals he'd once been blessed with had all but disappeared. Now, there was nothing he would not say or do to convince a landowner to sign an access agreement, but at night he was tormented and could not sleep.

CEGL scientists said that the methane extracted was colourless and odourless but Donny had been at well-heads where the leaking methane vapour was visible and sometimes the others gases released with it stank to the high heavens. He had seen more than half-a-dozen farmers collapse after breathing in the fumes around well-heads and he had heard and believed the stories of those who suffered blood noses, headaches and strange welts on their bodies. Donny always drove around well-head areas with his windows tightly wound up and hated it when he had to make follow-up calls to landowners after gas wells had been sunk on their properties.

While Moira Raymond had been mouthing off that morning, he had momentarily thought about telling her where she could stick her job but, as always, his generous salary, fully-maintained late-model car and large expense account managed to get the better of what was left of his conscience.

Chapter 3

Paxton did not utter a word on the way home from the funeral; instead he moped and schemed in silence. As he pulled the big Merc up to the front gates of the farm, a pitch-black dog came out of the shadows, whimpering like a baby. Paxton got out of the car and kicked the gates open in anger, which set Cosmos howling. 'You miss him boy, don't you?' he said, ruffling the massive dog's head. 'You know our little mate's gone, don't you?' This seemed to settle the dog but his face was sad and his eyes seemed full of tears and for a moment Paxton's anger subsided. He drove slowly up the long driveway to the house and the dog loped along next to the car, howling. Daylight was fading and the curtains had been drawn since Charlie's passing. Faye switched the hallway lights on and went out to the kitchen while Paxton went into the lounge room, grabbed a glass and a bottle of Jack Daniel's and settled himself into his favourite recliner, with Cosmos at his feet.

A few minutes later Faye came into the room. As she was about to turn the lights on, Paxton growled, 'Leave them off.' Then, 'I'm sorry love, I didn't mean to snap. I just want to sit here in the dark. Would you like something to drink?'

Faye did not drink alcohol but she envied her husband's source of escape. 'Would you like anything to eat?'

'I'm not hungry,' he said, although he had not eaten for the past three days.

'I'm going to bed then.' She hoped she'd find some solace in the Valium that Dr George had prescribed.

'Good night,' he muttered, downing a double shot of whiskey in one huge, throat-burning gulp. Two hours later he stared down at the empty bottle. He was surprised, because the alcohol had had no effect; he was clear-headed, not in the slightest tipsy and, when he stood up to go to the liquor cabinet to get another bottle of Jack's fine brew, he did not falter. Perhaps it was the coldness of his hate, his need for revenge or the plan that he had hatched. He settled back in the recliner, resting one foot on Cosmos's head. There was a grunt of approval. 'A few more drinks boy and then we'll show those mongrels a thing or two.'

It was nearly midnight when he slunk out through the front door, his hand tight around Cosmos's mouth. 'Shoosh boy,' he whispered. The cold air hit him hard and his attempt to creep silently down to the shed failed dismally when he stumbled and crashed to the ground. He glanced back at the house but fortunately no lights came on. Once inside the shed, he picked up a couple of five-gallon drums of petrol, a pair of metal cutters and a sledge hammer and stowed them in the back of the pickup truck. As always, the keys were in the ignition and he patted the passenger seat for Cosmos to join him in the cabin.

It was a moonless night and Paxton stayed on the dirt tracks, carefully working his way along the twenty kilometres or so to his target. He was decidedly woozy and rolled the window down in a forlorn attempt to clear his head. As he did so, he heard the rushing of the Blaxland River and knew they were close. He rounded a bend and there was the monstrosity less than five hundred metres from the lifeline that supplied the town's drinking water. He was inebriated and angry but even stone cold sober he could not fathom the logic that had allowed this poisonous mess of gas-producing pipes and valves to be sunk so deep into the ground and so close to the river. He pulled the truck off the track and parked behind a clump of bushes and then toiled up the hill, carrying a five-gallon drum in each hand, the sledge hammer under his arm pit and the pair of metal cutters in his back pocket.

Drawing closer, he could hear the well-head sputtering and hissing like some venomous caged reptile as methane escaped from its poorly-tightened valves. Head spinning and gasping for breath, Paxton sat down to rest and Cosmos snuggled up to him and licked his face. The light breeze coming over the well-head picked up the disgusting odour of hydrogen sulphide, better known as rotten egg gas, and carried it towards him, causing him to cough and violently dry retch. 'We're about to show 'em boy. I can't bring Charlie back but I'll make their life misery before I'm through.'

He carefully cut an opening in the galvanised mesh fence and pulled himself through and onto the pad that supported the well-head. Giving no thought to sparks or his safety, he lifted the sledge hammer above his head and with two mighty blows smashed the metering equipment and the valves. Methane surged from the broken pipes. He reached through the opening and picked up the drums of petrol, tipping one over the pipes, the well-head, and the separator. Then he tipped the other over the pad and the ground, clumsily spilling the final few drops on his arm as he backed some fifteen metres away from the enclosure.

'We're gonna have to run like the wind when I drop this,' he said, striking a match. A burst of flame removed every hair on his right forearm and then snaked across the ground as he stumbled drunkenly down the hill. He reached the pickup and looked back to see the petrol doing no more than burning superficially. He kicked a tyre and hung his head in disappointment. As he did, the ground shook and flames shot fifty metres into the air. Cosmos, who had stopped to sniff some grass, bounded down the hill and leaped into the back of the pickup without breaking stride. 'Yeah, that'll teach you bastards!' Paxton yelled, as he revved the pickup into action and drove slowly down the hill without lights, not increasing speed until he reached the gravel road. Glancing in the rear-vision mirror he caught sight of tail-lights but, when he looked a split second later, there was nothing. Maybe it was the whiskey?

Paisley shook, the streets lit up and the locals raced out of their houses and stared, fascinated by the vivid red glow in the sky. Then the smaller after-explosions started and more flames erupted into the sky. Senior Constable Josh Gibson, a ten-year police veteran, phoned his offsider, Constable Sandi Carlisle, and arranged to pick her up in five minutes. As he raced across town, siren blaring, he saw cars being reversed out of driveways and he groaned, knowing that many of the locals would be heading up into the hills. Josh had been born and raised in Paisley and when, after a few years in Sydney, the opportunity had arisen to get posted back home, he had jumped at it. Married with three kids, he could think of no better place in the world to bring them up. While only in his mid-thirties, Josh had let himself go since returning home and this was apparent by his heavy jowls, triple chin, and generous girth. In the six months that Sandi had been in Paisley, this was the first time anything remotely exciting had occurred and she was waiting at her front gate as Josh brought the van to a screeching halt. She had barely had time to brush her long, curly, auburn hair. Despite the lack of make-up, her face was glowing. She gave Josh a flashing smile as she strapped her willowy body in with the seatbelt. 'What happened?'

'I'm guessing one of the gas wells near the river blew up.'

'Holy hell!'

The only sealed road out of town that went up into the hills to the south was clogged with locals. Josh flicked on the siren and flashing lights and sped up the wrong side of the road, past the slow moving convoy of gawkers. 'Go Josh,' Sandi screamed. 'God, this was what I dreamed police life would be like.'

Josh and Sandi drew closer to the red light in the sky which was accompanied by sporadic spurts of yellow and deep rumbles. Josh swung the van off the road and onto the gravel track, where the rear wheels spun wildly and threw stones everywhere. They flew around a bend, nearly smashing into one of the many cars already parked at the bottom of the hill.

Josh glanced over at Sandi. Her face was lit up, totally entranced by the flames. He had never thought her particularly attractive but now she was flushed and her dark brown eyes shone with an almost unnatural intensity. 'Let's see if anyone knows what happened.'

'It exploded,' she giggled. 'You know the locals have been saying something like this would eventually happen.'

As Josh got out of the van, an older man yelled, 'Hey Josh, young Billy McGregor's been looking for you. Hey Billy, get over here.'

A skinny, scruffy kid with long, dirty blond hair, wearing a black polo shirt and faded blue jeans, sauntered over from the small crowd. He was holding hands with a pretty little blue-eyed redhead with freckles, a button nose and a silver stud in her right cheek. Following close behind was Steve Forrest, notepad in hand and recorder in his shirt pocket. 'Hello Karen,' Josh said. 'Do your parents know where you are? Hell, Steve, you sure got here in a hurry.'

Karen grinned. 'I dunno Josh. You're not gonna tell 'em are ya?'

'G'day Josh,' Steve said.

'He won't tell 'em,' the boy interrupted and then, looking over at Sandi. 'Hey Josh, ya partner's a bit of a fox. Does ya wife know about her?'

'He's Senior Constable Gibson to you kid, and you can address me as Constable Carlisle.'

'It's all right, Sandi. Billy and I go back a long way. I was his rugby coach for six years. So what is it you want to see me about, Billy?'

'She's hot and feisty too.'

'Billy!'

'Sorry Josh. Well I wus up here and saw the bloody thing blow sky high.'

'What were you doing up here?'

'We wus parking. Me and Kazza come up here for a bitta privacy … if ya know what I mean.'

'So you saw it too, Karen?'

'Nah, she didn't. Ya see I was at the back of the car having a snake's hiss and next thing ya know the ground shakes and there's flames exploding everywhere. Jeez, I nearly peed all over me new shoes.'

'Do you know how it started?'

'Dunno, but there wus one strange thing.'

'What was that?'

'Well, the explosion lit up the hill like it wus daylight and I saw this big black wolf against the flames. He wus in full flight.'

'There are no wolves in Australia. Are you sure it wasn't a dingo or a collie?'

'It wus a wolf all right.'

'It was a wolf,' Karen said. 'As soon as Billy got back in the car he told me about it. Said it was as black as death.'

'Did you see anything else, Billy?'

'Nothing, only the wolf.'

'Let's have a look at where you were parked.'

'Sure, me car's just down the hill a bit. Follow me.'

A few minutes later they were next to Billy's bright yellow Ford which had dual chrome exhausts and a lowered suspension. Josh looked up the hill. The flame lit up the area around the well and it would be easy to see a large dog. 'Billy, why don't you take Karen home before her parents start phoning us? You can come down to the station tomorrow and make a statement.'

A CEGL truck with flashing orange lights pulled up to the jeers of the crowd. Four maintenance men got out. Someone shouted, 'Where have you been?' and someone else, 'Are you happy with yourselves now, you mongrels?'

'How long before you get it under control?' Sandi asked the driver.

'I've got no idea, but we'll secure the site tonight and it won't be left unmanned until we've plugged it.'

Steve knew what had happened and wondered whether Josh Gibson had twigged. Josh wasn't all that sharp but there was only one dog in the valley that could be mistaken for a wolf. He drove slowly back to town, wondering what he should do, knowing that if he said anything there were those in the town who would blackball him and the *Chronicle*. *How could Paxton have been so stupid and how had he expected to get away with it?* Steve was convinced that when the truth came out, as it surely would, it would prove there was nothing wrong with the gas well and that Paxton had blown it to pieces. The government supported coal seam gas and its sympathy lay with CEGL, courtesy of the future royalty revenues it was salivating over. If it came out that the well had been sabotaged, government support would intensify and the pollies would have an excuse to bury the good work done by the Fisher Valley Protective Alliance.

Josh Gibson took a few minutes to decipher what Billy had said about seeing a big black wolf, before putting two and two together and relating his suspicions to Sandi. This had been her most exciting policing day and she did not want it to finish. 'So are we going to arrest Paxton tonight? Will we need to cuff him?'

'He buried his only son less than twelve hours ago and he's not going anywhere. We can wait until the morning.'

'So you don't think he's a flight risk?'

'I think you've been watching too many cop shows.' Josh wasn't looking forward to the morning. He had known and respected Paxton all his life and the thought of having to arrest him, particularly when he was still grieving, made him ill.

Steve had had a big day and was totally exhausted but, the minute he entered his second floor apartment, he smelt his favourite fragrance, *Allure*, and knew that Bianca had returned from Nepal and would be in his bed. They had been lovers on and off since university days and, while she didn't live with him, she had a key to the apartment and a wardrobe for a change of clothes and her toiletries. She was a stunning, voluptuous, young woman with olive-brown skin, jet-black hair, and a toned body from years spent mountain climbing. They had discussed marriage many times but her father, Norris Scott-Tempy, neither liked Steve nor thought that he was good enough for his daughter. It was rumoured that he had been christened Norris Scott Tempy but had added the hyphen because he thought the extended surname fitted his pretention to class.

Scott-Tempy had anticipated the coal seam gas boom and had borrowed to the hilt to buy cheap motels and housing in the valley. He'd then evicted the locals in anticipation of the surge of itinerant workers whose employers would pay double the going rental rates. He saw himself as a man about town but Steve thought of him as a slum lord. His wife, Bettina, was a beautiful, Maltese woman and Steve often wondered what she saw in the sour-faced, tight-fisted Norris.

One thing he was sure of was that Bianca's looks didn't come from her father. Steve's relationship with her was tempestuous, mainly because he couldn't keep his mouth shut when it came to her father but, when she turned up out of the blue like tonight, he thought himself the luckiest man in the world. Normally he would have snuggled up to her and made passionate love, but tonight was different. He felt the heat of her body and breathed in her fragrance but, amazingly, there was no desire, no stirring in his loins.

He silently cursed Paxton. What would Bianca think in the morning? He stared up at the blackness of the ceiling, listening to her soft rhythmic breathing as he struggled to get his head around the day's events. He was bone-tired but knew it was pointless trying to sleep – his mind refused to shut down. All Paxton's power and money wouldn't save him from a lengthy jail sentence once word got out about what he had done. Steve wondered who he could share his secret with, who he could talk to, and how long it would remain a secret? He momentarily thought about waking Bianca but stopped himself, not knowing how she would react, given her father's love of the coal seam gas companies.

Besides Steve, the *Paisley Chronicle* had one full-time employee, one part-timer and, when he felt like it, Steve's sexagenarian father, Len. The paper operated from a double-fronted shop on Main Street. It was rare for anyone other than Steve to work on Saturdays, and even rarer for them to be there at 7am, so he was surprised to find the door open. He was exhausted and wondered whether he'd forgotten to lock up the night before. As he entered the office, he heard sounds coming from the despatch section at the rear of the building. 'Hello,' he shouted.

'Steve, I thought I'd clean up and be gone before you arrived,' croaked a grey-haired man, nearly as skinny as the broom he was stooped over. 'Couldn't you sleep?'

'Dad, how many times do I have to tell you? I've got contract cleaners coming in.'

'Well, you'd better get rid of them, they're no good. What was the excitement about last night? I heard one of CEGL's wells blew up. I wish I had been there. I would've fanned the flames.'

'I was there and it was pretty spectacular.'

'So what happened? How'd it start?' His father's face was lined and his jowls were sunken but his green eyes were alert and twinkling.

'You can't breathe a word of what I'm about to tell you, Dad.' For the next five minutes, Steve related what had happened and how Billy had supposedly seen a big black wolf. 'That stupid Paxton will be caught before the week is out. He'll go to jail and the anti-CEGL forces in the valley will lose all credibility. Can you believe he was so stupid?'

'You did say the well exploded a bit after midnight, didn't you Son?'

'That's right.'

'Phew. It's lucky you didn't say anything last night then.'

'Why?'

His father sat down at one of the desks, rubbing his gnarled hands together. 'I was with Charles Paxton last night. I knew he'd need company so I went to his home around ten o'clock and didn't leave until two-thirty. We talked and had a few drinks. I think it helped ease his pain.'

'Dad! Dad, don't be as stupid as he is. You weren't at his home last night and since when have you been friends with him? You're too old to go to jail, so forget about this foolishness.'

'I'm telling the truth, Son. Have you considered that there might be more than one black dog in the valley?'

'Of course, but there's only one that looks like a wolf, and it wouldn't surprise me to find that it has a burnt coat.'

'I need a coffee.' The old man sighed, holding his head in his hands. 'But there's no milk in the fridge.'

'Are you all right, Dad?'

'I'm feeling a little dizzy, but it's nothing a good cup of coffee won't fix. I'll go and get some milk,' he said, stumbling as he stood up.

'Sit down, Dad. Take it easy. I'll get the milk. I want you to forget about Paxton. You'll only get yourself in trouble. I'll lock the door after me to stop anyone coming in and disturbing you, so why don't you put your head down and have a rest?'

'That's a good idea.' His father crossed his arms on the table and rested his head on them.

As soon as Steve closed the front door, his father staged an amazing recovery and, for one so old, showed amazing alacrity. He first called his wife. It was short and sweet and she had no hesitation in agreeing with him. His second call was to Paxton and the phone rang ten times before he answered, sounding slurred and hung-over. However it did not take him long to focus and express his gratitude.

Paxton hung up the phone and staggered out onto the verandah, nearly tripping over Cosmos lying across the door. He bent down and patted the dog's head, rubbed his tummy and checked his magnificent, shiny black coat. There wasn't so much as a burnt hair, let alone a singe mark and Paxton breathed a sigh of relief. The satisfaction of what he had done had disappeared; he had a crushing hangover and, if it were not for Len Forrest, he'd be in a lot of trouble. His actions the night before had done nothing to remove the aching pain from his heart and, while he cursed himself for acting impulsively, he was unrepentant and still seething.

There were half-a-dozen locals chatting in the milk bar while they waited for the newspapers from Sydney to arrive. Steve took a carton of milk from the refrigerator and then heard someone laugh and say, 'If you didn't know any different, that Paxton dog would pass for a wolf.' There was a murmur of assent and then someone else said, 'I think it's just what we needed. Now maybe those gas companies will clear out of the valley.' Steve paid for the milk, thinking, *so much for it being secret.*

Sandi patted the big black dog that so resembled a wolf, while her partner listened in amazement to Paxton. He said that he knew nothing about the destruction of the gas well other than that the explosion had rocked the house and that, along with Len Forrest, he had gone outside and they had seen a red glow in the sky. Other than that, he had not left his house.

It was only a short drive to the Forrests' place, where Len confirmed everything Paxton had said. Maggie, who was known to be as honest as the day was long, added that Len had left home before nine-thirty and, being the light sleeper that she was, she had heard him come in just after three o'clock. Josh was emotionally torn; he had not been looking forward to arresting Paxton but, by the same token, was shocked to find that three pillars of the local community could tell lies so easily. What was *big gas* doing to his community?

Paxton, while well respected, would never have won a popularity contest, but this largely changed overnight. People walked across the street just to say hello and others wanted to buy him a drink; storekeepers, restaurateurs and motel proprietors, who did a lot of business with the gas companies, were not so generous. Len Forrest had always been gregarious, happy and generous with his time and what little money he had. The locals slapped him on the back, high-fived him and there wasn't a winery in the valley that would charge him for a drink or a meal, but there were many in the town who disapproved of what he had done. Paisley had created two unlikely heroes and, to those who knew of Maggie Forrest's involvement, a heroine, but the 'heroes' were not universally popular or supported.

Billy McGregor and his hoon friends sat around the pub, drinking and talking, amazed at how popular the two old men had become with most of the townsfolk. Billy noted that they hadn't been charged or punished and instead were lauded. He rationalised that, if that was how it worked for *them*, maybe he and his mates should blow up a few gas wells too. Little did he know that Steve Forrest had warned his father that a consequence of his lies would be to induce others to commit the copy-cat destruction of more gas wells.

Chapter 4

Joanna Singer had just turned forty-four when she collapsed with a heart attack while cleaning one of her clients' houses. Paramedics responded to the emergency call within minutes but defibrillation was not successful and an hour later she was pronounced dead.

She had arrived in Paisley twenty-five years earlier, a single mother with two toddlers and had rented a shack on thirty-five acres on the outskirts of the valley, near the small town of Tura. Many said that the hard work she had taken on had worn her out.

Despite its rugged beauty, it was one of the few infertile areas in the valley, with an abundance of gum trees and tumbleweed and little else. The properties in the area had originally been granted by the government as residential allotments to soldiers returning from the First World War, who consequently became known as *estatees*. Originally there was a certain honour to the name but, as the years elapsed, *estatee* became associated with being poor, even though the residents never saw themselves in that light. Many of Joanna's neighbours lived on residential blocks as large as seventy-five acres and had moved there because they were hiding something from their past and looking for privacy on their own piece of paradise.

For Joanna it was quiet and peaceful, she loved the freedom and the rent was cheap. She was remarkably industrious and, with both kids in her old beat-up Volkswagen, she drove around the towns in the valley, offering to wash and iron clothes. It wasn't long before she had established a regular clientele. When young Danny and Carol were old enough to go to school, Joanna started cleaning houses in the area. She worked hard, didn't go out, didn't waste money and soon saved enough to put a deposit on the property she was renting. Her only indulgence was the plants and trailer loads of black soil she bought to create a stunning little garden around the house. She had no close friends and seemed to live her life solely for her children. However, once they left home in their late teens, she rarely heard from or saw them but, when she did, they were always after money. Sadly, when she was buried, only a few of her long-term clients were at her graveside.

Lawyers for Joanna's estate placed the requisite notices in newspapers and unsuccessfully used their best efforts to find Carol and Danny, who were Joanna's sole beneficiaries. Joanna had managed to pay off the mortgage and her estate comprised the property and a new second-hand Toyota Corolla that she had treated herself to in a moment of despair.

Four years before Joanna's death, 300 acres, a few kilometres to the west of her property, was bought, anonymously, by CEGL. No-one in the area was aware of this until it was too late.

A two-metre steel mesh and barbed wire fence was erected to encompass the property but, other than this, it lay undisturbed for twelve months, while CEGL lodged applications for coal seam gas exploration licences which ran to thousands of pages. The environment authority application by itself was nine hundred pages and was signed off by seventeen employees with illustrious titles like: Manager Engineering Upstream, Environmental Scientist, Manager Water Strategy and Sustainability, Senior Engineer Technical Interfaces and Legal Counsel Upstream. CEGL knew that the paperwork detailing the process was far more important than the process itself and they buried the responsible government departments in a mass of documents that they had neither the expertise nor the time to adequately assess. After the authorities and licences were issued, the only regulation was company self-regulation; not unlike licensing a fox to look after a chicken coop.

A placard, *Keep Out CEGL Construction Site,* was affixed to the gates and, soon after, workers began laying a gravel track and clearing a five-acre square section. Twenty portafabs, made up of offices, storage and ablutions, were placed around its perimeter. It didn't take long to drill the first of eight exploration wells.

A few weeks after Joanna's death, three CEGL trucks appeared on the red dirt track at the front of her property. One of the trucks was fitted with a seismic vibratory plate and it stopped every fifteen metres along the three hundred and fifty metre boundary where the plate was lowered to the ground. The other two trucks carried sophisticated computers and geophones, which were placed in a geometric array on the surface to detect the seismic signals from the changes in rock type or faults. CEGL knew that there were deep coal seams in the area and the seismic testing allowed their geologists to confirm and measure their extent and depth. However, before the volume of methane and its flow pressure could be measured, exploration wells had to be sunk.

While Joanna's lawyers had been unable to contact her children, CEGL's attorneys had no such problem, having more resources and a large, powerful client that desperately wanted access to her property. Within a week, a private investigator had located Carol and Danny, informed them of their mother's passing and offered to lease the property that they were going to inherit; a corporate client was looking for grazing land. Danny wasn't very bright but he had a nose for a dollar and told them he wasn't interested in leasing and that if their client wanted the property it would have to buy it. CEGL's management did not normally buy property when they could dupe landowners into granting access agreements, but thirty-five acres was a small allotment; it was cheap and would give them a toehold where they could sink another two exploration wells. They also knew that the wells, once sunk, would devalue the adjoining properties, making their subsequent work easier. By the time Carol and Danny marched into their mother's lawyer's office, they had come to an agreement to sell the property to CEGL. Two hours later they were back on the road to Sydney, not having been able to spare even ten minutes to visit their mother's grave.

Although Joanna's property was neglected after her death and quickly became over-run with weeds, the neighbours were surprised to see a bulldozer demolish the house and destroy what was left of the garden. Soon, huge trucks carrying gravel, arc lights and engineering equipment roared along the unmade roads at all times of the day and night, terrifying the locals and throwing up a constant haze of red dust. Progress, industry and exploitation took the place of peace and tranquillity. The flimsy, old front gates to Joanna's property were replaced with heavy steel gates that were padlocked, and large placards were affixed to them announcing: *CEGL Private Property Trespassers will be Prosecuted.*

It wasn't long before gangs of men employed by CEGL and an American company, Filliburton, were working on the property around the clock, seven days a week. Armed with heavy equipment and truckloads of gravel, they extended the track to the east and west boundaries, where they ripped the vegetation from the ground, levelled it, and constructed two large, hard-standing pads measuring one hundred metres square. Portafabs were quickly positioned around the perimeter of the east pad and light towers powered by diesel generators were installed. Two pits were excavated: one for collecting the saline-laden, toxic wastewater, and another for collecting drill cuttings and for flaring in case of striking methane pockets while drilling.

When the pits were completed, a convoy of semitrailers brought in components of the first drill rig. Under the direction of tough, hard-cussing area supervisor, Frank Beck, the men quickly assembled these in much the same way a child assembles a Meccano model.

Beck, from Colorado, was a Filliburton oil and gas veteran whose remuneration was based on the number of wells he could sink. An ex-marine of medium height and heavyset build, it was obvious that his nose had been broken many times and his sandy hair was cropped in a style that said he was still a marine.

After he quit the services, he got a job with Filliburton, working as a labourer on the oil rigs in the Gulf of Mexico. It wasn't long before he was promoted to assistant foreman, his toughness and ability to get things done coming to the fore. These attributes did not go unnoticed and he soon found himself in charge of installing drilling rigs on coal seam gas projects in Wyoming and then Colorado. Private landowners were no match for him and he sank countless wells on their properties.

Streams and aquifers were polluted, methane seeped into houses, and the sound of drilling and compressors was never-ending. Folk living in close proximity to the wells collapsed after breathing the heavily-contaminated air, and others were afflicted by cancers and dermatitis. The government, the EPA, and the Colorado Gas and Oil Conservation Commission, which were meant to protect citizens, did nothing. The landowners screamed, there were threats of legal action, there were death threats, there were rowdy town meetings and in some instances gas wells were sabotaged, but for Beck it was like water off a duck's back and he arrogantly stared the Colorado gas dissidents down. The good citizens of the Fisher Valley held no fears for him.

Drilling began two weeks after the first gang entered Joanna's property. The first rig drilled down to a depth of about ten metres before it was replaced with another rig with a smaller diameter drill which extended the bore to two hundred metres. Arc lights lit up the pad and the neighbours could see and hear the drilling twenty-four hours a day. Beck never left the site, shouting and cajoling his men to work faster. Hundreds of trucks roared onto the site carrying steel pipes to reinforce and enclose the well, and cement was forced down the bore hole to encase the exterior. A blowout preventer was installed at the surface and pressure-tested to confirm the integrity of the casing cement. This was done in an attempt to prevent gas or water leakage around the casing, as the consequences of toxic fracking chemicals entering the aquifers was too horrible to contemplate.

Hydraulic fracturing or 'fracking' is a process where water, sand and toxic chemicals are forced down well-bores in huge volumes under enormous pressure to break-up the coal seams hundreds of metres below the ground, so methane can be released. For the gas companies, the great thing about fracking is that, when the methane pressure and recovery decreases, the well can be fracked again and again; sometimes up to twenty times. The National Water Commissioner warned of the risks involved in large volumes of water being extracted, the depressurisation of coal seam aquifers and the disposal of large volumes of treated wastewater. However, when CEGL threatened to withdraw their massive investment from the valley, the federal minister rolled over in favour of the company and disregarded his commissioner's findings. This, despite the very real risk of contaminating the valley's drinking water, the Blaxland River and its tributaries and the water used for livestock, crops, vineyards and wineries.

It took just twenty-eight days to complete the drilling and then the steel pipe and concrete casing were perforated at the level of the coal seams so that the toxic fracking concoction could be forced through the perforations. Engineers and scientists employed by CEGL were adamant that the poisonous cocktail they were pumping into the coal seams could not escape or seep into the surrounding aquifers and streams. However, this was exactly what had occurred in Colorado.

When the first exploration well on Joanna's property was ready for fracking, trucks delivered sand and fracking chemicals while tankers brought in hundreds of thousands of litres of water to be pumped down the well-bore. Hydraulic fracking opens the cracks already present in the coal seams' gas reservoirs and the sand keeps the induced fractures open, ensuring an uninterrupted gas flow. No-one on site knew what the fracking chemicals comprised. Filliburton described them as additives and claimed they could not reveal their contents, as they were proprietary, just like *Coca Cola's* famous formulae.

Beck had fracked hundreds of wells but the process still excited him. Often the ground shook as the coal seams fractured, at other times a fizzling sound emanated from deep within the earth, and sometimes the physical impact was minimal. When the first well on Joanna's property was fracked, it was as if the area had been hit by a mini earthquake and Beck high-fived his workers and grinned with satisfaction. No-one from the government or EPA had attended the well-site.

Dean Prezky owned three properties to the west of Joanna's property, totalling about one hundred and thirty acres. He was a strapping young man in his mid-thirties with dark black hair, powerful chest and arms and a deep tan from the days he spent working outdoors as a carpenter. He had built a rustic house, complete with solar panels that powered his property for ten months and in the two coldest months he used a diesel generator. A water well had provided fresh drinking water since 1920 but Dean also installed two ten-thousand-litre water tanks that caught rain for use in the house, allowing him to use the well as a reserve. There were five dams on the properties and Dean and the kids used one as a swimming hole. Like Joanna, he too had bought rich black soil – but in far greater quantities – and had used it to build a large fruit and vegetable garden to make his family self-sufficient. He craved privacy and his goal was to buy the adjoining properties until he owned around five hundred acres, which he reasoned would finally put enough space between him and the outside world.

When Dean complained to Frank Beck about the bright lights on the well-pads on Joanna's property, he was met with profuse apologies and assurances that they would be repositioned so as not to shine into the windows of his house. Dean wasn't someone to stand in the way of progress and during the conversation with Beck he agreed to let Filliburton access his properties during the day to transfer materials and speed up the completion of work. He'd heard stories about how the gas wells would change life in the valley for the worse but he had ignored them, guessing that it was just the whining of a few millionaires trying to shield their hobby vineyards and horse studs. He had little sympathy for the Fisher Valley Protective Alliance and believed that the gas companies might one day provide his children with jobs.

Dean loved his lifestyle, had no intention of ever selling his properties and thought that finding gas would increase their value, enabling him to increase his borrowings to buy more properties. He was impressed that Filliburton was doing its best to control the red dust haze by using tankers to spray water on unmade roads and, when Beck asked him if he would like the tracks on his properties watered, he leapt at the opportunity. However, when asked if he would agree to pipes being laid under his property so that gas could be transferred to CEGL's central compressor station, he refused to even consider it.

As fast as they appeared on Joanna's property, the workers were gone, leaving behind two well-heads and ancillary equipment, enclosed by chain-link fences with warning placards attached. Flames burned from the flare stacks while meters measured the rate of gas flow, to determine whether the exploration wells would be converted into producers.

For Dean Prezky life was soon to become hell on earth.

Chapter 5

Six weeks after Beck and his workers departed, Dean and his kids broke out in nasty, itchy red rashes on their legs and upper bodies, resulting in ugly, painful, weeping wounds. The local doctor referred them to a dermatologist in Paisley who immediately diagnosed dermatitis and then questioned them about changes in their lifestyle and diet. Dean said nothing had changed and that the food and drink they consumed was the same as it had always been. The dermatologist was puzzled, as he had recently seen two other families from Tura who had displayed near-identical symptoms and who had been equally adamant that nothing in their lives had changed. He prescribed creams, lotions and tablets, some of which were not covered by the Pharmaceutical Benefits Scheme. By the time Dean headed home, he was out of pocket nearly $800, which he could ill afford.

That night he lay in bed scratching, tossing and turning. He heard the children going to the toilet and then washing their bodies while crying in frustration. Normally he would have told them to get back into their beds but he didn't say a word, knowing the hell they were going through.

Just before dawn the house was quiet. The kids had finally dropped off from exhaustion, but Dean was wide awake, staring up at the ceiling. Again he went over the dermatologist's questions and again he drew a blank. He listened to his wife's peaceful breathing and not for the first time wondered why Vicki had not broken out in a rash. What was she doing that was different? They did everything together: they ate the same meals, drank the same milk and water, tended the fruit trees and vegetable gardens and the only fertiliser they used was horse manure.

As sunlight filtered through the windows, he looked at the bloody streaks on the sheets and decided to take a quick dip in the dam. Then it hit him. The only thing Vicki wasn't doing was swimming in the dam, saying that the early spring weather wasn't warm enough for her to venture into the cold water. He sprang out of bed, threw on a pair of shorts and his work boots and went to the kitchen, where he found two of Vicki's bottling jars. He ran down to the dam, his muscular legs carrying him easily over the rough surface. At the dam's edge, he knelt down and dipped the jars into the water before holding them up to the early morning light. The water looked clear and he sighed in exasperation as he trudged back to the house.

The kids were usually up by now but he heard no voices, only Vicki moving around the kitchen and the whistling of the coffee percolator. 'You look like hell,' she said, staring into his bloodshot eyes. 'And what have you got in my good jam jars?'

He quickly explained his theory and his disappointment about the clarity of the dam water.

'Honey, you may be right. What did you expect to see? Amoebas floating around in the water? Just because the water appears clear doesn't mean that it's not contaminated and the only way you'll find out is by chemical analysis, which we can't afford.' She sipped her coffee.

'You're right. Just because it isn't murky doesn't mean anything. Perhaps I could phone Josh Gibson and see if he can get the police lab to analyse it?'

Vicki put her arms around his neck, her firm, full breasts pressing into his chest. 'The police lab's there to track down murderers and analyse the saliva of drunk and drugged-out drivers, not find the source of dermatitis.' She laughed. 'I'm not saying you're wrong and I think you and the kids should stop swimming in the dam.'

'You'd better get them up, or they'll be late for school.'

'They had a terrible night and I'm going to let them sleep. Missing one day won't hurt.'

'Good idea,' Dean said, deep in thought. 'But, if we don't get the water analysed, we'll never know if it caused the dermatitis. If it clears up, we'll just put it down to the medicine and creams.'

Two hours later, Dean was phoning the laboratories listed in the Yellow

Pages. From each call he learnt something and the standard question he was asked was what contaminants he expected the analysis to detect? He had no idea how to answer and, by the sixth call, thought that he was beating his head against a brick wall. It was then that he spoke to a technician whom he could tell was of advanced years, who patiently listened to his plight, occasionally asking a question.

'Have there been any road works recently undertaken near your property?'

'No.'

'Have there been any excavations on or near your property?'

'No.'

'Has any aerial plant spraying taken place in the area where you live in the past few months?'

'No.'

'I'm not sure we can help you, Sir. You say that you've been swimming in the dam for years without ever experiencing rashes before. There's been no disturbance to the land or air that might've changed the composition of the water, so it's highly unlikely that the dermatitis resulted from swimming in the dam.'

'Did you say disturbance to the land?'

'I did.'

'Well, they recently fracked two coal seam gas wells on an adjoining property, but they're about two kilometres from the dam, so I guess that doesn't help.'

There was no response from the technician. 'Hello, hello, are you still there?'

'Mr Prezky, if you send the water samples to me, together with a cheque for one thousand dollars, I'll see what I can do. It could be up to two weeks before we have any results and, even then, the analysis may not reveal anything. I do have something in mind though and, if I'm right, you'll have your results very quickly.'

'What do you think it is?'

'I can't say yet. Be patient Mr Prezky. I'll get the results to you as soon as I can.'

Dean wrote the cheque but didn't fill in the butt, knowing Vicki would go crazy if she discovered his extravagance, even if he could justify it. He taped the lids on the jars, tore some old newspapers into tiny pieces and packed them and the jars into a cardboard box, so they couldn't move or break in transit to Sydney. Thirty minutes later he was in Paisley, despatching the consignment.

That night, while the rashes remained inflamed, the itching eased and Dean and the kids finally experienced some relief. Vicki attributed this to the creams and lotions. By nine o'clock everyone was sleeping soundly. Five hours later Dean sat bolt upright in bed, awakened by the sound of *whirr, whirr, whirr* that he had never heard before.

'What's that?' Vicki groaned.

'I don't know, but it seems to be coming from CEGL's property.'

'They can't be drilling another well, can they?'

'We've never heard a noise like that before, so I doubt it.'

'Do you think it could be coming from the Thompsons' property next door?'

'Nah, old man Thompson hates the gas companies and said he'd put a bullet in the first CEGL employee that tries to set foot on his property, so it's not coming from there.'

'What are you going to do?'

'There's nothing I can do tonight. I'll check it out first thing in the morning.' Dean buried his head under a pillow.

'It's such a horrible, droning noise.'

'Go to sleep, Darling. There's nothing we can do about it tonight.'

Chapter 6

The *National Advocate* was the first major newspaper to question the veracity and safety of extracting coal seam gas in Australia. In a small article, hidden at the bottom of page twelve, it outlined the American experience, where oil and gas companies had sunk hundreds of thousands of gas wells, with support of legislation which exempted them from having to comply with either the *Clean Water Act* or *Clean Air Act*. The journalist wrote without passion about the poisoning of the water, the pollution in the air, the sickness and, in some cases, the unexplained deaths by cancer of those who had lived in the areas where gas wells had been sunk.

By midday the first emails and faxes, headed *Letters to Editor – Coal Seam Gas* were received, and by four o'clock they had reached avalanche proportions. They came from people living in the Fisher Valley, The Spurling Downs and townships in rural Victoria. Many correspondents were worried that their properties would be seized by the gas companies, others were concerned that national parks and forests would be littered with gas wells and some feared that the nation's precious aquifers would be contaminated or depleted. However, the majority were concerned about cancer and protecting the health and well-being of their families. The journalist and the editor were staggered by the community outrage, so the following day they published a follow-up article, which profiled the activities of some of the gas companies, including CEGL. This time it was on page three, together with twenty of the more colourful responses in the *Letters to Editor* section.

The reaction to this second article was more subdued; however, there were some responses from residents of the Fisher Valley accusing CEGL of using chemicals that were known carcinogens, which had resulted in the death of six-year-old Charlie Paxton. These responses were passionate and inflammatory – they were also libellous and could not be published. The journalist did, however, phone those who had sent the inflammatory emails to get the full story. The following day, the *Advocate* ran a carefully-worded article, which had been screened by its lawyers, that mentioned CEGL and its contractor's refusal to disclose what chemicals were being used in hydraulic fracturing, the explosion at CEGL's gas well and Charlie Paxton's death, without specifically drawing any conclusions – there was no need, as the article was both subtle and obvious.

CEGL had been in the Harbrow family for a long time and Spencer Harbrow was its third-generation CEO. His father, Winston, might still have been in that position had he not died in a car crash sixteen years earlier. Winston had openly admired the woman who was now Spencer's deputy, Moira Raymond, but Spencer was jealous of her and her abilities.

When Spencer became CEO, he demonstrated that he did not share his father's aversion to debt. He had a dream of turning CEGL from a small, family-controlled retailer of electricity, gas and appliances into a major gas producer. He borrowed hundreds of millions of dollars from second-tier lenders on unfavourable terms and at exorbitant interest rates. As his grand plans progressed, money was always scarce, so he raised more capital by issuing shares. The result was that his family's interest in the company declined from sixty to just eight percent, but the company's market capitalisation had grown to eleven billion dollars and Harbrow was eight hundred million dollars richer. He liked to boast that CEGL was the only Australian owned energy company, but its share register was dominated by foreign institutions. The financial press lauded him, but he was uncertain whether he could have achieved his goals without Moira Raymond's talents and toughness.

Harbrow was tall, slightly greying, tanned and, although pushing fifty-six, had not a wrinkle on his superficially friendly face. Sitting in his sixtieth floor office overlooking Sydney Harbour, he read the article in the *National Advocate* one more time before summoning his PA, Janet Bourne. He gave her precise instructions: get CEGL's Chairman, Harold Llewellyn, on the phone; get him a macchiato – which only she could prepare to his exacting standards; make sure he wasn't disturbed; and lastly, track down the other directors in the event that he might need to speak to them. As Janet scurried off, Harbrow paced over to the window, his thumbs pushed into the vest of his *Brioni* suit, and cursorily glanced down at the yachts being tossed around in the harbour. He had used his influence to appoint five, hand-picked, non-executive directors. They all controlled firms that did business with CEGL and were therefore both indebted to him and massively conflicted. The seventh director was Moira Raymond and she had been appointed by the board against his wishes, when he had been ill for three months with pneumonia.

He was anxious to talk to Llewellyn, whom he had appointed Chairman of the company shortly after his father's passing, because of his business and political connections. Llewellyn was senior partner of the blue-blood legal firm, *Braithwaite Ogilvie and Llewellyn,* and a former National Party minister who knew how to count the numbers and was a past-master when it came to networking and schmoozing. He had not practised law for years, finding managing the practice and being chairman of a number of public companies more befitting his prestige and expertise. Born of wealthy English parents, he was a throw-back to a bygone era: long, silver hair, a matching, floppy moustache, mutton-chop sideburns and florid cheeks. Even after a lifetime in Australia, he yearned for the class system of the old country. Llewellyn fervently believed that he was superior to all others, with the possible exception of the British Royal Family. He also liked to boast that he was one of only a handful of people who had the Prime Minister's direct number. Despite his pomposity, he was no-one's fool and was known around the firm as the *Silver Fox.*

Harbrow took off his suit coat and hung it on the stand behind his desk, carefully removing the diamond cuff links from his light blue hand-tailored shirt before rolling up his sleeves. The intercom buzzed: 'I have Mr Llewellyn for you.'

'Good morning Harold. Have you read that disgraceful article in that disgusting yellow rag? God, they're saying we were responsible for that boy's death. It's defamatory and I want something done about it.'

While he was talking, Janet quietly brought him a cup of piping hot macchiato which he picked up and sipped, neither acknowledging nor thanking her.

'Yes, and I feel the same way you do, so I took the liberty of running it past the firm's defamation specialists. I'm sorry, but they say it's obvious that the *Advocate* took legal advice before it was published. Unfortunately there are no grounds for mounting a successful action.'

The phone went quiet and after fifteen seconds Llewellyn pressed the receiver hard against his ear. 'Spencer, are you there?'

'I was thinking,' Harbrow said, offering no apology. 'Perhaps you misunderstood me. I'm not looking for damages. I just want to stop them publishing any more rubbish. Look, five years ago the company was worth less than two billion dollars and you well know why it's grown into the powerhouse it is today. It's because I had the foresight to apply for coal seam gas exploration licences on massive tracts of land all down the eastern seaboard. The last thing we need is any adverse publicity that results in slowing or stopping exploration like what's occurred in New York. You know what happened there: the greenies lied and said there was a distinct probability that the city's water supply could become contaminated. The press believed them and next thing you know the wells and exploration were on hold. I don't need to tell you that the value of your shares and options in the company will be significantly diminished if the same thing happens here.'

Llewellyn pondered this. It was true; he had made more money from CEGL in the last five years than he had from a lifetime in the law and politics. It also applied to the other directors, particularly Harbrow, who had almost become a billionaire. He didn't particularly like Harbrow, thinking him a Jekyll and Hyde character: smooth and charming with those in power who might be able to help him and sarcastic and demanding with those on his payroll, including directors. 'I'll ensure that a writ is issued before the day is out, claiming unspecified damages.'

'You said there are no grounds for legal action.'

'There aren't, but nothing focuses an adversary's senses like a well-worded writ and, after it's served, the *Advocate* won't be taking liberties with what they print.'

'It's a bluff.'

'Yes.'

'I like it, but what if they call your bluff?'

'They won't. However, if they do, we'll apply for an injunction restraining them from publishing further defamatory articles. We'll tie them up in the courts for weeks.' Llewellyn laughed, thinking that the litigation might turn out to be a nice little earner for his firm.

'Good.'

'Spencer, the Western Australian Premier's visiting next week. Would you like to have lunch with him on Thursday?'

'Set it up,' Harbrow said, putting the receiver back in its cradle while simultaneously buzzing Janet. 'Get me Clem Aspley.'

A few minutes later Aspley was asking, 'How can I help you, Spencer?'

Clem Aspley was an advertising genius who had twice been bankrupted after taking huge risks that would, had they been successful, have catapulted him to the top of his profession. Harbrow had known from the day they had met that any grandiose plans that he put before the board would have the overwhelming support of Aspley and he had moved quickly to ensure his appointment as a director. Harbrow had few close friends but, as he had got to know Aspley, he found they had many common interests; they were both divorced, they loved wine, they enjoyed the finer things in life and they were committed to making as much money as was humanly possible. Aspley looked and dressed far younger than his fifty-two years and often attended board meetings wearing ripped jeans, a polo shirt and sandals. He may not have been the first advertising executive to use the words 'clean' and 'green' in relation to coal seam gas, but the form in which he used those words, including the changing of the company's name, was brilliant, and the public perception of CEGL was that it was an environmentally friendly company.

'Clem, I'm very unhappy about those articles in the *National Advocate*. Did you see them?'

'Sure, and I agree that last one was a bit rough.'

'The *Advocate's* owned by the Maddock Group and we must be spending a fortune with them. They have magazines, regional newspapers, radio stations and an interest in Channel Twelve, don't they?'

Harbrow knew that Aspley would have guessed the purpose of his question and be thinking of subtle reasons to oppose it, as he hated changing schedules or breaking contracts. 'I think that's right.'

'No, Clem, you know it's right and you also know the name of every media outlet that the Maddock Group have an interest in. I want you to cancel every advertisement you have booked and let them know why.'

Aspley groaned. 'They're going to sue my arse off.'

Harbrow chuckled. 'No they won't. You own one of the biggest agencies in the land and they'll be worried about you slagging them off and cancelling contracts for other clients. Besides, if you're successfully sued, which you won't be, CEGL will pick up the tab.'

'Don't do it, Spencer. Robert Maddock doesn't like being stood over and has a history of retaliating against those who threaten him or his newspapers. It will be very bad for the company if they dig their heels in.'

'As if Robert's even going to hear about it. We're an awfully large account to lose, so let them know, when they stop publishing that rubbish, we'll reinstate all contracts.'

'You're gonna owe me one after this.'

'Clem, with what we pay you for your unique skills, together with director's fees, not to speak of the shares and options, I think hell will freeze over before this company ever owes you anything.' They were friends but Aspley, like the other directors, often needed to be reminded on which side his bread was buttered.

Harbrow put the phone down and smiled, knowing that, once the writ was issued and the advertising contracts severed, the smart-arse reporter and his stupid editor at the *Advocate* would be right in the firing line of those who controlled the cash at the Maddock Group. *There'd be no more derogatory or suggestive articles about CEGL published in the* Advocate. *It's always the cash,* he pondered, *and he who has the most gold always calls the tune.* He didn't have gold but something better – unlimited reserves of methane just waiting to be pumped from the ground.

Harbrow briefly thought about phoning the other directors, but he knew that they would support his actions and he decided not to waste his or their time. Sir Richard Crichton-Smythe was nudging eighty but had lost none of his mental agility or toughness, having started his career as an office boy with Newtower Iron & Steel, a company he now chaired. He had introduced Harbrow to his financial contacts in London when CEGL had been desperate for cash, on the conditions that the company appoint him as a director, issue him a significant number of options and purchase the huge quantities of steel pipe that it used in its gas exploration and extraction exclusively from Newtower Iron & Steel.

One of those London contacts was Joe Biederman, the head of the Royal Treasury Group, an institution that was CEGL's largest shareholder, with twenty-nine percent of the stock. Like everyone else, the Royal Treasury Group had made a fortune on its investment, but Biederman had never made the transition from highly-salaried employee to entrepreneur. Despite this, he had enormous influence and, while not a member of CEGL's board, major decisions were rarely taken without his tacit approval. About the same age as

Harbrow, his strengths lay in his uncanny knack to sniff out a good deal, an elephant-like memory, his ability to make figures talk without the need for computers and an overbearing negotiating style which centred on the deal being done at his price or not at all. In just fifteen years he had managed to increase the size of Royal fiftyfold. Shareholders loved him and he was on an enormous salary and options package but his one weakness ensured that his package was never enough to make ends meet. She was platinum blonde, a real-life Barbie twenty-five years his junior, who had been a hat check girl at one of the clubs when Joe, a happily married man, had walked in one night and fallen head over heels in love with her. The divorce was messy, drawn out and expensive, but not nearly as costly as marrying young Trish. She spent fifty thousand pounds a month on clothes and cosmetics, had a chauffeur-driven limousine and a passion but not a taste for art, on which she squandered millions. Joe Biederman was a brilliant investor and one of the very few men whom Harbrow deferred to.

Phillip Bancroft was senior partner of *Bancroft & Coulter,* a second-tier Sydney stockbroking firm. He had convinced his clients to take huge risks and buy shares in CEGL just as Harbrow was implementing his expansion plans. Not a cent of his own money was invested but he had made a personal fortune from the free options that had been issued to him for risking his clients' money. Those clients had made twenty times their initial investment and thought that Bancroft was an investment guru – had they known what he had done, they may not have held him in such high esteem. He was particularly sensitive about anything that adversely affected the company's share price and Harbrow knew he would support the actions he had taken to bring the *Advocate* to heel.

Harbrow had appointed Harold Llewellyn so that he could be introduced to and access heads of business, finance and government, whereas he had appointed the rough-around-the-edges Vic Bezzina so that he could be informed of the weaknesses of those powerful people, their hidden skeletons and what motivated them. Bezzina was an ex-federal policeman who had built a unique business, which provided discreet security itineraries and investigatory services for heads of corporations and government leaders. He employed ex-federal and state police, ex-ASIO operatives, ex-tax office investigators and even had two former CIA spooks on his payroll. Over the years, he had built up dirt files that Edgar Hoover would have been proud of, on senior industry and government figures and those who posed a threat to his exclusive clientele. One of his clients was Newtower Iron & Steel and, when the greenies and other radical groups started picketing CEGL's annual general meetings, blockading properties and generally making nuisances of themselves, Sir Richard Crichton-Smythe suggested to Harbrow that his problems might be solved if he met with Bezzina. Soon after their meeting, Harbrow had dossiers on all those in positions of power who were opposed to coal seam gas development, but what really impressed him about Bezzina was that he seemed to have the power to influence the Federal Police to hassle and restrain the green radicals who had been causing CEGL trouble. Like the other non-executive directors, Bezzina negotiated a very generous fee and a remuneration and benefits package which Harbrow did not attempt to bargain down, as he liked the idea of his directors being indebted to him.

He gave no thought to contacting the ruthlessly ambitious Moira Raymond, who openly aspired to his job. Unfortunately she had the ear and support of Harold Llewellyn who doted on her, and Harbrow often wondered whether they had been sexually involved. Sir Richard Crichton-Smythe also sang Moira's praises and, while Harbrow could have used his influence to remove her, he could not run the risk of his chairman and another 'distinguished' director resigning or creating a fuss.

Moira had in the past occupied the office next to Harbrow's and she had mistakenly thought that he had had the hots for her. *He'd wanted to bed her all right but his motivations weren't sexual but rather to show her who was boss.* She had flirted and led him on many times, only to reject him when things started to get serious and, the more she rejected him, the more determined he became to have her submit. Frustrated at the sight of her every day and wanting to move her on, he came up with the brilliant idea of putting her out in the field into situations that might be physically violent for a man but were unlikely to be for a woman. When she failed, which she surely would when dealing with hardened labourers and facing angry landowners, it would destroy her chance of ever sitting in his chair. He had not envisaged her making an outstanding success of those tough assignments and, when she did, she not only won the plaudits of board members but was seen by them as his successor-in-waiting. He vaguely recollected telling her one night that he would stand aside so that she could become the company's CEO, but he had only said it because he was trying to get her between the sheets and he promptly forgot the details after she had rejected him yet again.

Chapter 7

Much to Steve's disappointment, Bianca had left by the time he returned home. There wasn't a trace of *Allure* and it was almost as if she had never been there. Her response to a note that he had left, apologising for leaving early that morning, was that she would be busy at the weekend selling real estate and that she would phone him when she could. She had a healthy sexual appetite and he suspected that she must be wondering what was wrong with him.

The front page of Monday's *Paisley Chronicle* carried graphic colour photos of CEGL's gas well in flames. The accompanying article mentioned Billy McGregor and his sighting of a big black wolf but it did not draw any conclusions as to what caused the explosion. No mention was made of Karen. Most who read the article already knew what it contained and thought that it was boring. Many subscribers and advertisers phoned to express their disappointment and spoke to Steve's receptionist-come-girl Friday, Buffy Preston, letting her know in no uncertain terms that they thought he had wasted a golden opportunity to tip a bucket on CEGL. Steve was close enough to hear what Buffy was saying but he could not understand why she had broken into fits of laughter. She was a big girl who had been with him since she left school, and when she laughed her whole body shook.

'What's so funny?'

'Nothing,' she said, removing her silver, wire-framed glasses as she played with her plaits.

'I don't think so.'

'You really don't want to know.'

'Jeez, I dunno why I employ you. You can't type, you can't make coffee and you won't give me my messages.'

'You employ me because no-one looks after your back like I do, and who'd defend you from pissed-off subscribers if I wasn't here?'

He knew that was true. She was blindly loyal and could be downright intimidating – no-one could collect debts so effectively. 'Buffy, please tell me what was so funny?'

'All right, but don't say I didn't warn you. Old Mrs Elliot asked me how come your daddy was born with such big gonads but you didn't get any.' She burst out into laughter again. 'I'm sorry, but it's funny, especially coming from her, when she's so prim and proper.'

Steve felt himself going red and wondered what they expected him to do. Everyone knew that the well had been sabotaged, but they still wanted him to sink the boots into CEGL – to say that the gas wells were dangerous, poisonous and that they contaminated the air and water. Well, his parents had not brought him up to tell lies but, as he thought about this, he smiled at the irony of them having become such convincing liars themselves.

'Yeah, real funny, Buffy, I don't think,' he said.

The Fisher Valley Protective Alliance was a group of townsfolk and valley people vehemently opposed to the extraction of coal seam gas. It published a weekly newsletter and, unlike Steve Forrest, had no compunction about unleashing a vicious attack on CEGL and the safety of the gas wells dotted around the valley.

Paisley Police Station was a single-level brick building with a main office, a holding cell, a small, tight driveway and three car parks at the rear strictly reserved for police. 'No parking at any time' signs ran the length of the driveway. The window in Josh Gibson's corner of the office looked directly out onto the driveway and he groaned when a silver Porsche pulled up directly in front of him, completely blocking the driveway. He was glad that his two offsiders were out making calls, because he had a feeling that he would not like them to see what was about to occur. A middle-aged woman with sandy hair alighted, wearing a pants suit and silk scarf that would not be out of place in Paris. She quickly checked her perfectly applied make-up in the driver's door rear-vision mirror, but it failed to disguise the hardness of her features.

Josh had met Moira Raymond three years earlier when she had parked in exactly the same spot and he had told her to move or he would book her. As cool as a cucumber, she had pulled out her mobile, punched in a number and, while he was still shouting at her, she passed it to him. 'It's the Chief Commissioner. He'd like a few words with you.' It was the first and only time he had ever spoken to the state's top cop and he was told that Moira was a personal friend and that he should do everything he could to help her. Since then, he had watched her take the premier and senior government ministers on tours of the gas wells around Paisley on many occasions and later dine with them. Whenever she was with a politician, she was quick to spruik the benefits to the state and nation of extracting coal seam gas.

She was as comfortable drinking beer and telling crude jokes in the company of labourers she employed on gas wells as she was sipping Dom Perignon with oil barons. Moira was a complex mix of rapier-wit and charm, which she could turn off and on at a whim. In the not too distant future, with the proviso that she did not fall at a hurdle, she would be CEGL's CEO. She was grimly determined that those opposed to the extraction of coal seam gas in the Fisher Valley would not be that hurdle.

'Good morning, Josh.' Moira smiled through perfectly capped teeth. 'How are you this beautiful day?'

'I'm fine, Moira. What brings you here?' He knew that whatever had brought her here could not be good for him.

'Have you made any arrests yet?'

'No. We don't know that it wasn't an accident.'

'God, the whole town knows it was sabotage, knows who did it and knows Len Forrest is a liar. You know that, don't you Josh?' She rested a perfectly manicured hand on his wrist in the same way a mother restrains her child from straying into danger.

'No, I don't.'

Her icy blue, unblinking eyes locked onto him and she slowly shook her head. 'We plugged the well last night and guess what we found?'

'I don't know,' he muttered.

'A small melted mass of metal that looks like a petrol drum.'

'Don't your maintenance guys carry diesel and oilcans with them?'

'Are you saying that one of my employees left an oilcan at the well? It's not possible. They have to account for everything on a report sheet.'

'People make mistakes and what you've found doesn't prove anything.'

'My people don't make mistakes.' She scowled. 'I really hoped you'd be more cooperative. If any more of our wells are sabotaged, I'll hold you responsible.'

'Moira, there's three of us to cover the whole valley and we've got more to do than worry about your wells. If you're worried about sabotage, you better bring in your own security guards.'

'I might do that,' she said, walking to the door. 'But you won't like it Joshy, because, unlike you, they have their own ways of getting results.'

He watched the Porsche's tyres burn rubber as she reversed out of the driveway and he hoped he wouldn't see her again any time soon.

Five minutes later Moira entered the premises of the *Paisley Chronicle*. Neither Steve nor Buffy had met her but they both knew who she was – everyone in the valley knew who Moira Raymond was. She looked past Buffy and said, 'Steve Forrest?'

Before Steve could respond, Buffy smiled cheekily. 'Who will I say is calling?'

'That'd be me,' Steve said, glaring at Buffy.

'Your article was pretty weak, but I don't suppose you could call your father a liar when he owns the paper.'

Steve was about to protest, but Moira held her hand up. 'I'm not here to complain. I think you've been even-handed in the way you've reported on our industry and I'm guessing you resisted a lot of pressure to bucket us. That's right isn't it?'

'I'm sure you didn't come here to compliment me on my writing.'

'You're right about that. I want to book the centre pages of this Friday's paper for a community announcement about the benefits CEGL can bring to the town.'

'We … we can't,' Buffy gasped.

'I take it you're not the editor of this fine publication,' Moira said, eying Buffy disdainfully. 'So I presume it's not your decision.'

'Buffy plays a vital part in running this newspaper and she organises and allocates advertising space,' Steve said. This wasn't a total lie and at that moment Buffy wanted to hug him. She liked to think that she was tough in a nice way but the woman on the other side of the counter was a bitch: caustic and just plain nasty.

'I've got the copy with me,' Moira said, opening her *Hermes* handbag. 'There are twenty points, starting with the employment opportunities we'll generate and finishing with our undertaking that we haven't and won't contaminate the town's air and water.'

'You've already poisoned the water,' Buffy said. 'Look what happened to poor Charlie Paxton.'

Moira ignored Buffy and stared at Steve. 'You know that's not true. If it was, there'd be a lot more Charlie Paxtons in the valley. I feel sorry for the kid and his family, but his death had nothing to do with us. Are you going to run our advertisement this Friday, or not?'

'You've been here for nearly three years but you've never approached us before. Why now?'

'We looked at advertising a few years back, but your circulation barely exceeded three thousand then, so there was no point. You've done well in building up the readership and I'm going to reward you for your efforts by running weekly community advertisements for the next twelve months.'

'And it'll drop back to three thousand if we run your ads,' Buffy butted in.

Steve was pondering the pros and cons of this surprising offer and knew that he needed more time. The increase in advertising revenue would add significantly to cash flow and profits, which were still small, but, against this, it would be a real fight to hold on to subscribers and small advertisers.

'Thank you, but I need to think about your proposition and talk to my professional advisers before I can make a decision. I'm sorry, but I can't place your announcement in this Friday's paper.'

'That's very disappointing. Talk to your advisers, Steve, but don't think that my offer's going to remain on the table forever. Phone me.' She dropped her business card on the counter, turned on her heel and disappeared through the door.

'You can't do it, Steve. You'll destroy everything you've worked so hard for,' Buffy said.

'We'll see.'

Steve had only been home a few minutes, flicked the TV on, grabbed a coke from the fridge and put his feet up when the phone rang. 'Hello.'

'You can't do it! You just can't do it!'

'Dad, settle down. You'll do yourself an injury.'

'Listen to me. You not only won't have a subscriber left, you'll be the most hated man in the valley.'

'How did you find out about CEGL's proposition?'

'Word travels.'

'You mean Buffy phoned you the minute I left the office, don't you?'

'I didn't say it was her.'

'You didn't need to. Dad, we can use the additional cash flow and, if we handle it well, we won't lose many subscribers. I thought I'd do an editorial saying the *Chronicle* has to present both sides of the story.'

'That's baloney. I forbid you to accept that woman's money!'

'Forbid me? Dad, you put me in charge of the paper; now let me do my job.' Steve slammed the phone down, something he'd never done to his father before.

Chapter 8

The Federal Bank of Australia had been established in Paisley for nearly a hundred years in a large bluestone building on the corner of Main and Pedder Streets. The bank had an almost unblemished history of helping wineries, farms and small businesses through the hard climatic times that rural Australia was subject to. You could count on one hand the number of times the bank had foreclosed on a mortgage, and in living memory it had never forced anyone into bankruptcy. As the area expanded, the other banks set up branches in town but hardly won enough business to justify their existence. The FBA was the people's bank, the bank you could trust to help you through the hard times.

Craig and Jenny Orr operated a successful organic fruit and vegetable farm on fifty acres of prime land, and were not the slightest concerned when their good friend, Andrew Brown, FBA's branch manager, phoned on Monday and asked them to come in and see him. However, they were a little taken aback that Andrew had not said anything to them at the weekend, when he had attended the birthday of their nine-year-old son, Jarryd.

Usually, when they had a meeting with Andrew, he came out of his office and greeted them warmly. Today they were shown into his office by one of the tellers and they were surprised to see him wearing a suit and tie. He was usually tieless, shirtsleeves rolled up, with his shirt hanging loosely over his protruding stomach. He got up from behind his desk and shook Craig's hand but did not make eye contact, nor did he kiss Jenny on the cheek.

'Did you get a promotion or something, Andy?' Craig joked, his deep voice echoing around the room. In direct contrast to his tiny wife, he was a big man who, after years of hard work, didn't carry an ounce of surplus weight. His face was weather-beaten and drawn.

Andrew stroked his bushy salt-and-pepper beard nervously, picked at his ears and patted his long brown hair. 'It's a bit more serious than that.'

'You're worrying me Andy,' Jenny teased. 'You're not going to foreclose on us are you?'

'Head office has directed me to reduce the bank's loans to you by half,' he blurted out, looking down at his feet.

'You're joking,' Jenny said, but her face said otherwise. Lips pursed and eyes narrowed, she stared at Andrew and watched him cringe in embarrassment. Because she was small, there were those who ignored her, but Andrew knew better, having seen her outmanoeuvre suppliers who had mistakenly taken her for a soft touch. There was nothing soft about Jenny Orr when it came to business and she provided the brains in the Orr partnership, while her husband supplied the brawn.

'I'm sorry.'

'You're sorry. Why, Andrew, why? Have we ever missed a mortgage payment? Have we ever exceeded our overdraft limit? Have we ever missed a lease payment? What have we bloody-well done to deserve this?'

'They know that you've been model customers, but they're concerned about the security.'

'Are they stark raving mad? They have the property as security, the orchard as security, the vegetable gardens as security and the equipment as security. What do you mean they're worried about the security? Jesus, for every dollar we've borrowed, the bank's got two as security.'

'No, that's what it used to have.'

'I don't understand.'

'Jenny, you know that your neighbours, the Cleevers, signed an access agreement with CEGL, don't you?'

'Yes, of course I do. The poor old things were conned into signing and CEGL was never going to let 'em off the hook. They lost six acres of their land and inherited three bloody gas wells that they'd do anything to get rid of. But what's that got to do with us?' Jenny squeezed her husband's hand.

'The powers that be in Sydney had your property valued and those gas wells really knocked the value about. The valuer discounted your property on the basis of who'd want to buy it when there's three ugly, possibly poisonous gas wells right next door. Worse, the Cleevers' property is on the high side of the hill and you're both drawing your water from the same source.'

The Orrs were shocked. They had toiled from dawn to dusk on the property for nearly fifteen years and had never failed to increase its productivity and yield. They had been increasing the cash flow of the business while at same time thinking that they were increasing the value of the property.

'What about the value of the produce?' Jenny was stunned. 'We're going to have a record year and supermarkets and health food shops are paying premium prices for organics.'

Andrew felt gutted. He had not slept the previous night and had discussed with his wife, Sally, handing in his resignation; but where was he going to get another job? He had no university degree, had been with the FBA for twenty years, was approaching forty and the only chance he would have of getting another position was with another bank, but even that was doubtful. He had a low-interest-rate housing loan that he would have to pay out if he quit; a fully maintained car that he would lose; and he had three children to provide for. There was no way he could buck his superiors in Sydney, or resign.

'I'm sorry, but my bosses don't think you're going to be able to sell your produce as organic anymore.'

'All because of those bloody gas wells, which aren't even on our property?'

'Yes.'

'How long have we got?'

'Thirty days.'

'We'll find another bank.'

'I really hope you can, but you should know that they're also reviewing their clients' loan security.'

'What happens if we can't?'

Andrew felt Jenny's eyes glaring at him and he didn't have the courage to look directly at her. 'The bank will appoint a mortgagee in possession to sell your property.'

'And we'll get nothing for it. Only bottom feeders turn up to mortgagee's auctions. By the time the mortgagee in possession takes his fees and you recover your principal, interest and legal fees, we'll get nothing.'

'So CEGL's gas wells killed us,' Craig growled. 'How does that work?'

'What about the wineries?' Jenny asked. 'Did those hard-hearted bosses of yours get the wineries valued too?'

'I can't say.'

'You just did. How many, Andrew? How many wineries are you going to close? You're going to destroy families and land values throughout the valley.'

'I'm sorry, I can't say.' Andrew cringed, knowing that in the next month he would repeat this scenario at least twenty times with people who were friends and whom he had known for years. He fought the urge to puke and felt himself starting to choke. He wanted to say, *It's not me, it's CEGL and it's the gas wells,* but how could he? CEGL was one of the bank's biggest accounts in Sydney, its business far more valuable than the Paisley branch's thousands of accounts.

'Sorry? Is that all you can say? Doesn't our friendship mean anything to you?' Jenny's eyes watered in frustration.

'Honey, it's not Andrew's fau..'

'Shut up Craig. Come on, we're leaving. And Andrew, if you or Sally ever need any help with anything, don't even think about phoning us.'

After they had left, Andrew rested his head in his hands and wondered how he and his family were going to survive in Paisley.

The Orrs sat in their car and stared at the old bluestone bank. 'I can't believe that Andrew's doing this to us,' Jenny said.

Craig knew that it wasn't Andrew but, rather than risk feeling the sting of his wife's tongue again, he said, 'Me neither.'

Chapter 9

The Fisher Valley Protective Alliance, through its Chief Executive, Jack Thomas, hastily convened a meeting of valley folk and other interested parties in the Paisley Town Hall, after it became known that the FBA had served demands for repayment of loans on four wineries, a dairy farm and the Orrs. Thomas was a middle-aged Canadian with a lush mane of silky hair, a genial face and love of food and wine; equally obvious was his hate for the coal seam gas companies. It was rumoured that he had spies, or those friendly to his cause, in some of the gas companies and he always seemed to be a step ahead of 'the enemy'. When he stood to address the meeting, every seat in the hall was taken and it was standing room only, with the crowd packed six deep against the rear wall. Many attendees carried placards with the words, 'CEGL go to hell' and 'What gives CEGL the right to rape and destroy our properties?' One held by Charles Paxton as he entered the hall with Len Forrest had even some locals gasping, 'CEGL killing our kids,' but the gasps were drowned out by thunderous applause and calls of, 'Let's blow up a few more wells,' and, 'The government won't help us so let's take matters into our own hands.' Unlike the cheers his father received, Steve Forrest was met with loud whispers of 'traitor' and 'Judas' as he pushed his way to the front of the hall, and squatted down in the aisle. Billy McGregor and his mates parked themselves against the back wall, itching to belt the daylights out of any CEGL supporters stupid enough to show themselves. Josh Gibson stood nervously at the entrance to the hall and wondered if this was what a lynch mob looked like. Sandi Carlisle was next to him, mesmerised yet excited by the anger in the seething crowd.

'Order, order,' Thomas shouted, his deep powerful voice lost in the din.

'Give him a go,' a few locals shouted and the noise subsided to an angry murmur.

'I called this meeting to discuss what we're going to do to stop the FBA making more loan repayment demands. Because the demands stem directly from the actions of the gas companies, I've asked Dennis Fulton from *Save the Earth* to address you. Simon Breckenridge will handle any legal questions.'

The contrast in the two men was stark. Fulton, a former leader of the Greens in Queensland, was tall and slim with grey hair, blue eyes and a kind face. He was dressed in an open-neck shirt and jeans. Breckenridge was small with a face resembling a whippet's. He was bald but his thick black eyebrows had knitted together and matched his eyes, giving him a menacing look. He wore a single-breasted navy blue, pin-stripe *Zegna* suit, a matching tie and Italian hand-made black shoes that he could see his reflection in.

'We don't need a bloody greenie telling us what to do,' one of the graziers yelled.

'Yeah,' someone else urged. 'He's one of the mugs who stopped us clearing trees from our properties.'

'Order, order! Dennis has been fighting the gas companies in Queensland for the last three years, and many farmers and graziers up there didn't like him, but now, because of his sterling efforts, they love him. He's given up his valuable time to talk to you, so give him the courtesy of listening,' Thomas shouted and passed the microphone to Dennis.

'Thank you, Mr Chairman, I'm not sure you're right about the farmers loving me though,' Dennis laughed. 'But I like to think there's a mutual respect.' There were a few sniggers in the audience. 'I'm going to be brief and I know I don't need to waste your time by telling you about the evils of *big gas*. I will tell you how we thwarted them on the Spurling Downs though, which was to form a vigilante group of about 200 members connected by a good communication network, that we called *Barricade the Gate* and which we can activate within minutes.'

'Activate to do what?' someone yelled. 'Save the bloody trees?'

Dennis ignored the interjection. 'As I was saying, from the minute we knew the gas companies were moving to forcibly enter a property, we sent text messages to every member and then we converged on the property with trucks, trailers and cars to form a blockade in front of the gates. That stopped them in their tracks.'

Dennis could see signs of scepticism on the faces of many farmers and graziers. Amid the groaning, a man whom Dennis knew only by recent photos in the *Paisley Chronicle,* rose to speak.

'How did you know which properties they were going to enter?'

'Thank you for the question, Mr Paxton, and may I express my profound sorrow for your recent loss. We watch the main bases they've set up and when their trucks move we've got someone following. We also have our contacts in the gas companies' offices who feed us tipoffs which enables us to mobilise in advance. Ask yourself, what would you do if Australia was invaded by a foreign power and your properties were seized? You'd fight, wouldn't you? Well, your properties are being invaded by the gas companies, which are mainly foreign-owned, so what's the difference? Let me tell you – there is no difference! If we were invaded, the government would order the army to defend us but, because it's the gas companies stealing our properties and, because our governments are so desperate for the tax and royalties that they'll generate, they're actually encouraging them to rape and pillage our land.'

'So you think we should form a group like *Barricade the Gate?*' someone yelled. 'How's that going to help those of us who've already had our loans called up?' This was greeted with many 'Yeahs' and a few dissenting grumbles about doing something that a bloody greenie was suggesting.

'Yes, but you have to be smart. By all means barricade the gates with your vehicles, but you mustn't resort to physical violence because, if you do, you'll lose the public relations battle. Lose the public and you lose the war. For those of you who've had your loans called up by the FBA, I can only sympathise, but sadly I have no silver bullet that can help you. Perhaps Simon Breckenridge does.'

A smattering of begrudging applause went around the hall for Dennis as he handed over the microphone and sat down.

'Thank you Dennis. Sadly, there's not much we can do to help those who've already been served with demands,' Breckenridge said. 'Sure, there's legal tactics that can be used to stall the FBA, but they're expensive and in the end the bank will still win. What we have to do is make it as hard as possible for the bank to make any further demands.'

'We could always tar and feather Andrew Brown and run him out of town,' someone yelled, to laughter and cries of 'hear, hear.'

'Or we could punch his lights out,' Billy McGregor shouted, to raucous support from his gang, who had obviously taken no notice of Dennis.

'Look, what's happened has nothing to do with Andrew. There's nothing he can do; he's just following orders which I'm sure he tried to resist.'

'He should've resigned,' Jenny Orr spat out. 'He sold his friends out.'

'No, he didn't, Jenny.' Breckenridge sighed. 'He's been backed into a corner and he's just trying to survive, like you. There's no point in attacking Andrew and if anyone's thinking along those lines I'd counsel them to rethink. He doesn't deserve it and anyone stupid enough to assault him will most likely go to jail and we'll lose credibility and public support.'

A few boos echoed around the room.

'You'd be well advised to listen to Simon,' Tom Morgan drawled and the noise subsided. 'These demands have nothing to do with Andrew and if he's not making them the bank will soon find someone else who will.'

Breckenridge was grateful for the support but, as he stared at the faces in the crowd, he saw desperation and hostility and a shiver went up his spine. He did not fear for himself but for these normally peaceful farmers and vineyard owners who were being backed into a corner by unscrupulous gas companies advised by big-firm lawyers who in the main had never set foot in the valley.

'Thanks, Tom. If we're going to stop this occurring we have to keep CEGL and the smaller gas companies off our properties. Don't cooperate with them, don't sign their lease agreements and, whatever you do, don't sign their access agreements because, if you do, your actions will not only devalue your property but your neighbours' as well and, worse, you'll expose them to the same action taken against the Orrs. And don't forget, they'll tell any lie necessary to get onto your property. Some of the lies they tell are about provid …'

An old man stood up and banged his walking stick on the floor. His spectacles sat on his hawk-like nose. 'They tricked me! They said they wanted to do some minor exploratory work and that if my wife and I granted them access, they'd resurface the track to our house and replace the fencing on the south boundary. Before I knew it, the bastards had drilled three wells and when I complained, they told me to get lost. I had no rights.' Tears of anger welled up in his eyes. 'And they only resurfaced the track to help them bring their heavy equipment in, but the fence is still in a dilapidated condition and their workers told me they know nothing about it being replaced. I'm sorry Craig, I'm sorry Jenny. I never knew that when I signed that access agreement I'd be hurting you.'

'We know that, Mr Cleever,' Jenny said, feeling so sorry for the old man, whom she had hated ever since that day at the bank.

'They sank one of the ugly things about a hundred metres from my house and when they fracked it, I swear the house shook like it'd been hit by an earthquake. Emily and I were scared it was gonna collapse and every time we go out the front door we're staring at a gas well that we smell and hear every hour of the day. It stinks like rotten eggs and they warned us to make sure we left a house window open so we wouldn't get a methane build-up that might blow us sky high. Emily, who's been healthy all her life, now gets short of breath after walking twenty metres, I developed rashes on my chest and shoulders and we both lost our appetites and weight. When I complained, they said it was old-age and refused to help. Had I known what they were going to do, I would've been waiting at the front gate for them with my shot gun.'

'Thank you, Mr Cleever.'

'I'm not finished.' He banged his walking stick on the floor again. 'About three months ago, the water in our bores turned murky and CEGL had it analysed and told us it wasn't harmful and was fine to drink and wash in. So when two of their executives came to visit us we offered them a glass and they wouldn't touch it. You should have seen them run for cover.'

There was laughter around the hall.

'Anyhow, I told 'em I was going to the environment authorities and was gonna start writing letters to the newspapers. The following day they phoned me and said they'd install two water tanks on our property and deliver tanker water to us at their expense, but there was a catch. Me and the missus had to sign a non-disclosure agreement acknowledging that the contaminated water wasn't caused as a result of their drilling and that we'll never sue or be party to litigation against them. They told us that if we disclosed the contents of the agreement they'd walk away from their undertakings and stop delivering water to us. Well here it is, and if anyone wants to read it or make copies, you can see me after the meeting,' Cleever shouted defiantly holding the agreement above his head.

'Thanks, Mr Cleever. I couldn't have illustrated the gas companies' lies and trickery better,' Breckenridge said. 'This meeting sympathises with you.'

A number of people said 'hear, hear' and a few sitting close to Cleever patted him on the back as he sat down, breathing heavily.

'How do you know when a gas company executive is telling lies?' Breckenridge asked rhetorically.

Before Breckenridge could answer his own question, Len Forrest drawled, 'When you see his lips move.'

Some in the room laughed, others cursed and tears of anger and remorse ran down the leathery cheeks of old Artie Cleever.

'Let's hear from Don Carmody,' someone shouted. 'He runs the largest merchant bank in the country, so he should know how to beat the banks.' There was murmured approval.

A distinguished looking man in his early sixties, with receding grey hair and an open face, rose from his chair. He was immaculately dressed in a conservative, hand-tailored charcoal-grey business suit. Don Carmody had owned a vineyard and winery in the valley for more than twenty years and was vehemently opposed to the gas companies drilling in the rich rural areas of Australia.

'Friends, what you must understand is that every gas well sunk in this valley reduces the land available for primary production and reduces the water supply because, as you know, unlike us, the mining companies are not limited by water quotas. But worse, it increases the probability of aquifer contamination and the eventual destruction of the valley. This reduces the value of our properties and that's why the banks are acting to protect their loans.'

'We know that, Don,' someone growled. 'What we want to know is how to stop them.'

'As you know, they've been active in the Tura *estates* of late because they see the *estatees* as a soft target but, once they've established a foothold there, they'll advance across the valley like cane toads, devouring everything before them. Some of you aren't concerned about what happens around Tura because the land's infertile. You should be concerned, very concerned. We need to establish a beachhead there, support our neighbours, unify and draw a line in the sand. If we defeat the gas companies in the *estates* we defeat them in the valley.'

'Yeah, but how do we defeat them?'

'We establish a fighting fund, to be administered by Simon, where he instructs one of the major legal firms to act for us. I mean no disrespect to you Simon but, as you know, your firm doesn't have the personnel to cut it against the big firms acting for the gas companies and I think we should mount a significant action against them that stops them entering the *estates*.'

This was met by catcalls and then someone shouted. 'It's all right for you Don, you and the McLachlan Bank have got plenty of cash, but we're fighting to keep our heads above water.'

Someone else interjected. 'Simon, isn't it true that no matter how hard we fight, the courts will eventually side with the gas companies and order us to let them enter our properties?'

'Not necessarily and, if we could win a major case like Don is suggesting and establish a precedent, we might be able to throw them out of the valley but, if we lose, we'll be at their mercy, so there are great risks in adopting that strategy. I think a better plan is to stall them for as long as we can in the hope that, as the issue becomes more mainstream, public opinion forces the government to have a change of mind about the extraction of coal seam gas.'

There were groans from those more interested in taking direct and forceful action.

'I remind you that the premier is speaking on this subject in this very hall tomorrow fortnight, and this will provide us with an opportunity to demonstrate peacefully in front of the cameras,' Carmody said, and the catcalls were more numerous and louder. It wasn't only Billy McGregor and his gang who were looking for a violent solution.

Harry O'Brien had been in Australia for twenty years but still spoke in a rich Irish brogue. He owned a small boutique winery in the valley and to look at him you would think that he spent most days sampling his wares. 'What if we get rid of this Labor government and replace them with the conservatives?'

'It won't work, Harry,' Tom Morgan responded. 'This state is stuffed, services are terrible and the government's been running budget deficits for years. They've had to offer the gas companies five royalty-free years so they can steal an advantage over Queensland, but they're gonna get hundreds of millions in the future. And when you put a heap of cash on one side and an environmental issue on the other and ask a politician to make a decision, no matter which party he represents, the heap of cash is always gonna win. And don't forget the federal government will reap even more in taxes.'

'What about the Greens then?' O'Brien persisted.

'Yeah, they can help,' Morgan said. 'But they're not in a position to alter government policy. They can help with the media and maybe get us some coverage but, Harry, do you want to support a party that's into euthanasia, legalising gay marriage and taxing you out of existence?'

'Euthanasia's a good thing and I can think of a Porsche-driving gas exec I'd willingly inject,' O'Brien said, to cacophonous applause.

Dennis Fulton rose to defend the Greens but the firm hand of Jack Thomas on his arm caused him to sit down again. Thomas knew that this was a crowd that didn't need to be side-tracked or incited.

'Should those of us with unencumbered properties take our business away from the FBA as a show of protest?' A farmer sitting in the front row asked.

'According to Andrew Brown the other big banks will soon be taking the same action as the FBA,' Breckenridge said. 'So you'd need to give your business to one of the smaller regional banks. If it makes you feel good, then do it, but it won't have any impact on the FBA.'

'We need to get more press coverage, more documentaries on television; and more stories about the damage the gas miners are doing to rural communities and we need to get the city folk on our side. There's a brilliant documentary, *Gasland*, showing at the Majestic, that sets out the American experience and you should all get along and watch it,' Len Forrest said, before his gravelly voice was drowned out by groans.

'Did it help the Americans get rid of the gas companies?' someone asked. 'I don't think so.'

'If we wait that long, it'll be too late for most of us,' someone else said.

'You can groan all you like,' Len said. 'But when I was young, people power brought our country's participation in a war to an end. One hundred thousand people massed in Melbourne to oppose our involvement in Vietnam and the government brought our troops home. If *they* could stop our participation in a war, then surely *we* can garner enough support to stop the gas companies.'

'Charles. Charles Paxton,' someone asked. 'What do you think we should do?'

There was an excited buzz and someone else said, 'Let's blow up a few more gas wells.'

'I can't think of anything that will make the FBA withdraw their demands but I think we should form a group along the lines that our friend Dennis Fulton suggested, which can act at short notice to blockade the gas companies at the gates to any property they're trying to enter. If we stop the gas wells, hopefully we stop the bank from making any fresh demands.'

'I'll be in that,' Billy McGregor yelled, thrusting his fist into the air. 'We'll call it *Smash the bastards!*'

There were numerous calls of 'Good onya Charles,' as if he, rather than Dennis Fulton, had come up with the idea.

'We'll call it *Lock 'em out* and that's what we'll be doing,' Paxton responded.

'Yeah, but if they resist, we might have to do a bit of persuading,' Billy persisted, punching his fist into his palm.

'Order, order!' Thomas yelled, seizing the microphone. 'We can barricade the gates with our cars and trucks, but in the end the gas companies will go to the courts and get orders requiring the police to remove us. We mustn't attack or assault their employees or the police, because that will set our cause back years. I implore you to act within the law.'

This brought a wave of booing and one of Billy's gang said, 'Let's go to the pub,' and twenty young men pushed towards the entrance, taking many others with them.

'Does anyone have anything else they wish to raise?' Thomas shouted over the din of moving chairs and shuffling feet. When there was no response he declared the meeting adjourned and this was greeted by faint, uninspired applause.

'So what do you think of the gas companies now?' Len Forrest asked, grabbing his son's arm as they left the hall. 'It's their bloody gas wells that have destroyed property values and forced the bank to act.'

'Dad, I'm not sure that you're right. There's a massive glut of wine nationwide, too many grape vines and the competition from the French and Americans on world markets is intense. There'd be lucky to be ten percent of the wineries in the valley turning a profit. I'm sorry for those who've had their loans called up but the bank has to protect itself and you can't expect it to carry loss-making businesses.'

'Is that what they taught you at Harvard? Didn't they teach you anything about people, families, their lives and their hopes, or couldn't they translate that into the almighty dollar? Are you going to tell me that the gas companies didn't destroy Bill Morrisey's dairy farm?'

'And how did they do that?'

'His yields are way down and his cows are sick. Two years ago he was getting an average of twenty litres per cow per day and then CEGL conned him into letting them sink two gas wells on his property and the yields plunged. Bill said that two of his dams were bubbling after they installed the wells and his cows must've drunk from them. What do you think of that?'

'Dad, it's common knowledge around town that he lost his major contract to supply Murray Valley Dairies and that's the reason his farm failed.'

'Yes, because the quality of the milk he was producing deteriorated. How can you be so blind to what's going on around you?'

'It's progress, and you can't stand in the way of progress.'

'What about the Orrs, Mr Smarty Pants? Andrew Brown told them that their loan was being called in because the bank bosses didn't think they could maintain their licence to produce organic foods, because of the close proximity of gas wells. Don't tell me that wasn't the gas company's fault.'

As they walked past the car park, Steve caught sight of Jenny Orr with her arms around Tom Morgan's neck and tears rolling down her cheeks. Craig had a hand on Morgan's shoulder, his expression a cross between disbelief and relief. Steve paused, looked over and pondered what might be going on.

'Dad, that's disturbing and I'm not sure that the bank didn't over-react. You've gotta admit that some of the rumours about the destruction coal seam gas will unleash on the community have been exaggerated and maybe the bank was spooked.'

'You're living in a fool's paradise, Son. You need to see *Gasland,* and then you'll find out about the misery that the big oil and gas companies in America unleashed in Pennsylvania and Colorado. Poison in the water, poison in the air, people lighting their drinking water, sickness, cancer and animals th..'

'I went to see it last night,' Steve interrupted. 'It's so biased and one-sided, I'm not sure it's believable. The oil and gas companies weren't given a chance to put their side.'

'Yes they were. Were you asleep when that guy, Josh Fox, phoned the gas companies, trying to get an interview, and they knocked him back or wouldn't take his calls?'

'And you actually believed that?'

'Why wouldn't I?'

'Because it's a fix-up. Michael Moore does it in his docos and Al Gore did something similar in *An Inconvenient Truth.* They make it look like they're trying to get the other side's opinion but it's the last thing they want. It's far more effective to create the smokescreen of a cover-up and the illusion of evil.'

'Unbelievable. What's it going to take to convince you?'

'Dad, look; I agree with you that the mining companies shouldn't be able to force their way onto properties and I've written articles expressing that view, but until the legislation changes they're not breaking any laws.' Steve put his arm around his father's shoulders. 'One of the guys I did that management course with at Harvard lives in Denver and I'm going to Skype him tonight and find out what's fact and what's make-believe in Colorado.'

'At last some good news. I'm guessing by the morning you'll have changed your mind.'

'Perhaps.' Steve smiled, not having told his father that his friend in Colorado was an investment banker. 'Oh, and by the way, I'm going to accept CEGL's offer to buy advertising space.'

Len Forrest clenched and unclenched his hands. 'I never thought you'd do that to me, Son.'

'It's a business decision, Dad, pure and simple. The *Chronicle* can't afford to knock back that type of revenue and, besides, it'll speed up getting rid of your debts.'

'With the blood and sweat of those folks that the gas companies are running out of the valley,' his father snarled, wiping a tear from his cheek. 'Thanks, but no thanks.'

'Wait until you see how I handle it, before judging me.'

Chapter 10

Dean Prezky woke from a broken sleep to the sounds of birds tweeting and the humming of the bush but he could still hear the *whirr, whirr, whirr,* even though it wasn't as noticeable as it had been in the silence of the night. He climbed into his rusty Toyota four-wheel-drive and headed to the CEGL site office, where the noise was loudest. He pulled up and looked out of his window at a heap of neatly configured steel pipes and four compressors surrounded by a chain-mesh fence and instantly knew the compressor station had been commissioned. The eight gas wells on CEGL's property had been converted from exploration to production and methane was being piped to the compressor station. Filled-in trenches, where pipes had been laid, extended to the property's boundaries and methane was most probably being received from wells on surrounding properties. Dean knew that, had he agreed to have pipes laid under his property, gas from the two wells sunk on Joanna's property would be pumping to the compressor station, and he guessed that pipes would eventually be laid under the dirt road. He had no idea where the compressed gas was being pumped to, or whether it was for domestic use or export, nor did he really care; his only concern was the noise. He climbed out of the four-wheel-drive and knelt down, closing his eyes, as he listened to the *whirr, whirr, whirr,* shocked by its intensity. *Surely this breached whatever laws determined the noise level? Perhaps the noise would abate after the compressor station had been running for a few days.*

At the rear of the property he could see bulldozers and excavators clearing a massive area. He didn't know what they were doing but would later find they had been constructing a huge, hundred-acre, lined pond, where CEGL would store the toxic, saline-laden wastewater from the wells in the area.

That night, Dean tried to block his ears with his fingers, but the drone of the *whirr, whirr, whirr* continued to deprive him of sleep. Vicki, who was a heavy sleeper, tried to bury her head under the blankets and the kids were up all night going to the fridge or the pantry, or getting glasses of water. At nine o'clock the following morning, Dean, cranky and tired, was on the phone to a CEGL environment officer who told him that they had measured the noise levels of the compressor station after it had been commissioned and that it complied with environmental guidelines. After Dean complained more vociferously, he was informed that there was nothing that could be done. When he told the officer he was going to lodge a complaint with the council, he heard a distinct chuckle, followed by 'Good luck' and the sound of dial tone.

The lady he spoke to at the Tura Council was sympathetic but advised that the planning department was rarely even notified about exploration and development licences for coal seam gas. These were issued directly by the Department of Industry and Investment. Yes, he could lodge a complaint with Council, but it would have to be in writing and it was unlikely that CEGL would have breached the conditions of their licence or the mandated noise levels, so was it worth it? Dean was fuming at the injustice and snapped at her, 'Well, if you won't help, I'll go to the environment authorities.'

'Sir, I never said this, but you're not going to find anyone in any government department willing to take on *big gas*. There's far too much money involved to rock the coal seam gas boat.'

'How can that be?'

She lowered her voice. 'I can't help you, but you should talk to someone at the Fisher Valley Protective Alliance.'

'I don't have anything in common with a bunch of rich farmers and vineyard owners.'

'I have to go, Sir. Think about what I said.'

Dean did not move from his chair as he pondered the two conversations; the arrogance of the CEGL employee, the helplessness of the council officer and her use of the two words he hadn't heard before, *big gas,* in a tone that suggested she might just as well have been talking about the *Mafia*.

His thoughts were interrupted by Vicki. 'Honey,' she yelled, from the kitchen, an edge to her voice. 'We're a thousand dollars short in our cheque account. Do you know anything about it?'

The last thing he needed was a fight with Vicki. 'No,' he lied. 'I have to go into Tura to pick up the mail and fill the Toyota. I'll go through the cheque butts when I get back.'

'I've already been through them and the butt is blank. I'll have to phone the bank. Aren't you going to work today?'

'It's too late; half the day's already gone.'

'Another day off,' Vicki whined. 'We've got no money and you're not working.'

'We'll be fine.' He kissed her on the cheek, anxious to get out of the house.

Tura was a typical small country town with about twenty-five shops, a service station, hotel, two motels and a third nearing completion. As Dean pulled the Toyota up to the diesel pump, he saw a Filliburton truck parked at the adjoining pump. Frank Beck and a few of his workers were at the door to the service station shop, arguing heatedly with a group of men. One, a solidly built young man with a mop of unruly, ginger hair, was red-faced and gesticulating angrily. It was a hot day and he was wearing overalls over a long-sleeved flannel shirt, and heavy work boots. Standing next to him was an older man – unshaven, with grey straggly hair and a roll-your-own cigarette hanging out of the side of his mouth. He was more appropriately dressed for the weather, in a flimsy white T-shirt and jeans, and he was clearly supporting the younger man.

As Dean watched, he realised that the others were all on Beck's side. It wasn't Beck who was surrounded, but the odd couple. He didn't know who the two men were but he sauntered over, intending to talk to Beck – whom he had always found reasonable – about the compressor noise.

The younger man was rolling his eyes and shouting and, when he started to unbutton his shirtsleeves, Dean, convinced it was a prelude to fisticuffs, moved quickly to intervene. As he reached the group, he saw the man pointing at his bare arms, which were covered with ugly red welts. 'You poisoned our water, you bastard,' he roared. 'I'm covered with these things and so are my kids. And to think you made yourself out a big man when you watered our roads and tracks to get rid of the dust, when all you were doing was saving the cost of getting rid of your contaminated wastewater. Bastard!'

'You poisoned all the dams in the area,' the older man added, spitting in the gap between Beck's feet, while rolling another cigarette.

Beck lolled up against the door sneering, his well-muscled body barely contained by his tight, short-sleeved shirt. The man next to him looked over at the younger man and said, 'Jeez Shawn, Filliburton and Frank are good for the town. Look at all the business they've brought to it and you don't know what you're talking about. God, as if a respected American company like Filliburton would poison your dam. Why don't you apologise to Frank and get back to the *estate*?'

'You must be selling an awful lot of newspapers these days, Jason,' the older man said.

'Keep out of it, Mick,' another man said.

'Ah, Bill, I hear you've doubled the rents on your motels since the gas companies came to town, and business is so good that you're building another one.'

'Shut up, Mick. You're nothing but a trouble-maker.'

'Have a look at this,' the younger man bellowed, slipping his overalls down to his waist and removing his shirt to reveal a body covered in red, weeping welts. 'My kids are covered in 'em as well. They scratch all day and can't sleep at night and we only got 'em after Filliburton's tankers watered the tracks with that toxic wastewater.'

'You don't know that, Shawn,' the newsagent scoffed.

'Yes he does,' Dean said, pulling his T-shirt over his head to show the scars on his well-developed chest. 'I don't swim in my dam anymore and me and my kids have been on tablets and creams for weeks. And to think I thought you were doing me a favour with that water, Frank, you slimy piece of shit!'

'Well,' Beck drawled, 'it seems we're no longer welcome in Tura, so I'll have to relocate my men to Paisley. If this town's not prepared to support Filliburton, we're not prepared to support the town.'

'No, no, Frank,' the motel owner pleaded. 'They don't represent the town; you don't need to go to Paisley.'

'That's right,' the proprietor of the hardware store said. 'Apologise to Frank for making those ridiculous claims, Shawn. You probably got those bloody things on your body because you don't wash properly?'

'Well that applies to me too,' Dean snarled. 'Are you saying me and my kids don't wash ourselves?'

'He didn't mean anything,' the newsagent interrupted. 'Look, Shawn, just say you're sorry and we can get things back to normal again. Frank's a big enough man to accept your apology and let bygones be bygones, aren't you Frank?'

'I ain't ever apologising to that bastard.'

'And nor should you.' Dean struggled to stop himself from crashing his fist into Beck's sneering face.

'That's right,' Mick chipped in, firing off a squirt of saliva that landed next to the hardware man's shiny shoes.

'Come on boys, let's get packed and out of here,' Beck said, striding off towards the motel, with the townspeople following close behind, begging him to change his mind. He smiled. *Divide and conquer – it always worked. No matter what part of the world you were in.*

'How come I haven't seen you before?' the older man asked Dean. 'I'm Mick Petheridge. I've gotta place out in the west *estates* and this is one of me neighbours, Shawn Rosen. Shawn's kids' bodies are covered with welts, their noses bleed at night and they've been vomiting uncontrollably. Poor little mites.'

'Good to meet you. I'm Dean Prezky. Me and my kids got welts all over our bodies too, but I never knew how until now. Jeez, I came to the *estates* looking for privacy. I just wanted to be left alone with my family.'

'Mate, we all came here for that reason. I've got thirty acres and young Shawn's got seventy just down the track from me. We've been here for years, but we've only got to know each other in the last year because of those bloody gas companies,' Mick said. 'We formed the *Tura Defence Association* eighteen months ago, created our own website and we've built up to nearly 200 members.'

'From the *estates?*'

'Hardly. Our members include farmers, graziers, millionaire vineyard owners, conservatives and greenies from the valley; all with one thing in common, a passion to stop *big gas* in its tracks.'

'Mick's our tactician and General.'

'General? You make it sound like a war.'

'That's what it is, Dean, and while you mightn't know it yet, you're in the middle of the warzone. Have a look at our website and see what you think. We're always looking for new members and it don't cost nothin' to join.'

'It was nice meeting you guys. I'm sorry, I have to get to the post office, but I'll have a look at your website.' Dean climbed into the Toyota. He was seething but had no intention of joining any group that might seek to control his actions, no matter how good its intentions.

The heat haze rose from the bitumen as the Toyota rolled down the road towards the post office. It was a small timber building with a flat corrugated iron roof that extended over the footpath to protect the mail boxes from the elements. Dean opened his box and removed a dozen or so envelopes that he flicked through, knowing that they were bills, but the last one bore the name 'Pitcher Laboratories' and he hastily tore it open. The words benzene and toluene meant little to him but they sounded nasty, and he was even more suspicious when the report stated that their levels significantly exceeded the norm. As he looked up, he saw the hardware man, newsagent and the motel owner staring at him from across the road, their faces drawn and glum. Clearly they weren't happy with him.

Nor was Vicki and, as he drove up the driveway, she came out the front door, crossed her arms and glared. She had phoned the bank seeking details of the thousand-dollar cheque and, when they'd told her that the payee was Pitcher Laboratories, she knew exactly what had occurred.

'How could you do it? I thought we agreed that we couldn't afford to have that damn dam water analysed.'

'No, Vicki, we didn't agree. You told me, and you know how much I hate being told I can't do something.'

She was about to ask him where she was going to get the money to meet the mortgage, but his face was black, his bottom lip was quivering and his arms were at his sides, hands formed into tight fists. They had been together for fifteen years and, while he had always been stubborn, he had also been docile and easy-going. Vicki had only ever seen him lose his temper twice and it had been like Vesuvius erupting. Somehow he had managed to physically control himself on both occasions, but the vitriol that had poured from his mouth had been destructive and terrifying and the recipients of his attacks had cowered. For the third time in her life, she watched him fighting for self-control and knew this was not the time to chide him.

'Have you eaten?' she asked.

'I'm not hungry; I'm going on the Net. Make sure the kids don't disturb me.' He strode past her and tromped down the hallway to the tiny room they called 'solitary confinement'. It had been a storeroom that Dean had converted into an office. It housed a small trestle table, an old laptop computer and a canvas chair; nothing else. He crawled under the table and pulled himself up onto the chair on the other side. There was less than ten centimetres wiggle room between the back of the chair and the wall behind it.

Vicki did not know that Dean had received the chemical analysis of the dam water and she wondered what had happened in town to upset him. He would tell her in his own good time – he always did – and, in the meantime, she would make sure that not a peep was heard from the kids.

Dean started the computer, pulled out the chemical analysis, and googled 'benzene' and saw that it was found in gasoline, insecticides, pesticides, paints, other gasoline derivatives and cigarette smoke. Next he googled 'toluene', discovering that it was a component of many petroleum products and used as a solvent for paints, coatings, gums and resins. He scratched his head, wondering why these chemicals had been highlighted in the report. He'd assumed that they had to be toxic but his research indicated that they were used in everyday products that could be bought from the service station or supermarket. When he searched for 'Filliburton +benzene', nothing came up on the Filliburton website, but many other sites referred to BTEX, a group of chemical compounds made up of benzene, toluene, ethylbenzene and xylene.

As he continued to pore over the sites, he found that Filliburton used BTEX in their fracking fluids which, as far he was concerned, proved that when they had sprayed the dirt roads and tracks they had contaminated his dam. Next he googled 'BTEX + health hazards' and was staggered when he got more than 20,000 hits, many blaming Filliburton for life-threatening illnesses like leukaemia, brain tumours, liver cancer, kidney cancer, lung cancer and numerous other nasty conditions, depending on the level of BTEX absorbed. *What are these lunatics doing pumping this stuff into the ground and why are the Australian governments letting them get away with it?* According to one website, coal seam gas was being exploited by the gas companies in thirty-eight states in the US, leaving behind a trail of discontent, destruction and sickness. Dean could not help but notice that the main culprits were Filliburton, Plumberjay and SK Services, all large American companies that had subsidiaries operating in the valley.

He felt sick as he googled 'illnesses + symptoms + BTEX', already anticipating the result, but hoping the symptoms would not confirm his worst fears. Skin and sensory irritation, tiredness, dizziness, headaches, loss of coordination, eye and nose irritation appeared on the screen, all symptoms that he and the kids had experienced. He said a silent prayer for his kids, before the thought of them contracting cancer as a result of Filliburton and CEGL's deceit drove him into a cold fury. He had thought that, once they had stopped swimming in the dam, they would be safe, only to realise they could be exposed to BTEX in the air through evaporation; he wondered whether his rainwater tanks were contaminated.

It was close to midnight, he had not eaten but wasn't hungry, his head was aching and some of the information on the websites had been too scientific for him to understand. He rationalised that, because Vicki had not come down with any symptoms, the rainwater tanks were probably okay; but he could not be sure and it did nothing to ease his fury. Frustrated, angry and exhausted, he shut the computer down and staggered to the bedroom, threw off his clothes and flopped onto the mattress next to his restless wife.

As Dean put his head on the pillow, the *whirr, whirr, whirr* was louder than ever. He rested his hands on his temples and tried to massage his headache away, but the unrelenting *whirr, whirr, whirr* droned on, making sleep and any respite impossible.

Chapter 11

Breckenridge & Priestley had been the Forrest family's lawyers for over thirty years. However, Simon Breckenridge was shocked when Steve Forrest phoned and asked him to prepare a short agreement between CEGL and the *Chronicle*. There was a short, sharp exchange, finishing with Breckenridge telling Steve that he should find another firm to act for him. After reflecting for a few minutes, the lawyer came to the conclusion that he was the best person to prepare the agreement and he quickly phoned Steve back, apologised and said he would be happy to act.

Steve had been expecting a three-page agreement, confirming the discussions he had had with Moira Raymond. The document he received was more than thirty pages and the *Chronicle* had the right to decline any advertising copy and to retain any monies received, while CEGL was virtually without rights. Steve doubted that Moira Raymond would sign the agreement but, within seventy-two hours of sending it to her, it was back on his desk, duly executed without amendment. Attached to the agreement was the announcement she wanted to run in the next issue, with a cheque for the first year's advertising. Steve should have been happy but, instead, he was uncomfortable and suspicious. *Why had she signed such a one-sided agreement and why had she paid a year in advance?*

The twenty-point announcement for the double-page spread was innocuous and merely set out the economic benefits that CEGL had brought to the community, the employment opportunities, the business it had brought to the local towns, the donations it had made to charities, hospitals and schools, the building boom that the valley was experiencing and that clean gas was far better for both the economy and the environment than extracting and burning coal.

Buffy was frosty and had hardly spoken to Steve since she had found out that he had accepted Moira Raymond's offer. When he showed her the editorial that he had painstakingly prepared for the same edition as the CEGL announcement, she curled her lower lip and shook her head, without voicing an opinion. The editorial was headed 'Both Sides':

You will notice that today's edition of the Paisley Chronicle *carries an announcement from CEGL setting out the economic and environmental benefits that its management claims to have brought to the valley. The* Chronicle *carefully considered the content before agreeing to publish and, while not expressing any opinion on the claims made, believes that, in the spirit of free speech, CEGL has the right to express such claims on the same basis that any other advertiser with this newspaper does. These announcements will become a weekly fixture in the* Chronicle *for the next twelve months, but will always be subject to amendment or change by this newspaper's editorial staff. As you are aware, the* Chronicle *accepts advertisements from the Fisher Valley Protective Alliance and, by agreeing to publish CEGL's announcements, we are doing no more than allowing both sides of the coal seam gas debate to express their views, and keep you, the reader, fully informed.*

Within minutes of the newspaper hitting the streets, Buffy was fielding phone calls from irate readers, subscribers cancelling their subscriptions and advertisers who wanted to break their contracts. She agreed with most of the opinions expressed but, despite this, she fought tenaciously to hold on to every subscriber and advertiser. Old Mrs Elliot, who was supposedly going senile, provided some light relief when she phoned to tell Buffy that she was disgusted with the announcement, the editorial was a cop-out and that she had been right: Steve had no balls.

Len Forrest came through the front door, shouting. 'You don't think that stupid, bloody editorial is going to have any effect do you? Folks are laughing at you and saying you'd publish anything if there was a buck in it. I've never been so embarrassed.'

'Settle down Dad.' Steve was cut by his father's comments. 'This little storm will blow over.'

'Little storm? Did you have anything to do with that crazy editorial, Buffy?' The old man knew that she had not.

'No, Mr Forrest.'

'You're a smart girl. If you listened to Buffy, you'd run a far better newspaper, Steve.'

Len was red-faced and wheezing, and Steve knew there was nothing to be gained by arguing with him. After a few more minutes, having exhausted his chagrin, he stormed out the door, yelling, 'I don't know how I'm going to be able to face my friends.'

Steve hung his head and ran his hands through his hair, wondering whether he'd done the right thing, when the phone on his desk rang. 'Bianca for you,' Buffy said coldly.

'Hi honey,' he said, 'how are you?'

'Probably better than you.' She giggled. 'I did an early morning aerobics class and you were the talk of the gym. Don't worry, though; Daddy said your editorial was very good.'

'Is that meant to make me feel better? Look, I'm really busy. Can I phone you tonight?'

'Don't be like that. Daddy's just being supportive and he's invited us to have dinner with him and Mum at the Barclay on Friday night. I think he wants to celebrate some big deal.'

Steve paused. The Barclay was very expensive and not a restaurant that Norris Scott-Tempy would normally go to, unless someone else was paying. 'I'll have to check and get back to you.'

'No you don't. I've already accepted, so I'll see you there at eight o'clock. And, before you moan, it's smart casual, so you don't need a tie or jacket. Steve, Daddy really defended you and your editorial, so you owe him. When you get to know him better, you'll see that he only wants to help.'

He thought he was about to puke. *Why did Bianca see her father through rose-coloured glasses when it was blindingly obvious what he was?* 'I gotta go.'

'You are coming, aren't you?' she asked, with a tinge of annoyance.

'Do I have a choice?'

'No. See you on Friday night.'

By the end of the day the *Chronicle* had lost $1800 a week in subscriptions and advertising revenue, which was significantly less than CEGL had paid for their announcements. Steve had expected a larger loss and he remained confident that within a few weeks the subscribers and advertisers would return. He was pleased, his satisfaction only slightly tarnished by the words his father had used to belittle his editorial; and the forthcoming dinner with Norris Scott-Tempy.

The first weak rays of sunshine were breaking through the early morning haze when Moira Raymond, on her way to CEGL's offices, stopped at the local newsagent and bought a copy of the *Chronicle*. She, too, was pleased with the editorial. Steve had told her that he was going to write something expressing the *Chronicle's* view, but had refused to let her see the content prior to publishing. She could not have wished for better. Her advertisement had achieved exactly what it was designed to do: divide the community. Steve's attempt to exonerate himself would do nothing but pour petrol on the flames of dissent.

In her opulent office on the top floor of the Fidelity Insurance building, the tallest building in Paisley, Moira reclined in her comfortable chair, a mineral water in one hand and a remote control in the other. She switched the large, flat screen television on and found an item from the previous night's news. An image of her boss, Spencer Harbrow, appeared. He was standing in front of a field full of wind turbines with the Premier of South Australia, his wife and the Federal Environment Minister.

'CEGL is proud to have developed this wind farm in the fine state of South Australia and, as a company, in the long-term we remain committed to the environment and to replacing the use of fossil fuels with green power.' The premier thanked him, they shook hands and cameras flashed.

Moira felt sick at the sight of Harbrow. She knew that wind and solar power represented less than one percent of CEGL's business and that the company's involvement in producing environmentally friendly power was purely for PR purposes.

She envied her boss for his job, which revolved around entertaining government ministers and merchant bankers, and flitting around the world in the company's luxuriously fitted-out Boeing 737. For all his polish and charm, he was a hard, uncompromising man, used to getting his own way in the boardroom and the bedroom. Moira had resisted his numerous advances and curried favour with the non-executive directors to progress through the company. Now Harbrow was all that stood between her and the top job. He had promised her that he was going to retire when he turned fifty but now, six years later, he appeared no closer to retirement. Given his cushy lifestyle, that was hardly surprising.

She smacked the table with her open hand when she thought about the ugly crowds she had faced, the community hostility, and the hard decisions she had had to make at her boss's direction, while he kept his soft hands clean. He made the bullets and she fired them and she doubted that he had heard a cross or angry word for years, other than from her or one of the many lovers whom he had dispensed with.

On Friday night, the NSW Premier would appear at a community meeting in the Paisley Town Hall to announce the government's approval of CEGL's twenty-billion-dollar investment in a three-hundred kilometre pipeline and an LNG plant on the south coast's Kravis Island. Moira had warned Harbrow that there were those who hated the thought of a pipeline running through the valley and that the meeting might become hostile. He had ridiculed her, hinting that perhaps she had an ulterior motive for not wanting him to attend what would be the most important event in the company's history.

Andrew Brown's children had lost most of their friends at primary school and, when one of the other students called Andrew a dirty scumbag, his eldest son, Billy, retaliated to defend his father's honour. When Billy arrived home that afternoon, he had lost one of his front teeth and his eyes were black and swollen. Sally broke down in tears when she saw him, knowing that he and his siblings, Emily and Ron, were being picked on nearly every day.

Sally knew what it was like to be ostracised: people she had known for twenty years crossed the street when they saw her coming, refusing to make eye contact. She was a fine horsewoman who helped out at the local equestrian school but, when Jenny Orr and a number of other parents had withdrawn their children, the owner had had no choice but to sack her. People who had once been friends made cutting remarks or stared through her as if she did not exist. Sally hated CEGL but, because of her husband's position, she had no way of expressing it. *Perhaps he should have resigned, because nothing could be worse than what she and her family were going through.*

When Jenny Orr phoned Andrew at the bank, he was apprehensive about taking her call and then surprised when she informed him that she would be discharging all debts with the bank the next day. She asked him to fax the total amount due, including any fees. He was relieved and congratulated her but she was cold and business-like, even addressing him as 'Mr Brown'. She told him she would be at the bank at ten o'clock in the morning with a bank cheque.

Jenny arrived precisely on time wearing a smart blue business suit. 'Good morning, Jenny,' Andrew said, coming out of his office. 'Would you like to come in?'

'I don't think that will be necessary, Mr Brown,' she said loudly enough to ensure that everyone else in the bank could hear. 'I have your cheque. When can I expect the return of the titles to our property?'

Andrew had been wondering who had lent the Orrs the funds; however, when he looked at the cheque, it was drawn on an American merchant bank not normally engaged in mortgage lending – so it told him nothing. 'They're in Sydney, but you should have them within fourteen days.'

'Not good enough. We've discharged our debts and I want our titles back within forty-eight hours. You can have them couriered to us.'

He felt his staff and the customers in the bank looking at him and he started to turn red. 'Very well, I will,' he responded, not knowing whether it was possible but anxious not to give Jenny another reason to continue embarrassing him.

'Make sure you do and, while I'm here, I want to close our trading account. Please make out a cheque for the balance.'

'I … I'll have to make sure all the deposits have cleared.'

'We haven't made a deposit with you for over a week so everything's cleared. I want my money now!'

Andrew nodded at one of his clerks who scampered off to organise the cheque. 'Won't you come into my office while you're waiting?'

'No, Mr Brown, I'm quite happy here, but please hurry with my cheque.'

As she walked out of the bank, cheque in hand, Jenny felt a twinge of conscience. When Tom Morgan had offered confidentially to discharge the debts due and take over the mortgages on the night of the fiery meeting at Paisley Town Hall, he had made her promise that she would not demean Andrew Brown. She knew she could have transferred the funds electronically, but she had wanted to attend the bank in person so she could pay him back for the grief he had caused her and her family.

Before the day was out, most folks in Paisley knew that Jenny had made Andrew Brown look weak and foolish.

Dean Prezky had spent the previous night plotting his revenge on those who had put his family's health at serious risk and who had compounded their misdemeanours by depriving them of sleep. He had rummaged around the house until he found the antique battery-powered taperecorder that, despite Vicki's pleading, he had refused to throw out. With a little TLC he had managed to get it recording and playing like new. It was 4.30am and the *whirr, whirr, whirr* that had kept him awake most of the night seemed louder than ever. He rolled out of bed, threw on a pair of jeans and an old black T-shirt, slipped his feet into a pair of thongs and tucked the taperecorder under his arm. A few minutes later, with the lights of the four-wheel-drive turned off, he pulled up outside CEGL's site office. He got out and crept over to the fence closest to the compressor station. The *whirr, whirr, whirr* was loud and he recorded the noise for two minutes.

Vicki, who was barely talking to him these days, was in the kitchen making coffee when he returned. She did not bother asking where he had been or what he had been using the old taperecorder for, knowing he would either grunt or ignore her. The bills kept coming in, the mortgage had to be paid and the house insurance was due, but the wages that Dean brought home, on the occasional days he deigned to work, fell far short of making ends meet.

'Are you working today?' she asked, more in hope than in conviction.

'Tomorrow. I know it's tough, but if I don't do something we'll never get any peace. I'll work longer days and make up what I'm losing. Don't worry. Everything will be fine.'

'Honey,' she said, softening her tone. 'There's nothing you can do. CEGL is a huge company with millions and millions of dollars and we can't even pay the mortgage. You can't win and we'll just have to get used to the noise.'

'It's more than the noise; it's the poison they're putting into the water and the air.'

'We could always shift.'

'This land, the trees, the animals: it's our little haven and I'm not going to be run off it. I've got a plan. I just need to spend a little time on the Net.'

'I'll get you a coffee.' She was relieved he wasn't going to take any more days off – at least she thought he wasn't.

CEGL's website had photos and details of all of its directors and senior managers and Dean was surprised to find that, with the exception of Sir Richard Crichton-Smythe, their private phone numbers were listed in the

White Pages. The CEO, who Dean thought looked like a smooth, slimy creature, resided in the exclusive suburb of Point Piper. He wrote down all the numbers in his diary and then sauntered down the hallway whistling loudly before saying, 'Honey, I'm off to work for the rest of the day. I'll make up the time I lost this morning, so I won't be home until late. Don't worry about dinner; I'll grab fish and chips in Tura.'

It was just after eight o'clock when he arrived home and thirty minutes later he was sound asleep on the couch with the television partially drowning out the compressor noise. At 1.45am, when the alarm on his wristwatch went off, the TV was still on. When he turned it off, the *whirr, whirr, whirr* was more intense than ever and he flushed with anger. He washed his face in the kitchen sink, grabbed his prepaid mobile phone and a torch and hastened out to the Toyota. Sitting on the passenger seat were the taperecorder and his diary. The first number he phoned was Spencer Harbrow's and after a few rings he heard a sleepy, 'Hello, who is this?'

'Did my phone call wake you up?'

'Who is this?' Harbrow barked.

'It's no fun being woken up in the middle of the night, is it, Spencer?'

'Who is this?'

'Well, your bloody compressors keep me awake every night,' Dean growled and turned his taperecorder to maximum volume. The *whirr, whirr, whirr* echoed around the Toyota. 'How do you like it, Spencer?'

'Phone me again and I'll report you to the police,' Harbrow yelled.

Nine phone calls later, Dean was well pleased with himself. He had not known it, but Moira Raymond was an insomniac who valued every minute of sleep and was furious at having been woken from a rare, deep sleep. 'It's terrible being woken up in the middle of the night,' he said, as he flicked the taperecorder on.

In the early hours of the following morning, Dean repeated the exercise and was surprised that only three of the numbers were engaged, indicating that the phones had probably been left off the hook. He told Moira Raymond that, when she turned the compressor station off at night or silenced it, he would stop making the phone calls. She had choked with anger.

On the fourth night, the first two numbers he phoned were answered by a woman who enquired whether he would like to leave a message. He had anticipated that they would secure private numbers, but they had obviously contracted with a call centre, which was now fielding all his early morning calls.

He smiled to himself as he phoned Harbrow's number again and, when asked if he would like to leave a message, he screamed, 'This is an emergency, there's a gas well about three kilometres to the east of CEGL's site office in Tura that's blown sky high and there's flames erupting everywhere. Get someone out here right away.' Twenty minutes later, a convoy of CEGL trucks and water tankers raced down the road. Dean knew that CEGL did not want to attract attention and would not call the fire brigade – he also knew they could not run the risk of not checking to see if one of their wells had exploded. He planned to continue making random calls until they silenced the compressors.

Charles Paxton had not fully understood the autopsy but he knew the words benzene, toluene and xylene. As he sat quizzing Dr George Bingham in his surgery, he was ropeable. 'What do you mean, only traces?'

'The traces found in his kidneys and liver were within acceptable levels.' Dr George sighed.

'And what is an acceptable level for a six-year-old boy?' Paxton brought his fist crashing down on the desk. 'Would a six-year-old living in Cronulla, Manly or even Western Sydney have any traces of those chemicals in his body?'

'I can't answer that, Charles, but do you use diesel or gasoline on your farm?'

'You know I do. Every farmer does. What kind of question's that?'

'Benzene, toluene and xylene are naturally occurring chemicals found in diesel and gasoline.'

Paxton paused, his face darkened. 'Spit it out, George! What are you getting at?'

'As I told you, the traces were too small to be toxic and there's nothing to say they came from the gas wells and, yes, it is possible they came from the supply of diesel you have on the farm.'

'No it's not. You know as well as I do that Charlie either drank or breathed something that came from those bloody gas wells. I know that, if those gas companies had never set foot in the valley, he'd still be alive,' Paxton shouted, as he stood up and stomped towards the door.

Chapter 12

Steve set the alarm for 3am so he could Skype his friend in Denver, where it was nine o'clock in the morning. The conversation was depressing:

Yes there had been some illness and maybe a few deaths but coal seam gas was a boon to the American economy. It was providing cheap energy, replacing oil imports from the Middle East and the share prices of companies engaged in exploring, developing and extracting were going through the roof.

When Steve asked how many deaths it would take for his friend to change his mind, the response was:

It's the price of progress, Buddy, and the Greens are just blowing everything out of proportion, exaggerating and telling lies. Hell, if we listened to them, we'd all be living in mud shacks and eating daisies. There were deaths when they built the Hoover Dam, there were deaths in the nuclear power stations, but you can't let a bunch of hillbillies selfishly sit on something that provides so many benefits to the masses. You've phoned at the right time, because we're promoting a small company that has some highly prospective licences around the Colorado River and I can put you into the shares at the right price. If the exploration is successful, it'll almost certainly be taken over by one of the oil giants and you'll do very nicely.

Steve declined the offer. He had learnt very little, but his friend's cavalier attitude and callousness gnawed at him. This, together with being unable to think of a credible excuse to get out of having dinner with Norris Scott-Tempy, made getting back to sleep impossible. Frustrated and needing to write, he got up at 4:30, showered, and headed for the office.

Writing did not come easily to him and he would wrestle over words for ages, only committing them to print after much painstaking self-editing. He had penned many articles about landowners' rights versus the rights of the state, always marginally coming down on the side of landowners.

Perhaps it was the early morning peace, the unwanted compliments from Scott-Tempy or the impending visit of the premier that drove him, but for once the words flowed easily and his typing fought to keep pace with his brain. The article was far from marginal and accused governments and *big gas* of selling landowners out for 'thirty pieces of silver.' Steve questioned whether governments should have the right to grant mining licences over private property but, if they did, he argued, that landowners needed to be fairly compensated for the loss of their quiet enjoyment of the land. He raised the matter of paying compensation to the owners of properties that adjoined or were in close proximity to land where gas wells were sunk. He discussed the Supreme Court decision that had determined that all parties with an interest in property had to sign land access agreements before they were valid. The decision had infuriated the Mining Association and it had lobbied hard to have it overturned. In the amazingly short time of three months, a bill to set aside the court's decision was introduced into the parliament. Steve concluded by questioning who was running the state, *big gas* or the government. He made a few minor changes, read it for the last time, and changed the headline from *Landowners' Rights* to *Stolen Rights* .

Buffy had hardly spoken to him since he had agreed to run CEGL's announcements and the atmosphere in the office had been chilly. As she came through the front door just before 9am she pretended not to hear his breezy greeting.

He dropped the article on her desk. 'Can you have a look at this? I want to run it on the front page tomorrow morning.'

'When I get time,' she responded curtly. However, the headline caught her eye and, by the time he had sat down, she was already half-way through the first page. A few minutes later she swivelled her chair around. 'Steve, I never knew you could write like that, it … it's so passionate, it's marvellous.'

'I didn't either.' He blushed. 'Did you pick up any errors?'

'Not a one. Would you like coffee?'

~

The following morning, compliments flooded in and Buffy signed up over one-hundred new subscribers.

Len Forrest called in and embraced his son warmly. 'I knew you'd eventually come around, Son.' Steve nodded, not having the heart to tell his father that he still wasn't opposed to the extraction of coal seam gas and that the intent of his article had been to highlight the injustices that landowners were subject to under the existing legislation.

Moira Raymond read the article and slammed the paper down on her desk. It was well written and heartfelt and would likely unify landowners; but her real fear, even though she considered it highly unlikely, was that one of the major publishing groups would syndicate it.

Norris Scott-Tempy hurled his copy of the *Chronicle* across the room. *God! He had stuck his neck out and defended the kid and this was the thanks he got for it. The old man had always been a loser and his kid was no better.*

The NSW election was only three months away and it would take a miracle for the Labor Party to retain power. When the powerbrokers from the Right Faction summoned the premier, he had wasted no time responding. Now, late in the afternoon, he sat opposite the campaign director while they both sipped tea.

'Jeez, Clarrie, I could use a whiskey rather than this bloody bath water,' the big man croaked. He had an open, honest face; proof that looks could be deceptive.

'After, Nick,' Clarrie Driscoll replied from the other side of the desk. In direct contrast to the premier, he was a small, sharp-featured man. 'First I want to talk about the campaign that we're going to run that'll keep you and us in office.' He looked over the top of his horn-rimmed glasses at Nick Gould and marvelled that this hard-drinking gambler and womaniser had been premier of Australia's most populous state for nearly fifteen years. And all because of one day at the Sydney Cricket Ground in the early eighties, when playing for the Kangaroos, he had crashed through the seemingly impenetrable English defence, after all hope was lost, to score the winning try for the game and series. That day, Nick Gould became a legend who could do no wrong and, when he got drunk or caught in one of his numerous affairs, the public just said *that's Nick*. If anything, his popularity increased and without him the NSW Labor Party would have been consigned to oblivion long ago. Even though the government was in chaos, he was still the preferred premier, commanding opinion poll support in the high sixties.

'I understand you're speaking in Paisley on Monday night and that you're going to announce that the government's approved CEGL's development applications.'

'That's right.'

'Bill Warburton's not happy. He's worried about holding his seat. With the three other seats in the Fisher Valley solidly theirs, the Nationals could easily take Penroy as well.'

'Yeah, Bill wants me to tone my speech down. He's shitting himself, and told me that if he loses his seat, it'll be because of the bloody coal seam gas companies.'

'He's right Nick. CEGL's pipeline's going to go through another five electorates on the way to Kravis Island. We hold two, the Greens have one and the conservatives have the others.'

'Yeah, yeah, what's your point?'

'The numbers men don't see us holding either of our seats and we're sure not going to take any off the conservatives.'

'I thought that was what you were going to say.' Nick put his massive hands behind his head and stretched. 'I have a bad feeling about these coal seam gas projects and I can feel the negative momentum getting stronger every day. Did you see those letters in the *Advocate*? Perhaps we've backed the wrong horse this time. Maybe I should steer clear of Paisley and get one of my junior ministers to make the announcement on Monday night.'

This would be Driscoll's sixth and last campaign before he made the big move into the federal arena, and he was determined to go out a winner. 'Nice try Nick.' He grinned while running his fingers up and down his long, pointed nose. 'The only reason we've got any campaign funds is because of the resources companies. If you shaft one of the biggest, they'll not only withdraw their support, but they'll come after you as well. I can just see CEGL's advertisements screaming to the voters that their government is depriving them of cheap, green power and gas.'

'Yeah, I know. If we upset the pricks, they'll redirect our share of campaign funds to the conservatives. But if we lose those three seats it'll be bloody near impossible to win.'

'Channels Six and Twelve are going to be covering Monday night, so you're going to have to pacify the live audience while speaking to those in the suburbs who'll be watching their tellies. Our pollsters say that we've got a slim chance of picking up some seats in the east, which might just be enough to get us over the line for another four years. You're a strong speaker and you should be able to blunt any audience hostility. The local and federal police will be there and we're setting up metal scanners at the entrance.'

'Don't piss in my pocket, Clarrie. I know I'm no Mandela but what you've got planned will just make me look scared and weak,' the Premier bellowed, jumping out of his chair and towering above the smaller man. 'Hell, have you forgotten what the media did to John Howard when he wore that stupid bulletproof vest? You make damn sure there are no bloody metal scanners.'

'I … I wa … was thinking of your safety.'

'Well, don't! Hey, maybe we should get someone from our side to take a pot-shot at me. The sympathy vote would be enormous.'

'You're joking.'

'Yeah, I am, Clarrie. Come on, it's time for a real drink.' Nick sat down, pushing his cold cup of tea away. 'Are you coming with me on Monday night?'

'I wouldn't miss it.' Clarrie opened a bottle of *Chivas Regal* and poured two shots.

'Be at the helipad at five o'clock and don't be late, because I won't be waiting for you. Fill this up and don't skimp this time.'

Chapter 13

The Barclay Restaurant was surrounded by five acres of rolling lawns, beautiful rose gardens, native trees, paths and fountains. It was opulent but purposely understated and the cuisine was to die for.

The car park was nearly full when Steve arrived. Norris Scott-Tempy's glistening old Rolls Silver Cloud stood out like a sore thumb. It hadn't been expensive but he loved driving it, knowing that it attracted a lot of attention.

The maître d cast a frosty eye over Steve, obviously not approving of his designer jeans and custom-fitted light blue shirt. 'Do you have a reservation, Sir?'

'I'm with the Scott-Tempys.'

Without looking at his booking sheet, the maître d nodded and a young waiter materialised. 'Please show this gentleman to Mr Scott-Tempy's table.' As Steve followed the waiter up the stairs, his stomach was churning and he wondered how he was going to get through the night without losing his girlfriend or his temper, or both. He was determined to choose the most expensive courses on the menu, just to upset Scott-Tempy. The room was packed with diners, with the Scott-Tempys seated right in the middle. Bettina greeted him with a warm smile and he bent down to kiss her on the cheek, wondering what she had ever seen in Norris. He brushed his lips over Bianca's and gave her a gentle cuddle, saying, 'You look beautiful,' before extending his hand to Norris, knowing that the older man would try and crush it.

Scott-Tempy was wearing a three-piece, navy blue suit with a silver fob watch hanging from the vest and a blue-and-red diagonally striped Paisley Grammar tie. 'Steven, are they the best clothes you could find?'

Bianca started to protest but Steve held his left hand up as if to say, *don't worry about it,* and then squeezed her father's sweaty hand tightly and watched him flinch in pain, before releasing it. 'I'm sorry, I always seem to disappoint you, Mr Scott-Tempy.'

'Daddy, I told Steve it was smart casual.' Bianca pouted.

'I was joking,' her father lied, 'and Steve, you don't disappoint me. I thought your editorial about CEGL was excellent, but then you came out with that rubbish about stolen land rights. I'm not sure that journalism is your forte but chartered accountants are in great demand and you should think yourself lucky that you're still young enough to resume your former career.'

'I have no intention of ever returning to accounting and I didn't realise you were an expert on journalism.'

'I'm not,' Scott-Tempy replied, his bifocals slipping down his bulbous nose, 'but how many of your articles have been syndicated by either of the national publishers?'

He was like a fat toad with beady, black eyes, a few strands of oily patted-down hair, massive jowls, a huge neck and a stomach that was at war with the vest that was meant to be containing it.

'None,' Steve replied, biting his tongue hard.

'I rest my case. Surely the national newspapers would've published at least one of your articles if your writing was any good.'

Steve was about to ask the slum lord how many exclusive properties he owned on Park Avenue when Bettina said, 'The waitress has been to our table twice. Can we please order, Norris?'

'We know what we're having. We went over the menu before you arrived,' Bianca said, placing her hand on Steve's, while he opened the menu with his other. His eyes ran down the prices. 'I'll have the Alaskan king crab cocktail entrée and the black lip abalone steak meuniere.' He grinned at the waitress as he ordered. A few minutes later the wine waiter appeared and as Steve reached over to take the menu from him, Scott-Tempy's hand shot out and snatched it.

'You do understand that CEGL and the other, smaller companies are good for the valley?' Scott-Tempy said.

'How is that?'

'They provide a cheap and plentiful source of energy that's very beneficial to the state, particularly to the working classes.' Scott-Tempy sniffed dismissively at the words 'working classes'. 'And don't forget the employment they're providing in our towns.'

'That's funny; I thought CEGL was building a plant on Kravis Island so it could ship LNG to India and China.'

'Yes, that too. Very beneficial for the state and national economies, don't you think?'

'I don't know. Would you dig up your own backyard to help your neighbours ten thousand kilometres away?'

'That's a stupid analogy.'

Blood rushed to Steve's face and he was about to let fly, when he felt Bianca's hand on his arm. 'Honey, are we going to talk about gas companies all night?'

'Sorry. Have you adjusted from climbing mountains to selling houses yet?'

'It's like I never left, except we're so much busier and house prices are going through the roof.'

'Why's that?' Steve sipped his chardonnay, while wondering how she would respond. *Would she be honest enough to say it was because of the gas companies buying up the better houses in the towns for their executives and middle management and the lesser ones for their site workers?*

'I guess we're going through a growth spurt,' she responded, refusing to take the bait.

He was about to pursue her further when the waitress served their entrées: Half-a-dozen oysters Kilpatrick for Bianca, soup for her parents, and a tiny crab cocktail for him which was going to set Scott-Tempy back fifty-five bucks.

'Bon appetit,' he said, grinning at the older man, who slurped his soup so loudly that he drew glances from those seated at the adjoining tables.

'Mum, have you been spending much time at the hospital lately?' Bianca asked, before Steve could return to quizzing her about real estate.

Bettina was a volunteer at the Paisley Memorial, helping the sick kids. She was kind, bubbly and still an attractive woman, with long, brunette hair and large, laughing brown eyes. 'Yes, I've been bathing some of the children and reading to them. It's strange, there have been so many coming in with large red welts on their bodies and the poor little things can't stop scratching.

Some of them can't hold their food down, and they suffer terrible diarrhoea attacks and nose-bleeds. One poor little girl, Kristy Conrad, has shown no improvement in nearly three weeks, which is very unusual. Most of the kids get better in about ten days and are back home within two weeks.'

Under the disapproving eye of Scott-Tempy, Steve reached over and picked up the wine bottle, asking if anyone would like a top up, before pouring a generous glass for himself. He was upset about what he had just heard and took a large gulp of wine. 'What's causing it?'

'No-one knows, but the children are being admitted on the referrals of dermatologists and some GPs.'

'Have any of the referrals come from oncologists or cancer specialists?'

Bettina looked surprised. 'I don't think so. Why do you ask?'

'Little Charlie Paxton had some of the symptoms that you described.'

'Oh no! You do ... don't think that ...?'

'He's scare-mongering about the gas wells again,' her husband interrupted. 'The doctors at Paisley Memorial would know exactly what the boy died from and it's obvious the kids you're looking after are fortunately in no danger of suffering the same fate. The kid's demented father blamed CEGL for his death but there wasn't a skerrick of evidence to support his opinion. He's just a bitter man looking for someone to blame.'

God, you must hate Charles Paxton for blocking your admission to the exclusive Fisher Valley Country Club, Steve thought. Paxton was President of the club and it was rumoured that he had used his casting vote on two occasions to deny Scott-Tempy membership.

'You're right; they know Charlie died from cancer of the kidneys and liver but they have no idea how or why it attacked him and many of his symptoms were the same as those that Bettina just described.'

Scott-Tempy wasn't used to being challenged or contradicted and he didn't like it. 'So you're not only a Pulitzer Prize-winning journalist but an oncologist as well? So, let me repeat what I just said. Charles Paxton has no evidence that his son's cancers resulted from anything that CEGL or the other gas companies did. The fool even blew up one of their gas wells?'

'I didn't know that. When was he charged?'

'Don't get smart with me.'

There was an uneasy silence at the table, which was broken by the waitress bringing their meals. Steak for Scott-Tempy, barramundi for Bettina and her daughter, and for Steve, at a cost of $125, abalone, which he'd never before laid eyes on, let alone tasted. Steve handed the empty wine bottle to the waitress and asked her to bring another. Bianca hated it when he drank too much and he could feel her eyes on him.

'Are you two doing anything at the weekend?' Bettina asked, anxious to get the conversation going again.

'I'm taking Steve to look at some houses,' Bianca replied.

Scott-Tempy coughed loudly and his hand went to his throat.

'No, Daddy. It's not what you think.' Bianca laughed. 'Steve wants to move out of his apartment and we have some good houses on the books. We're not ...'

'Thank God for that. It's not that we don't like you, Steve, but you're running a two-bit newspaper and, well, how can I put this? Neither you nor the paper seem to have much of a future. It would be different if you were a partner of an accounting firm or financial controller of a large company.'

Wow, Steve thought, *this is the ultimate insult; the slum lord actually thinks I'm not good enough to be a member of his family.* He glanced over at Bianca, but she wouldn't make eye contact and he wondered whether she had known what her father was going to say. Probably not, and now she was embarrassed.

'I'm sorry you think that way, but at least what I do is honest.'

'I hope that's not a snide inference about my business, young man. I pay my taxes, provide good-quality accommodation and contribute to reducing unemployment. Anyway, I'm branching out into a totally new field that has enormous potential for expansion, and that's why we're celebrating tonight.'

The alcohol was starting to affect Steve and he was unable to conceal a dopey, cynical grin. The quality accommodation was a number of dirty, second-rate dives and Scott-Tempy's contribution to reducing unemployment was giving jobs to four goons who collected his rent, made pay-day loans for him at exorbitant rates of interest and coerced others at auctions not to bid against him. Steve was dying to call him Norrie because he knew it would drive him mad, but he hadn't imbibed enough.

'So, Mr Scott-Tempy, what is this grand new venture we're celebrating?' Steve swept his arm clumsily over the table.

'I'm going into the gas business,' he gloated. 'I bought the Morrisey dairy farm and did a deal with CEGL for them to sink eight gas wells on it. I'm getting rent plus royalties for the wells. However, the real beauty of the deal is that I get to convert the farm house and sheds into permanent, motel-style accommodation for CEGL to house their employees as they expand in the area.'

'Bu … but how?' Steve slurred. 'The Morrisey's property is going to a mortgagee's auc … auction. Jeez, your firm's handling it, Bianca.'

'I'm as surprised as you are,' she said flatly.

'Bianca knew nothing about it. I convinced old Morrisey that he'd get a better deal with me than with the bank. I treated him real well,' Scott-Tempy crowed.

'You hadn't done the deal with CEGL before you bought the property, though.' Steve groaned, knowing he almost certainly had.

They were interrupted by the waitress offering the dessert menu, but Scott-Tempy waved her away.

'That's confidential.' However, his body language made it clear that he and CEGL had well and truly stitched Morrisey up. 'Let's toast my success with a port.'

A few minutes earlier, Steve had been feeling tipsy, but he quickly regained his mental faculties.

'You did the deal with CEGL first and then went and screwed poor Morrisey when he was down and out. Bastard,' he muttered under his breath.

'What did you say?' Bianca asked angrily.

Ignoring her, Steve glared at the smirking toad. 'You know the value of the properties close to the Morrisey farm will fall significantly when word of this gets out. God, how could you do it?'

'Why would I be concerned? It's how business is done. Everything I've done is legal. I don't know who owns the adjoining properties but, even if I did, it wouldn't change anything. I'm sure when they do a deal they don't worry about how it's going to impact on me. Anyhow, what are you on about? You're always saying in that rag of yours that the valley can't stand in the way of progress.'

Steve now regretted what he had said but he had only supported the extraction of coal seam gas where landowners and those on surrounding properties were adequately compensated, and the mere fact that Norris Scott-Tempy was involved removed any possibility of that.

'You apologise to Daddy for what you said.'

'What did he say, Darling?'

'Norrie, let me tell you,' Steve said, standing up and glaring, 'I said …'

'What'd you call me?'

'I said you were a low-life scumbag who makes his money by renting out bug-infested rooms to the poor and by making pay-day loans to the suckers who can't live from week to week, Norrie. That's what I said, Norrie. Did you get that, Norrie?'

'Stop it, Steven.' Bianca glared. 'What's got into you? Apologise!'

'Good night, Bettina. Good night, Bianca. I'd normally thank you for dinner, Norrie, but we both know Ian Morrisey paid for it, so I'll pass,' Steve said, heading for the stairs.

He stood outside, wrestling with himself, undecided if he should risk driving or take the safer option of walking. He had earlier hoped that Bianca would drive him home, but knew he had blown any chance of that. The restaurant doors swung open and he felt a solid push in the middle of his back. He jerked around with his right fist cocked only to see Bianca, dark eyes flashing, mouth contorted and her exquisite breasts heaving with anger.

'You ungrateful bastard. How dare you insult my father.'

He had never seen her looking more beautiful. Lust and the alcohol made him think about falling to his knees and begging forgiveness in the hope that they might go back to his apartment for make-up sex, but then his sense returned.

'Everything I said was true. Your father's a parasite who lives off the misfortune of others and I'm not sure you're any better. How did he find out about the Morrisey property and what price he'd be able to steal it for?'

'I told him nothing. I didn't even know we'd been appointed to handle the sale.'

'I don't believe that.' Steve knew that they were way past the boundaries of reconciliation. 'Maybe the next time you're in Nepal you should drop Ian Morrisey a card, thanking him.'

'I've paid for all my own trips. My father always said you and your family were losers and I used to defend you. What a fool I was!'

He wanted to say *your father and the goons he employs ought to be in jail.* 'I'm sorry I didn't live up to his gutter standards, but I like what I see in the mirror every morning, and what a bloody cheek he's got telling me to get out of journalism. At least what I do is honest.'

'You imbecile! He's never done anything illegal and all he was trying to do was give you some good advice.'

'You mean he hasn't been caught yet, and what gives him the right to tell me what to do?'

'Someone has to or you're going to end up running the *Paisley Chronicle* when you're sixty-five. Some future!'

Steve had pondered the futility of his future in Paisley many times, but it was always too hard to contemplate, so he merely put off thinking about it.

'I'm happy doing what I do. I'm not going to go through life counting beans just because your father says I should.'

'I'm sorry you feel that way,' she said, putting her hand on his wrist.

That was all it took for the lust to return and his eyes dropped to her breasts and then to her tiny waist. Maybe there was still hope.

'What about us?'

'There is no us. My father will never forgive you for publicly insulting him and I could never do anything that would hurt him.' She stretched up to kiss him on the cheek. 'Good-bye, Steven.'

He watched her walk back into the restaurant and momentarily regretted what he had called her father. *Perhaps he had got it wrong and maybe he was a hard but honest businessman and had been fair with Morrisey. He detested Scott-Tempy with such a passion that perhaps it had clouded his judgment. God, Bettina and Bianca could see something about him to love, so could he be all that bad?* And then he thought back to the time when Scott-Tempy had physically evicted a young pregnant, deserted mother and her two young kids from a rat-infested, fibro house on the outskirts of Tura. *Yes, there was no doubt he was all bad, and no, his judgment hadn't been clouded, and yes, Norris Scott-Tempy was without any redeeming features.*

Belatedly, he remembered what he had meant to do the minute he left the restaurant and he took out his notebook and wrote down Kristy Conrad's name.

Chapter 14

Moira Raymond looked up at the helicopter, shaking her head as if to send the pilot a message not to land. Standing next to her, as reward for selling Norris Scott-Tempy the idea of purchasing the Morrisey property, was Donny Drayton, hoping that the weather wouldn't cost him the opportunity of meeting the premier

It was late in the afternoon and the pilot wrestled with fierce winds as he hovered above the helipad on CEGL's rooftop. He glanced over his shoulder at the five white faces of the press secretaries, personal assistants and campaign director, but the premier, whiskey in hand, was totally unfazed and appeared to be enjoying his staff's discomfort.

'Clarrie, I don't like being summoned,' he shouted over the noise of the rotor. 'And certainly not by Spencer "bloody" Harbrow. I'm the Premier, ya know!'

'He di … didn't su … summon you. He … he said that he thor … thought it'd be good if you could spen … spend a few min … minutes with him before the meeting.'

'And you jumped and said okay without talking to me.' Nick drained his glass. 'Ya know what he wants to see me about, don't ya? He wants to tell me what to say tonight. Bloody cheek! If he wasn't making donations to the party I wouldn't even talk to him. I betcha, because the polls have got the conservatives in front, he's making even bigger donations to them. Public opinion opposing coal seam gas is growing and, if it wasn't for the future

96

royalties and cheap energy, I'd cut him loose.'

'Boss,' the pilot shouted. 'It's too dangerous to put down here. I think we should head to the airport.'

'Bullshit Jack! Put it down or I'll take the controls and land it myself,' the premier yelled. He grinned at the panicky faces around him.

'We … we only lose thir … thirty minutes by pu … putting down at the airport,' Clarrie said. 'Thi … this isn't a game of rug … rugby, Nick, where a bad play only cos … costs you the game.'

'Put it down now!' the premier bellowed, as a gust of wind tipped the copter to one side. The pilot, sweat pouring from his forehead and using all his skill, finally managed to land. As he cut the engine, a large, meaty hand patted him on the back. 'I knew ya could do it, Jack. Well done.'

The others looked relieved but sick and Clarrie muttered, 'Bloody fool.'

'What'd you say?'

'Nothing, Nick. Nothing.'

Nick Gould leapt from the chopper and embraced Moira. He liked what he felt. Even though he had never got far with her, he enjoyed the hunt.

'Are we having a drink after this bloody palaver's over?'

'I wouldn't miss it, Mr Premier. I'd like you to meet Donny Drayton. He's one of your greatest supporters and biggest fans.'

'It's an honour, Sir,' Donny said, gulping as Nick pounded his back.

'G'day kid. Hey, Moira, where's your boss?'

'He's in the boardroom, preparing,' she lied, knowing Harbrow had said he wasn't going to waste his time waiting on the rooftop.

Nick Gould scowled and thought *who does this prick think he is? He mightn't like or respect me but where does he get off disrespecting the office of the Premier?* His mood didn't improve when he entered the boardroom to find Harbrow sitting at the head of the table, a position that he thought should be reserved for him.

'Hello, Nick. How are you?'

Bloody hell! What a bloody cheek. In public everyone calls me 'Mr Premier', 'Premier' or 'Boss'. 'I'm well,' he said, without any warmth, as his entourage took seats around the table.

'I'd like a quick word in private. Let's go into Moira's office while she entertains your troops,' Harbow said, relishing the opportunity to exclude and put her down.

'Sure, but I want Clarrie to hear what you've got to say.'

In Moira's office, Harbrow showed them to seats around the coffee table. Much to Nick's chagrin, he did not offer them drinks.

'The election's on a knife's edge and could be won or lost by one or two seats,' Harbrow said.

'We know that,' Clarrie responded.

'The growing public opposition to coal seam gas companies isn't helping,' the premier barked. 'We look like losing the only seat we hold in the Fisher Valley and another two on the pipeline route.'

'Yes, I realise that we're not popular and the greenies are scare-mongering about supposedly dangerous air and water pollution. It's complete rubbish! But, as you know, if enough mud's thrown, some will eventually stick. That's where I think we might be able to help each other.' He picked up a company report from the table and handed it to the Premier. 'There's a small company, Hercules Gas, that has some licences in Tura. Have you heard of it?'

Harbrow had their full attention. Clarrie leaned across to see the report. 'No, but go on.'

'The guys who run Hercules have just fessed up to the environment authorities that they've found benzene, toluene, ethylene and xylene in their water samples and the few locals who know about it are jumping up and down screaming. They're worried that the chemicals might be in the aquifers or their drinking water.'

'Aren't they used in fracking?' Clarrie asked.

'They can be, but they can also occur naturally in minute and harmless quantities and that's what happened with Hercules. When the water analysis comes back in a few weeks, that's what it'll reveal. I know, because we took our own samples and we've already had them analysed.'

'Christ, how's that going to help me win or retain any seats in the valley?'

'Bear with me, Nick, I'm coming to that. If you were to launch a personal attack on gas companies engaged in unsafe fracking, it'd go down well with the greenies, nutters and farmers in the valley.'

'Yeah, I can see that, but it wouldn't help you, so why are you raising it?'

'We've already made an announcement to the Stock Exchange, stating that the processes we use are totally different to those used by Hercules and that all of the water samples we've tested at our wells are clean.'

'But you said it wasn't the process and that the chemicals detected were naturally occurring,' Clarrie said, looking puzzled.

'I did say that, didn't I?' Harbrow smiled. 'But the greenies and landowners out in Tura will never believe it and, if Nick was to announce a full-scale investigation into Hercules, it'd have wide community support.'

'Yeah, and it'd ruin the company. The share price would go through the floor and Hercules might have to sell assets to stay afloat,' the premier said grimly. 'It'd present a perfect opportunity for some opportunist to buy the company for a song.'

'I'm glad we see eye to eye, Nick.' Harbrow picked up the report and turned to the financial statements. 'And what you say is correct. Hercules is severely undercapitalised and any bad news will most likely tip it over.'

'I don't like the smell of this one little bit.' The Premier stood up and paced around the room. 'I don't like it.'

'It'll save Bill Warburton's seat and might even save the government,' Clarrie said. 'We don't have a choice.'

'Yeah, and what happens when the analysis is issued in a few weeks and it's found that the chemicals occurred naturally? The press will slaughter me.'

'The only analysis that counts is the one performed by the state's environment authorities. Just make sure it's not completed before the election and don't worry, I can assure you there'll be no complaints from Hercules after you've been re-elected.' Harbrow smiled through tightly pursed lips.

'Shit! You're actually asking me to help ya steal the company and its licences.'

'No I'm not. I'm giving you some advice that might help you retain your premiership and govern the state for another four years.'

'What if we lose and the conservatives get hold of the analysis? They'll crucify me.'

'Nick, if you lose this election, Hercules will be the least of your problems,' Clarrie said. 'You don't have a choice. This will give us a chance in three, maybe four seats we hadn't counted on and that may be enough to get us over the line. You have to do it. Jeez, Spencer, have you ever thought about going into politics?"

'Never. I like to be properly remunerated for the work I do,' Harbrow said sombrely. 'If you want to get maximum exposure, you'll make the announcement about Hercules tonight.'

When Buffy put the call from the Maddock Group through to Steve, he had immediately been suspicious. 'Now, really, no joking, who are you?'

'As I said, I'm Amanda Simpson from the Maddock Group and we'd like to publish your article about land rights in the *National Advocate* and eighty-six other newspapers around Australia.'

Steve started to laugh. 'Look, I don't know who you are, but I'd sure like to know who put you up to this.'

'Mr Forrest, we're not getting anywhere, so I'm going to hang up. We're willing to pay you a generous fee for your article and we'll publish without any amendments or deletions. That's a real rarity. If you're as smart as I think you are, you'll phone me back within the next ten minutes. I'm based at head office in Pitt Street and I'll be waiting for your call.'

A few minutes later Steve was amazed when the receptionist at the Maddock Group said that yes, Amanda Simpson was a senior executive. As he was waiting to be put through, he was still doubtful, as perhaps some prankster had phoned him using her name, but he soon heard her lilting voice. 'Do you believe me now?' Steve was stunned and only wished that the overture had been made before he'd had dinner with the obnoxious Norris Scott-Tempy.

Paisley Town Hall was bursting at the seams again but this time a bank of loudspeakers carried the speeches out to the street so that those who could not cram into the building didn't miss anything. There were television crews in attendance, more than a dozen reporters, eight federal police, and a small group of locals who supported the coal seam gas companies, including Norris and Bianca Scott-Tempy. Bianca had got to know Donny Drayton when he was negotiating the Morrisey deal with her father and they were sitting together, chatting comfortably.

There was a vacant seat reserved for Harbrow on the far right of the front row near the steps to the stage, while Moira sat on the far left, with CEGL executives occupying the seats in-between. Josh and Sandi were again stationed at the front doors, scanning the crowd. All the regulars who had attended the Fisher Valley Protective Alliance meeting three weeks earlier were there, but this time the mood was subdued and restrained. Josh sensed it was the calm before the storm and that it would take little for it to become violent.

As an introduction, the mayor spoke for a few minutes about what an honour it was for Paisley to have 'the Premier, the Honourable Nicholas Gould, and the chief executive of CEGL, Mr Spencer Harbrow, take time out from their busy schedules to address us about an important development in the valley.'

As Harbrow took the microphone, there was a smattering of applause.

'Ladies and gentlemen, I'm not here to make an announcement, that is for the premier to do. However, I know some of you have concerns and I want to give you an undertaking that my company will not do anything unsafe that might jeopardise the health of the community or the environment.' He paused for impact and there were a few boos and catcalls. 'I understand your apprehension, but be assured that my family has been in the gas industry for nearly one hundred years. We're vastly experienced; we don't make mistakes and our processes are fail-safe.' What he didn't say was that for over ninety years the company had been a gas retailer and it had less than ten years' experience in exploration. 'Careful planning and experienced personnel remove the risk from the projects we're involved in and I give you my personal assurance that you have no reason to be concerned. I'll now hand you over to the Premier.'

Harbrow left the stage and the ever-popular Nick Gould took the microphone. There was spontaneous applause from a large section of the audience and a smattering of begrudging handclaps from those who knew what he was about to say and opposed it. He may not have been Nelson Mandela but he knew how to control a meeting. His gravelly voice, the legacy of smoking far too many cigarettes which he was trying to give up, and drinking too much whiskey which he had no intention of giving up, echoed around the hall. He thanked Harbrow, spoke about CEGL's investment, the jobs it would create, the increased prosperity that those in the valley would enjoy and then, looking directly at the cameras, said, 'This project will provide cheap gas and power to all those who live in our great state and more particularly to those in suburban Sydney.'

'And to the bloody Chinese and Indians,' someone shouted from the audience. The cameras swivelled in a vain attempt to find the interjector.

'Yes, and what's wrong with that?' Nick barked. 'It helps the state by providing the funds to invest in hospitals, schools and other infrastructure, while helping our neighbours to the north achieve a better lifestyle. I'm not about to apologise for that.'

There was a lot of shifting in seats and muttering, which gave Charles Paxton an opportunity to interject. 'And, Mr Premier, does your approval of this development justify killing our kids?'

Nick had been briefed on Charlie's death and was prepared for the question. 'Mr Paxton, I cannot tell you how sorry I am for your loss, but I am informed that doctors and scientists have been unable to find any direct link between coal seam gas and what befell your poor son.'

Paxton jumped to his feet again and was about to read from the autopsy, when the Premier held his hands up.

'Please let me finish. I promise I'll take questions at the end of the meeting.' Nick could feel the tension and knew that it would only take one or two hotheads to inflame the crowd and then anything that he had achieved by way of the television cameras would be lost.

'Quiet,' someone in the crowd shouted. 'Give him a go.'

'Let me just say that safety is of paramount importance to this government and, if we thought there was any possibility of jeopardising the health of those of you who live in the valley, we would have never approved this project. Why, only today I asked my Minister for Industry to launch a full investigation into the processes of one of the gas companies operating in the valley, Hercules Gas, and, pending the outcome of that investigation, I intend to suspend its licence. I want to stress that I'm not prejudging Hercules and its processes might well be up to standard, but a little delay won't hurt the company while we determine whether it's operating safely or not. So, as I said,' Nick beamed at the audience, 'safety is paramount and we have no intention of jeopardising anyone's health or well-being.'

Moira looked along the row at Harbrow, bewildered as to how he'd convinced the premier to make an announcement that would surely destroy Hercules. There were a few gasps from the audience and some subdued clapping, but Tom Morgan and Simon Breckenridge immediately smelt a rat. So did Charles Paxton, who was back on his feet and about to speak when there was a disturbance at the back of the hall.

Josh and Sandi had been standing on tip toes watching the Premier. They had their backs to the street, when a man barged past them. He was wearing a gasmask and a white boilersuit with the words *chemicals killing our kids* embossed on the front in large black letters. He pushed his way through those standing at the rear and ran down the aisle, shouting, 'You're a bloody disgrace, Nick Gould. CEGL poisoned me and my kids and you're not only licensing them to poison the valley but Kravis Island as well. You're a bloody disgrace!'

Josh and Sandi raced after him, but the feds were quicker and already had him covered, with two of them behind and two in front of him. They would have liked to eject him but they had been warned not to use strongarm tactics that would make the premier look bad, unless it was a matter of life and death. One of them snapped at Josh, 'Get back to the front door, and this time try to stay awake.' Camera flashes went off like strobe lights as photographers fought to get closer to the man in the white boilersuit.

Harbrow recognised the voice immediately as the phantom early morning phone caller and cursed the police for letting him turn a perfectly-scripted meeting into a total disaster.

The man continued shouting, while opening the front of his boilersuit to reveal the scars on his body. 'Filliburton and CEGL did this,' he screamed, as the television cameras zoomed in on him. Billy McGregor and his gang started yahooing and yelling and someone threw an egg at the premier. It whistled over his head and splattered harmlessly into the wall behind him. Norris Scott-Tempy was hurling abuse at Charles Paxton and the man in the gasmask was being swamped by reporters firing questions at him. In fifteen years Nick Gould had never lost control of a meeting. He stood on the stage, angry and open-mouthed in astonishment at the pandemonium. He felt someone tugging on his sleeve and looked around to see Clarrie and two feds, 'Come on, Boss, let's get out of here.'

'Shit, what just bloody well happened? I need a drink, real bad.'

Steve pushed his way through the crowd to get closer to the man who was the centre of attention, catching a fleeting glimpse of Donny Drayton with his arm around Bianca, protectively steering her towards the exit. As he drew closer, Steve recognised the man in white; he didn't know him but had seen him around town.

Harbrow had been going to stay in town overnight, but now he was anxious to get out as soon as could, ordering his driver to take him to the airport where, he hoped, his crew would have readied the jet for take-off. He'd had enough of Paisley to do him for a lifetime.

The premier and his entourage were staying at the upmarket Blaxland River Motel, where Moira had booked a function room so that they could share a few celebratory drinks. As she handed her car keys to the valet, a sense of dread overtook her. She knew that Nick Gould could be a real pig when things didn't go his way, particularly when others were at fault. She had asked the motel to cater for fifty but, when she entered the room, it was like a wake, with only the premier's entourage and half-a-dozen freeloaders there. The premier beckoned her over to where he was holding court at the bar, his face black with rage. He downed a whiskey in one gulp and told the waiter to 'keep 'em coming.'

'Who was that prick?' he growled. 'Christ, how'd he get in wearing that stupid boilersuit? Where was security? Where were the cops? What happened, Moira? What happened?'

Before she could answer, he held his hands up as the theme music for the Channel Six late-night news played on the flat screen televisions. A female reporter led in with the premier's attendance at a meeting in Paisley to announce the approval of CEGL's twenty-billion-dollar development in the Fisher Valley and Kravis Island, before the image of Charles Paxton appeared, asking if the *approval would justify killing our kids.* Then there was footage of a man wearing a gasmask running down the aisle shouting. There wasn't a word about the supply of cheap power and gas to suburban Sydney or the investigation into the operations of Hercules Gas.

'Get me another whiskey,' Nick demanded, resting his forehead in his hands and muttering, 'I'm finished, I'm gone.' Then he heard the reporter ask, *Mr Prezky, why did you attack the premier?* He looked up to see a rugged, dark-haired man still wearing the white boilersuit.

Because Filliburton and CEGL poisoned the air and the water in my dams when they were exploring for coal seam gas and me and my kids got very sick. And we're not the only ones; there are many families around Tura who have recently been struck down by ailments that leave them with red itchy welts on their bodies, bleeding noses and diarrhoea.

Filliburton and CEGL are big, responsible companies and they say that the ailments have nothing to do with them. Why are you so certain that they're responsible?

There was no sickness in the valley until the gas companies started sinking gas wells. In my case, Filliburton dumped wastewater on the tracks on my property, which seeped into my dams. When I had my dam water analysed, it contained dangerous chemicals used in fracking.

Why didn't you complain to the company?

I did, and they told me to get lost, and the local council said that the big gas companies had the government in their pocket. They built a compressor station near my home that runs twenty-four hours a day and it makes it impossible for me and my family to sleep. Worse, I've since found out that it vents invisible toxins into the air. They don't seem to have to comply with any laws, so I guess they're not worried about noise and air pollution.

The camera panned back to the reporter, who was biting her lower lip and scowling. *Unbelievable,* she said, before going to an ad break.

'That prick just cost me the election. God, Moira, where was the security?'

He was right. The television footage was damning and Moira was glad that she had remained in close contact with the leader of the conservatives.

'I think you're overreacting, Mr Premier. I'm sure this will blow over. We had nothing to do with the security; your people organised it. I promise I've never heard from or seen that man before,' she lied. She had not recognised his voice earlier but, as soon as he'd mentioned the compressor station and lack of sleep, she knew it was the 'nutter' who had made those late night phone calls.

'Did you have a hand in this, Clarrie?'

'Boss, you told us to get rid of the metal scanners. If we'd kept them, this never would've happened.'

'Bullshit! How would they've stopped him? He would've run through them in the same way he ran through the doors. Was anyone manning the front doors?'

'The feds organised it,' Clarrie muttered nervously, anxious to deflect the blame. 'They put two local cops on the front doors, and they were watching you when that imbecile broke in.'

The presenter for Channel Twelve's *Today in Politics* appeared on the television screens and, sitting in the chair to the right of him, was the troublemaker. *Dean Prezky, welcome to* Today in Politics. *Can you tell us a little ab ...?*

'Turn those bloody televisions off,' the Premier yelled to no-one in particular and the screens were instantly black. 'Clarrie, you're the bloody imbecile. Get out of my sight and take the others with you.'

'Bu ...'

'Now, Clarrie, now!'

'Where's ya boss, Moira? Why isn't he here commiserating with me?'

They were alone except for the bar staff. 'Nick, Spencer had already organised to fly out toni ...'

'Don't lie to me,' he whispered, surprising her. He wasn't angry, but sad, and reminded her of a big, despondent bloodhound. 'If it had gone well, he would've been here taking all the credit. You know it was him who came up with the idea of tipping a bucket over Hercules, so that I could show the government was serious about safety.'

'I didn't, but I guessed it when you were speaking. He's had his eyes on Hercules' licences for ages and he usually gets what he wants.'

'Has he ever got you?'

'Never.'

'Well at least I've got something in common with him,' he said, getting maudlin as he slipped an arm around her waist. 'How about coming up to my suite for a nightcap?'

'I'm sorry, Nick, I couldn't do it to Maureen. I'd just feel so guilty.'

'Come on, you hardly know my wife. You wouldn't have talked to her more than three or four times in your life.'

'Yes, but I really like her.'

'How long has it been since you've been with a real man?'

'That's none of your business.' She laughed and pushed his hand away. 'I'm sorry, it's getting late and I have to get home.'

'I'm bettin' it's a long time,' he slurred. 'You're married to that bloody company and the top job, aren't you? Well, I hope they sack that up-himself Spencer "bloody" Harbrow and give it to you. Now can we go upstairs?'

'You're incorrigible.' She had seen him in nasty moods many times before, but tonight he was sad and trying to make light of it. She didn't think that he even wanted her to go up to his suite, but was just carrying on with the charade to show her he hadn't lost his manliness. Maybe not, but she knew he was about to go through a huge change after having been the most powerful man in the state for the past fifteen years.

'Is that a no?'

'Goodnight,' she said, giving him a peck on the cheek. 'Don't forget, a week is a long time in politics.'

Billy McGregor and his gang had decided before the meeting that they would create an almighty ruckus and drown out the last few minutes of the premier's speech. They felt sure this would attract the attention of the television cameras and, if they were outrageous enough, they might even feature on YouTube. However, the main reason for their planned antics was that they were seeking to become as popular as Len Forrest and Charles Paxton. They were annoyed that yet another 'oldie' had gatecrashed what they saw as *their* party.

Chapter 15

The morning peak hour snarl brought Sydney's traffic to a standstill. Half the drivers had their radios tuned to 2ZL, listening to its famous talkback presenter, Aaron James. He was speaking about the disastrous fall of one folk hero, Nick Gould, and glowingly about the anointment of another, Dean Prezky, before unleashing his invective on the coal seam gas companies.

'What's been overlooked in last night's debacle is the sheer stupidity of Nick Gould and his government granting licences to a foreign company, CEGL, to plunder our food bowls in pursuit of coal seam gas for export to India and China. This is a dirty, inefficient gas with a low calorific value that CEGL lie about by calling it clean. Contrast this with Oilside, whose offshore wells in the west produce high calorific, genuinely clean gas. Twelve of their wells produce the equivalent of four thousand coal seam gas wells that destroy hundreds of thousands of acres of our land.

'CEGL, and its partner in crime, Filliburton, pump a concoction of water, sand and toxic chemicals, like hydrochloric acid, acetic acid and naphthalene, an ingredient used in napalm, deep into the ground in a process called fracking which forces the methane to the surface. Half this toxic mix remains in the ground and no-one knows what happens to it, but in America it's been known to poison water wells. The half that comes to the surface is not only toxic but full of saline and has to be environmentally disposed of, something CEGL and its cronies pay scant regard to.

'And to think some fool in government has issued exploration licences to explore for gas in Sydney and its eastern suburbs.

'I've been swamped with correspondence from the Fisher Valley and let me quote from one letter. "The gas companies are without morals and integrity. They ride roughshod over us, do not consult with the community, tell blatant lies and have no respect for the people who have invested their lives in establishing tourist, wine and farming businesses."

'Another letter says, "How can we allow the government to destroy this beautiful valley, a major tourist attraction and internationally renowned wine-making area?"

'CEGL has seventy-five percent of the licences issued in the Fisher Valley, covering two million acres. One company with seventy-five percent, it makes you wonder doesn't it? It was announced last night that they're going to run a pipeline through some of the finest agricultural land in the world, but the farmers are told nothing, despite the potential damage to the nation's bread basket. It doesn't surprise me to find the chairman of CEGL, the right dishonourable Harold Llewellyn, or should I say Sir Lunchalot, up to his neck in this. The only reason he ever got to be a senior federal minister was the farmers and now he's selling them out for a fist full of roubles, and this in the heartland of the National Party.

'The same thing's happening in Queensland and the Federal Minister for the Environment recently approved a fifteen billion dollar project on the Spurling Downs, after ignoring his own department's advice that there was a real risk of land subsidence, water pollution and the destruction of fauna and flora. It seems governments are unable to resist the lure of the enormous taxes and royalties that coal seam gas will generate. Bloody fools!

'Let me tell you how the state government and its gas company cronies use a well-intended piece of legislation to achieve their tawdry goals. Part 3A of the Planning Act gives the Planning Minister the right to forcibly acquire or access properties for, say, a freeway or bridge. You guessed it! They're going to use this legislation to run a pipeline directly through rich fertile land to Kravis Island, because that's the most cost-effective route. The pipeline could be laid under stock routes, tracks and adjacent to roads but, no, that's too costly, so these economic and environmental vandals choose instead to destroy our food bowls.

'The gas companies know that, if they can dupe a few landowners in an area into voluntarily signing land access agreements, they can then make application under the infamous Part 3A, claiming that those landowners who haven't signed are impeding projects of state significance. The minister virtually rubber-stamps these applications and the aggrieved landowners get stuck with arbitrated agreements.

'Despite CEGL's dominance, there are another twenty companies, mainly smaller ones, who have been granted licences, and Nick Gould made a big deal about suspending the licence of Hercules Gas last night, but he did it after the horse had bolted. I doubt that CEGL and Filliburton have the expertise to safely drill these noxious gas wells and I'm absolutely certain their smaller peers don't. Yet here they are drilling through our aquifers and next to our rivers, where, if something goes wrong, we'll have the onshore equivalent of the Exxon Valdez.

'The *National Advocate,* which I rarely see eye to eye with, is, like this radio station, owned by the Maddock Group. Recently, the *Advocate* published some very instructive articles about coal seam gas and CEGL. This resulted in a defamation writ, which I have in front of me, being issued against my employers by the supposed blue-chip legal firm of *Braithwaite Ogilvy and Llewellyn,* and, yes, the Llewellyn is none other than Sir Lunchalot. The writ is specious, without foundation or merit and is an attempt by CEGL to silence the *Advocate* from reporting the truth. It's an abuse of the legal system and accordingly my employer has reported this distasteful action and the shyster lawyers who instituted it, to the Law Society.'

Listeners were treated to a few seconds of the sound of tearing paper, before James' voice came over the air again.

'As you've just heard, I've disposed of the writ in a way that measures its true worth. You would've thought that issuing the spurious writ was enough but it wasn't, because CEGL's advertising agency, *Aspley & Partners,* whose senior partner, Clem Aspley, also serves on CEGL's board, cancelled all CEGL-related advertising contracts it had with my employers. There are some major differences between my employers and CEGL; my employers are ethical, they're not bullies, and they use real lawyers skilled in drafting contracts and recovering damages, which *Aspley & Partners* will soon discover.

'And to think this is a company that Nick Gould supports. Well, we'll soon have an opportunity at the ballot box to tell him what we think. We have to go to an ad break. I'll be taking calls when I return.'

The switchboard operators were flooded with calls.

~

The call for Josh Gibson wasn't from the Commissioner this time but from a superintendent, who berated him for 'taking your eye off the ball' and 'letting riff-raff disrupt the premier's important announcement.'

Josh suspected it would not be long before he was demoted to constable and walking the beat in Sydney again. When he put the phone down, he momentarily lost it and tore into Sandi for not properly keeping watch. She ran out of the station in tears. As he reflected, he knew he would have to apologise to her and again pondered what *big gas* was doing to his community.

The front pages of the Sydney dailies carried pictures of Dean Prezky, in full attire of white boilersuit and gasmask. They universally captioned him the *gas-man*. Early morning television presenters and radio talkback hosts fell over themselves to interview him and, while he'd had no training, he took to the media like a professional.

The *National Advocate* ran the story on its front three pages and pulled Steve Forrest's article, deciding it would have far more impact if they ran it the following day when a little of the frenzy about the *gas-man* had died down.

Steve wrote what he thought was a balanced article about the night's events in the *Paisley Chronicle,* only to be told by Buffy that she was really sorry that he'd reverted to his boring old style. He had not reported it, but Prezky's claim that he, his children and his neighbours had the same symptoms that Bettina Scott-Tempy had described in relation to the children in the Paisley Memorial Hospital, had seriously disturbed him. Was it the start of an epidemic in the valley and did it prove that exploring for and extracting coal seam gas wasn't only unsafe but downright dangerous? Or were they isolated instances where the gas companies had illegally, or out of the ignorance of their employees, sprayed toxic water on roads and tracks? If it was the latter, then those responsible needed to be held accountable, but it was something that could and would be stopped and, that being the case, he saw no need to lobby for the closing down of the gas companies' operations. If, however, it was inherently unsafe and dangerous, as his father and others claimed, it needed to be banned. He had always been against those who opposed progress and now he thought that they might be right. However, he didn't know how he'd be able to confirm or set aside his suspicions.

The next day, he bought four copies of the *National Advocate* and read and reread his article on land rights, which took all of page three. He folded one copy to the relevant page and put it in a large envelope, addressing it 'private and confidential' to the attention of 'Norrie' Scott-Tempy. A second envelope was addressed to Bianca Scott-Tempy. He intended to drop the third copy off to his father. The last copy was for the archives he was starting today.

It had been nearly forty-eight hours since Dean 'Nobody' had metamorphosed into Dean 'Celebrity' and Vicki was struggling to cope. The phone hadn't stopped ringing, he was on the radio and television, reporters were at the front door at all hours and he was far too busy to go to work. What had happened to her recluse of a husband, the man who couldn't stand neighbours, the man who wanted to buy more property so that he could get even further away from them? How were they going to survive?

Every one of the many organisations that opposed the coal seam gas industry in New South Wales phoned, emailed or door-knocked the *gasman,* all eager to have him join or be associated with them. He feared they would try and control him, so all invitations were politely declined. When Jack Thomas finally phoned, he was aware that Dean had rejected many other associations, so he asked for and spoke to Vicki for a few minutes. He was warm and charming and by the time he asked if he could speak to her husband, he had a fair idea of the state of the Prezkys' finances and marriage. Dean was tired and grumpy, and the thought of being controlled by a group of rich vineyard owners and horse breeders did nothing for him. When he said he didn't have time to talk, he was far from polite.

'Don't be too hasty,' Thomas cautioned in his broad Canadian brogue. 'We can probably do more for you than you can do for us?'

'How so?'

'You said on television that you sent water samples to Sydney for analysis. That wouldn't have been cheap and I have a hunch that you might want some more samples analysed soon. We have people in our group who can get liquids analysed at no cost. Is that of interest to you?'

'Go on,' Dean said grudgingly.

'We also have lawyers, a Queen's Counsel and two Federal Court judges who are members of our group.'

'I don't need them.'

'You're a smart man. While you don't need them now, who's to say you won't in the future. Think about it.'

'Yeah, yeah.'

'Dean, we're no different from you. Jeez, Charles Paxton lost a son who had some of the symptoms that you and your family suffered. We're fighting a common enemy.'

'If I join your group, I won't stand for having my actions or words censored.'

'We don't want you to join us. From what we've heard about you, it might be downright risky,' Thomas chuckled, 'for us! I phoned to offer you our services unconditionally, but you'd be welcome at our blockades and if you felt inclined you could address our members. After all, you're a media personality now. What do you say?'

'I never look a gift horse in the mouth,' Dean responded, but his voice reflected his suspicions. 'I'll think about it.'

'I have one last piece of advice. There's a guy who lives out your way, Mick Petheridge. He heads up the *Tura Defence Association*. He's very clever and someone you should get to know.'

'The General. I already know him and he phoned me today. I'm surprised you blue bloods know him, though.'

'When you get to know us, you won't be. Phone me when you need our help.'

It was eight o'clock when Vicki, who was worn to a frazzle, took the phone off the hook and put the kids to bed. She could still hear the *whirr, whirr, whirr* from the compressors, but the sound was muffled. She craved sleep but was desperate to talk to Dean, who had adjourned to the room they called solitary confinement. He was hard at it on the Net, doing more research on the evils of coal seam gas. Vicki stood in the doorway, looking in as her husband banged away on the keyboard. While he knew she was there he did not look up.

'Honey, I know the last two days have been hectic, but there's no money coming into the house. We missed the mortgage payment and I'm getting worried.'

'The bank can wait. It's not as if they're going to foreclose because we're one payment in arrears, is it?'

'It's not only the bank. I don't have enough money to buy food and the kids' clothes are in tatters.' She wanted to say *you promised you'd return to work* but knew that he would call her a whinger and it would lead to a fight, which was the last thing she wanted. 'Do you remember when AMEX sent you that credit card with a $5000 limit and we resolved never to use it unless we were absolutely desperate? I think we've reached that point.'

He tried to shift the chair but got nowhere and fared no better when he made a belated attempt to stand up. Vicki, standing in the doorway, made the room even smaller and he felt trapped.

'You still have it, don't you?'

'Sure,' he said, looking uncomfortable.

'What's wrong? My God, you haven't spent the five thousand have you?'

'Not yet, but I'm going to use it tomorrow to buy some essential items.'

'Essential items?'

'Yeah, I have to buy a small hand-held methane detector and a camcorder with a telescopic lense.' His tone told her he would brook no interference.

'Have to?' she snapped. The tension in the tiny room increased. 'We have to eat, we have to clothe our kids and we have to pay our rates. What's happened to you? Has being a media personality for a few days gone to your head? You've had your fifteen minutes of fame but you have to come back to reality and we need that credit card for food.'

'It's not about me. Don't you understand? If we don't stop the gas companies, we'll have nothing, our property value will halve and the bank will foreclose on us and here you are worried because we missed one mortgage payment.' He sighed. 'Do you know that they have to comply with 1500 state and federal conditions before they can frack a well? What a joke! They tick 1500 boxes and then couldn't care less about them once they have their precious licence. If I can film them breaching those conditions, I can stop them. I know I can.'

'You can't beat them. They're huge.'

'I already have. Listen to how muted the compressor noise is tonight. Why do you think that is? It's because I attacked CEGL on Monday night and they've spent the last two days putting buffers around it.'

'Why does it have to be you who takes them on?'

'It's not just me; there are groups all over the valley fighting to stop them. They're mounting petitions, writing to politicians and the press and even barricading the gates of properties. What I'm going to do is different. I intend to prove that what they're doing is undeniably dangerous, that it will poison the aquifers and destroy the valley as a place to cultivate food. My boss wants to stop 'em as badly as I do and says that I can work on a casual basis whenever I want, and I've got a part-time job at the pub pulling beers three nights a week. I'm not gonna let you down honey, but I really need your help and support on this.'

She knew there was no use arguing, because his mind was made up. 'How much is this stuff you're buying going to cost?'

'About $2500. Maybe a little more. The hard drive will record for sixteen hours but I'll need backup memory cards and multiple battery packs that I haven't priced, and I don't know whether I'll have to buy anything extra to download onto the computer.'

'God, you sound like Richard Attenborough. While you're on this spending binge, can you go to the bank and get five hundred dollars on that credit card as well, because *we have to eat?*'

'Sure can.' He grinned and a little of the tension lifted, 'You're a good sort. Thanks.'

She stretched over the table and kissed him goodnight. 'Don't stay up too late.'

Chapter 16

Janet Bourne was always busy on the days the board met and her boss invariably made last minute-submissions and today was no exception. The previous night Mr Harbrow had been agitated when preparing a submission about the action that the company should take against the Maddock Group and Aaron James. He had also made a recommendation to the board regarding the takeover of a small company, Hercules Gas. There was a fourteen-seat boardroom table and Mr Harbrow and Mr Llewellyn always took chairs at either end while the other five directors spread themselves out between them. Janet distributed the last-minute board papers accordingly.

Being a non-executive director of a large public company is considered quite an honour. Often committees of directors are formed to ensure that invitations to join the board are only made to those candidates of the highest calibre and integrity. These committees invariably nominate candidates whom they already know, resulting in a relatively small number of directors sitting on numerous boards. These directors are commonly referred to as being members of 'the old boys club' – a very lucrative club.

Harold Llewellyn and Sir Richard Crichton-Smythe sat on a multitude of boards. Fees paid to these supposed doyens of the community were extraordinarily generous; purportedly to compensate them for the risk and responsibility they were taking. Harold Llewellyn, as chairman of CEGL, was paid the princely sum of $800,000 per annum while each of the other non-executive directors received $200,000. However, this was only the tip of the iceberg and the huge money was made from participating in generous option and share schemes. Directors are meant to ensure that companies act honestly and ethically and this is usually achieved by ensuring compliance with a cumbersome document known as a corporate governance protocol. It is also critical that directors act independently and be without conflicts of interest.

In the case of CEGL, Spencer Harbrow made all appointments, lip service was paid to corporate governance and all directors were massively conflicted. Harbrow came from the 'greed is good' school and those who sat on the CEGL board met this philosophy in spades. Years earlier, the company's consulting geologists had discovered coal seams in the Margaret Hills region of Western Australia but, to their surprise, Harbrow had shown no interest. A few months later, a private company applied for and was granted licences over huge tracts of land in the area. It was impossible to connect Harbrow with the company, which had two lawyers as directors and another two companies registered in Lichtenstein as its shareholders. The Margaret Hills tenements were Harbrow's insurance against the unforeseen and it had never entered his mind that he was stealing from CEGL.

Moira Raymond had flown in the night before on a commercial flight and took her seat in the boardroom at 9.30am, thirty minutes early. She had long thought that the company should replace nearly all its non-executive directors with candidates who were genuinely independent. Conflicts of interest abounded and yet she could never remember a director excusing himself from voting on a resolution in which he had an interest. Ironically, she could not make any attempt to remove them until after they had appointed her CEO and, until that occurred, she would have to tread a careful path. Whether her ambition and the sacrifices she had made over twenty years were eventually rewarded, largely depended on Harbrow. With his charisma he had dominated board meetings, using them to inform his co-directors of the deals he had put together since the last meeting and then basking in their praise. There would be no praise at today's meeting and Moira suspected it would be like no meeting she had attended before.

Phillip Bancroft was the first of the non-executive directors to arrive. He was a weedy little man with receding salt-and-pepper hair, bulbous, green eyes and sunken jowls, who looked older than his forty-eight years. Moira didn't like him but still greeted him with a pleasant, 'Good morning, Phil.'

'The stock price is down fifteen percent, what's good about it?'

A few minutes later, a grim-faced Sir Richard Crichton-Smythe joined them. For one so old, he glowed with good health and his sparkling blue eyes lit up when he kissed Moira on the cheek. When Sir Richard had phoned her during the week, he had asked if she had had anything to do with the Maddock debacle and whether she thought Harbrow was losing it. She had been diplomatic, saying that she wasn't totally aware of the circumstances that had led to Aaron James's savage attack and, until she knew, would prefer not to comment. He had persisted, asking her how an article in the *Paisley Chronicle* had found its way to national prominence, leaving her in no doubt that he thought she was to blame.

Spencer Harbrow and Harold Llewellyn entered the room together. The tension between them was palpable and it was obvious to the others that they had already met and that whatever they had talked about had been acrimonious. It was only 9.55 but Llewellyn snapped impatiently, 'Where are Clem and Vic?' No-one answered. CEGL's board meetings were normally full of 'bonhomie' in anticipation of news that would make those sitting around the table wealthier and more highly thought of, but today they were all worth a lot less than they had been five days ago; and, worse, the company was being torn apart by the media.

Vic Bezzina arrived with a minute to spare and was greeted with cursory nods and a cold greeting from Llewellyn. He had black hair, a slightly bent Roman nose, a strong, protruding jaw and he was wearing a fitted white shirt that showed off his muscular body. As he sat down, he winked at Moira and she returned a fleeting smile. She liked him and valued his work. He was the only director she would retain after she had the top job.

Janet Bourne sat away from the table and to the right of the chairman, with her recorder and notebook in hand.

When, at five minutes past ten, Clem Aspley joined them, Llewellyn growled at him as if addressing a schoolboy. 'You're late.'

'Don't bloody start, Harold. I've been fielding phone calls from the Maddock Group all morning and they're going to sue my arse off. They're also talking to my other large clients and suggesting they find another agency if they want continuity. Continuity! Jesus, they're planting the seeds that I mightn't be around for much longer. You got me into this Spencer, now you've gotta get me out of it.'

'If you'd been on time, you would've been able to read what I have planned for them and that smart-arse, Aaron James.'

'Let me brief you, Clem,' Vic Bezzina said, reading from the documents in front of him. 'Spencer wants to seek injunctions restraining the Maddock Group and James from making further defamatory comments. He then wants so sue them for defamation, libel, slander and anything else he can think of.'

'We're going to be in the media for months, maybe years, and the share price is going to hell,' Bancroft groaned. 'My clients and I have hundreds of millions of dollars in the company. They're not happy.'

'And how did they get those hundreds of millions? Because I increased the share price thirtyfold. They put comparatively little in for huge returns and they've little to complain about,' Harbrow sneered, refraining with great difficulty from adding, *and you put nothing in, Phil, so what've you got to complain about?*

Moira had never been to a board meeting that was even remotely like this. Insults and accusations were flying around the table, and Harbrow, who was normally never questioned, was under severe attack; and the chairman had completely lost control.

Sir Richard thumped the table and demanded order. He asked directors if they would like to dispense with the agenda and move to the matters that had been widely canvassed in the media over the past four days. There was unanimous agreement and he asked Harbrow to explain the background of his proposed legal action. The explanation went back to the defamatory nature of the original articles by the *National Advocate* and the discussions with Llewellyn that had resulted in the issuing of a writ.

'I knew that we had little chance of winning in court, but Harold told me that the bluff would curtail the *Advocate* from publishing further derogatory articles. He also said that, if the Maddock Group challenged the action, his firm would bury their lawyers in a mass of paperwork. Clearly I was misadvised.'

Llewellyn's normally red face turned purple. 'You never said that you were going to cancel millions of dollars of advertising contracts as well. I was trying to win a small battle and, if you'd told me you were going to declare war, I would've advised against the legal action. You backed them into a corner and they have nothing to lose by retaliating.'

'Crap,' Harbrow responded.

'Don't talk to me th ...'

'Order,' Sir Richard growled. 'Order.'

'You never said anything about suing for defamation when you ordered me to cancel those advertising contracts,' Aspley moaned. 'Harold's right. You declared war on them and no-one stands over the Maddock Group without getting hurt.'

'Rubbish.'

'It's not rubbish, Spencer,' Llewellyn said.

'And don't forget you promised that CEGL would indemnify me for legal costs and damages,' Aspley said. 'And while we didn't talk about it, I expect to be compensated for any clients I lose.'

'Did you promise that?' Sir Richard asked, with an expression that said 'how dare you?'

Harbrow was seething; *after all he had done for them. How quickly they had forgotten that he was the only reason they were even sitting at the table.*

'Yes, he did,' Aspley responded. Then, looking over at Janet, 'I want that minuted.'

'So the reason you took your actions was to deter the *Advocate* from publishing any more articles about the company and coal seam gas?' Bezzina asked.

Harbrow thought *what a stupid question, wasn't it obvious?* but he controlled himself. 'Yes, Vic.'

'I'm not criticising your motive, but the mainstream media, with incessant pressure from the Greens, is gradually waking up to the coal seam gas story. I've heard that *Your Nation* is producing a documentary that will paint certain gas companies, including us, and the Queensland Government, in a very bad light. It's going to air in four weeks.'

'What story?' Bancroft asked.

'Air pollution, water pollution, sickness, death and land rights for starters, and that guy the media's calling *the gas-man* is getting huge coverage. I also read an article that came out of Paisley, that the national newspapers picked up about land rights.'

'None of it's true,' Harbrow said, 'and that thug they call *the gas-man* will soon be yesterday's news.'

'Hear, hear,' Sir Richard added.

'So, Sir Richard, you wouldn't mind if one of the gas companies started sinking gas wells on your Tamworth farm,' Bezzina asked.

'Ah ... ah, that's different.'

'Really?'

'Harold,' Sir Richard asked, anxious to change the subject, 'what are the chances of success with the litigation that Spencer is proposing?'

'That big-mouth, Aaron James, defamed CEGL, my firm and me.' Llewellyn leaned back and tweaked his moustache to conceal his anxiety. 'And the transcript of his program proves it. It's open and shut.'

'Sorry, I didn't hear what he said and I haven't read the transcript,' Bezzina lied, tapping Moira's ankle with his foot. 'What did he say about you, Harold?'

'He called me one of the worst-ever leaders of the National Party and dishonourable.'

'And "Sir Lunchalot".' Bancroft smirked.

A little of the tension lifted, and some of the directors smiled while others looked down at the floor.

'Yes.' Llewellyn glared.

'If you want to avoid publicity, you'll drop all thoughts of litigation,' Aspley said. 'When the McLachlan Bank took on Aaron James, he read out their letters and those of their lawyers on the air and mocked them. The more threatening the letters, the more he sent them up, and in the end the bank dropped the action and begged him to stop trashing them. Spencer, if I'd known about the initial litigation, I would've implored you not to go ahead with it. This might go away if you turn the other cheek but, I warn you, don't give Aaron James a reason to attack you.'

'I don't listen to popular radio,' Harbrow responded with disdain, 'but I'm not going to stand by and let some loud-mouth talkback presenter defame the company.' As an afterthought he added, 'Or Harold.'

'Oh, he's far more than that,' Bezzina said. 'He's got more than two million listeners in Sydney alone who love him, and his program goes into every state and hundreds of country towns. He's the king of national radio and there's not a politician in the country, from the PM down, who wouldn't jump if he asked them to appear on his program. Harold, you're connected with those in the corridors of power, but James actually tells them what to do and, if you're unwise enough to pick a fight with him, by the time he gets through with you, you'll be lucky if your next door neighbour's still talking to you.'

'He defamed me,' Llewellyn said defensively. He knew how powerful James was – everyone did, with the exception of Harbrow – and, while not relishing the fight, his pride would not let him back down.

'The longer this stays in the public eye, the more the share price will fall,' Bancroft said. 'I'm with Clem and Vic and definitely not in favour of litigating.'

'Well I am,' Sir Richard said. 'Why should we turn a blind eye to the defamation of the company and its chairman? This James fellow may be very powerful in his own medium but that won't help him in court.' He glanced over at Moira. 'By my count that makes three in favour of litigation and three against.'

Moira had purposely not participated in the debate, because she knew that whatever she said would alienate someone, but she had not anticipated being left with the deciding vote. Some of them blamed her for Steve Forrest's article reaching national prominence, but no-one had suggested how she could have stopped it. For a split second, abstaining went through her mind, but she knew this was something leaders never did. *Her two greatest supporters were Llewellyn and Sir Richard and they both supported litigation, so the wise move would be to vote with them, but she sensed the former wasn't as 'gung ho' as he made himself out to be. There was no doubt that Harbrow wanted his day in court and she felt him staring at her; she pondered what those around the table would think if she supported him. Would they see it as acquiescence and weakness? However, if she voted against him, would they see it as bloody-mindedness and vindictiveness? She wasn't scared of Aaron James but nor was she scared of a lion, provided it was securely leashed, and that thought helped make her mind up – why would she want to unleash James so that he could vent his vitriol about CEGL and the coal seam gas industry to his massive audience, unrelentingly as he surely would, morning after morning?*

'If we withdrew the current legal action and didn't issue writs in respect of James's comments, we still couldn't be certain that he would stop his tirade against the company, and against Harold and his firm.'

'My thoughts exactly,' Harbrow said, knowing that she wouldn't dare defy him.

'I haven't finished,' she said, not trying to conceal her annoyance at having been interrupted. 'But what we can be absolutely certain of is that, if we issue legal proceedings against him, he'll have his researchers investigate us and the history of the industry and then he'll unleash a sustained campaign that will have us in the news for weeks, possibly months. For that reason I cannot support litigation.'

In the sixteen years he had run the company, Harbrow had never suffered a defeat in the boardroom and there was nothing gracious about the way he took it. 'Fools,' he muttered, already planning how he would get rid of the three non-executive directors who had voted against him; but his real fury was reserved for Moira, who had openly betrayed him. Progress with access agreements and Part 3A applications in the Fisher Valley had been painfully slow and she had been unable to control the local press. He may not be able to remove her from the board, but he certainly could relieve her of her executive responsibilities. Perhaps it was time to move her on.

Sir Richard's mobile rang and he apologised for answering and then apologised again when he finished the call. 'I'm sorry, a minor emergency has arisen at home and I won't be able to stay, but there are two matters I'd like to raise before leaving. That James fellow said that the gas companies are telling landowners lies to induce them to sign land access agreements. I don't know whether it's true, but I'd be very disappointed if our land access consultants are telling lies.'

The three architects of the company's policy, Harbrow, Llewellyn and Moira, looked at each other, none wishing to respond. Then Harbrow said, 'Sir Richard, I can categorically say that I've never heard one of our land access consultants tell a landowner a lie.' Given that he was never in the field, this was hardly surprising.

'Thank goodness. I'm relieved. Janet, I'd like that minuted. I'd also like to know whether Nick Gould losing government will adversely impact the company.'

'I'd rather the devil we know,' Harbrow said, 'but Nick's run his race and we just have to move on. The good thing is, the conservatives and Labor have a bipartisan approach to taxes and royalties. It's called "greed" and "get as much as you can and hang the consequences". We might have to spend a little time courting the conservatives but I can assure you it'll be business as usual.'

A smattering of laughter went around the table and Sir Richard stood up. 'Good, I'll see you all at our next meeting.'

Moira Raymond thought it was strange that Sir Richard had isolated the treatment of landowners and then wanted the discussion minuted. The devious means used to coerce landowners might not ever have been discussed at board meetings, but every board member knew about them. She suspected that Sir Richard was indulging himself in a little personal arse-covering and she wondered why?

'Can I take the minutes of the last meeting as being read and confirmed?' Llewellyn asked, returning to the formal agenda.

Buffy Preston could not stop giggling as she smeared thick white paint onto her boss's face before reaching for a tube of vivid red to apply to his lips.

'I don't know how I let you talk me into this crazy idea.'

'Shoosh up, Steve, or you'll end up with red paint on your nose; and don't worry, you're going to make a great clown. That costume and enormous yellow shoes you hired make you look like Ronald McDonald. The kids will love you.'

'You mean, if I get to see them?'

'Where do you keep your tissues?' she asked, glancing around the kitchen of his apartment. 'And don't worry, I'll get you in.'

'You're not coming.'

'Of course I am. You won't be able to drive once you put those shoes on and I'm not waiting in the hospital car park while you're having all the fun.'

'Some fun.'

'Yeah, sorry, that was thoughtless,' she said, applying black paint around his eyes before affixing a bright green bubble nose. 'You're all done and I can't wait to see you once you've put the costume and wig on.'

It was just after 5pm when Steve stumbled out of his bedroom, wearing a red-and-white-striped top and blue overalls embossed with multi-coloured patches, but it was the bright orange curly hair that brought everything together.

'Fantastic.' Buffy laughed. 'I've got the colouring books and toys. Let's go.'

Steve struggled to walk in his huge shoes and, when they arrived at Paisley Memorial, Buffy dropped him off at the entrance while she parked the car. They had timed their visit close to dinnertime in the hope that there would be no visitors in the children's ward. As doctors and nurses walked in and out of the foyer, they were all smiles at the sight of the clown and this eased his apprehension about being refused entry.

When Buffy had found out about Kristy Conrad, she had phoned the hospital and got the girl's ward number: west 6c. She marched up to the reception and asked for directions; when the receptionists looked at Steve there were more smiles. He pondered the absurdity of a clown costume creating instant trust. For all they knew, he could be an axe murderer. A few minutes later, they entered a small ward in which there were two small children in beds and another five clustered around an Xbox, playing games.

'Hi kids,' Buffy said. 'Bozo the clown's here to visit you.'

Steve flicked his recorder on, as little faces lit up and a chorus of 'Hello Bozo' echoed around the ward.

'Hey Bozo,' one of the little boys shouted. 'You've got a really big mouth.'

'All the better to eat you with,' Steve said, and there was a burst of laughter.

'And a really big nose,' a little girl said.

'All the better to smell you with.'

'Oh, that's off Bozo,' Buffy joined in. 'Isn't that off kids?'

'You're off Bozo,' the kids chorused.

'Are your feet really that big?' a little girl whispered, touching them. Steve saw the welts on her arms and legs. She was timid and looked to be sicker than the others.

'Yes, and they stop me falling over,' he said, purposefully stumbling and nearly falling, to the sounds of raucous laughter. 'What's your name?'

'Kristy.'

'Kristy Conrad?'

'Yes, how did you know?'

'Bozo's a very clever clown,' Steve said.

The boys booed, and shouted, 'No you're not, you're dumb.'

'That's right kids,' Buffy said. 'Bozo's a Bozo.'

A little boy pulled at Bozo's overalls and, when Steve looked down at him, he saw that his face was covered with a nasty rash and he was bleeding from his tiny nose. 'I want to be a clown when I grow up, Bozo,' he said, brushing the blood away with the back of his hand.

Buffy bent down and wiped his nose with a tissue, her eyes welling up with tears. 'What's your name?'

'William … William Aston.'

'How long have you been here?'

'I don't know. Mummy and Daddy told me the hospital would make me better. Do you know I have my own horse at home?'

Buffy didn't need a clown suit to attract the kids, as she had that one thing that all kids loved: she was as silly as they were and could communicate at their level. She was soon surrounded.

Steve looked up and saw a pale little girl sitting up in bed, but still under the covers, looking at him. 'Hello.'

'I like you Bozo, you're funny.' She smiled wanly.

'And I like you too, Jessie,' he said, reading her name off the bed chart. 'Would you like to do some colouring with me?'

'I can't,' she said, taking her hands from under the covers and showing him her palms. The skin had peeled away and her hands and arms were covered in light gauze, all the way up to her elbows. Steve looked at her cute little face and felt his stomach knotting.

'I'll leave a book for you to colour when you're better.'

Two nurses wheeling a trolley entered the ward and caught sight of Buffy. 'I'm sorry, it's dinnertime, but you can come back at seven o'clock for an hour if you like,' one said, and then, seeing Steve, 'Oh, how lucky are you kids to have a clown visit you?'

'That's Bozo,' the kids screamed.

'Well, thank Bozo for coming,' the second nurse said, picking William up, which caused his pyjama top to rise and reveal red welts on his back.

'Thank you Bozo,' they choroused, and then roared with laughter as, even with Buffy's assistance, he nearly tripped over his feet on the way to the door.

As they walked down the corridor, Steve said, 'Did you see that little boy's back?'

'It was horrible. I saw you reading the medical charts on the ends of the little tykes' beds. Did you find anything?'

'Nothing of relevance,' he responded, but he was coming around to the view that *big gas* was responsible for the ailments that beset the young children of the valley. The man the press labelled the *gas-man* had blamed CEGL's spraying of wastewater on tracks and roads for his and his kids' symptoms, but that spraying was supposedly isolated and had stopped. Maybe, as Steve's father claimed, every gas well released toxins into the water and air.

'Well at least we know their names and where they live. Don't you think it's strange that they all live on rural properties? None of them live in the towns. I'm guessing we'll find gas wells on their properties or nearby.'

'Yeah, you might be right,' Steve frowned. 'I'll tell you what I find even stranger is the lack of outrage. Why aren't the parents screaming? Why hasn't this strange outbreak of skin diseases received more publicity?'

'You're the boss of the valley's main newspaper. Have you published anything?'

'I've just found out about it and I still don't know the cause.' Steve glared.

'Maybe there haven't been enough cases or perhaps the community's doctors have been unable to establish a link between the rashes and the gas wells, or perhaps that's your answer,' she said, stopping in the foyer and pointing at a polished timber board that listed the names of the hospital's large donors. CEGL appeared at the top and the gold paint seemed fresher than that used on the names below. 'Looks like a recent and very large donation to me.'

'God, Buffy, they're the biggest company in the valley and they've made a lot of donations to community projects. It's part of appearing to be a good corporate citizen and all large companies do it. You don't really believe that they made a donation to the hospital to buy the doctors off, do you? They're not the evil empire, you know.'

'Appearing to be a good corporate citizen? Says it all doesn't it and I wouldn't be so sure that they're not the evil empire.'

'I'd like to go to Colorado and find out what's really happening, but the only contact I have loves the coal seam gas companies, so he's hardly likely to be helpful. Besides, I can't afford it and I don't have the time.'

'Why don't you go to Queensland? There are 4000 gas wells on the Spurling Downs and plans for another 40,000. You won't have any trouble getting help up there and I'm sure that guy from *Barricade the Gate*, Dennis Fulton, will be happy to show you around. I'm betting you'll find kids up there with the same symptoms as those poor little mites we've just seen.'

'Great idea, Buffy. I'll phone Fulton. Remind me when I get back to give you a bonus from the money I save.'

Chapter 17

The *National Advocate* had reported the events that took place on the night the *gas-man* became a folk hero, without detailing the content of the speeches. After the heat had died down, they printed Harbrow's short speech verbatim, in which he guaranteed the community's safety, under the insipid headline *A Solid Assurance*.

The sting was in the article immediately below, which carried the far larger headline *A Disgrace* and a large photo of a village in which houses were enveloped by a sea of mud to roof level and which revisited a 2006 Indonesian disaster in which the large Australian oil and gas producer, Santos Limited, was involved.

Four years after the drilling for gas in Sidoarjo, East Java, by a consortium in which Santos Limited had an eighteen percent interest, went badly wrong, mud is still spewing at the rate of fifty Olympic-size swimming pools per day. Scientists say that it may not abate for thirty years and in a worst case scenario might be in existence for thousands of years, even if its flow rate subsides. The cause is thought to be a blowout of the gas well.

An Australian team was unable to plug the spill and massive ponds built to contain it were breached, causing mud to flow over the roads and inundate villages.

The mud volcano has killed thirteen people, buried twelve villages, destroyed 13,000 homes, displaced more than 42,000 residents and wiped out two thousand acres of densely populated farming and industrial land. The whole region around the vent hole is sinking by two to five centimetres each day due to the rising mud level, causing more damage to villages and triggering frequent bursts of flammable gas around homes. Damage caused by the mud, which has been devouring land and homes in Sidoarjo district since May, 2006, is estimated at about five billion dollars.

Santos exited the project in December, 2008 and a spokesman said it had paid an Indonesian firm twenty-two million US dollars to support long-term mud management efforts at the site.

Most readers who read the second article thought that Harbrow's assurance amounted to little more than hot air.

Chapter 18

Dean Prezky was able to get a part-time job in the pub only because the gas companies employed most of the valley's competent workforce on exorbitant wages. Proprietors of small businesses were left to fend for themselves, and in many cases had to employ the unemployable. Shop assistants in Tura were rude and lazy but the only way small business owners could get a break from working hundred-plus-hour weeks was to hire these ungrateful incompetents. Motel owners, building contractors, hardware suppliers and employees of the gas companies were on the gravy train, but not everyone was so fortunate. CEGL's employees had covered up the logos on their shirts after a young female employee at a fast food shop had been caught spitting in their hamburgers.

It was 11pm when Dean finished balancing the till, mopping the floors and locking up. He'd received three text messages from activist groups, informing him that Filliburton trucks carrying fracking chemicals had been rumbling through the town in convoys and, as he stood on the pub's verandah, three more roared past him. Movement by night was standard practice for the gas companies, as they tried to hide drilling locations, and they were even more careful when about to frack, fearing community disruption and backlash. The drivers of the trucks were told to drive away from the well-sites if they were being followed. Another convoy sped past and Dean made up his mind. He quickly went back into the hotel, took three large bottles of water from the fridge and left ten dollars next to the till. He ran to his old four-wheel-drive and turned the engine on, glancing back over his shoulder to make sure the large bag and back-pack that he had packed the night before were still there. Then he sent a short text to Vicki to let her know that he might be gone for a couple of nights.

It was only a few minutes before the next convoy appeared and Dean gunned the Toyota and took off. He dared not turn the headlights on. A few minutes later, they left the bitumen and accelerated onto an unmade dirt road. The Toyota struggled to keep up and the only vision he had was the tail-lights of the third semitrailer.

His windscreen was being peppered by stones and covered in red dust; he rolled down the window and stuck his head out, only to have his face blanketed. He turned on the windscreen-wipers, hoping that he had filled the wiper water container; a few seconds later there was a small, clear patch at the bottom of the windscreen. The whole time he squinted to the left and right looking for kangaroos and emus, knowing, that if he hit a big one, it would probably bounce up on the bonnet and crash through the windscreen, and he would be a dead duck. Still the trucks sped on and he yearned to flick the lights on to see how long he'd been driving and how far he had travelled. He was soaked in perspiration, as he sat on the bumper of the third semitrailer, fearing that it might suddenly brake.

The dirt track had become rougher and Dean's head bounced against the roof as he hit numerous pot holes; a few minutes later he thought the Toyota would shake itself to pieces as it rattled over a long, corrugated section. The trucks hardly slowed and Dean imagined the terror the driver of a small car coming in the opposite direction would feel on seeing these monsters. Visibility was almost zero and he turned the wipers back on, but the red dust and water had formed into a solid mass across the windscreen and they did nothing to remove it. He rolled the window down and with his fingers tried to clear a patch to see through, just as the third truck braked to take a sharp turn. Dean jammed his foot on the brake and felt the Toyota tip and start to spin. He fought furiously to regain control, finally straightening it. The trucks had disappeared.

Sweat was pouring from him as he pulled off the track, and checked the odometer – he was one hundred and sixty kilometres from town. He grabbed a torch from the glove box; got out and tried to clean the windscreen. At first he had panicked when he lost the trucks but, after he'd calmed down, he realised there would be more convoys coming along the track. He hoped that the drivers he had been following had not seen his brake lights and got on their two-way radios.

A few minutes later, the high beam lights of the truck leading the next convoy lit up the bush and Dean waited, his foot poised above the accelerator, hoping he would be able to catch the last trailer before its tail-lights disappeared. As the third truck flew past, he slammed his foot down and the Toyota jolted into action. Even though the convoy was drawing away, he kept the last semitrailer in sight, building up momentum and closing the gap.

Ten kilometres further on, the convoy started to slow and, as he rounded a bend, he saw them turning off at a T-intersection. They were heading for a drill rig that was lit up like a Christmas tree. Clouds of red dust hung over the track and he could not see a thing or use his brakes for fear of being seen as he sped past the intersection. Working down through the gears he reduced speed and slowly worked his way along the track, keeping the brightly-lit derrick in his rear-vision mirror. Once he was out of sight, he turned his lights on and looked for somewhere to hide the Toyota. He soon found a clump of densely-packed bushes and trees and he concealed the vehicle with broken branches. It was 2am when he took a swig of water and put the bottles in his back-pack, which also contained a packet of jelly beans and a box of smarties that he had bought as a special treat for his kids. He also had a groundsheet, a mosquito net, and a can of insect repellent which he sprayed over his arms and face. It was quiet but he could hear the sound of running water; he was close to the Blaxland River or one of its tributaries and he wondered why these lunatics always drilled so close to water.

He threw the bag containing the camcorder equipment over his shoulder and was soon striding down the track in the direction of the drill rig. He stopped, took another small swig of water and continued walking close to the bushes and trees so that he could quickly hide if a truck suddenly appeared. As he drew closer, he could hear the rig groaning. He got off the track and worked his way through thigh-high grass and shrubs, looking for a clearing that would be shaded during the day yet provide an unimpeded line of vision for his camcorder.

Trucks continued to roll onto the well-pad and a dozen or so men worked feverishly, making adjustments to the rig. Dean circled the well-pad, eventually finding a clump of bushes below a monstrous old gum tree. He spent twenty minutes tearing out long grass until he had a roughly cleared area of about three by three metres. It was nearly 3.30am when he set the camcorder up on its tripod and resprayed himself with insect repellent. He lay down on the groundsheet and, using the back-pack as a pillow, he pulled the mosquito net over his body and face, hoping to grab a few hours' sleep before dawn.

He woke to the warmth of the rising sun, a cloudless blue sky, the sound of the drill rig, the buzzing of cicadas and the hum of bush insects. It was going to be a clear, hot day and he was thankful for the canopy of gum leaves above him. He popped a few jelly beans into his mouth and took a long gulp of water, before crawling over to the camcorder and adjusting the lens. In contrast to the night, there was little activity and most of the men were obviously sleeping or having breakfast in the huts around the perimeter of the well-pad. Dean guessed that little would happen during the day, but that by nightfall the trucks would again be rolling in and the well would be fracked.

Despite the protection of the gum tree, he felt himself cooking and he was sweating profusely, his throat was parched, and tiny insects stung his hands, arms and face. He swatted heaps of large, aggressive bush flies but it didn't dent their army and they continued to swarm around him. Putting the water in the shade had not helped; it was tepid and unrefreshing, although without it he would be dehydrated within hours.

The adrenalin that had driven him the previous night had been replaced by heat and boredom; early in the afternoon, he finally succumbed to fatigue and fell into a restless sleep. When he awoke, the sun was setting and he could hear shouting coming from the drill-pad. He rolled over to the camcorder, looked through the clearing and saw Frank Beck getting out of a Filliburton Hummer. This confirmed the well was about to be fracked and he was relieved that he would not have to spend another day in the blistering sun. However, he had no idea how he was going to get a sample of wastewater. He rolled back over to his back-pack and finished the first bottle of water. He fished around for the smarties, deciding he'd have half now and the other half when driving back home in the morning. He opened the top, annoyed and disappointed to see a mess of melted chocolate. Carefully he tore the box completely open and licked the chocolate from the cardboard. By the time he finished, he was sipping the second bottle of the water. At least he still had the jelly beans.

A few hours after nightfall, convoys of trucks began arriving. There were more men than the night before and Beck's booming voice carried over the noise of the rig. A small group of men set up a pump next to the wastewater pit, but Dean had no idea what it was for. Midnight passed and, despite the activity, the well still had not been fracked. Dean fought the encroaching sleepiness, anxious to get his water sample and be gone before sunrise. Finally he could sit up no longer, so he turned the camcorder on and set the alarm on his watch. He crawled under the mosquito net and closed his eyes, knowing that a thirty-minute power nap would restore his energy.

He was lying on his side when the first rays of sunshine played across his face, the alarm having failed to wake him. As he forced his eyes open, he was aware of the presence of something moving in the clearing. It was a snake, within arm's length. It was one of the biggest he had ever seen; around two metres long. It sensed his awakening and reared up in a distinctive S shape, mouth open and fangs bared, ready to strike. Dean froze, knowing that if he made even the slightest movement he was dead. He had seen hundreds of common eastern brown snakes and this one was grey with a black stripe across the head, but what identified it beyond doubt was its orange-spotted cream underbelly. He knew its characteristics – nervous, aggressive and apt to strike more than once when threatened. He also knew that it was one of the ten deadliest snakes in the world and, if antivenin wasn't administered within thirty minutes, its venom was nearly always fatal. Sweating heavily and too scared to blink, he watched it swaying back and forth. Each time it moved forward he waited, frozen, for the blindingly fast and painful hit that he knew was surely coming. It seemed to be working itself into a rage and he felt urine seeping through his underpants. A kookaburra landed in the tree above him and started to laugh, briefly giving him a glimmer of hope. He knew they ate snakes – but not one as big or as deadly as the monster in front of him. The cicadas kept singing, the insects buzzed and the bush flies swarmed around him; the denizens of the bush were oblivious to the deadly drama being enacted in their midst. Maybe he was imagining it, but the snake appeared to be edging closer with each sway of its fluid body. Unable to keep his eyes open any longer, he slowly closed them and prayed. He wasn't a religious man but knew some of the words of the Lord's Prayer, *Our father who art in heaven, hallowed be thy name, thou shall be done on earth as it is in heaven, forgive us our trespassers as they forgive us.* Not knowing any more, he repeated the same words over and over. It was less than two minutes since he'd closed his eyes but it felt like hours. He slowly opened his right eye and, through the slit, saw the snake's tail disappearing into the long grass next to the camcorder. He started to sob and then he cried uncontrollably. He thought of Vicki and the kids and how tenuous life was. He started to cough and dry retch and then pulled away the mosquito net but was unable to move more than this; he spat phlegm on the ground next to him.

It was ten minutes before he could kneel and take off his sweat-drenched T-shirt, his jeans and underpants. He laid them on the groundsheet to dry, never taking his eyes off the grass around him. He pulled his boots on and, despite his nakedness, felt some small sense of security. There were insect and mosquito bites all over him, the legacy of spending two nights in the outback, and he resolved that there would not be a third night. Fear had destroyed his appetite but he realised that he had to eat and drink, so he drained the second bottle of water and ate half of the remaining jelly beans.

He knew he would eventually have to check what was happening on the well-pad, so he forced himself to crawl over to the camcorder. Eyes peeled and his pink bits dangling below him, he stole a quick glance around the tripod, fortunately seeing no movement. He crept back with the camcorder to the centre of the clearing and inserted a fresh battery into it.

He rewound to the time when he had fallen asleep and started watching. The trucks kept rolling in, Beck was shouting and angry and Dean guessed it was because the well had not been fracked. But what captured his attention was a small group of men placing a length of heavy black tubing into the wastewater pit. By fast-forwarding, he watched the three hours, recorded before the battery ran out, by which time his clothes had dried. He dressed and carefully replaced the camcorder on the tripod. It would be eight hours until nightfall, but he knew there was no chance of falling asleep again – flashbacks of the snake haunted him every few minutes. If the well wasn't fracked tonight, he was leaving and wasn't coming back. He had never been scared of snakes, but was dreading the thought of sneaking through the long grass to the wastewater.

By 9pm three more semitrailers arrived at the well-pad and Beck's shouting echoed through the bush as his men ran around like furious ants. Dean turned on the camcorder and ten minutes later felt a small tremor ripple below his knees and the noise level go up threefold, as he watched wastewater explode from the well like an oil gusher, soaking everyone around it. There was a look of exultation on Beck's face as the men adjusted pipes and valves, ensuring that the wastewater was directed into the pit.

Dean, famished and feeling weak, ate the remaining jelly beans, took a swig of water from what was left in the last bottle and put it in his back-pack, along with the mosquito net and groundsheet. He still had not worked out where he'd get the courage to creep down to the pit, but he still prepared by cutting two lengths of string and tying them around the necks of jars, so he could dip them. While he was doing this, he heard a new thumping sound and, when he peered through the grass, he saw men standing around the now-activated pump. He still had no idea what its purpose was. Just after midnight Beck went to one of the huts, returned with two slabs of beer and shared them around. They were only about fifteen metres from the wastewater pit. Soon some of them drifted off to their huts but a small, hard core kept drinking and Dean started to fret, wondering if they were going to booze on all night. Around 2.30 Beck pointed to the huts and the remaining few men reluctantly finished their beers and trooped off to bed.

Dean packed the tripod, put the two jars in the back-pack, hung the camcorder from his shoulder, waited another ten minutes while he built up his courage and then he was off. He ran through the long grass in a low crouch, trying to keep his feet as light as possible. There were no lights on in the huts but Dean was on edge, and wasted no time dunking the jars into the wastewater pit, withdrawing them by the strings, capping them and putting them in his back-pack. Beck's Hummer was on the pad, about twenty metres away. Moving like a cat, Dean reached the passenger side rear wheel and let the tyre down, even though he wasn't sure why. Striding back past the rig, he saw the black tubing on the other side of the pit running through the long grass towards the track and, while hesitant to follow it, at least it appeared to be lying in the same direction he was going. He took a deep breath and charged into the long grass, following the thick black tubing until he heard the sound of slushing water. It was pouring out of the end of the tubing and he gasped at Beck's audacious disregard for licence conditions and environment laws. It was almost certainly toxic, saline-laden wastewater. He could hear the river and surely there were aquifers nearby; this irresponsible fool and the company he worked for were poisoning them. He took a third jar and filled it. Turning the camcorder on, he filmed the hose and slush heap, before he ran through the last fifty metres of long grass to the side track that the convoy had turned into two nights earlier. He was still having flashbacks but at last he could put the fear of stepping on an unseen snake behind him. Reaching the T-intersection, he looked up to see a sign: *CEGL Private Property Trespassers will be prosecuted.*

Dean was exhausted, and the trek back to the four-wheel-drive felt like it would never end. By the time he threw the branches off the Toyota, dawn was starting to break. He drove slowly without turning the lights on, worried that there might be an early morning riser in the Filliburton camp. As it turned out, Frank Beck was up doing his early morning exercises and was stunned when he saw the small approaching dust cloud – all the land for kilometres around was owned by CEGL and no-one ever came out this far. The old, white four-wheel-drive was adjacent to the well-pad, and Beck, meaning to find out what was going on, jumped into his Hummer and gunned it, only to feel the *clunk, clunk, clunk* of a flat tyre. He quickly surmised that the unusual activity and flat tyre had to be more than coincidence.

Once around the bend, Dean turned the headlights on and increased his speed but drove nowhere near as fast as he had when following the convoys. He was spent, but the sight of herds of kangaroos in the trees and bushes and the occasional one or two on the edge of the track forced him to fight through his need for sleep. Three hours later he drove up the long bumpy gravel trail to his house. Vicki raced to the front door to see her husband almost fall out of the vehicle and lurch towards her like he was drunk. His eyes were bloodshot, his face drawn; he stank and was filthy with red and grey dust caked on his heavy facial growth.

'Wha … what happened to you?' Concern was etched on her face, and she put an arm around his waist to support him.

'Not now. I need a shower, something to eat and then a long sleep. God, I need sleep.'

He struggled to keep his eyes open as the lukewarm water and a large cake of soap washed away the three-day build-up of grime. The soft feel of the towel on his skin was something he had never before thought of as a luxury. He opened the bathroom door, breathed in the aroma and headed for the kitchen, where a huge plate of bacon and eggs and two pieces of thick, already-buttered pieces of toast and a mug of steaming coffee were waiting for him.

'Slow down,' Vicki said, 'slow down. You'll make yourself sick,' but he ignored her, wolfing down pieces of bacon and toast like a ravenous dog. He had never tasted anything so good. A little life returned to his face as he sipped the coffee and savoured the aroma and taste.

'Where have you been?'

'After, Sweetie, after. I'm going to bed. Don't wake me. Let me sleep, no matter how long I'm out to it.'

Frank Beck wasn't a man to take risks or leave openings for others to exploit. By 9am he was on the phone to Filliburton's environment manager, explaining that some of his men had accidentally and inadvertently discharged wastewater into the bushland and in the circumstances it might be prudent to notify the environment authorities and stress that the company was sorry and would ensure it didn't happen again.

'Did someone see you?' the officer asked.

'I'm not sure, but it's better to play safe and fess up, rather than have someone report us, isn't it?'

'Consider it done.'

It was six o'clock the following morning when Dean finally awoke to the sounds of birds singing and Vicki preparing the kids' breakfasts. He felt reinvigorated and bounded down the hallway to the kitchen. 'Good morning, Honey,' he said, putting his arms around her waist and kissing her on the cheek. 'I'm starved. What's to eat?'

'You're so rough.' She laughed. 'Why don't you go and shave and I'll make you an omelette, and then you can tell me where you were and what you've been doing since Friday night.'

He didn't waste any time in the bathroom, giving himself a few small nicks, before he was back sitting at the kitchen table. While he devoured his ham and tomato omelette, he told Vicki everything that had occurred but toned down the encounter with the snake, telling her that it had appeared in his little clearing and that he had chased it away. When he finished, she sat looking at him, grim-faced, shaking her head and wondering why she had to be the one who was married to this one-man vigilante squad. What were the other husbands on the *estates* doing?

'Honey, I have to do this. I need you to understand and support me. Come on, cheer up; I'll try and get home from work early tonight.'

She softened a little, knowing that he was trying hard to balance his work, family and gas company commitments. 'I'll try, but don't disappear like that again. I was worried sick.'

'I promise I won't.' He glanced at his watch. 'Sorry, Honey, I have to fly.'

As Dean drove away from the house, he was already on the mobile to Jack Thomas, telling him what he had seen and asking if he could drop the wastewater samples off for analysis. 'I want you to report Filliburton and Beck to the environment authorities.'

'It'll give me great pleasure. I'll say I got an anonymous tip-off and ask them to check it out.'

'You can say it was me. They don't worry me, criminal pricks!'

'Dean, I know where you were; it was on private property owned by CEGL and the wastewater you're going to give me is their property and you stole it. Now do you understand why my source must remain anonymous?'

'You're saying they could have me charged?'

'I'm not a lawyer, so I don't know how many laws you broke, but I do know it was plenty.'

'Hell, how am I going to use what I filmed?'

'With great care and anonymously. We can talk about that when you drop the samples off.'

'Sure.' Dean wondered if he'd nearly lost his life for nothing.

Dennis Fulton said that he would be pleased to show Steve around what he described as the 'ugly coal seam gas fields of South East Queensland'. Anxious to find out whether his fears were well-founded, Steve took an early morning flight to Brisbane the next day. Soon after landing he was on the freeway in his rented SUV, heading towards the small town of Marra, four hundred kilometres inland on the southern boundary of the Spurling Downs. It was an unusually overcast day and the cloud cover played havoc with the dash-mounted GPS, taking him off the freeway and onto a narrow, crumbling road with gravel shoulders. A few minutes later he was banked up in heavy traffic on another thoroughfare where workmen had closed off one lane while they effected what looked like temporary repairs.

As he drew closer to Marra, the roads continued to deteriorate, suggesting there were little or no funds available for infrastructure, so there were plenty of reasons for the government bending over backwards to accommodate *big gas* and its royalty dollars. By the time he reached the large town of Hallby, the GPS still wasn't working, so he stopped at the Information Centre to ask for directions. When the little, middle-aged lady behind the counter asked him why he was going to Marra, he replied that he was a Sydney reporter doing a story on the gas wells and was meeting someone there.

'You're fifty kilometres from Marra,' she said, pulling out a map and marking it with red crosses. 'The gas companies have made such a difference.

They've provided jobs for the young and brought wealth and growth back to the town. It was dying until they discovered those coal seams.'

'Oh, I didn't think they were very popular,' Steve said. 'I heard something about them pumping toxic chemicals into aquifers.'

'Hmmph. If that was right, everyone in town would be sick or dead, wouldn't they?'

'So, no-one has come down with skin or respiratory problems?'

Her face clouded over and she squinted and wiggled her nose as if in deep thought, before responding. 'Mister, I've been in this town for twenty years and there have always been those with skin problems and asthma but there aren't any more now than there was when I first came here.'

'So there were kids with red welts all over the body and nose bleeds then?'

'We don't need greenie Sydney trouble-makers up here,' she replied, as a young couple came into the centre. 'I have other people to look after.'

As he climbed back into the SUV, he thought that her remarks typified what was happening in the Fisher Valley, with those in the towns supporting the gas companies and those on the land hating them.

Marra was a tiny town with a few houses, a hotel and a freight depot. Dennis Fulton had his office in the back of the faded, weatherboard post office. In the adjacent room there was a mattress on the floor and a mosquito net. Dennis greeted Steve warmly, asking him to take a seat on a plastic kitchen chair, while he continued to pound the keyboard of his old computer. Clearly *Barricade the Gate* was not rolling in cash and Dennis obviously had to be a frugal dissident.

'Have a look at this,' he said, pointing to the screen.

Steve walked behind the desk and saw an overhead shot of the Colorado River and thousands of gas wells surrounding it, all joined by gravel tracks. It was like looking at a massive peg board with all the pegs joined by pieces of string.

'I've seen it before.'

'I thought you might've, but I wanted to refresh your memory. I've gotta farmer mate who has a light plane and he's taking us up this afternoon. You're going to see a near-identical grid on the Spurling Downs. Hard to believe, isn't it? There are 4000 wells already and the fools are looking to drill another 40,000 on what is some of the best agricultural land in Australia.'

Steve took what he'd just heard with a grain of salt, knowing that zealots supporting a cause, no matter how good-hearted, were always prone to exaggerate.

'I was on Source Energy's website last night and they've got testimonials from landowners who've entered into access agreements with them. They all seem happy. How's that work?'

'Ignorant fools! They're all graziers, you know, and I bet you didn't see any testimonials from crop growers. When their livestock starts dying and the calves they breed are deformed, they'll wake up, but by then it'll be too late.'

Steve wasn't happy with that answer; it smacked of Dennis saying he knew more than the graziers who had signed up with Source Energy.

'You said on the phone that there are many families suffering from skin and respiratory problems.'

'Sadly, yes there are.'

'The lady at the Information Centre in Hallby told me that the gas companies had been good for the town and that there's been no increase in skin and respiratory ailments in the twenty years she's lived there.'

'God, ignorance is the biggest problem we have. I'm going to introduce you to a family that had never experienced a day of sickness until gas wells were drilled on the property across the road from them, and I'll show you a few other things that you won't believe. We've got a ninety-minute drive to the airstrip, so we'd better get a move on.'

Chapter 19

Jack Thomas had no time for the state environment authorities, whom he saw as mere sycophants to their political masters. However, there were times, like now, when he had irrefutable evidence of a serious environmental crime, that he relished the thought of bringing them to account. He asked the receptionist to put him through to a senior environment officer with whom he'd had many run-ins. Angry at having been kept waiting for nearly five minutes, he blurted out his accusation. The officer condescendingly responded that they already knew about the spillage, that the company had reported it, that it was accidental, that damage was minimal and that Filliburton was making its best efforts to minimise the impact of the spill. Thomas silently cursed; someone must have seen Dean spying, as the gas companies never fessed up to anything unless they knew they had already been sprung. He put the phone down, his earlier ebullient mood replaced with dejection.

The crushing sorrow weighing on Charles Paxton had threatened to derail him, and it was only the warm feeling he got from thinking about taking the law into his own hands that kept him from completely losing his mind. He mused about blowing Spencer Harbrow's head off with his double-barrel shot gun, smashing his pick-up truck into Moira Raymond's car and pummelling Frank Beck to death with his bare fists, but his upbringing and character would never let him act these thoughts out. Every day he woke up grieving for Charlie, his marriage was on the rocks, the farm and winery were neglected and his only companion was Cosmos, who never left his side. He had taken the autopsy to his local and federal members of parliament, the EPA, lawyers and cancer specialists, all to no avail. Just like Dr George, they told him that the level of toxins found in Charlie's liver and kidneys were within normal parameters. In his mind there was no such thing as a normal level of poison in the body of a six-year-old and he knew, without the slightest smidgeon of doubt, that CEGL had killed his son.

He was glad that he had taken it upon himself to organise *Lock 'em Out* and it was only when he was recruiting, circulating phone numbers and planning tactics, that the ever-present misery eased. One of the men who had signed on without any prompting was Mick Petheridge, an *estatee,* who headed up the *Tura Defence Association,* and who turned out to be a very clever tactician with an amazing knowledge of what the gas companies were doing. They had hit it off immediately and barely a day went by without them meeting or talking on the phone.

Paxton accepted Billy McGregor and his larrikin mob only after they swore they would not beat up the gas companies' employees, but deep down he didn't really care. Tom Morgan was another who had signed on without needing to be asked and soon there was a small army of 250 ready to move at short notice.

Morgan's phone call, when it came, was brief. Gentle Lady's water had broken and she was about to foal. Besides providing him with the thrill of winning big races, she was, like her name, quiet and gentle, and he could still see Charlie riding her around the paddocks. He loved her. He jumped into the car with Cosmos next to him and headed to Morgan's stud. He knew from an early ultrasound that she was about to give birth to a colt, that would, no doubt, grow to be a magnificent, good-natured racehorse.

A large brass plaque worded *Portman Stud* was affixed to one of the two enormous rendered pillars that formed an imposing entrance to one of the finest properties in the valley. Paxton drove past the black, wrought-iron gates underneath the elms that were showing the first signs of spring and up to Morgan's countrified mansion. The garden beds that housed the rose bushes were weedless and the lawns were manicured. Morgan's glistening red-and-white Sikorsky sat on a helipad adjacent to the gardens. The stables were at the rear of the mansion; a little further on was the training track, which was the equivalent of any city racecourse. It was surrounded by lush paddocks where Morgan's horses could enjoy their freedom. The opulent twenty-stall breeding facility was a hive of activity when Paxton entered; Gentle Lady was lying on a bed of straw and Morgan, two vets and three stable hands were around her.

'You're just in time,' Morgan said. 'She's straining but the vets say that she's doing fine.'

Strangely, Cosmos started to whimper and Paxton put his hand on his head and told him to shut up. 'Sorry, Tom, he's never carried on like this before and if he keeps it up I'll put him outside.'

Gentle Lady was groaning and letting out the occasional whinny but this wasn't unusual, given that she was pushing a thirty-five kilogram foal through her birth canal. What was unusual was that Cosmos kept on whimpering. Paxton led him to the door and pushed him out.

'There's one of the front hooves,' shouted a stable hand. It was distinctly visible through the white transparent sac and was soon joined by the other.

'Good girl, good girl,' Morgan encouraged, but his sharp horseman's eye detected what looked like a deformity in the foal's knees and he prayed he was wrong. A few seconds later the head and nose appeared. He was a chestnut with a white diamond forehead. Gentle Lady let out a huge sigh and stopped pushing. Ten minutes went by before she started straining again and the shoulders appeared.

'Wha … what's than on his neck?' Paxton said. 'Bloody hell, what is it?'

They had all seen the ugly, protruding lump but no-one wanted to answer. Only the rear legs were left in the birth canal and Gentle Lady and the newborn foal paused for a rest, while the grim-faced men looked on, unable to take their eyes off the deformities in the front knees and neck.

'What's wrong?' Morgan asked, directing his question to the two vets.

One shrugged his shoulders and the other said, 'I've seen half-a-dozen deformed calves in the past year, but I've never seen an ulcer like that on a newborn foal before.'

As they were talking, the mare struggled to her feet and broke the umbilical cord. The foal tried to stand but kept falling over. 'He's no good and he'll never be any good,' Morgan said, a tear running down his cheek. 'The kindest thing we can do is put him out of his misery.'

'No, I owe Gentle Lady for all the pleasure she's given me and Charlie,' Paxton said. 'She's a part of him and so is her foal.'

The foal was still on the ground when the vet gave him a pain-killing injection, before lancing the growth on his neck. Grey, murky fluid, tinged with blood, poured from the small incision.

'Make sure you get a sample of that muck,' Paxton said. 'I want it analysed.'

'I was going to.' The vet ran his hands behind the foal's front legs. 'It's not his knees, they're okay. It's his tendons. Just like the calves, they're short and he may never walk.'

'Are you sure you want to keep him, Charles?'

'I'm positive, Tom.'

Paxton turned to the vets. 'I want you to treat them with tenderness and care. Think about what can be done for the foal's legs. I know he'll never race, but I want you to do everything you can to ease his discomfort. Money is no object.'

Cosmos was still whimpering at the door and Paxton ruffled his big head. 'I don't know how, but you knew, didn't you boy?'

'I've never seen anything like that before, Charles. We've had fifteen foals this season, every one of them perfect.'

'Nor me and, if I'd hadn't heard about those deformed calves, I would've put it down to a freak of nature. I feel so sorry for the poor little bugger. No animal deserves to come into the world like that. Let's hope the analysis of that muck proves what we already know and that we never see anything like it again.'

A healthy colt out of Gentle Lady by Achilles would have been worth in excess of $800,000 but neither man mentioned the money. Their burning passion had been to breed a champion that they could cheer for in big races.

There were a few small planes on the grass tarmac when Steve drove through the rusted gates of the tiny airport and along a gravel track to where an old, reddish-brown, four-wheel-drive was parked. The man standing next to it ambled over, hand extended, the bow in his legs suggesting that he spent a lot of time riding horses. 'Lang McRae', he said. 'So you're Steve Forrest. I heard you wanted to see some gas wells. Well you're gonna see plenty. G'day Dennis. The weather looks like it's coming in, so we better not loiter.'

The plane was an old four-seater, single engine Cessna Skyhawk with patches on the fuselage and on one wing, and Steve, who was no fan of light planes, started to have second thoughts. However, the interior was spotless and looked like it had had a complete makeover; its four black leather seats still smelt new.

'Lang's got an eight-thousand-acre cattle property,' Dennis volunteered, as they taxied along the runway. 'He's worried that the gas companies are working their way towards him and he wants to stop 'em where they are. He's one of the founding members of *Barricade the Gate* and every time we've blocked the bastards he's been there.'

'If we don't stop 'em, they'll ruin the country. They're stealing and destroying the land and when they're not poisoning the water they're depleting it, and our bloody useless politicians are helping them,' Lang said, as the little plane hit turbulence. Steve gripped the armrests tightly, glad that he was sitting in the back where the other two men couldn't see him.

'God help us all if they pollute the Great Artesian Basin,' Dennis said. 'Look out your window, Steve. Can you see them?'

Steve strained his eyes, but all he could see was green; it was hard to distinguish the grass from the trees, let alone see a gas well. 'Sorry, I can't.'

'I'm at eight thousand feet. I'll take it down lower when we get near the Owens' place. They've got ninety wells on their property and there are plans to double that.'

'Did they sign an access agreement?' Steve asked.

'Nah. Up here the land access consultants know more about the law than the lawyers, but the landowners are only allowed legal representation when negotiating an agreement and then only if the gas companies consent. Have you ever heard anything so bloody one-sided and stupid? Anyhow, the Owens told them to get lost and Source Energy applied to the Land Court to have an agreement determined. Now listen to this. Once the application was filed, Source had the right to give the Owens notice, telling them that they intended to enter the property within ten business days, which they did. The mining and gas companies have the right to enter landowners' properties before the Land Court has even made a determination on their applications. It's ludicrous legislation enacted to favour the gas companies and screw the farmers.'

'Why didn't you block them?'

'We hadn't formed *Barricade the Gate* back then, but we've stopped them in their tracks many times since, haven't we Dennis? We've cost the bastards plenty and they haven't liked it, so they whinged and whined to their buddies in the Government, who rushed through draconian legislation in an attempt to stop us. Any person blocking a gas company from entering a property is now liable to a fine of $50,000.'

Dennis laughed. 'And if you're someone who can't or won't pay, like me, they'll jail you for two years. We've got nearly 500 members and I can't wait for them to try us on. Can you imagine the media's reaction when they try to put us all behind bars?'

'We'll be over the Owens' place in a minute, so I'm gonna take it down.'

It was obvious to Steve that governments were desperate for cash and he wasn't surprised that they were selling out their primary producers for royalties and taxes. What did surprise him were the risks they were prepared to take with the Great Artesian Basin, the aquifers and the health of their constituents. As the plane completed its abrupt descent and levelled out, he could see the tracks between scores of gas wells.

'There's the Owens' place,' Dennis shouted. 'God, look at the bloody wells. They're on every property in the area.'

Steve thought that it was like looking down on the land adjacent to the Colorado River, except the grid was more widely spaced.

As if reading his mind, Dennis said, 'And the mongrels are hell-bent on increasing the concentration. Look at the size of that wastewater pit half full with God knows what.'

It was so large that Steve had thought that it was a dam – hundreds of acres of enclosed land, containing a grey, grimy solution.

'It's on a flood pain,' Dennis continued. 'If it ever floods up here, the land will take years to recover. That's if it ever recovers. And to think they want to sink gas wells all over the Downs. Bloody fools!'

There was a flash of lightning on the horizon and Lang yelled, 'It's time to head back.' The little plane started to climb, labouring through the rain and the wind. Steve gripped the armrests even tighter as hailstones battered the fuselage and wings, and he resolved that this would be the last time he'd get into anything smaller than a 737. Forty minutes later the storm was over and Lang made a perfect landing in bright sunshine. 'Are you coming back home for dinner?'

'Sorry, Lang, Steve has to get back to Hallby. I'm taking him out to the Lairds' place in the morning.'

'Poor buggers,' Lang muttered, shaking Steve's hand. 'I read your article in the *Advocate* young fella and it was very good. You need to follow it up with something about the damage to the environment and to people's lives that the bloody gas companies cause once they force their way onto our land.'

Steve thanked him but didn't respond. Sure, he'd seen a lot of gas wells, heard some terrible stories and thought it inequitable when landowners had their properties stolen from under them, but they did provide cheap gas for the masses here and overseas, there were economic benefits and they created employment. He also knew that, if he was going to be true to himself and his craft, he needed to remain open-minded.

Chapter 20

Beautiful one day perfect the next was a slogan used by travel agents to describe Queensland's weather and as Steve rolled back into Marra just after 8am, he thought it was so appropriate. There wasn't a breath of wind or the sign of a cloud, the sun was already warm and the sky was a perfect, clear blue; a real contrast to the smog he had left behind at Newtower Airport the previous morning. Dennis was waiting for him, looking like one of those tall, lean movie stars from old western movies. Steve knew he was a radical Green who had fought to save the forests, and that he'd spent many nights in the cells over his beliefs. He had delivered hell-raising speeches opposing what the coal seam gas companies were doing to Australia's health, its food security and its water. As they drove towards the small town of Pinilla, Steve stole a glance at Dennis squished up in the passenger seat; he looked so peaceful and calm, that you might mistakenly think he was harmless.

'I know of no family that has been as badly mistreated as the Lairds,' Dennis said, trying to stretch his body. 'Some of their neighbours signed access agreements and next thing you know the gas companies, with the authority of the Land Court, were on their property. Now there are gas wells all over it and they have some major problems. You'll like Annie and Peter; they're the salt of the earth.'

'What type of problems?'

'It's better that you hear about them first-hand. You're going to be amazed.'

'That's all the briefing I get?'

'You'll understand why, after you've heard them tell you their story.'

As they approached Pinilla, Steve said, 'Do you feel like stopping for a coffee?'

'Nah, we'd have to wait ages, it'd taste terrible and be cold by the time we got it. This town employs the dregs, the unemployable. Anyone who's any good is earning a fortune working for the gas and coal companies. The mining boom has created a society of *haves* and *have nots* and God only knows what will happen to these towns when it ends. There are three service stations here and they all close at 6pm because the owners can't get anyone to work at night, and to think there are fools who call this progress.'

Steve didn't respond, thinking of all the times he had said *you can't stand in the way of progress*. A few minutes after leaving town, they were on a bumpy, red, dirt track.

'Just stay on this track for another eighty kilometres and when you see the first gas wells we'll be getting close. I'm going to have a snooze. Don't worry, you won't have to wake me.'

It was rich land but the scenery never changed – kilometre after kilometre of grassy fields, gum trees and bushy shrubs. Steve was starting to feel bored when he saw the first gas well about a hundred metres off the track. A little further on, there was a large blue sign with the words *Nordic Gas, Safely Developing and Promoting your Community,* but the key words had been painted over with *Swiftly Raping and Pillaging your Community.* He wondered if there had ever been a more hated industry in Australia?

'Slow down, the entrance to the Laird's place is coming up on the left,' Dennis said, yawning.

A few minutes later, Dennis got out of the SUV and opened a large gate to a gravel driveway, and Steve drove across the cattle grid. There were gas wells connected by tracks as far as the eye could see, on pads that were surrounded by mesh fences bearing white placards with large red-lettered *Keep Out* warning signs. Dennis opened three more gates before they arrived at a white, weatherboard farmhouse which was badly in need of a fresh coat of paint. A wiry, auburn-haired, middle-aged woman with a freckled face, came down the steps from the verandah, her fair skin protected by a wide-brimmed, dark brown Akubra. 'G'day Dennis,' she said.

'Hello, Annie. This is Steve Forrest, the reporter from Paisley that I told you about.'

She extended her hand and Steve was struck by the intensity of her piercing, black eyes. 'Pleased to meet you,' he said.

'I've read some of your articles on the Net and you seem to be a bit of a fence-sitter. We ain't got much time up here for those who play both sides.'

'Annie, Annie,' Dennis said. 'He's coming around and, after he hears what you've gotta say, he'll be a fully-fledged convert. Don't worry, Steve, her bark's worse than her bite. She once told me that, if I ever set foot on her property, she'd blow my head off with a double-barrelled shotgun.'

'And I would've,' she said, grinning for the first time. 'Come inside and we'll have a cuppa. Pete's down in the paddocks but he knows you're here and will be up as soon as he can.'

The house was cool, with high ceilings, large draped windows and deep brown, polished floor boards and, as she showed them to the carved timber dining table, Steve was struck by how spotless everything was. A strange combination, he thought; run-down on the exterior and immaculate inside. It wasn't long before tea and biscuits were on the table.

'Before I take you around the property, I want you to read this.' Annie handed Steve a letter on Nordic Gas letterhead.

It was a concise demand, accusing the Lairds of not exercising due care in protecting Nordic's property, namely the fence surrounding well-head number 54A, which had been knocked over. Nordic sought the sum of $1,700 in recompense, with a threat of legal action if payment wasn't received within fourteen days.

'They come onto our land without our permission, they poison our cattle, ruin our breeding, contaminate and deplete our water and, when a few of our bulls accidentally knock one of their fences over, they can't demand their money fast enough. We have to protect their equipment that we never wanted on our land in the first place. I hate them.'

'And so do I,' a stocky little man, with a creased, leathery face, said. 'We're the fifth generation of Lairds to own this property and if the other four could see the hell we're going through they'd be turning in their graves. G'day, Dennis. Jeez you look like you could use a good feed.'

'G'day, Pete. This is Steve Forrest.'

Peter Laird had taken his boots off, which was why they had not heard him come in. He wasn't much taller than his wife and had a head full of black, curly hair, and dark, almost black skin. Steve braced his hand for the handshake that he knew was coming and wondered if it was some rite of passage peculiar to farmers and graziers.

'I'm not gonna bullshit you, Steve, and all I ask is that you write the truth about what I show you. Let's get going, there's a lot to see and we'll start with Old Faithful.'

Steve gulped his tea down and wondered what a geyser in Yellowstone had to do with gas wells.

A few minutes later they were flying along in Pete's dark green Land Cruiser.

'We've got nearly fifty thousand acres and have a look at the bloody things, they're everywhere.' He nodded at the gas wells on his right. 'They dug trenches all over the place so they could lay their pipelines and, after backfilling, they topped up with gravel so their trucks can get in to do maintenance; not that they ever do any after the wells start to flow. Old Faithful's coming up on the left.'

They got out of the Toyota and walked over to the first of two fenced enclosures surrounding a well-pad, which was set back forty metres from the inner enclosure. There were warning signs all over both fences. 'This is a rogue well,' Pete said. 'They drilled it four years ago but have been unable to control it, and they've been trying to plug it ever since. They've just wasted another three weeks pouring cement. Come over here, Steve, and get your camera ready. Just watch the ground between the outer fence and the pad.'

As they drew closer, the ground seemed to take on a life of its own, lifting and subsiding over and over. Steve watched, gobsmacked.

'It's the gas under the ground trying to escape, but it's got nowhere to go and it's spreading. If they can't plug it, they're going to have to build a third fence even further back and then, who knows, maybe a fourth. Yellowstone's Old Faithful blows every sixty-five minutes, but our Old Faithful never stops blowing. I dunno where it's going to end.'

'That's four acres of land they've enclosed and you know how much compensation we got? Not a red cent,' Annie said.

'Did you complain?'

'Steve, you don't understand, Nordic don't listen to us,' Pete said. 'They treat us as if they own the land and we're their tenants. You know what they called this? "A minor seep." They said they'd get back to plug it when they have time. Fact is, they can't plug it. You know, the gas companies have a commitment to restore the land and return it to the owners when the wells stop producing in twenty-five years or so. There'll be 100,000 wells by then and this won't be the only rogue. I'm guessing they'll conveniently forget their commitments, and the government, whatever side's in power then, will be too gutless to force them. Come on, let's go. I'll be sick if I stay here any longer and I want to show you how they're depleting our water.'

As they climbed back into the Land Cruiser, Pete said. 'Annie, did you tell Steve what CD you put on every time we get a visit from Nordic?' Before she could answer he went on, 'It's *Lies* and her favourite lyric is *Lies, lies, I can't believe a word you say.* It really pisses them off.' Pete's ironic humour wasn't shared by his wife.

Dennis had talked about falling water levels and pressure, but Steve hadn't understood and had been unwilling to show his ignorance by questioning him. A few minutes later they stopped at a small enclosure with a dome-like lid in the middle.

'This one's ours,' Pete said, unscrewing the lid. 'This is where I check our water levels and we should have twenty metres, but you'll see when I dip it that there's only seven metres left to pump. Our cattle are dependent on this water and it's been subsiding ever since Nordic came onto our property.'

'But how?'

'I've been pondering that. Maybe they use it for fracking, rather than bringing in hundreds of thousands of gallons of water in tankers like they should, or perhaps it's depleted after they've fracked and the water's exploded to the surface.'

'Did you confront Nordic?'

'It's like dealing with Colonel Klink. "I see nothing! I know nothing!" They're in total denial,' Annie said.

'Us farmers and graziers have water quotas but there are no restrictions on how much the mining and gas companies can use. It's a bloody joke,' Pete said, walking over to a large, fenced bore. 'I had to enclose this because it's full of methane and I can set the water on fire.'

Steve had seen the same thing in Colorado in the documentary *Gasland*, but had not understood how it occurred. As if reading his mind, Pete added, 'The water pressure holds the methane in the aquifers but, when the water levels are depleted, the coal seams are exposed and the escaping methane that fills the void between the level of the water and the surface has to find a way to escape. My family's been drawing water from this bore for over a hundred years and this has never happened before.'

'What'd Nordic say about it?'

'Their scientists said it was genetic.'

'Genetic?'

'Naturally occurring,' Dennis chipped in. 'The fact that it's never happened before, and that it only occurred after they'd started drilling, meant nothing. They emphatically denied that they were to blame.'

'Unbelievable.'

'I'd love to be able to say you've seen it all, but you ain't seen nothing yet.'

'They've destroyed our lives,' Annie snapped, as Pete nudged the four-wheel-drive through a herd of Black Angus that were wandering on the track.

'Steve, we're heading to a neighbour's property about twenty kilometres away and, if you aren't a convert after what you see, you'll never be,' Pete said grimly.

After opening and closing five more large gates, they stopped in front of another well-pad. Steve scanned it carefully, looking for movements in the ground, but he didn't see any. Pete glanced over at Annie. 'Why don't you tell Steve what happened, Darling?'

Annie clenched her hands and muttered, 'Bastards. We hadn't been well. Pete had been having trouble breathing, the kids had picked up rashes that caused them to scratch all the time and Tony, our youngest boy, bled from the ears. Then we found out that Nordic fracked this well about six months ago and that it went badly wrong, but they never said a word. We only found out about it because one of their workers got drunk in the Hallby pub one night and mouthed off. It turned out that they'd poisoned an aquifer, which joins up with the one under our property. The gas companies have always said that it's impossible for this to occur and Nordic, once they knew about it, had a legal and moral responsibility to report it but, instead, they tried to cover it up. So much for self-regulation. They didn't tell old Sam Arnold, who owns the property; they didn't tell us, despite knowing that we were drawing water from an adjoining aquifer, and they didn't tell any of the others who were taking water from these two aquifers. After they found out that we knew what they'd been up to, they owned up, saying it was an unfortunate accident that they'd overlooked reporting. Liars!'

'And surprise, surprise. The environment authorities and government took no action; not even a public admonishment,' Pete said. 'Instead, they got stuck into us.'

'Yeah, we found out that they'd pumped one hundred and fifty litres of

THPS down the well and, while we didn't know what it was then or if it was dangerous, we soon found out,' Annie continued. 'It's toxic. It can result in death, severe eye inflammation, skin allergies, irritation of the mouth and gastro-intestinal tract and can cause chemical pneumonia. If we'd been drinking bore water, they might've killed us. I'm so bloody angry. Luckily we draw our drinking water from rainwater tanks, but that didn't help our cattle: they not only lost condition, but clumps fell off their coats and they looked like walking patchwork quilts. What were the idiots thinking when they pumped this poison into our water? Half the fracking chemicals remain below the surface, in the coal seams, and we know they can move through the ground water. It terrifies me when I hear numbers like 100,000 wells in Queensland.'

'And you know what the authorities and our esteemed government did?' Pete said. 'They banned us and our neighbours from selling our cattle or having them slaughtered until tests had cleared them of contamination. Then they issued a belated warning telling us not to let our animals drink the bore water, even though they'd already been drinking it for six months. They should've thrown the book at Nordic, but they were scared they'd pull their money out of the development and go back to London. Money really talks up here and there's no shortage of willing ears in this pathetic government. Some of the smaller companies are occasionally rapped on the knuckles as a government face-saving exercise, but the big ones, like Nordic, are untouchable.'

'Incredible isn't it?' Annie said, taking up the story again. 'The same government that says the extraction of coal seam gas is safe, and that there's no risk to the Great Artesian Basin and the aquifers, couldn't get to us fast enough to stop us selling our cattle. Anyhow, we weren't convinced that THPS was the only poisonous chemical used. So we applied to the government to look at the company's data sheets and, after they'd tried to wear us down by procrastination, they eventually released them. It was then that I noticed that the data sheet on THPS was American, ten years out of date and missing critical information. We took the rest of the data sheets to an Australian specialist in chemical management and she said they didn't meet Australian standards and were in breach of the *Dangerous Goods Safety Management Act* and the national code for material safety data sheets.'

'The data sheets form part of the environmental applications don't they?'
'Yeah,' Pete laughed. 'The gas companies have got 'em down pat and

they run to thousands and thousands of pages and they know that neither the authorities nor the government have the personnel or the expertise to examine them. Tell me one other reason why Nordic could get away with copying a foreign company's incomplete data sheet, typing their name on the top and then submitting it as if it was their own, and it's not detected? Spare me.'

'What action did the government take against Nordic?'

'You're joking,' Annie said. 'Nothing, of course.'

'Let's go back to the house for drinks and I'll show you a file that you might find interesting. By the way, Steve, did you notice anything strange about the herds of cattle here and on our property?'

He was no farmer but racked his brain for an answer. The cattle on this property were brown and white, while the cattle on the Lairds' property were black, but surely that wasn't the answer. 'Sorry, Pete, I didn't.'

'There are no calves in the herds. Our breeding started to fall away four years ago, then we went through a spate of stillborn calves and the occasional few with deformities. In the past twelve months, we haven't had one newborn.'

They were all silent for a few minutes until Pete, entering his property through another entrance, said, 'If you look out to the right, you'll see the well-pad fence that our bulls flattened. I won't stop, but I want to show you the next two wells.' Slowing down, he drove off the track again, stopping fifty metres away from another well-pad. 'I don't want to get too close to this one and you'll soon see why.'

Steve could hear the hissing as they strode through the grass towards the well-head, 'What's that?'

'It's a methane leak, a big one, and it's escaping straight into the atmosphere. This is the worst one, but half the well-heads on our property are leaking and no-one gives a damn. This stuff is highly volatile, so we fenced off twenty acres to stop the cattle getting down here. If those bulls had accidentally knocked down *this* fence, we might've had a major disaster on our hands. The fence posts and the equipment are made of steel and all it would take is one small spark.'

'All your problems are with one company, though. Surely they're not all like Nordic?'

'They're all the same. I could take you to properties all over the Downs where the owners have suffered dreadfully, like we have.' Pete paused and spat on the ground. 'Well, maybe not as bad as us, but CEGL, Source, Javelin and a heap of the smaller gas companies have made life miserable for farmers. They're not regulated in any way and, after they've lodged their environmental applications, they just do what they want. Then, to rub salt into the wounds, we get to watch some dopey government minister on the six o'clock news telling us that they're subject to the harshest regulations ever enacted and have to comply with 1500 conditions. Christ, I'm getting depressed. Let's go and have that drink.'

They were barely back on the track, before they saw a cloud of red dust coming towards them, as it drew closer they saw that it was a blue and white Nordic truck with a dozen or so workers on board. The driver waved but was ignored and Annie muttered, 'Bastards.'

'Where are they going?'

'Look at the gum trees coming up on the left. You can see the top of a drill rig. I'm guessing they'll frack it in the next few days.'

'We've got Nordic employees all over our property every day of the week, exploring, drilling, fracking, laying pipes and gravel and disturbing the cattle, but they do nothing, not a damn thing, to maintain their existing wells,' Annie said.

Steve had planned to be on a flight out of Brisbane that night, but the tour had taken longer than anticipated; as they pulled up to the house, the sun was dipping behind the horizon.

Dennis had hardly spoken, but now he smiled at Steve. 'Are you a convert?'

'You knew I would be.'

'Yeah, anyone who can't see that Annie and Pete have been dealt the rawest of raw deals wouldn't have a smidgeon of compassion in their body, but remember, when you write your article, that they're just a microcosm of what's happening to families all over the Downs.'

Annie smiled. 'Welcome to the clan, Steve. Are you going to join us for tea?'

'I'd love to,' he said, as Pete dropped a fat, two-ring binder in front of him, saying,' Have a flick through that.'

There were medical bills from GPs, dermatologists and pathology laboratories for blood tests, that ran into the thousands of dollars, along with photos of them and their two boys. There were pictures of their younger son, Tony, with red welts all over his body and blood oozing from his ears and others of Roger, their older boy, lying in bed with blood pouring from his nose.

'That happened before we found out about the THPS in the water,' Annie said, 'but we couldn't prove it caused the boys' ailments or get Nordic to admit they were responsible. When we accused them, we got letters from their highfalutin' lawyers, not only denying liability but threatening legal action, in the event that we made any defamatory remarks about their client.'

'That's the standard procedure they adopt against anyone who challenges them,' Pete added. 'They intimidate and coerce knowing that most farmers don't have the time or money to brief a big firm of lawyers to fight 'em.'

'What did you do?'

'What could we do? We're struggling to make ends meet, we haven't seen a newborn calf for over a year and our once-fertile land is being destroyed in front of our eyes,' Annie sniffled, her face contorted in anger. 'It's so unfair.'

'We sent the boys to boarding school in Southport so they could get away from this environment, something we really couldn't afford to do, but we didn't have a choice.' Pete said. 'Ironic isn't it? It used to be thought of as healthy to send your kids to work on a farm or station. Well, it sure ain't now. In some ways we're lucky, because we own this place unencumbered. Had we had a mortgage, we wouldn't have been able to continue. We've got no intention of selling; besides, there wouldn't be any buyers and the property's lost half its value in the past five years.'

'But how did you get sick? You said you never drank the bore water.'

'No, but we used it to wash and shower. After we found out about the THPS and other chemicals, I connected all of the outlets in the house to the rainwater tanks and within six weeks the welts had gone, the bleeding had stopped and we were almost back to normal. It's only a matter of time before the gas companies kill someone.'

Steve didn't respond, but his mind went back to Charlie Paxton and he thought, *they probably already have.*

'I expect to see your article in the *Advocate*,' Pete said.

It was nearly nine o'clock when they said good-bye to the Lairds. After Dennis closed the last gate and climbed back into the SUV, he looked over at Steve. 'I'm totally beat. I'm gonna have a sleep. Aim for Pinilla and you'll see signs to Marra once you get there. Oh, and keep an eye out for kangaroos and emus.'

Chapter 21

Dean Prezky had just got home from a long day's work when Jack Thomas phoned, telling him that Filliburton had already fessed up to the environment authorities and that someone must have seen him spying. Dean said it wasn't possible, before slamming the phone down and again musing whether the risks he had taken had been worth it.

He recalled the two-and-half days; he'd been well hidden, and was certain that he had not been detected. Then he thought back to the morning when he drove past the well-pad. Someone must have seen his old Toyota and put two and two together. If only he had got away in the dark as he had planned and then it dawned on him – he had evidence on film to prove that the disposal of wastewater had been anything but accidental. Bugger what Thomas had said about stealing, he had proof of a crime and surely the authorities would not be so stupid as to charge him with some misdemeanour that he may have inadvertently committed.

If necessity is the mother of invention then for Dean injustice was the mother of enlightenment. He wasn't computer literate but he persisted and eventually fathomed out how to download the camcorder's hard drive to his laptop and edit the footage. By midnight he had condensed nearly twelve hours of film to eight minutes.

Spencer Harbrow lobbied CEGL's major institutional shareholders in London, seeking their support to remove the three non-executive directors who had dared vote against him. The shareholders empathised with him but would not back his planned coup and this irritated him but he was careful not to vent his feelings, knowing he could not afford to upset them. The *National Advocate* had eased up on its vendetta after CEGL dropped its legal action and reinstated the advertising contracts. They had even published an article about Hercules Gas and its unsafe processes and finished, surprisingly, by saying that its takeover by the much larger CEGL was something that the community should welcome.

Harbrow was fed up with the delays in the Fisher Valley and being held up by a no-account group called the *estatees* and he was determined to crush them. In a detailed memo to Moira Raymond he set her the near-impossible task of having at least four wells drilled on the *estates* within ninety days. He knew that she would almost certainly fail, after which he would terminate her services. She would rue the day she had voted against him. He would then employ Frank Beck to break the *estatees'* resistance by any means necessary. When the share price resumed its upward climb, as it surely would with Beck's clandestine help, he would also rid himself of the others who were no longer team players.

Steve Forrest's flight touched down at Newtower Airport and thirty minutes later he was crawling through heavy early-morning traffic, listening to talkback radio. When he reached the outskirts of the city, he accelerated and two hours later he was pleased to see the *Welcome to the Fisher Valley* sign. He was soon flying past the massive open-cut and underground coal mines and watching clouds of steam pouring from the coal-fired power stations.

The news came on and he turned up the volume. *The Ministry for Primary Industries yesterday dissolved the Tura Community Coal Seam Gas Consultative Committee, without any explanation or community consultation. Residents are outraged that this Committee, seen as essential by the former minister to ensure proper communication between residents and the gas companies, could be abolished in such a cavalier manner. The Chief Executive of the* Fisher Valley Protective Alliance, *Mr Jack Thomas, said it was a black day for democracy and that it was more than just a coincidence that the gas giant, CEGL, held licences over seventy-five percent of the land in Tura. "The executives of CEGL have never been totally open with the community but with the stroke of a pen the Minister has licenced them to operate in secrecy without public scrutiny or accountability."*

There were five committees operating in the valley and Steve could not understand why only one, admittedly the most aggressive, had been shut down. The residents of Tura would be enraged and the decision might drive them to take matters into their own hands. Perhaps this was what the government and CEGL wanted, or maybe the premier was cosying up to his gas company buddies for a cushy consultancy after he lost the forthcoming election, which, in the absence of a miracle, he most certainly would.

Steve had been so absorbed by the news that he had not noticed the police car behind him until he heard the siren and saw the flashing lights. He breathed a sigh of relief when he saw Josh Gibson walking towards him.

'G'day Josh, how are you?' He grinned.

'We clocked you at one hundred and eleven. Why were you exceeding the speed limit?'

He started to laugh, but then noticed Sandi standing behind Josh and knew that his friend wasn't going to be able to turn a blind eye. 'I wasn't concentrating.'

'Lack of concentration is one of the prime reasons that we have so many accidents,' Josh said. 'Do you have your licence?'

Steve handed it over and Josh passed it to Sandi, saying, 'Check this and the vehicle registration and then write him up.'

As Sandi walked back to the police car, Josh said under his breath, 'Sorry, mate, I can't be seen to be doing favours in front of a junior officer.'

'That's okay, Josh, I understand,' he said, still watching Sandi. He had paid her scant attention the night the gas well exploded, but now there was something about her that caught his eye. She looked up and caught him staring and smiled, before going back to writing the ticket.

She returned and handed him the ticket. 'There's one demerit point with this and you don't have all that many left, so you need to be careful.' Her eyes were twinkling and she touched his fingers, holding the ticket for a split second longer than necessary.

'That's good advice,' Josh added. 'Make sure you stay within the speed limits from now on.'

As Steve neared the outskirts of Paisley, his mobile began to ring. He pulled off the road to answer it.

'My name's Dean Prezky. You don't know me but I need to see you.'

'Everyone knows who you are, Dean. I've been meaning to ask you for an interview. What's this about?'

'You'll see when we meet. When are you free?'

'Tomorrow morning at nine o'clock.'

'At your office?'

'Yeah.'

Moira Raymond knew from the formal tone of her boss's memo that there was more to it than met the eye. She picked it up, drew the drapes on her windows and poured herself a stiff scotch, before flopping into a recliner. As she read it again, its intent was obvious and clearly it had been drafted for the eyes of others, so that her boss, if pressed to justify his actions, could say, *Look, these are the instructions I issued and she failed to deliver.* He was smarmy but he was also clever and a master of subtleties, but to Moira there was nothing subtle about his memo. Others might not understand it, but Harbrow was blatantly telling her, *You crossed me and now you're for it.* Well, she had no intention of failing and the law was on her side; if she had to crash through the *estatees* by force, she would. Not only would she deliver the four gas wells on the *estates,* but another eight on Scott-Tempy's property and, in doing so, smash the resistance to *big gas* in the valley once and for all. She would need Frank Beck's assistance, but that would not be a problem.

She knew how big her boss's ego was and it would never have entered his mind that the dissent at the last board meeting might ultimately cost him his job, but it had not escaped her. The door to the job that she coveted had been nudged open and she wasn't about to waste the opportunity to ingratiate herself with those who counted.

Clem Aspley and Phillip Bancroft had never been great supporters of hers and she had not phoned either of them at home before.

Aspley answered the phone on the second ring and sounded far from happy at having had his evening disturbed.

'Moira, whatever it is, I'm sure it could've waited until tomorrow.'

She wondered if she was making him late for a hot date. 'I'm sorry. I just wanted to thank you for your decisive comments at the board meeting. They saved us from an embarrassing defeat in the courts and, needless to say, some very bad publicity and a pummelling on the stockmarket.'

'Yes, yes. Is that all?'

'I'm sorry, Clem; you're obviously busy so I'll let you go. I really admire your courage though. Bye.'

'Hold on. I'm not sure I know what you mean.'

'You're very modest. I'm sure you realise that opposing Spencer is not an everyday occurrence and I can't ever remember him being on the wrong side of a resolution before. I bet he's given you a real chewing out.'

'Well, actually no, I haven't heard from him.'

'You haven't heard from him?' She paused.

It had been a week since the board meeting and Aspley had given no thought to Harbrow not contacting him but, on reflection, it *was* unusual. Harbrow would phone at all times of the day or night to talk about cars, wines, women, and sometimes to organise a date or to invite him to come for what he described as *a quick spin in my jet.* 'He's probably just been busy.' There was a tinge of doubt in his voice.

'I'm sure you're right,' she said, intentionally replying too quickly.

'You don't believe that, do you? Has he spoken to you since the meeting?'

'No.'

'He's probably sulking. I wouldn't read too much into it if I were you,' he said without conviction, resolving to phone Phillip Bancroft and Vic Bezzina to see if Harbrow had called them.

Moira could sense the cogs spinning in Aspley's head. CEGL had made him rich and he enjoyed the perks of office. 'Oh, I wasn't reading *anything* into it,' she said. 'I just wanted to thank you for promoting such a tough decision. I doubt anyone else on the board could've championed the resolution in the way you did.'

Aspley had been so stressed about the pressure the Maddock Group had applied to him that he could not remember what he had said, but he didn't like what he'd just heard. 'I think you're placing far too much weight on what I did.'

'Have it your way, but I know that, thanks to you, and to a lesser extent Phil and Vic, we came to a decision that best served the interests of the company, and that's something I'd like to think we could do again.'

'I don't see why we couldn't.'

She had not won him over, but, before, he would have sided with Harbrow without giving her any thought. Now he would think long and hard.

'Have you spoken to any of the other directors about this?' he asked.

'No, but I do have to call Phil.'

'Let's keep what we discussed as our little secret.'

'Sure. Good night, Clem.'

'Good night, Moira.' His tone displayed none of his earlier aggression.

Fifteen minutes later, she took a long satisfying sip of whiskey, after having praised Phillip Bancroft for unflinchingly proposing and supporting the contentious resolution. When she put the phone down, she was well satisfied – she knew that Harold Llewellyn and Vic Bezzina would support her in any showdown and two more votes would see her boss shown the door.

Billy McGregor's gang were restless and had been at him night after night in the pub with their plan to hurl a Molotov cocktail through the window of the Paisley Real Estate Agency, which was full of advertisements for forthcoming mortgagee auctions of farms and vineyards. Billy was wild and loved a fight, but he wasn't a fool or inherently bad. Knowing there'd be no community support for such a wanton act of destruction, he had baulked at burning down the agency and instead came up with the idea of graffitiing the windows and gluing the locks. As they played pool and waited for the clock to tick around to closing time, Frank Beck and three of his Filliburton mates sauntered in, ordered a jug of beer and sat themselves down at the bar.

'How long are you kids gonna be on that table?' Beck yelled.

'It's a challenge table, Mister,' Kazza replied, blowing a large chewing gum bubble. 'Ya gotta put your name on the board.'

There were about a dozen names on the board, all members of Billy's gang.

'We don't want to challenge, we want to play against each other.'

Billy knew who Beck was and who he worked for. After CEGL, Filliburton was the most hated organisation in the valley. 'Okay,' he said, glancing at the board. 'As soon as the challenges are over, it's all yours.'

'Kid, you don't want me to come over there.'

'If you come over here,' Billy said, smacking the butt of the pool cue into his palm, 'you're going down.' His gang jumped to their feet as if they were one.

Beck turned purple and bounced off his stool, but his mates restrained him, knowing they were outnumbered five to one.

'Bloody ape man,' Billy said, smacking the cue a little harder.

'Your mob's not always gonna be around to protect you, you skinny little smart-arse.'

Billy laughed and turned back to the pool table, subtly nodding to two of the gang, who disappeared through the back door. For the next two hours an uncomfortable tension hung over the bar, with Beck seething, while the unruly gang provoked him. Three minutes before closing time, Kazza looked over at Beck and said, 'The table's all yours,' to raucous roars of laughter.

'Come on,' Beck said to his mates, 'let's get out of here; I've had enough of these jabbering idiots.'

The publican watched Billy and his gang follow them out to the car park, fearing that all hell was about to break loose, but the young larrikins, other than shouting out a few smart remarks, clambered into their cars. Beck stormed across the bitumen as the cars screamed off, with the gang giving him the finger and plenty of abuse, while his mates stood glumly looking at the Filliburton Hummer with four flat tyres.

It was after midnight when Josh got the call to attend an incident in the car park of the Paisley Hotel. When he arrived, a roadside assistance vehicle was next to a Filliburton SVU, with the mechanic crouching next to one of its flat tyres. Surely he hadn't had his sleep wrecked for something as minor as this. As Josh got out of the van, Beck strode towards him. 'I want those young punks in the pub charged with destruction of property.'

'Jeez, Frank, getting your tyres let down is hardly property destruction.'

'Christ, I know that. The idiots filled the valves with gunk and we can't get any air into the tyres. What are you going to do about it?'

Josh fought to hide a grin. 'Did you see who did it?'

'No, but it was that blond kid; he was in the pub looking for trouble. I'll break his neck if I ever get my hands on him.'

'If you take the law into your own hands you'll have me to answer to.'

Beck was about to argue, when the taxi he had phoned arrived and he jumped into the front and rolled down the window, while his mates got into the back.

'Josh, this is no joke. I want those kids caught and charged. They're in the pub every night on the pool table, so it shouldn't be too difficult, even for you.'

'Prick,' Josh muttered under his breath, anxious to get home and back to bed. Try as he might, he couldn't get back to sleep and it was still dark when he showered and left for the station to catch up on some paperwork. He was enjoying the peace and ploughing through a build-up of reports, when the quiet was broken by the phone ringing. The caller, the manager of the Paisley Real Estate Agency, was irate. Someone had defaced his front window and had poured glue into the locks on the doors, front and rear, and it was impossible to get into the building. Five minutes later, Josh brought his van to a halt in front of a window covered with the words *parasites, traitors* and *scum* in heavy black paint. The little man standing on the footpath and gesticulating furiously was obviously the manager and his staff looked bitter, but most folk passing by were smiling.

Chapter 22

The normal format of the *Paisley Chronicle* was to feature a major current news item on the front page and to run an editorial on a contentious issue, which was really Steve's personal opinion, on page three. Such was the importance of his findings in Queensland and his new-found passion in opposing *big gas,* that he dispensed with protocol and headed the front page with the editorial *Too much at risk.*

The editorial compared the symptoms of the children in the Paisley Memorial with those of the kids on the Spurling Downs, and followed up with the plight of the still-born calves, those born with deformities and the deterioration in breeding.

The third page continued in the same vein. Steve described the failure of the gas companies to plug wells, the methane leakage into the air and the depletion and poisoning of the water, before concluding that the exploration and extraction of coal seam gas in the Fisher Valley and Australia generally was far too risky – it should either be banned or, at the very least, there should be a moratorium until *big gas* could unequivocally prove it was safe.

On page two was a petition demanding that the government cease to issue any new licences and that exploration for, and the production of, coal seam gas in the Fisher Valley be halted pending an investigation into the health, safety and environmental issues that resulted from it. It was a call for unity and it asked subscribers to mail completed petitions to the *Chronicle,* which would submit them to the government.

Buffy thought the article was Steve's finest, but was disappointed when he told her that he was going to run it by his lawyer before publishing. She need not have worried, as Simon Breckenridge waxed lyrical, telling Steve that if defamation action was brought against him, which was unlikely, he would defend him *pro bono*.

The phone call from Jack Thomas was succinct. The contents of the three jars had been analysed and contained a cocktail of chemicals, including boric acid, methanol and hydrochloric acid which, according to him, 'were all bloody dangerous'.

'Send me the analysis report,' Dean said. 'I want to look them up on the Net and see what harm they do. Is the analysis of the three jars all the same?'

'Identical.'

'We've got 'em then. We'll put the footage together with the analysis and then see if the lying bastards still claim it was an accident.'

'I want to nail them and their mates in the government just as much as you do, but you don't want them to find out you were on their land spying, because they'll make your life hell.'

'I'll be careful, Jack. You leave it with me.'

Paisley was abuzz about the article and petition in the *Chronicle* and circulation was a record exceeding 12,000. Len Forrest was overjoyed and carried a copy under his arm, needlessly telling anyone in town who would listen, that it was his son who penned it.

Charles Paxton read about the deformed calves and felt the blood rush to his face. He had suspected that *big gas* was responsible for Gentle Lady's deformed foal and now, despite not having the laboratory results, he knew he was right.

Moira Raymond cursed. CEGL's strategy was to divide the community, but this article called for unity in opposition to *big gas* and she wondered if she had underestimated Steve Forrest. There was nearly nine months of the advertising contract with the *Chronicle* to run and she decided she would write a rebuttal of the editorial in the form of a community announcement and insist that Steve print it.

When Buffy said there was an Amanda Simpson from the Maddock Group on the phone, Steve had no hesitation in taking the call.

'So you don't think it's a trick this time,' she teased.

'No, Amanda, I don't. What can I do for you?'

'I think you already know.' She laughed.

'Perhaps.'

'We'd like to publish your article, without the petition and with a few minor deletions and changes. I'm emailing the changes to you and I'd like your return email consenting to the amendments.'

'Providing there's nothing major, it should be fine,' he responded, fighting to keep the excitement from his voice.

'If you ever decide to quit that quaint little paper, give me a call. You have a real way with words … when you're passionate about something.'

'Hello Dean,' Buffy said. 'You're here for your appointment with Steve. Can I get you a coffee, tea, anything?'

'No thanks. Do I know you?'

'No, probably not. I'm Buffy Preston and I've seen you on telly and I really admire you.'

Dean Prezky was a private man, still coming to grips with his new-found celebrity status and struggling to cope with the many strangers who addressed him by his first name as if they'd known him for years. 'Thanks,' he said.

Steve watched this exchange without saying anything, as he tried to get a handle on the man at the counter who, the major dailies said, had brought a premier down. He exuded nervous energy and obviously wasn't given to small talk.

'Come through.' Steve extended his hand. For once it wasn't crushed and their hands barely touched before Dean was undoing his computer bag and firing up his old laptop.

'It'll take a minute or so,' he said, as a statement rather than an apology. 'That was a good article you had in the paper this morning and you might want to follow up with what I'm going to show you.'

A gas rig eventually appeared on screen, illuminated by light towers and surrounded by Filliburton trucks and employees.

'Where'd you get the footage from?'

'That's unimportant. Just watch it.'

When it was over, Steve sat shaking his head in disbelief. He'd discounted some of the more outrageous stories he had heard on the Spurling Downs but now he knew they were true.

'That rig's less than a kilometre from the Blaxland River. Can you imagine what might happen if that crap seeps into it?'

'How did you get that footage?'

'You don't need to know. You just need to run the story and have the disk and chemical analysis as support. They're yours for two thousand dollars.'

'Who was Filliburton drilling for?'

'CEGL'

'Are you sure?'

'There was a *CEGL trespassers keep out sign* on the entrance to the well-pad.'

Steve had never paid for information, but two thousand dollars for this damning evidence wasn't much and the Maddock Group would almost certainly pay the *Chronicle* another healthy fee for the exposé that he was already writing in his mind. He regretted ever entering into that advertising contract with CEGL, because he felt obligated not to mention them in the critical articles that he'd written about the coal seam gas industry. It seemed morally indefensible to take their money with one hand while attacking them with the other.

'All right, I'll buy it but, before I write anything, I'm going to show it to CEGL's management and give them a chance to put their side of the story.'

'Are you completely mad?' Dean scowled and reached over for his laptop. 'You do that and they'll stop you from publishing and there'll be a lot of questions about how the footage came to be in your possession.'

Steve knew, that unless Filliburton had acted unilaterally, Dean was probably right, and that he would most likely be hit with an injunction from CEGL. But he could not take their money and not give them the opportunity to respond. If only he had listened to Buffy and his father, he would not be in this compromising position. 'I think you're over-reacting Dean.'

'Maybe, but I risked an awful lot to get what you just watched and I'm not going to let you jeopardise the prospects of the public hearing about it.' Dean stood up and threw the computer bag over his shoulder. 'I know CEGL run big advertisements with you but I never thought you'd put dollars before the public interest. The disk is no longer for sale. Well, not to you anyway.'

Josh Gibson knew that Billy McGregor had been behind the sabotage of Filliburton's SUV and the Paisley Real Estate Agency. All of Paisley knew, and Billy knew that Josh knew but, as they sat eyeing each other in the police station, Billy, with a huge grin, denied everything.

'I never left the pub, Josh. Ya can ask the publican; he'll vouch for me. I never touched that big ape's vehicle.'

'You mightn't have yourself but you sent someone out to do it. Who was it?'

'Hell, ya make me sound like the godfather or something. I ain't got that type of power. Wish I did.'

'Where were you when the real estate agency was trashed?'

'Dunno. What time did it happen?'

Josh knew he wasn't getting anywhere. 'Billy, I mightn't be able to prove it, but I know it was you. You think you're smart but you're not. If that guy, Frank Beck, had gotten hold of you last night, he would've broken your neck. I want you to knock it off; it's not up to you to be fighting the gas companies.'

'But it is for Charles Paxton, huh? Why didn't ya charge him, Josh? You knew the wolf I saw that night was his dog, didn't ya? But he was never charged.'

'That's got nothing to do with you.'

'Didn't ya read the *Chronicle* this morning? They're poisoning our water. I reckon everyone should be fighting 'em and if I knew who was running around with that glue last night I'd be the first to congratulate 'em.' Billy stood up. 'I sure hope ya don't catch 'em Josh.'

It was common knowledge that the producers of Channel Six's *Your Nation* were producing an exposé on the coal seam gas industry and that they'd been filming in Queensland for the past fortnight. After Dean Prezky had his run-in at the *Paisley Chronicle*, he'd drawn the conclusion that if a little newspaper owed *big gas* favours it was likely that the larger Sydney newspapers would be in the same boat. It was then that he thought of approaching *Your Nation* with his footage, knowing that, if they picked it up, the public would get to see what he had seen rather than reading what some journo had converted to print. The producers had fallen over themselves when he told them who was calling and what he had. They asked him to email it to them but, when he declined, they invited him to come to Sydney so he could show it to them in person.

'Honey, I'll only be gone for a day,' he protested, when Vicki got into a tizz.

'You'll kill yourself before this is over. It's a three-hour drive, you'll be there all day, and then you'll be driving home at night. You'll be exhausted.

If *Your Nation* is so interested in your footage, why can't they come here?'

'It doesn't work that way. Don't worry, I'll be careful and if I get lucky they might pay me something. That'll make it worthwhile, won't it?'

'Not if you're dead. Maybe you should find a cheap motel and drive home in the morning?'

'We can't afford it, Honey, you know that. I'm leaving at five o'clock; I'll try not to wake you.'

'I'll be up. I'll make you a thermos of coffee and some sandwiches.' She kissed him on the cheek. 'I love you, you damn fool.'

The disdain on the parking attendant's face at the entrance to Channel Six's executive car park suggested that he wasn't used to seeing dirty, battered four-wheel-drives but, once Dean told him who he was, it was, 'Yes, Mr Prezky, let me show you where to park and they're expecting you on the twentieth floor. After you've parked, I'll show you to the lifts.' Dean smiled to himself.

Two production executives were waiting for him when he left the lift. They introduced themselves as Brent and Troy and showed him into a meeting room. After asking if he'd like coffee or tea, which he declined, they moved straight to the business of the footage and sat engrossed through the eight minutes.

'Don't you want to know how I got it?'

'No,' Brent said quite sharply. 'We'd prefer not to. Show it again, please.' This time they asked Dean to freeze the film at certain stages while exchanging knowing glances.

'We need to cut it to about sixty seconds, Troy.'

'Exactly what I was thinking.'

'Sixty seconds! Are you mad? You'll lose the impact. Didn't you see that pump, the wastewater, the tubing and the mess? And you're going to have to show the Filiburton trucks and employees. It can't be done.'

'Yes it can,' Brent smiled. 'After we add some suitable music and Libby Hanover's introduction, I promise it'll be a powerful piece of film.'

All Dean could think of was that they were cutting his three days of hell to one minute, and he wanted to pack up his laptop and storm out. But, then, would any of his footage ever be shown? While he was brooding, a mid-fortyish, blonde woman entered the room.

'I'm Libby Hanover,' she said. 'I've been so looking forward to meeting the famous *gas-man.*' Her big blue eyes shone and she had an infectious smile.

'I'm not famous.' He grinned. 'If the truth be known, I just got fed up with coal seam gas companies ruining my life and probably over-reacted.'

'And brought down a premier?'

'If that turns out to be the case, it was unintended because the conservatives are no better.'

'So you're apolitical?'

'I hate coal seam gas and what it's doing to me and my family.'

'You've certainly made that obvious. Can I have a look at this footage that I've heard about?'

'I can hook the laptop up to the big screen,' Troy volunteered.

'Yes, do that.'

Libby sat entranced while viewing the film.

'What do you think?' Dean asked.

'It's compelling. When you add it to what we've filmed on the Spurling Downs, it'll blow the roof off this industry.'

'We need to trim it to about sixty seconds,' Brent said.

'I dunno.' Dean sounded despondent. 'You can't cut that much and have any impact. Perhaps I should see if your competitors have any interest?'

Libby put her hand on his forearm and gently squeezed it. 'Television time is incredibly expensive and it doesn't matter who you take it to, it'll be cut to a minute or perhaps even less. We're happy to pay a fair price for the footage and I think you'll be more than pleased with what we go to air with. These two gentlemen are the best in the business and I can guarantee it'll definitely have an impact.'

She was one of those people with enormous charisma and charm, whom you felt you could trust immediately.

'All right,' he said reluctantly.

'We're filming the final segment in the Fisher Valley next week and, if you're available, you might like to show us around.'

'I'd like that.'

'It was a pleasure meeting you, Dean. I have to fly, but Brent will fix up the paperwork.'

It was just after 1pm when he climbed back into the four-wheel-drive. He held a copy of a contract in which he'd signed over the rights to his eight minutes of footage to Channel Six, along with a cheque for $5000. Once out of the car park, he phoned Vicki to tell her that he'd be home early and that he would take her and the kids out to dinner. He didn't tell her about the cheque. That would be another surprise.

Steve Forrest often took the long route to the post office rather than run the risk that old Mrs Eleanor Elliot might be sitting on the porch of her cottage, ready to chew his ear about an article in the *Chronicle*. However, today, for some reason, he'd completely forgotten about her.

A widow for fifteen years, Mrs Elliot liked to peer over the top of her frameless spectacles while she interrogated anyone unlucky enough not to avoid her, although a few people, like Len Forrest and Buffy, enjoyed talking to her. She knew all about the goings on in town, but Steve did not appreciate her comments about his courage and his nether regions.

As he walked around the corner, she said, 'Good afternoon, Steven. I so enjoyed your article about the Spurling Downs.'

He looked up at her sitting in her rocking chair. *Bugger, why hadn't he gone the long way?* 'Thank you, Mrs Elliot.' He fought the urge to cringe. 'How are you?'

'As if you care,' she cackled. 'You purposely avoid walking past my house. Buffy tells me everything.'

'That's not true.'

'Never mind. I'm pleased to see that you've finally seen the light. But why are you still running their advertisements?'

'That's private and confidential, Mrs Elliot, and something I can't discuss, other than to say that after the end of September they'll cease.'

'And not before time. My Arthur, God bless his soul, used to always say that it was all right to make a mistake so long as you fixed it as soon as you realised the error of your ways. Is that something you believe in, Steven?'

'It's something I've never thought much about. I'm sorry, Mrs Elliot, I have to get to the post office.'

'No you don't. It doesn't close for another three hours. You just want to get away from me.' She removed her spectacles to wipe away an imaginary tear.

He knew it was an act, yet he still felt sorry for her.

'No I don't.' he responded, wishing he was nasty enough to have said *yeah, that's right.*

'Would you like a cup of tea?' she asked. Before he could respond, she followed up with, 'Who are you taking to the mayor's annual dinner dance, now that your beautiful ex-girlfriend has taken up with that land access consultant?'

God, he'd never gotten a guernsey to the mayor's dinner dance before, as invitations usually just went to Paisley's rich and esteemed, and he guessed he'd only been invited because of the articles that he'd had published in the *National Advocate.* He hadn't even told Buffy about the invitation, so how did Mrs Elliot know? He had been intending to try and make up with Bianca and then ask her, having no idea that she and Donny Drayton were now 'an item'. 'I should offer you a job as a reporter on the *Chronicle,* Mrs Elliot.'

'Oh, I couldn't accept, Steven, because that would mean I'd have to pry into other people's affairs.'

He fought back the urge to laugh as he looked at the frail little lady rocking back and forth on the porch. 'I do have to go; I have to get back to the office.'

'All right, all right; but who are you going to take to the dinner dance?'

'I really don't know. I'll find someone.'

'I think that nice policewoman who booked you for speeding will say yes, if you ask her nicely.'

'Good-bye, Mrs Elliot.' He scurried away, wondering if there was anything that occurred in the valley that she did not know about.

Chapter 23

Your Nation's exposé on the coal seam gas industry was heavily advertised on Channel Six in the week leading up to its screening and those who lived in the rural areas of Queensland and New South Wales were glued to their televisions. Their neighbours in the smaller, more densely-populated Victoria were more laid-back. After all, the scourge which was the coal seam gas companies had barely scraped the surface of their state.

The program commenced by summarising the havoc that the oil and gas companies had wreaked in Colorado and Pennsylvania. It showed them entering and destroying properties that, under the notional laws of human fairness, they had no right to be on.

A woman living on one of the properties contracted the rare condition known as Conn Syndrome, a benign tumour in one of her glands, which she put down to bad luck. Later she would find that her condition was directly linked to the chemicals that the oil and gas companies had used to extract methane.

The presenter said that the perpetrators in Colorado were the same companies driving the industry in Australia: huge American companies like Filliburton, Plumberjay and SK Services.

Libby Hanover appeared on screen, wearing dark blue jeans, a light blue shirt and riding boots. She was standing on a grassy mound with a drill rig and two gas wells in the background. 'How would you like it if *big gas* rolled onto your land without your authority or permission and then proceeded to jeopardise the health and livelihood of you and your family? It'd be bad enough if it was happening in a third-world country, but it's happening right here in Queensland, aided and abetted by laws enacted by politicians more interested in collecting royalties and taxes than protecting the health, property, water and food security of the community.'

Next, the program showed aerial footage of the lush, fertile land on the Spurling Downs. The area was defiled with thousands of gas wells. Libby, sitting next to the pilot in the helicopter, in an incredulous voice said, 'This on land that produces wheat, maize, millet, cotton, soybeans, sorghum, carrots, grapes and watermelons and is a major sheep, cattle and dairying area and the home of many horse studs.'

The camera panned to Libby interviewing the Queensland Minister for Mines, who was perspiring heavily, and whose incessantly-blinking eyes darted everywhere but the camera. 'Minister, do you know what chemicals are being pumped down into those wells?'

'Yes.'

'You know what chemicals are used?

'Well, not exactly, no.'

'Shouldn't you?'

'Uhmm,' he turned up his palms expressively and shrugged.

These were moments that journalists lived for and Libby had no intention of letting the minister off the hook. 'Shouldn't you know what chemicals they're pumping down those wells?'

'Well, what I'm assured about is the processes they employ are appropriate for the extraction of coal seam gas.'

One of the cameramen was heard to laugh in the background and whisper, 'Gas company self-regulation, the regulation you have when there is no regulation.' Clearly the producers could have edited this out but chose not to.

The camera then picked up Libby sitting opposite a tall, gangly man, with receding black hair. 'Gareth Mumford is a hydro-geologist from Queensland University. He is seriously concerned that coal seam gas extraction might impact on Australia's vast reserves of underground water.'

'A lot of communities around here,' Mumford said, 'are dependent on ground water and the coal seams are quite close to where people are pumping water from.'

'Then what's the worst case scenario?'

'If it were to happen, the depletion and pollution of the Great Artesian

Basin would rank high amongst the world's worst environmental disasters. Millions of acres of fertile land could be rendered useless and the Basin might never recover.'

Turning back to the minister, Libby asked, 'Doesn't drilling wells fragment the water tables?'

'That's one of the assertions that has been made.'

'Isn't it true?'

'Sorry,' he said, wiping the sweat from his brow, still not looking into the camera.

'Are you saying it's not true?'

'Well there is …'

Libby interrupted him. 'You're the minister but you don't know, do you?'

'No, no, there are two bodies of opinion. One that says that water extracted from coal seams causes water to be released from the Great Artesian Basin and another that says it doesn't.'

'So, you don't know, but you're still issuing exploration licences. Minister, why are you taking such a risk?'

'I … I'm not, we ha … have a very vig … vigorous monitoring regime.'

'Isn't it a fact that when gas wells are drilled there are thousands of megalitres of water released that is contaminated with saline, fracking chemicals and pollutants, and that this is caused by removing the water pressure on the coal seams? That being the case, isn't there a possibility that the aquifers and the Great Artesian Basin might not only be severely depleted but poisoned as well?'

'I … I reject that.'

Libby smiled. 'So, minister, like your federal counterpart, you reject the findings of the National Water Commissioner. Perhaps you'd like to outline the evidence, if any, that disproves the Water Commissioner's findings.'

'Uhmm … aah … well it's …'

'Thank you, Minister. I think that opinion sums up a precarious situation very nicely.'

A few seconds later she was standing in front of a water bore with a gas well in the background. 'This bore has been in use for over a hundred years without any problems but since coal seam gas wells were drilled on the property it's been bubbling,' she said, nodding to a man holding a long pole with a burning rag attached to the end of it. He held the rag over the bore and the water exploded into flames.

'It's really flowing,' he said.

'That's methane and it can be inhaled or ingested through drinking or eating and it's deadly,' Libby said, gravely.

The man, his adult son and Libby then clambered into a four-wheel-drive and drove to the gas well, stopping about fifty metres from the pad. As they walked through the grass towards it, the hissing became louder and louder, 'That's methane escaping into the atmosphere,' she said.

The man forced the gate open and held a methane detector next to the valve on the well-head and the gauge flickered wildly. 'This stuff's highly flammable,' he said, 'and if it ignites we're for it. I'm getting out of here.'

They scampered back to the four-wheel-drive. 'Don't get in, we can't risk a spark,' the son said to Libby. 'We're going to push it fifty metres away before we kick it over.'

The camera panned to an aerial shot of Paisley and back to the interior of the Channel Six helicopter, with Libby sitting next to a dark-haired, heavily-tanned man. 'Dean Prezky, better known as the *gas-man*, is passionate about protecting the Fisher Valley and Australia from the ravages of coal seam gas. He bought his little piece of paradise in the Tura estates but finds it under threat from the huge international company, CEGL, which has a licence to come onto his property and drill five exploratory wells. Dean, didn't you initially support the gas companies?'

'Not really, but I wasn't opposed to them and I thought that one day they might provide jobs for my kids.'

'You hate them with fervour now. What brought that on?'

'They knowingly poisoned my dams, and my kids and I got very sick.'

The helicopter zoomed over vineyards and farms before following the rapidly-flowing Blaxland River north. If anything, the valley was even more picturesque and abundant than the Spurling Downs and the gas wells were fewer and more sparsely spaced.

'CEGL's contractor, Filliburton,' Libby continued with voice-over, 'admitted to the environment authorities that they accidentally released wastewater which, as you can see, has totally destroyed many acres of surrounding land. The toxicity of this wastewater can be best exemplified by the huge gum tree directly below us. It has lost its foliage and is obviously dying. What's really worrying is the dumping of this water so close to the Blaxland River. You might wonder what action the environment authorities and government took against CEGL for this supposedly accidental release of poisonous water. I can answer that in one word – nothing. We can actually see how this gas well was drilled and you can determine for yourself if the discharge of wastewater was, as claimed, accidental.'

Dean's edited footage appeared on screen, accompanied by chilling music. Frank Beck appeared on the well-pad shouting at his employees installing the pump and then directing them to lay the black tubing in the wastewater pit and run it through the long grass, where water was seen flowing into the vegetation. Conspicuous was the huge, distinctive gum tree in its previously healthy, flourishing condition. Any concerns Dean had had about the editing vanished.

The camera panned back to a close-up of a grim-faced Libby in the studio. 'We were able to obtain a chemical analysis of the wastewater that Filiburton pumped into the environment, that destroyed the bushland and that huge gum tree. The complete analysis can be seen on our website, but some of the chemicals were boric acid which can result in chronic poisoning, hydrochloric acid which may be fatal and can cause severe damage to the skin and eyes, methanol which if ingested might cause death or lead to blindness, and acetic acid which can cause severe burns to the eyes and skin.

'The industry would have you believe that of the total solution hydraulically pumped into the ground, only two percent are fracking chemicals and that may well be right. Doesn't sound much does it?' She paused. 'But what if I told you on average every time a well is fracked, nineteen tonnes of these chemicals are pumped into the ground with fifty percent returning to the surface and the balance remaining in the ground? Think about this. The 40,000 gas wells planned for Queensland could result in seven hundred and sixty thousand tonnes of this poisonous muck being pumped into the ground, through and adjacent to aquifers, the Great Artesian Basin and rivers. And this assumes that these gas wells will only be fracked once, when we know that this could occur up to twenty times before their productive lives are over.

'We've seen what these chemicals can do on the surface but what I find really scary is what's left behind below the ground. In the longer term, where will the chemicals eventually seep to, what will they contaminate, will they poison our livestock or, worse, will they lead to human deaths? Already in the Fisher Valley there have been claims, admittedly not yet proven, that one little boy struck down by cancer before his seventh birthday may have been the first victim of this insidious, uncontrolled industry.' She paused again.

'That's our program for this week and I'm pleased to say that next Sunday we'll tell you the heartwarming story of the McEvoy quins, which for me will make a pleasant change.'

The following morning the *Your Nation* program was front page news in the Brisbane and Sydney dailies and across all the talkback radio stations. It barely rated a mention in Melbourne's newspapers, being seen as an unfortunate malaise impacting its cousins to the north, but having no direct relevance to its smug citizens.

Harbrow fumed when he saw what Filliburton had done, not because the environmental effects concerned him in the slightest, but because they had been stupid enough to get caught. Someone had unlawfully trespassed, used recording equipment without permission and had stolen water samples, but he knew that *Your Nation* would claim journalistic privilege and refuse to disclose their source. He already suspected it was that *gas-man* idiot, and, if it was, he intended to make his life a misery in the courts.

All of Harbrow's power centred around making others rich. As the share price eroded before his very eyes, his ability to push others around and get his own way deteriorated. He'd already fielded a phone call from Phillip Bancroft, whining about all the money that his clients were losing on CEGL's stock and daring to tell him that he had better get his act together. He'd get his act together all right and, when he did, Bancroft would be the second director shown the door, right behind Moira Raymond.

Frank Beck was stunned when he saw himself shown on the well-pad shouting instructions at the others to break environment laws and regulations, and was surprised when his bosses took it in their stride. 'Take a few weeks off,' he was told. 'You need a break.' When he queried them about what the environment authorities were going to do, they said, 'Don't worry, the state needs us more than we need it. There'll be an outcry, we'll blame a few low-level employees for issuing you with erroneous instructions and then sack them. We'll give them nice pay-offs, they'll sign confidentiality agreements, and, when you come back from leave in three weeks, it'll all be forgotten. The government's with us, Frank. You've nothing to be concerned about and you're going to need a break because we've got a big assignment for you when you return.'

Sandi Carlisle, wearing low-cut jeans, a clinging black T-shirt and matching sandals, arrived suitably late at the Valley Wine Bar for her first date with Steve. It was cosy, with an open brick fireplace, subtle, dimly-lit tan-leather cubicles around the walls, and cattle hides over the polished timber floorboards. Steve was in one of the cubicles at the rear. He stood up as she came through the door and looked around as if to check everything out, before slowly approaching and kissing him lightly on the cheek.

'Wow. Didn't you want to be seen with me?'

'I actually thought it was romantic.'

'Romantic huh? How come it took you so long to phone?'

'I'm not with you.'

'Oh, come on! That I day I booked you, you never stopped leering at me. It was embarrassing.'

'Was I? It must have been subconscious. But I do remember you almost holding my hand when you gave me the ticket.' He laughed.

'Subconscious my foot.' She leaned over and gently pushed his forearm. He felt a charge shoot through him and momentarily dropped his eyes to her tightly-fitted T-shirt. She wasn't stunningly beautiful or voluptuous like Bianca, but there was something indefinable about her. 'Excuse me! There's certainly nothing subtle about your staring, is there?'

The waitress interrupted and they ordered two glasses of one of the Fisher Valley's finest house reds and a platter of crackers and assorted cheeses. As soon as the waitress left, Sandi said, 'Well?'

'Guilty, constable. You're an attractive woman.'

For the next hour they talked and joked, while nibbling and sipping.

'You've hardly touched your wine,' she said, 'You don't drink, do you?'

'You can't talk.' He nodded towards her glass. 'But that's right, detective. I hardly drink, but on rare occasions I've been known to lash out. I ordered the wine because some women won't drink unless their date does.'

'I'm not inhibited or lacking in confidence, so the last thing I need is alcohol. I would've been happy with coffee.'

He thought she was provocative but also sensed vulnerability and false bravado.

Unexpectedly, she asked. 'What did you think of *Your Nation*, Steve?'

His smile was replaced by a frown. 'It was an opportunity lost. Communities all through history have killed their adult populations almost with impunity, but I know of no advanced society that has ever tolerated the slaying of its children. *Your Nation* did a great job, rightly scaring the bejesus out of everyone about the toxic fracking chemicals, but then they should have taken their cameras to the Paisley Memorial Hospital and filmed and interviewed the sick little kids. If they'd done that, the government would've had to declare a moratorium on the exploration and production of coal seam gas.'

She reached over and placed her hand over his and he felt the energy shoot through him again. 'You're passionately opposed to the coal seam gas companies, aren't you?'

'I'm ashamed to say that I wasn't, but that changed after I met those poor children. Let's not spoil the night talking about it. There's a great gangster movie on at the Majestic on Friday night and I was wondering whether you'd like to come with me. You might learn something.'

'Very funny, I don't think, and, yes, I'd love to go.'

'Good. While I'm running hot, would you like to join me at the mayor's annual dinner dance?'

She burst out laughing. 'I'm sorry. Josh told me all about it and said it's only for the elite and that in all his time in Paisley he's never come close to being invited. And here I am, been here for less than a year, and I'm going.'

'I'll take that as a "yes" and it's not just the elite, whoever they are, who get invitations.'

'It's getting late. It's been fun but I have an early start in the morning, so I'll have to get going.'

'I'll take you home.' He got to his feet and waited for her.

'That's alright. I have my car parked out the front.' She slid out of the booth. As he followed her, his eyes were drawn to the tautness of her body and her long legs. Out on the footpath, she turned and gave him a quick kiss on the lips, saying, 'Thank you. Phone me if you like.' Then she ran across the road to her car.

Tom Morgan knew his friend would be furious when he found out that naphthalene had been detected in the muck taken from the foal's neck and had also been detected in the blood of Gentle Lady, and that they both had contracted haemolytic anaemia. He wasn't wrong and when Charles Paxton roared, 'Bastards, I knew it was them!' he had to pull the phone away from his ear.

'Settle down, Charles, we can't prove it was fracking chemicals.'

'I don't understand.'

'Naphthalene's used in diesel and th …'

'No! No! I've heard it all before. Hell, tell me something that's not an ingredient of diesel? You know as well as I do that Gentle Lady didn't get poisoned by diesel.'

'I know, Charles, but when we analysed the bore water only minute traces of naphthalene were found and they were within acceptable levels.'

'Acceptable levels! There are no bloody acceptable levels. The aquifers are connected, the naphthalene content of the water has obviously been diluted since Gentle Lady ingested it or the contaminated water has moved from one aquifer to an adjoining one. How many wells are near the stud and were they being drilled when Gentle Lady was in foal?'

'I've installed additional rainwater storage for the horses and fenced off all the bores. Charles, you should know that Gentle Lady's foal is still the only deformed newborn we've seen.'

'And I hope with all my heart that you don't see another. The only thing the deformed calves here have in common with those on the Spurling Downs is the bloody gas wells, you know that. Gentle Lady couldn't have been the only mare in foal to drink that toxic water. We have to stop them, Tom, before their avarice turns this beautiful valley into one huge chemical cesspit. We just have to stop them.' Paxton was fighting back tears.

Chapter 24

The domineering Norris Scott-Tempy was no match for Bettina when it came to religion. She insisted that he join her every Sunday for early evening mass at St Stephens, where they always sat in the front row. She liked Father Michael O'Rourke; he was a popular gospeller who sometimes supplanted his personal views for that of the Vatican's. The church was invariably packed for his masses but Norris found Father Michael boring and often snoozed through his sermons.

'Today,' he thundered, 'I'm going to speak about greed, an evil force dividing the community and the need for neighbours to unite and support each other.' Scott-Tempy closed his eyes and was about to shut the priest's words out, when he heard, 'Those in the coal seam gas industry have divided us, set neighbour against neighbour, and despoiled our land, by their rapacity and underhand tactics.'

Scott-Tempy sat bolt upright, totally shocked, as the old fool urged his flock to support primary producers in the valley by joining *Lock 'em out.* He wasn't going to listen to another word of this garbage and he nudged his wife in the ribs, mouthing, 'We're getting out of here.' She responded by giving him a filthy look and putting a finger to her lips.

'Some of you may be tempted by the money on offer, but I beg you not to take advantage of your neighbours.' As Scott-Tempy looked up, the priest was staring at him with his unwavering, cobalt eyes. He tried to hold his gaze but couldn't and dropped his eyes to his feet, wondering whether the priest knew about his business dealings. With all the donations he'd made to the church, he deserved better and he fully intended to complain to the Bishop. The silly old bugger was long past his use-by date and he would suggest to the Monseigneur that it was time he was replaced with younger blood.

There was a pile of empty fifteen-litre, clear-plastic water containers stored at the pub waiting to be picked up by the springwater company. Dean borrowed one when he was locking up, knowing that it would not be missed.

The following morning he was up as dawn broke. He managed to stretch a pair of Vicki's rubber gloves past his wrists and halfway up his forearms and took the water container down to the dam. He dipped it and it filled with water which was cloudy, bordering on grey. He capped the container tightly and walked briskly back to the four-wheel-drive and placed it on the back seat. He momentarily thought about asking Jack Thomas to get a sample sent to the lab, but then reverted to his original plan.

It was 11am when Dean pulled up at the front of CEGL's Paisley headquarters. He was dressed in full *gas-man* attire with the container of water under his arm, and was greeted by a Channel Six team and two local radio station news crews whom he had tipped off. They trailed after him through the foyer to the lift, attracting many strange looks. When the doors of the first available lift slid open, none of the many waiting office workers entered with this strange group.

The doors opened on the eighth level to an expansive, white marble reception counter; the teak panelled wall behind bore the CEGL name in big, gold letters. The young receptionist, wearing headphones, looked up apprehensively. Dean politely said, 'This is an emergency. I need to see your senior environment manager immediately.'

Without responding to Dean she punched a number into the console in front of her. 'Mr How ... Howard, there's a ma ... man in reception who say ... says that there's an em ... emergency and he need ... needs to see you immediately.' Then she whispered, though everyone could hear. 'It ... it's that *gas-man* person.'

'Mr Howard will be here soon.' The colour had drained from the receptionist's face.

'Sweetie, don't worry. I promise you I'm not here to hurt anyone.'

As Dean was speaking, the lift doors opened and a heavy-set man, with distinct spider veins and a large, red nose, got out. 'What do you want?' The button on his collar was open and the knot on his tie was to one side. He was trembling with rage.

Dean could not believe his luck. 'I've got something for you.' He attempted to pass the container of murky water to the man, who shied away from it.

'What's that?'

'It's the wastewater your contractor sprayed into my dam and I'm here to return it to you.' Dean advanced while unscrewing the cap.

'Don't you open that,' the man shouted, and then, looking at the receptionist, 'Mandy, phone the police.'

'Can I take it that you don't want this water in your offices?'

'Get it away from me!'

'I'm sorry. So it's all right for you to dump this toxic crap on my property but, when I try to return it, you can't back away fast enough. That's right isn't it?'

That night Moira Raymond watched the Channel Six news and cursed her heavy-handed environment manager, knowing that her company and the industry were losing the public relations battle. She was desperate to change this.

Artie Cleever had been trampled on by CEGL. After he had blown the whistle on them at the Hunter Valley Protective Alliance meeting, they stopped providing him with tanker water. They knew that he was too old and did not have the funds to take them on in court. The methane in his once crystal-clear water bores bubbled twenty-four hours a day, but CEGL denied liability, claiming that it was naturally occurring.

Artie was a sick man, having been diagnosed with extreme levels of gas-related toxins in his system; his doctor had told him to get off the property or he would surely die. Worse, toxicity tests run on his wife indicated levels that exceeded the norm by more than 150 times and she was deteriorating before his eyes. His dogs had initially lost clumps of fur and then died and the koalas, goannas and lizards that once thrived had vanished. The three gas wells and the forty-metre easement over the pipeline that CEGL had run through his property made it virtually unsaleable; he had no money and could not shift away. He was without hope when he entered the offices of *Breckenridge & Priestley*.

Simon Breckenridge listened in silence as the old man, nearly in tears, told him the sorry saga that had all started after CEGL's land access consultant, Donny Drayton, had conned him into signing a land access agreement.

'How much was your property worth before CEGL sank their wells?'

'I had it valued three years ago,' the frail old man rasped, pushing a well-thumbed property valuation across the desk. 'Half-a-million dollars. I wouldn't get a bid for it now other than from that bloody gas company and it wouldn't be more than $200,000.'

'Would you be happy if I could get you the valuation amount?'

'That would be wonderful, Mr Breckenridge, but I don't have any money to pay you.' Artie hung his head in shame.

'Don't worry about me. I can't promise you anything, but why don't you leave your papers and medical reports with me?'

'You're going to help me?' A flicker of hope appeared on the old man's face.

'I'm going to try. I'll phone you within a fortnight. Good-bye, Mr Cleever. Try not to worry.'

Within minutes, Breckenridge was dictating a letter to CEGL offering to sell Artie Cleever's property to them for half-a-million dollars, pointing out that this option would prove less expensive than the litigation that he would bring in respect of his client's health problems, loss of peace and well-being and diminution in property value, should his generous offer to settle be declined.

Buffy saw the Porsche pull up in front of the *Chronicle* office. She turned around. 'Steve, it's that CEGL woman.' Steve groaned.

Moira barged through the front door, totally ignored Buffy and looked across at Steve. 'I've got the copy for our announcement this Friday.'

'Thanks, Moira, give it to Buffy. She'll need to edit it.'

'I don't deal with the hired help and this is to be published as is. No editing. Do you understand me?'

Buffy had never thought of hitting anyone before, but she would have sacrificed a week's pay to slap Moira Raymond's face. 'You heard Mr Forrest. I have to approve all advertising copy.'

'It's all right, Buffy.' Steve strode over to the counter; the last thing he needed was a cat fight. 'Okay, Moira, let's see what you've got.'

Like the first announcement, there were twenty key points but they had changed from the regular feel-good homilies.

'Just make sure that there are no changes.'

'I can't run this. It's not true. It says there's no evidence to support the spurious claims that the extraction of coal seam gas has led to an increase in the incidence of dermatitis in the valley. As you know, I made those claims in my recent editorial and I have no doubt about their authenticity. Have you visited the children's ward of the Paisley Memorial Hospital lately?'

'As a matter of fact I have. I've even spoken to the doctors and they don't agree with you. They say there's no proof to support your far-fetched claims and that the gas-related toxins in some of the kids' blood most likely came from water bores on their properties that are kilometres away from any drill rig or gas well. For an investigative journalist, you don't do much investigation, do you?'

'CEGL appears on the hospital's notice board as being its biggest donor and I'm sure the doctors know the size of your donations. How much exactly do you give each year?'

'I'm not going to give that absurd question the time of day. I warn you, if you fail to publish my copy, our lawyers will make your life a misery.'

'You obviously didn't read the contract,' Buffy chipped in.

'You stupid girl. A piece of paper put together by a firm of yokel bush lawyers. It won't help you.'

Simon Breckenridge was a smart attorney and Steve knew the contract he had prepared would stand up, but he also knew what big city legal firms without budget limits did for their influential clients, which was to file costly multiple actions, designed to wear the other party down. 'You're right. I didn't talk to the doctors but wh …'

'I knew it. You were scaremongering. If you had any principles, you'd print a full retraction of that rubbish you wrote.'

'I was going to say that what I did do, though, was talk to some of those kids' parents and they told me CEGL was picking up all their medical bills, providing they didn't go to the media.' Steve was gambling that the rumours he had heard around town were true.

'Who told you that? It's a lie.'

'I promised I wouldn't mention their names but, if this ends up in court, I'll have no choice but to subpoena them. It'll make CEGL look mighty magnanimous, paying the medical bills of sick little kids for no reason.'

'You think you're so smart, you skinny, big-nosed jerk, but you just made yourself a very bad enemy.' Moira stormed out of the office.

'Good riddance,' Buffy said.

'Buffy, work out how many weeks are left on the contract and send a cheque to CEGL. We won't be running their announcements anymore.'

'Yeah, yeah,' she said, thrusting her fist into the air.

'Oh, and buy me the minimum number of CEGL shares that I need, to get notice of their annual general meeting.'

Spencer Harbrow had used his power and influence to continually defer CEGL's annual general meeting, while he unsuccessfully tried to lobby the London institutions for the votes that he needed to replace his dissident directors. He had organised the nomination of three 'yes' men as replacements but, without the support of Joe Biederman's Royal Treasury Group, the company's largest shareholder, their nominations would be pointless. He had made countless phone calls to Biederman, knowing that the other institutions would follow his lead, but it was to no avail. When he offered to come to London, he was surprised to be told that it wasn't worth coming.

Harbrow was not a man to accept the word *no*. He told Janet to contact the crew of the corporate jet and tell them to prepare for take-off to Farnborough at 3pm the next day. The crew comprised the captain, a first officer, a cordon bleu chef and two stewardesses, one to take care of Mr Harbrow and one to look after the crew. Janet would ensure that a chauffeur-driven Bentley or Rolls was waiting at the private terminal at Farnborough Airport and that a suite was booked at Claridge's.

The 737 with CEGL livery was ready for take-off when he arrived at the Mascot terminal. A golf buggy ferried him onto the tarmac. He carried no luggage, as there was a full wardrobe of *Brioni*, *Zegna* and *Armani* on the plane with *Louis Vuitton* suitcases that would be packed and sent to Claridge's as soon they landed. Bounding up the stairs, he was greeted by a tall, ash-blonde and a curvaceous, tanned brunette, wearing white jackets embroidered with the red letters CEGL on the lapels and matching red dresses. He acknowledged them with a curt nod and walked briskly down the aisle, past the lounge and dining room, the fully-equipped cubicles for guests, and his stateroom, until he was in his office; this contained nearly every electronic business device known to man. A few minutes later, the plane began to taxi down the runway and he strapped himself in, hit a button on the remote and watched the take-off on a monitor before turning his attention to the screens showing Reuters, The Australian Stock Exchange and Fox. An hour into the flight, he phoned Joe Biederman and told him he had some business in London and invited him to dinner the following night.

'I hope you're not coming especially to see me, because I'm not changing my mind.'

'Of course not.'

He left his office just before the stopover in Bangkok and strode into the lounge, where the two stewardesses were reading magazines. 'Can I get you anything, Spencer?' the brunette asked.

Harbrow liked beautiful women, but looks unaccompanied by brains did nothing for him and both girls had commerce degrees, had read all documents on the public record about CEGL and were valuable assets when he was entertaining VIPs.

'I'll have a *Glenfiddich*, Trudy.'

She knew exactly how he liked it and added a touch of crushed ice before handing it to him. 'Sit down,' he said, and then, addressing the blonde, 'Barbara, I'll have dinner one hour after we've departed Bangkok. I'll have spinach lasagne, the wagyu fillet mignon, and tell Jacques I don't want to see any blood this time, strawberry soufflé, latte and I'll finish with a *Ferreira*.'

'Yes, Spencer.'

'Trudy, I'm having dinner with Joe Biederman and his wife tomorrow night at the hotel. You'll join me. I won't require you after I turn in tonight, so I suggest you do the same.'

'Will there be anything else?'

'Put CNN on,' he said, leaning back and taking a long sip of whiskey.

They touched down at Farnborough just after 2pm. After a cursory customs inspection and stamping of their passports, Harbrow and Trudy were soon walking across the tarmac to the waiting Bentley. It was damp and overcast and they pulled their coats up around their necks in a futile attempt to ward off the bitterly cold, cutting wind. Seventy-five minutes later they pulled up at the front of the beautiful old, red-brick Claridge's Hotel. As they walked across the foyer, Harbrow was greeted by the assistant manager who informed him that his suitcase had arrived and had been unpacked. Harbrow turned to Trudy. 'Come up to my suite at ten to seven. I don't want to be late tonight.'

Just before 7pm they entered the Gordon Ramsay-managed restaurant done out in classic art deco style. A waiter showed them to their table, casting an admiring but discreet eye over Trudy, who could have passed for a fashion model. They had barely taken their seats before they were standing to greet the Biedermans. Joe had a genial face, was slightly overweight and without a hair on his polished dome, which matched his smooth, cherubic complexion. He warmly shook hands with Harbrow and kissed Trudy, whom he knew from earlier dinners, on the cheek. The much younger Trish Biederman was wearing a silk turquoise dress that barely contained her breasts. Harbrow kissed her stiffly, brushing his lips over her cheek, whereas Trudy embraced her warmly and complimented her on her dress. Harbrow wondered what Joe saw in his loud-mouthed wife, physically beautiful though she was, refusing to believe that her looks and proficiency in the bedroom could ever justify marriage. The men ordered whiskey while Trish scanned the wine menu, before settling on a *1998 Krug Clos de Mesnil,* that she could barely pronounce, at a mere fourteen hundred pounds for herself and Trudy.

'What brings you to London, Spencer?'

'Oh, there's an opportunity to get involved in a joint venture in the North Sea that I'm looking at.' Biederman knew this was a lie. 'And I didn't want to miss the opportunity of having dinner with Trish and you.'

'You two aren't going to talk boring business all night, are you?' Trish pouted.

'No darling.' Her husband took her hand as the waiter brought their drinks.

'A toast,' Harbrow said, 'to success.'

'To life,' Trish interjected.

Harbrow flushed. He wasn't used to being interrupted or having his toasts changed and certainly not by a playboy bunny with plastic boobs, but he daren't upset her husband. 'To life and success,' he proposed, and they clinked glasses.

An hour later they had finished their entrées, the girls were onto their second bottle of champagne and the mood around the table was decidedly more relaxed. There was no subject that Trudy could not converse on and she seemed genuinely interested in Trish's trivial chatter about what she had recently bought and how much she had spent. Biederman was gregarious, engaging both ladies in small talk, as he shovelled down his spiced lobster ravioli. Harbrow impatiently picked at his salmon, wondering if the women were ever going to 'powder their noses', when Trish finally said, 'Excuse us. We have to go to the little girls' room.' Harbrow knew that Trudy would stay away as long as possible, giving him every opportunity to make his pitch to Biederman.

The women had barely left the table, when he said, 'Joe, I need your support.'

'I told you that we can't help. The share price is tanking and you want to get rid of half the board, which will put it in free-fall.'

'Royal's made an awful lot of money on its investment.'

'And so it should have. We took a huge risk backing you. I have people on my board telling me to sell your stock, that it's peaked and it's time to move on.'

The last thing Harbrow needed was a large block of stock on the market and he had never thought that Royal could be a seller. 'That'd be a big mistake. The best years are still ahead of us. I've never asked you for a favour before, but I need you to back me.'

'You're not listening, Spencer. You get the share price back up and I might be able to help.'

'That's bullshit! There's no way you'd support a board change then. Anyhow, I can't increase the share price while I'm carrying three laggards.'

'You appointed them!'

Harbrow had anticipated this remark. 'I did, there's no denying that. They were great appointments when the company was smaller, but they've outlived their usefulness.'

'I won't help you get rid of them and that's final.'

'What if I could offer you something personally?'

'I hope you're not trying to bribe me.'

'Of course not. Just hear me out. There's a small private company, let's call it XYZ, which owns some very valuable coal seam gas tenements in the Margaret Hills. It's looking to go public and could use your expertise.'

'Go on.'

'The directors owe me some favours and I've been authorised to offer five percent of the company's stock to the right person, and you're on my short list.'

'What's it expected to list at?' Biederman asked, expecting an answer of twenty to thirty million.

'Five hundred million.'

Biederman could not conceal his astonishment. This could solve all his money problems. His mind went into overdrive, processing the ethics and morals of accepting. The amount was almost too large to be called a bribe. 'How much of XYZ do you own?'

'I don't have any interest,' Harbrow lied, knowing his ownership could not be traced.

'Didn't CEGL abort some exploration work in the Margaret Hills some years back?'

Harbrow was amazed that Biederman remembered. He ignored the question. 'Are you interested Joe, because if you aren't, I'll have to find someone else.'

'It's risky.'

'Bullshit! You're a master of international finance and know you could hide your interest behind a maze of companies and trusts.'

'Is that what you did?'

'I told you I don't own any shares.'

'Yeah, you did, didn't you?'

'Are you in?'

'It's a very attractive offer, Spencer, but I have a responsibility to the shareholders of Royal and, as I told you, a messy and disruptive annual general meeting won't help CEGL. I'm sorry I can't help you.'

Harbrow was stunned; it was beyond his understanding that anyone could reject such an offer. 'Are you sure you don't want to reconsider?'

'Positive.'

What was happening? For sixteen years Harbrow had got everything he wanted but, in the space of a month, his board had voted against him and the company's major shareholder would not support him. 'Is there anything I can do to change your mind?'

'I might be prepared to help secure the resignations of your dissident directors after the AGM, but it would have to be handled in a low-key manner. The board can fill casual vacancies, which achieves what you want in a more convoluted but private way.'

'Might be prepared to help?'

'Spencer, I'll only help if I can be sure that it will not result in any publicity that is detrimental to the company and its stock price. That shouldn't be a problem.'

'You want me to buy their silence with generous farewell packages?'

'That's obvious.'

'I don't need your help to do that.'

'I wouldn't be so sure.' Biederman grinned. 'I expect that, despite your generosity, you could meet some resistance, and a phone call from me might help.'

'And you want the shares in XYZ on the off-chance that you might have to make a phone call? Jesus!'

'It's a little more than that, Spencer. It'll secure your future as well. Do we have a deal?'

Spencer Harbrow didn't like being subtly threatened but he hadn't anticipated Biederman remembering the Margaret Hills exploration and he didn't want him sniffing around, digging up long-buried skeletons. He reached across the table and grasped the other man's hand. 'We have a deal, conditional on the removal of the dissidents and the appointment of my three nominees.'

He had given an awful lot for a less-than-optimum result. He would have to be patient and forget about removing the incumbents at the annual general meeting. However, he had seen something in Biederman's face that the financier had been at pains to hide: greed, pure greed. Harbrow knew that he would not have to wait too long before he got his way. As the women returned, he beckoned the waiter over and asked for the dessert menu.

'Joe can't have sweets and I don't want to get like him,' Trish butted in, patting her wash-board stomach, 'so none for me either, but we'll have coffee, short black.'

Thinking of Joe and how he was being controlled by his wife, Harbrow ordered a large platter of cheese for the table and coffees all round. Thirty minutes later they said their farewells. On the way out, Harbrow muttered, 'I'm glad that's over. I'm having another coffee. What about you Trudy?'

'I won't sleep if I do. I'll stick with water.'

She'd seen him pensive like this before. While she had not been at the table when the negotiations were going on, she knew that he had not got what he wanted. He was a strange man, slightly aloof; he never flirted with her or any of the other girls, despite the rumours that the jet was his flying bordello. He'd had some beautiful women on the plane with him, who had shared his stateroom, but in public he rarely put his arm around any of them or showed even the slightest affection. Trudy thought that he was a cold fish, driven by money but, like the other girls, she found him very sexy. She wasn't sure why. Maybe it was because he showed no interest or perhaps it was the power he exuded. Most men in his position would be hitting on her but from him there was nothing even mildly suggestive. 'I don't understand how Joe let's her walk all over him.'

'It's simple. He loves her.'

'Why?'

'Who knows what makes two people fall in love.'

'All men have at least one weakness,' he said. Then, thinking about himself, added, 'Nearly all men.'

She didn't respond, wondering whether this man ever let his guard down for even a second. As if reading her mind, he said, 'Phone the captain and tell him I want to be out of this godforsaken place by nine o'clock and, Trudy, we'll be checking out at seven, so you'd better get to bed.'

Chapter 25

The foyer of the Paisley Town Hall was decked out in multi-coloured roses and ribbons with a large, red banner announcing *Welcome to the Lord Mayor's Dinner Dance* affixed to the wall. The last time Steve and Sandi had been at the town hall was when the *gas-man* had run amok, and they had hardly known each other then. Now she was clinging to his arm, wearing a full-length black dress, backless to just above the cleavage of her bottom. She loved the dress, but it was so daring that she had wrestled with herself, trying it on three times before finally plucking up the courage to buy it. The door attendant checked the invitation and gave her an admiring glance; he then looked at Steve with a *how did you ever end up with her* face? 'You're on table twenty-six, just to the left as you enter the hall.'

The tables were elegantly draped, bearing silver candelabras with matching cutlery. A six-piece band was belting out an old Sinatra number at the front of the hall next to three tables reserved for VIPs. Steve and Sandi were a little late and most guests were already seated.

'How come we aren't up the front?' Sandi pouted.

'Are you rich and powerful?' Steve responded, catching the pleasing sight of Charles and Faye Paxton laughing and chatting with the mayor. Rumour had it that they had been near separation after Charlie's death, but maybe they were trying to get it together again.

As they located their table, a small man, built like a bull, stood up and said, 'Hello Steve.'

Steve's hand went involuntarily to his nose. 'G'day John,' he responded begrudgingly. He glanced around the table and saw that he knew nearly everyone; they were all finance and accounting types.

'I'm John Leckie,' the squat, oily-haired man said, extending his hand to Sandi. 'And you are?'

'Steve's partner,' she responded coldly, sensing that her boyfriend didn't like this brash man.

Steve squeezed her hand. 'Sandi Carlisle,' he said, 'I don't want you to take any financial or taxation advice off this lot.' Then he introduced her to everyone at the table.

'What do you do for a job, Sandi?' Leckie asked.

'I'm a police officer.'

'You can handcuff me anytime you like,' Leckie guffawed.

She took no notice of him, instead bringing his wife into the conversation, 'That's a stunning ring. Is it a sapphire?'

'If only.' She smiled. 'It's topaz.'

'It's beautiful.'

Steve interrupted. 'Let's dance.'

As they walked to the dance floor, he saw Norris and Bettina Scott-Tempy, Moira Raymond with a man he didn't know, and Donny Drayton and Bianca sitting at the table to the right of the Mayor's. He surmised that all those at that table were coal seam gas supporters, while those at the table to the left, where Charles Paxton and Tom Morgan were sitting, were passionate haters.

He held Sandi close to him and she rested her head on his shoulder. Her perfume intoxicated him as they swayed to the beat of the music. She fitted perfectly against his body and moved with an instinctive rhythm; he felt himself becoming aroused.

'You don't like that creep, Leckie, do you?'

'He broke my nose playing football years ago when I wasn't looking.' He was enjoying the feel of her supple body. 'Let's not talk about him.'

He felt a tap on his shoulder and turned to see a pimply-faced young man in his early twenties asking to cut in. He wanted to tell him to get lost but, instead, stood aside for a respectable two minutes before cutting back in. He had barely got back into the swing when someone else tapped him on his shoulder. Sandi looked at Steve and shrugged as if to say *what can I do?* He stood watching and wondered whether he'd be lucky enough to get another dance with her.

As Donny and Bianca took the floor, he felt a tinge of jealousy, which he forced himself to resist. Bianca was glowing and he thought how fortunate he had been, being her lover for so many years. What could she possibly see in the anaemic, harmless Donny? He knew how demanding she could be, and he wondered how Donny was coping. The thought was almost too much for him: she had probably given the lucky little weasel instructions, something she had never needed to give him. He tapped Donny hard on the shoulder who turned around and gave him a weak smile before slinking off to his table.

'Hi Bianca, you look great,' Steve said, unable to stop his eyes dropping to her ample cleavage. Whether it was her flashing eyes or her seductive smile, she flaunted her sexuality like no other woman he had ever met.

'Thanks,' she responded coolly, making sure he did not get too close.

'Did Norrie enjoy the article I had published in the *Advocate?*'

'If you must know, he threw it in the rubbish bin without reading a word.'

'Why doesn't that surprise me? How's he doing in the gas business? Has he managed to rob any more downtrodden farmers lately?'

He felt her stiffen. 'You really are odious, Steven, and if you're going to make unkind remarks about Daddy, you'll be dancing by yourself.'

'I'm sorry,' he said sarcastically. 'How come you're still going out with that loser? You can do far better.'

'Not that it's your business, but Donny treats me really well and, unlike you, respects my father and values his opinions. We're getting engaged at Easter.'

'God, what's he got that I can't see?'

'Don't be vulgar. You had your chance.'

'You always said I had no future and yet you're going to marry some dimwitted land access consultant who's got no prospects. And you know he can't satisfy you.'

'That's how much you know. Donny's been working closely with Moira Raymond and, when she takes over as CEO of CEGL, he's going to be her assistant, Mr Smarty Pants. Anyhow, you can't talk. It's hardly like that skinny, underdressed clothes horse you're with is ever likely to be Chief Commissioner,' she sniggered.

'Envious, are we? Unlike Donny, Sandi's sexy and savvy.'

'Touchy about her, aren't you?'

'Why don't you tell me about this big promotion of Donny's,' he said, ignoring her barb. 'When's this big move going to happen?'

'A lot sooner than you think.' She paused and looked concerned. 'I shouldn't have said anything. No-one else knows. You won't say anything, will you?'

'You know me,' he said, as Donny tapped him on the shoulder. 'Thanks for the dance, Bianca.'

There were more than fifty couples dancing and he caught sight of Bettina dragging old Norrie around the floor. Her movements were fluid and rhythmic while her husband looked bored to tears and had all the finesse of a wooden plank. It took Steve a few seconds to find Sandi, who was in the middle of the floor trying to restrain the groping John Leckie. He pushed through the crowd, grabbed Leckie by the shoulder and pulled him away. 'Get away, you bloody schmuck,' he said, eyes blazing.

'Settle down, Stevie. We were just having a little fun. That's right isn't it, honey?'

'Don't make a scene, Steve. He's not worth it.'

'Yeah, and you know what happened to you the last time you took me on.'

Steve had never been a fighter, but he was trembling and dying to smash his fist into Leckie's smirking face.

'Dance with me, Steve,' Sandi said, as Leckie swaggered off the dance floor. 'I shouldn't have worn this silly dress, but I knew Bianca was going to be here and I wanted to show you I could be sexy too.'

'You look fantastic. You're the sexiest women in the hall and, don't worry, I'm not leaving your side for the rest of the night.'

'You're sweet, but I don't want to stay. That creep's going to keep drinking and making foul comments and you'll end up hitting him. I don't want to have to arrest you. Why don't I go back to the table and get my bag? Then we'll split.'

'I'll get it, but what are we going to do?'

'We could go back to your place and watch a DVD.'

'That sure leaves this for dead.' He grinned.

When he returned with her bag, after wearing a few parting smart-arse comments from Leckie, she was chatting to some of the young men whom she had danced with. He took her elbow and steered her through them to the foyer and out onto the street.

'For someone who's worried that she's not sexy, you sure know how to attract a crowd.'

'I'm sorry for spoiling your night,' she said, leaning over and kissing him. He put his arms around her and hungrily crushed her full, inviting lips to his.

'Not here, Steve. Let's go to your place.'

Five minutes later, bodies entangled, they stumbled up the two flights of stairs to Steve's apartment. 'Have you got anything to drink?'

'I thought you said you didn't drink?'

'I don't, but sometimes I get the urge.'

'Me too. I've got a bottle of Johnny Walker and a semillon. What do you prefer?'

'I'll have wine.'

'So will I,' he said, taking two flutes from a shelf.

She kicked her shoes off and curled up on the sofa with her feet under her. 'How was your old girlfriend?'

'Okay.'

'Okay? You seemed to be engaged in pretty intense conversation.'

'I made a few comments about her father that she didn't like, that's all.'

'Do you still love her?'

'No, but I still care for her.'

'Good answer. Come and give me a cuddle.'

He did not need to be asked twice. It had been a long time since he'd had anything resembling romance in his life and she felt good. They kissed passionately and, when she eased him away to take a sip of wine, he was breathing heavily.

'Slow down. We've got all night. Let's not spoil it.'

He was flushed and his forehead had broken out in a light sweat. 'Sorry, it's been a long time since ...'

'Me too, that's why I want to take it slowly.'

In their half-a-dozen dates she had said very little about herself, but he was sensitive enough to detect that she felt like talking. She was an only child, her family lived in Coffs Harbour and she had an arts degree from Newtower. She drained her glass and Steve quickly refilled it, as he listened to her talk about the man she had loved and spent two years with in Sydney. He was a big businessman working on complex security systems for ASIO and the Pentagon, and it was impossible for her to phone him while he was supposedly on one of his numerous interstate or international trips. They had talked about having children, building a house and spending the rest of their lives together. Then, one day in the waiting room of her dentist, she flicked through an old copy of the *Woman's Day* and there he was with wife, kids and dog. It had nearly killed her and she quit her job, vacated her apartment, got a new mobile phone and disappeared. Looking for something to ease the pain, she had joined the police force for the excitement, only to end up directing traffic and doing paperwork. The bastard could have found her had he wanted to, but she never saw or heard from him again. She would have rejected any advances but it exacerbated her hurt, knowing that he had not even bothered looking for her.

'That's some story.' Steve gently put his arm around her. 'What an arsehole.' He had been right; her outwardly confident manner was a mask to conceal her hurt.

For a few minutes her smile and vitality disappeared. 'I just want to ask you one question,' she said in mock seriousness. 'You're not married, are you?'

'Who'd marry someone with a honker like this?'

'It suits you; very Owen Wilson-like if you ask me.' She uncurled her legs and stood alluringly in front of him. 'Let's go to bed.'

Five weeks out from the election, the polls were grim for Labor. Nick Gould, despite the urging of Clarrie Driscoll, was only campaigning half-heartedly, knowing that the conservatives had an insurmountable lead. Whiskey in hand, he looked up at the big screen on his office wall to see the leader of the conservatives berating the government and prattling on about what he was going to do to fix roads and public transport. 'Have a look at the little prima donna, Clarrie. I'd like to swat him.'

'You can still win, Nick, if only you'd campaign. The people think the party stinks but they still love you.'

'No-one could ever accuse you of being a pessimist.' The Premier laughed. 'Nah, we've had our day. You saw the polls after that lunatic's performance in Paisley. We're dead, mate, dead as a doornail.'

'I just wish you'd have a go,' Clarrie responded, glancing at the screen. Then, in astonishment, 'Have a look at who's just entered the auditorium!'

The screen showed the *gas-man*, fully attired in white boilersuit and gasmask.

'So what? He's not shouting and screaming like he was when he went after me. He's probably supporting that little weasel.'

That is what the conservative's leader must have thought, because he came down from the stage and, playing up to the viewing audience, put his arm around Dean and said, 'Here's an example of Labor's policies. This poor man is being chased off his property by the big gas companies, aided and abetted by this avaricious government.'

Dean forcefully shrugged the little man's arm from his shoulders. 'Get away from me, you prick. Your policies about *big-gas* are no different to the government's, so don't try and paint yourself as the saviour of us landowners. Why don't you tell the audience how much the gas companies contributed to your campaign?'

There are times in most politicians' lives when they wish they hadn't said or done something and the leader of the conservatives was regretting the second he had left the stage. 'Uh-uh that's not right, we're going to protect landowners.'

'Liar! How much money did those plunderers put in your pocket? How much?'

One of his minders came to the rescue and steered the beleaguered politician back to the stage, but the damage had been done. Nick Gould had his feet up on his desk and his body shook with mirth. 'Can you hear the talkback jocks and see the newspapers in the morning, Clarrie? They're going to slaughter him and we might just be back in the race. Where are we campaigning tomorrow?'

'You're speaking in five marginal electorates, you've got one radio interview after the midday news and two minutes on *Australia Today* tomorrow night.'

'Bugger that! Hell, we've got an election to win,' the Premier said, bouncing out of his chair. 'Get me on as many early morning radio programs as you can, squeeze in more speaking engagements and let the television channels know I'm available any time. Come on, Clarrie, pull your finger out.'

The letter from *Braithwaite Ogilvie & Llewellyn* denied liability for all the matters that Simon Breckenridge had raised, and completely ignored his offer regarding the sale of Artie Cleever's property for $500,000. Instead, they offered $180,000 'as a generous first and final offer by our client to expeditiously settle this matter.' It was what Breckenridge had expected and he knew that, if he commenced litigation against CEGL, *Braithwaite Ogilvie*

& Llewellyn would use every legal avenue to stall the action and, by the time it reached court, the Cleevers might be dead. What the big city legal firm didn't know was that he had never intended that this matter be determined by the courts.

He picked up his recorder and dictated:

Create a letterhead for Mr Arthur Cleever and address this letter, private and confidential, to Mr Aaron James at 2ZL. Dear Mr James, attached are copies of letters from my lawyers, Breckenridge & Priestley *and response from CEGL's lawyers,* Braithwaite Ogilvie & Llewellyn. *Also enclosed is a copy of a non-disclosure document that I was forced to sign before CEGL would provide me with tanker water in replacement for the water in my bores that they had contaminated. They have since reneged on their undertaking. New Para.*

I seek your assistance to right a grave injustice perpetrated by CEGL. I am eighty-one years of age and my wife is four years younger and we were tricked by a land access consultant into signing an access agreement to our property. There are now three wells and a pipeline on it and my wife and I have medical reports certifying that we are being poisoned by gas toxins. We are both very sick and just looking to be fairly compensated for our property so that we can shift away from this coal seam gas area and live our remaining few years in peace. New Para.

Our property was valued at $500,000 as per copy of the attached valuation before drilling commenced, but CEGL have seen fit to offer us $180,000 on a take it or leave it basis. They know we cannot afford to litigate and that even if we could they would stall such legal action until we are too sick to appear in court or perhaps dead. New Para.

Any assistance that you can provide will be greatly appreciated and perhaps you can do what our legal system cannot. Sign it 'yours sincerely, Arthur Cleever' and, after you've typed it, phone him and get him to come in and sign it asap.

Chapter 26

It was 10am on a muggy Sydney day and, while CEGL's annual general meeting wasn't due to commence for an hour, the entrance to the Centurion Building was surrounded by about thirty placard-carrying demonstrators. Dean Prezky attired as the *gas-man* struck up the chant, *CEGL go to hell*, which was soon picked up by the slowly circling protestors. Don Carmody, the chairman of the McLachlan Bank, was carrying a placard, *CEGL destroying our food bowls*. Steve Forrest entered the building to the puzzled looks of those who knew him.

Channel Six arrived ten minutes before the meeting was due to commence, by which time the ranks of the demonstrators had swelled to nearly a hundred. On seeing the cameras, they lifted their noise levels by a few decibels.

A young journalist conducted a brief interview with Don Carmody, asking him if he found it strange that Greens, farmers and graziers, and right-wingers like Aaron James, and he himself, were all on the same side fighting *big gas*.

'Not at all, young lady. We're all fighting for fairness and equity, which transcends political affiliations. The coal seam gas companies, many of them foreign-owned, are destroying our land and, worse, they're ruining the lives of hardworking Australians and being assisted by greedy governments blinded by dollars.'

Dennis Fulton, carrying a placard, *Big gas destroying the Great Artesian*

Basin, noticed a thickset, dark-suited man taking photos of him. 'What the bloody hell do you think you're doing, mate?' he growled.

The man took off his sunglasses, reached into his suit pocket and flashed his wallet. 'Federal police,' Dennis exclaimed, looking at the badge. 'What do you want with me?'

'You're a person of interest.'

'A person of interest?'

'Yeah, an agitator. You've been making trouble in Queensland for years. Why don't you take yourself back there? We don't need your type down here.'

'I don't know what you're talking about. Who put you up to taking the photos? Are you on duty or moonlighting?'

'Don't get cute with me and if you keep carrying on like a smart-arse I'll throw you in the lockup.'

Dennis turned and saw the TV cameras pointed right at him. 'Go for it. Then you can explain to the television reporters what you're doing disturbing a peaceful protest and how much CEGL are paying you?'

The Fed covered his mouth with his hand. 'Bastard! There'll be another time, without the cameras, and then we'll see how smart you are.'

Meanwhile, on the sixtieth floor, Harold Llewellyn was chairing the meeting, sitting along the middle of a long table with Spencer Harbrow on his right and Moira Raymond on his left. The meetings were usually brief and, after formal resolutions were passed, Llewellyn usually made a short speech about another successful year and then everyone adjourned to an adjoining room for refreshments. This was his sixteenth meeting and in every other year the share price had risen, but it had fallen nearly twenty percent over the past year. As he looked at the larger-than-usual audience, all he could see were glum faces. They were like vultures and fired off questions about the company's fall in profits, its massive expansion program and its fights with landowners. They all led back to one thing: the company's share price.

Harbrow was brooding; these people had made a fortune thanks to him and now, when for the first time the company's performance was less than stellar, they were baying for blood. *How dare they, these piddling little shareholders criticise him after what he had done for them?* Someone raised the matter of the demonstrators and Llewellyn promptly put them down as unrepresentative riff-raff, but the questioner followed up with, 'Is that how you'd describe the chairman of the McLachlan Bank?'

Before he could answer, Steve Forrest chimed in with, 'I'd hardly call Tom Morgan and Charles Paxton unrepresentative riff-raff.' Only Moira Raymond knew him and she was quick to pass the information onto Llewellyn.

'Perhaps that description is a little harsh,' Llewellyn offered. 'But these people, despite their standing in the community, are ill-informed. This company is a good corporate citizen that creates jobs, provides opportunities, pays taxes and makes generous donations to the communities in which it works.'

'If the company's so good, why do farmers and graziers hate it so much? Isn't it ruining their land and poisoning their water, and hasn't there been a link drawn between exploiting coal seam gas and an increase in skin problems and cancer?'

'Are you here as a reporter or shareholder, Sir?'

'I'm a shareholder and you, more than anyone, should know that I am perfectly entitled to ask questions. I'd like an answer please.'

Harbrow was seething and started to get to his feet, but Llewellyn put his hand on his shoulder and whispered, 'I'll handle this.'

'Many landowners have signed access agreements with the company and there is no evidence to suggest that the extraction of coal seam gas leads to illness or health problems.'

'Why then is the company the largest donor to the Paisley Memorial Hospital and why is it paying the medical bills of sick children in the Fisher Valley?'

'I have no idea what you're talking about.' Llewellyn blustered.

'You should ask Ms Raymond, then.' Steve grinned. 'Mr Chairman, why is the company running pipelines through prime agricultural land when they could be laid under stock tracks?'

'That's confidential and relates to the company's operations and it is not appropriate to discuss it in this forum.'

'Mr Chair …'

'No, no more questions from you. You've had more than a fair go.'

'I was finished,' Steve said, pulling his recorder from his shirt pocket as he strode towards the door. 'I was going to say that I'd be pleased to help ensure the minutes of the meeting are accurate. I'm happy to email you a copy if it'd help.'

'No recording devices are allowed,' Llewellyn shouted.

'Sue me,' Steve laughed, pushing the door open.

The next morning, Aaron James was in full flight. 'I want to tell you a disgraceful story about a big international company screwing one of our diggers. Not to put too fine a point on it, these bastards are trying to steal his land. I spoke to this man yesterday. Artie Cleever's his name and he's lived peacefully with his wife on their property in the Fisher Valley for forty years. He didn't want to talk about it, but I found out that he lied about his age in the Second World War and enlisted in our infantry as a fifteen-year-old and saw action in the Philippines under MacArthur. What a hero!

'Anyhow, our friends at CEGL thought he was old and ripe for the picking, so they conned him into signing a land access agreement, then sunk three wells on his property that contaminated his air and water and caused him and his wife to become extremely ill. Let me read you an exchange of letters between his lawyers and the Sydney shysters who have plenty of form in this area of the law, *Braithwaite Ogilvie & Llewellyn*. But I warn you, when you hear them you'll want to puke.'

Five minutes later, 2ZL's switchboard was choked with callers wanting to trash CEGL and its lawyers.

'Here's what I suggest,' James ranted. 'Anyone with a CEGL gas or electricity account should cancel it and switch to another provider. Let's boycott the bastards and see how these fat cats like it when we hit them in their hip pockets and I promise you, I'll raise this matter every morning until Artie Cleever has been paid his half-a-million dollars. If this is happening to poor old Artie, it's happening to others as well, so, if you're getting fleeced by *big-gas* or know someone who is, phone me.'

No-one else could get away with what Aaron James did, but he had a history of ridiculing lawyers and their clients when he was supporting good causes, to the point that the bullies withdrew, bruised and battered, long before reaching court.

'Buffy, how would you like your own column?' Steve asked.

'What's the catch? What do you want me to put my name to that you're too scared to put your own on?'

'You're very cynical. I'm thinking about resurrecting *Heard Around Town*, but I'm not sure you could rake up enough gossip to justify a regular column. What do you think?'

'Of course I could and, if I ever ran short, I'd phone Mrs Elliot.'

'So you want to run with it?'

'I'd love to have my own column.'

'Good. I've already drafted the first article, under your name of course.'

'I knew there was a catch.' Buffy groaned. 'Who am I attacking on your behalf?'

'Read it for yourself.' Steve pushed a single A4 page towards her:

Heard Around Town

Heard around town that a Porsche-driving, Paisley-based executive is about to make a tilt at her company's top job and might soon be leaving the Fisher Valley for the greener pastures of Sydney. Rumour has it the company's board of directors are none too happy with the long-serving incumbent and a change at the top is imminent. I'd like to say that when she goes she'll be sadly missed, but I was brought up not to tell lies, so I can't. Good riddance and God speed.

'I'm hoping it might create a bit of tension.'

'I love it. But is it true?'

'Yes, I heard it around town.' Steve laughed, ducking a stapler that came whistling past his ear. 'You'll need to write two more articles to complete the column but, remember, they have to be filled with innuendos and you can't specifically identify anyone.'

'How many female executives in Paisley drive a Porsche?'

'Good point, Buffy. Why don't you change it to sports-car-driving female executive?'

'Thanks boss. If you'll excuse me, I have a column to write.'

Chapter 27

CEGL's phones were jammed as punters from all over the state phoned in to cancel their energy accounts. The television, radio and print media had picked up the story of Artie Cleever and the 'hard-hearted international corporation' that was trying to rip him off. Harbrow paced around his office while Harold Llewellyn replayed the Aaron James indictment on his laptop. It had outraged Sydneysiders and sent CEGL's share price tumbling again.

Harbrow abruptly stopped pacing, 'We never conned the silly old goat or forced him to sign an access agreement. Harold, I want to sue that big-mouthed prick this time.'

The older man slowly shook his head. 'We can't win. If we sue, he'll ridicule us every morning, he'll make a mockery of the legal action and, in the end, we'll withdraw and he'll crow for weeks. He's done it before to bigger companies than us.'

'He called you a shyster. You can't let him get away with that.'

'We offered Cleever less than fifty percent of the value of his land before we started drilling. Do you want to listen to some of the calls that James took from his legion of listeners? "Shyster" is tame compared to some of the language they used.'

'I'm not interested in listening to peons, Harold, but are you advising me not to take action against this loud-mouth?'

'Yes, and not only that. We need to pay Cleever his half-a-million dollars and get out of the media spotlight as quickly as we can. Aaron James will move onto another campaign once we've settled. He'll find another cause and forget about us but, if we don't, he'll be at us day after day.'

'And then we'll be a soft touch for every other sod farmer in the land. Maybe I need to take some legal advice from a more aggressive firm.'

Llewellyn rarely lost his cool, but he had to restrain himself from saying, *if you hadn't taken the Maddock group on in the first place we wouldn't be in this predicament.* 'You think you can beat Aaron James because you have a lot more money than he does. He doesn't care about that. He controls the media and he's like no other talkback presenter in the land. Don't you understand? He doesn't report the news, he makes the news. You can go to another legal firm if you like, but don't come running back to me when your nose is bloodied and James has his foot on your windpipe, crushing the life out of you.'

'Settle down, Harold.' Harbrow placed his hand on his chairman's forearm. 'I was joking. Sure I'd like to take James on, but when have I ever not taken your wise counsel? If you say we should pay the silly old goat out, then pay him out we shall.'

'On another matter,' Llewellyn said, still miffed. 'Did you see the latest polls? Nick Gould's campaigning hard and he's closed the gap to four points. I hope you didn't cancel that donation to the Labor Party.'

'I know what Nick can do on the election trail and I never considered cancelling,' Harbrow lied. He had read the same polls and reinstated the cheque.

Llewellyn got up to leave and the two men shook hands, each thinking the other had outlived his usefulness. The door had barely closed before Harbrow was again reading the small article in the *Paisley Chronicle* that had so peeved him. So, Moira was bragging that she was about to unseat him. Well, if his plans worked out, she'd soon be fighting to keep her own job, let alone be worrying about his.

Moira also read the article and cursed, while wondering where that rude, overweight girl had got her information. Someone with loose lips had talked and she'd soon find out who it was. Fortunately, Spencer Harbrow was hardly likely to read the *Paisley Chronicle,* so she was unlikely to have lost the element of surprise.

Andrew Brown, once the popular bank manager around town, was now reviled and life at home, other than for the children, was loveless. Sally had twice raised divorce in the past month. She wanted her friends and lifestyle back and was constantly at him to quit the bank, but knew that he couldn't and the feeling of being trapped drove her to despair. Andrew was ill-tempered with his staff, made mistakes, and forgetfulness crept into his work. Each morning when he left home, he wondered whether he would return to an empty house. He dreaded Monday mornings, because there was always an email instructing him to implement a fresh batch of foreclosures.

Andrew flicked through the nine files that had sat on his desk for the past two days, dreading the phone calls that he knew he would eventually have to make. For the folks of the Fisher Valley, receiving a phone call from Andrew Brown was thought to be only marginally better than receiving one from your Maker. Well, he'd put them off long enough. Once he had finished his appointment with Tom Morgan, he'd grit his teeth and get on with the dirty job the bank was paying him to do.

As one of the clerks showed Morgan into his office, Andrew wondered what he wanted. He'd never banked with the FBA and was advised by some of Sydney's finest merchant bankers. Not that he needed much advice, because he had always known how to make a dollar. He was dressed in a black jacket that he hung over the back of a chair, a red-and-blue flannel shirt, frayed jeans and black workboots. Andrew thought that he must be the most unlikely-looking billionaire in the world.

'What can I do for you, Tom?' he asked.

'Andrew, I'm running very short of time,' Morgan said, glancing at his watch. 'And it's not what you can do for me but what I can do for you. The stud is taking more time than ever; it's losing its enjoyment, because I'm getting bogged down in paperwork and administration that any competent manager could handle far better than me. How would you like to come and work for me?'

'I ... I ... I'm flattered,' Andrew responded, seeing a glimmer of hope in his otherwise futile circumstances. 'Bu ... but there's so much to discuss. What does the job entail and how much d ...'

'Sixty-five thousand dollars a year.'

It was less than the bank was paying him but not by much. 'What about a car?'

'You won't need a car. There's utilities, four-wheel-drives and trucks on the property and if you need to use one you can take your pick.'

The fully-maintained car from the bank was such a big deal. Andrew estimated that it saved him nearly $20,000 a year and Morgan's offer had just lost any attraction. His disappointment must have shown, because Morgan said, 'There's a four-bedroom manager's residence on the property. It needs some sprucing up and TLC but you could sell or rent your house in Paisley and use the money to buy a car. But, I'm telling you, you won't need one.'

'You expect me to live on the property?'

'Of course. I didn't think I'd need to spell that out. If I remember rightly, your wife's a fine horsewoman and I might be able to offer her something around the stud, on a casual basis to start with, but who knows where it might lead. There's a small primary school about two kilometres away.' Morgan pushed an envelope across the desk. 'I have to fly. It's all in here. Read it carefully and if you've got any queries phone me, preferably at night. I've got a lot on right now.'

'If I accept, when would you like me to start?'

'Tomorrow.' Morgan grinned. 'Let me know as soon as you can.'

'I will. Thanks, Tom.' Andrew's mind was already made up and he hoped Sally would share his enthusiasm. After Morgan left, he opened the deepest drawer of his desk and dropped the files into it. With luck and good timing he might never have to make those nine phone calls.

The man sitting in Dr George Bingham's surgery was about forty-five years old, wiry, with a burnt, wrinkled face, the legacy of working outdoors for years. He had complained about bringing blood up in his saliva. The doctor examined his mouth and throat and then placed his stethoscope on his chest and his back. 'How long has this been occurring, Mr Martin?'

'Call me Jake, Doc, and about six months.'

'Why did it take you so long to come and see me?'

'Didn't think it was anything to be worried about, and then I began losing weight, so I thought I betta get checked out.' The man grinned nervously.

'When did you have your last full medical?'

'No offence doc, but I don't like doctors. I don't reckon I've been inside a surgery for ten years and, if it wasn't for my wife's nagging, I wouldn't be here today.'

'How's your appetite?'

'I used to eat like a horse, but now I rarely feel like eating. I put it down to getting older.'

'What about your bowel movements?'

'Irregular and sometimes I don't go for days, but I guess if ya don't eat you don't ...' He didn't complete the sentence.

'What do you do?'

'I work for Filliburton on the gas wells. I was up on the Spurling Downs before I came down here. Got a promotion to assistant supervisor, ya see, and had to come down here cos the money was too good to knock back.'

'When a well's fracked and the water gushes from the ground, have you ever got any on you?' Doctor George asked, his face clouding over. He wasn't one to jump to conclusions, but coughing up blood, losing weight and loss of appetite were symptomatic of cancer and he didn't like what he'd heard.

Jake laughed. 'You're joking aren't ya? Anyone within twenty or thirty metres gets saturated. I can't remember working on a rig where I haven't been soaked and I reckon I've worked on hundreds.'

'Do you wear safety gear?'

'We can wear wet-weather slicks, but they don't keep the water off your face and they're so bloody hot that no-one ever bothers.'

'So you're not forced to wear safety gear?'

'Doc, we're usually drilling hundreds of kilometres from nowhere. Who's gonna force us?'

'Do you have a trade union?'

'Sure, the Gas Workers Union, but we never see anyone. The company deducts our subs and we get a monthly newsletter and that's about it.'

'I'm booking you in for a full set of X-rays, scans and blood tests at Paisley Memorial at 8am tomorrow. They might take two to three days, but you'll be able to go home at nights.'

'Tomorrow? That soon?'

'Try to get a good night's sleep.' Doctor George put his hand reassuringly on Jake's shoulder.

'Wha ... what do ya think it might be Doc? Ya must have some idea.'

'I'm sorry, I don't,' he lied. 'I'll know more once the results of the tests are back.' Five minutes after the man had left, the doctor was still at his desk, perusing Charlie Paxton's file. He had been hoping that little Charlie was a 'one off', but the man's symptoms were identical and he knew what the tests would reveal.

Aaron James gloated after contracts were exchanged between CEGL and

Artie Cleever for the purchase of his land. Old Artie phoned in and broke down in tears as he expressed his gratitude to Simon Breckenridge and to James. This resulted in James unleashing another tirade against CEGL and *Braithwaite Ogilvie and Llewellyn* but, just as Llewellyn had predicted, another crusade soon beckoned and two days later neither were mentioned. The public relations disaster was, in the short term, over.

Norris Scott-Tempy stood at the front gates of the old Morrisey property like some feudal lord, waving in convoys of CEGL's trucks carrying huts, generators, light poles and components of drilling rigs, to be erected on the well-pads that had been constructed the previous week. The activity on the pads was more than matched by gangs of labourers who had been promised huge bonuses to clear the trees at the rear of the property and extend the gravel tracks. There was an eight-well plan for the property on a very tight deadline and Moira Raymond had let her supervisors know that she would take no prisoners if they dared fail her.

Some objectors had sought to block the gates, but they knew they had no rights and the police had moved them on with a minimum of fuss. Adjoining neighbours had agitated and one had even threatened Scott-Tempy with physical violence, but he wasn't worried, the law was on his side. If he got the opportunity to buy these whingers' properties at depressed prices, he most certainly would. He had gone from being disliked to being hated, but it was like water off a duck's back. He was well-off, some might say rich, but he'd always dreamed of being mega-wealthy and, with the help of *big gas,* the realisation of his dream was in sight.

Frank Beck spent three weeks in Noosa, where he hit the surf every morning at 6.30 for two hours before having breakfast. On most days he was on the golf course before midday and back in his luxurious beachside apartment early enough to take a quick swim before dinner. It didn't take him long to strike up a relationship with a tawny, long-legged, forty-something divorcee trying to forget a bad marriage. The sex was torrid but she was insatiable; he'd soon had more than enough of her and was ready to get back to work. He kissed her goodbye at the airport, promising to stay in touch, knowing that he would never see her again.

At Newtower Airport he picked up copies of the *Chronicle* and the *National Advocate* and skim-read them, looking for anything relating to the illegal discharge of wastewater by Filliburton. As his bosses had predicted, his misdemeanours appeared to be have been swept under the carpet. On the drive back to the valley, he received a phone call from a man whom he knew of but had never spoken to before, Spencer Harbrow.

On Monday morning, he'd just finished telling the receptionist about the weather and surf in Noosa, when the phone rang. She put her hand over the mouthpiece. 'Moira Raymond for you.'

'Good morning, Moira.'

'I need to see you. Twenty minutes. My office.'

She was tense and wasted no time on pleasantries before directing him to take a chair. 'Frank, we've wasted far too much time on the *estates* without getting anywhere. As you know, despite having exploration licences and arbitrated land access agreements, nearly every time we've tried to drill, those fools calling themselves *Lock 'em out* have barricaded the gates, blocked the roads and let down the tyres on our trucks. Well, enough's enough. We need to make a decisive move to establish ourselves in the heart of the *estates*.'

This was the type of challenge that Beck thrived on. 'I agree. What do you have in mind?'

'I've selected a property.' She opened a map and pointed. 'This one's a little larger than the norm for the *estatees*. It's seventy acres and we can get four wells on it. I want you to put a team together and get ready to move, but you mustn't breathe a word about the location until you're ready to roll. Every time we've planned something in the past, word has leaked out and those nutters have been waiting for us. Only three of my executives know where you're going to strike and I've sworn them to secrecy. From now on, in emails, letters and phone calls, we'll refer to it as Project Genesis, and don't worry about your bosses, they know something big is on but they don't know what and they won't ask you about it.'

Beck started to laugh. 'I know the property. It's owned by a young troublemaker named Shawn Rosen, who I've had some run-ins with. I'm going to enjoy this.'

'Will he be a problem? We can choose another property if you think he'll cause trouble. You can't fail on this assignment, there's too much hanging on it.'

'He'll cause trouble all right but nothing I can't handle, so you've got nothing to worry about. After we're equipped and ready, we'll move in the early hours of the morning and be driving through his gates at 4am. He'll never know what hit him and by the time he does it'll be far too late. I'm gonna enjoy this.'

'Frank, I can't stress how much is riding on this.'

'Hell, you know the hard part is actually getting into the property but, once we're in, nothing can stop us. Don't worry, nothing's gonna go wrong.'

She had been hovering over the map, but now she eased back in her chair and the tension that had been in her face evaporated. She smiled. 'Good. If you pull this off, how would you like to come and work for CEGL?'

'Not if, when,' he corrected her. 'I'm always open to offers. What did you have in mind?'

'This is highly confidential and, if it's ever raised outside this office, I'll deny that I said it. Are you clear about that?'

'Mum's the word.'

'I expect to be moving back to Sydney after we finish drilling on the Scott-Tempy property and you've sunk your four wells, so my position in Paisley will become vacant. How would you like the job?' She was watching him like a hawk.

Frank Beck was a good card player and his face didn't reveal anything, but he was laughing inside. When Spencer Harbrow had phoned him in Newtower he had also sworn him to secrecy and then offered him Moira's job, in the event that she unexpectedly left the company. 'It'd be quite a promotion, but I'm sure I'll be able to handle it.'

'Frank, I just wanted to sound you out. We can discuss the details after you've successfully completed our little project.'

'Is the offer conditional on that?'

'You betcha! You've got a lot of planning to do so I don't want hold you up. Remember, the fewer people who know what you're doing, including employees, sub-contractors and suppliers, the better.'

'Sure. I'll treat it as if I was back in the marines.' Beck marched confidently to the door, knowing he was in the middle of a power struggle and that he would need to play both sides until a clear winner emerged.

Chapter 28

Saturday's edition of the *National Advocate* always included a glossy magazine titled *Long Weekend*. Steve rarely read it, but the photo of an exploding oil platform captioned *Is the BP disaster finally over?* caught his attention. He sprawled out on the couch, with his coffee on the floor beside him, and settled in to read the five-page treatise.

In April, 2010, BP was drilling an exploratory well in the Gulf of Mexico to a depth of fifteen hundred metres, when a methane bubble under extreme pressure flew up and out of the drill column at enormous velocity, where it expanded on the platform before igniting and exploding, killing eleven workers. Efforts by multiple ships to douse the flames failed and thirty-six hours later the platform sank. For the next three months, the equivalent of five million barrels of crude oil gushed from the well while all attempts to cap it failed. As the oil spread, it caused massive damage to wildlife and marine habitats, as well as the Gulf's fishing and tourism industries. Nearly a year after the explosion, tar balls continued to litter the shore, the crude oil on the ocean floor did not seem to be degrading and dead dolphins were washing up along the coast. Many described it as the worst man-made environmental disaster in the history of the US, and BP committed to spend forty billion dollars in the clean-up, but, despite this, there were those who thought that the Gulf would never recover. The White House Oil Spill Commission found that BP and its contractors had done things on the cheap, which helped trigger the explosion and the leakage that followed. The drilling rig's last line of defence was a massive three hundred tonne blowout preventer sitting on the ocean floor, designed to cap the well, that BP had described as 'fail-safe', but which had still failed, albeit by only centimetres. The writer concluded that, while the oil had stopped gushing, the disaster would be with the folk of the Gulf for another twenty years.

The words 'fail-safe' troubled Steve and he turned his laptop on, looking for the transcripts of the speeches given the night Nick Gould had announced CEGL's twenty-billion dollar investment in the coal seam gas industry. He soon found what he was looking for. Spencer Harbrow had guaranteed that CEGL's processes were fail-safe and that CEGL would not do anything that might endanger the health of the community or the environment. *How could he, when CEGL was using toxic chemicals and drilling thousands of wells through aquifers and near the Great Artesian Basin?* The oil in the Gulf of Mexico had spread over eleven thousand square kilometres; the Great Artesian Basin was over 150 times larger and, if contaminated, would be impossible to restore. *How could governments be complicit in developing coal seam gas wells when it was impossible for* big gas *to guarantee that the underground water would not be ruined for future generations?*

Chapter 29

Sally Brown and the kids jumped at the opportunity to get out of Paisley to make a fresh start on Tom Morgan's stud. Andrew wasn't a devious man but the following day he phoned his boss and complained of severe work-related anguish and said that he desperately needed to get away for a few months. He emphasised that he didn't even know if a long break would cure him. His boss was uncaring, fearing that Andrew was setting the bank up for a big WorkCover claim for stress-related mental illness. He suggested that, if Andrew was away for an extended period of time, it would be difficult to hold his job in Paisley and that on his return he might have to be relocated to another branch, which could prove disruptive.

'I don't want to upset the bank.' Andrew sniffled, as if stifling a sob. 'You've been so good to me but I don't know if I can go on. I could resign, but that wouldn't help, because I'd still have to work another month and I'd lose so many benefits.'

There was a long pause. 'Andrew, your health is paramount. If you think resigning and getting away will help, we wouldn't be so churlish as to withhold anything that was due to you.' Then, for the first time in ten years, he complimented him. 'You've been a fine employee.'

'But I'd lose my last month's pay if I left immediately.'

'Not at all. Given the circumstances regarding your health, we'd be happy to pay you a month's salary in lieu of notice and you could finish up tomorrow.'

'That's very generous of you.'

'Andrew, when you get better, phone me and I'll see if I can find a position for you.' He hoped he would be seeing the last of this weak-willed manager who procrastinated about enforcing foreclosures.

It took no time at all for the Brown family to rent their house out and move into the manager's residence at the Portman Stud. The children loved their new school and the open spaces. While Sally knew they would never regain the friends they had lost, they would not lose any of the few remaining and, hopefully, would no longer be reviled. Andrew felt as if an enormous weight had been lifted from his shoulders and each day family life became a little happier.

The community had been outraged by *Your Nation's* exposé of the coal seam gas industry and the program's producers had immediately started work on a follow-up program which, courtesy of Dennis Fulton, they called *The End of a Dirty Line*. Recently completed, it had been extensively advertised and had drawn a massive peak-time Sunday night audience.

Libby Hanover was seated in the front of the Channel Six helicopter. 'This is Kravis Island, a beautiful semi-tropical atoll and home to over 200 species of fauna, including birdlife, wallabies, wombats, goannas and a near-extinct possum-like marsupial. Fifteen kilometres from Newtower, it's only accessible by air or boat via the Tapered Straits. It is home to 600 species of flora, huge towering eucalypts and native grasses and flowers. The lagoon is a fisherman's paradise teeming with fish and marine life.'

The camera panned over the lush, green island and vividly-blue lagoon, surrounded by pristine, yellow beaches. 'This is nature at its most perfect and it's where the methane extracted three hundred kilometres away in the Fisher Valley is going to be piped, before being processed and consigned to huge tankers for shipment to China and India.'

She paused, as the camera panned low across the dense foliage, before coming to a huge, cleared area. There were hundreds of men, bull dozers, cranes, trucks, huts, three recently-poured massive concrete slabs and a number of partially-erected buildings. 'The ugly scar you're looking at is a designated liquid natural gas precinct, set aside by the government, so that CEGL can construct a gas liquefaction plant and a deepwater port for huge tankers. The pipeline from the Fisher Valley will run to Newtower and then continue under the Tapered Straits and across this stunning island to the liquefaction plant. Ecologists claim that the dredging of the straits has destroyed the seagrass and so far has resulted in the deaths of one hundred turtles, five sea lions and four dolphins. Fish are diseased with lesions on their bodies; fishermen are going broke and wholesalers are refusing to purchase their catches. The government denies this and says that it has completed ecological studies and that the laying of the pipeline has not impacted on marine life. Spin doctors for the same government announced that the grant of land to CEGL on Kravis Island amounted to only one percent of its area, but, what they didn't tell us, was that it amounted to seven hundred acres. Seven hundred acres!

'The workers you can see are building three processing plants known as trains, which convert the gas to liquid by cooling it to minus one hundred and sixty-two degrees centigrade. This reduces its volume to one six-hundredth of its gaseous state, making it very profitable to ship.'

The camera panned back to Libby. 'One of the many problems associated with producing this supposed clean energy is the enormous usage of power in the cooling process and the reconversion back to gas at its eventual destination. Needless to say, this will spew carbons into the atmosphere – exactly what our esteemed political leaders say they're trying to stop.'

The next shot was of Libby standing with the ubiquitous Dennis Fulton, backed by 300 greenies and outraged locals, noisily protesting. They were about fifty metres from the gates to the construction site, with twenty police between them and the cyclone and barbed-wire fence; there were a similar number of private security guards behind it.

'Dennis Fulton, the last time you were on this island you were jailed after you chained yourself to a bulldozer. I hope we're not going to see a repeat performance.'

'I spent a night in the Newtower police cells.' He laughed. 'And the following day I was heavily fined by an overzealous magistrate.' He didn't say that, like the many other fines he'd incurred, it remained unpaid.

'He said he'd jail you if you appeared before him again, didn't he?'

'He did,' Dennis said, a huge smile on his face.

'You've championed many green causes,' she said, over the din of noisy protestors chanting *go to hell CEGL*. 'But you seem to be devoting every waking minute to stopping the coal seam gas industry.'

'This is the greatest environmental threat of our lifetime. Think about it. What other industry is licenced to steal and destroy hundreds of thousands of acres of prime agricultural land? To deplete and contaminate our aquifers? To pump methane into the atmosphere and poison the air we breathe? To cause dermatitis, other serious illnesses and cancer? To destroy marine life? To scar a beautiful island? To use obscene amounts of power, converting gas to liquid? And to think those liars in the industry and greedy fools in government call it green energy.' He pointed to the construction site. 'Do you know what that is, Libby? It's the end of a dirty line!'

The cameras panned back to Libby in the studio. 'We invited the New South Wales Minister for Industry and the Federal Minister for the Environment to appear on the program, but unfortunately they had prior engagements.'

Before Sandi Carlisle moved in with Steve Forrest they drew up a set of rules. The main ones were that he wasn't to publish anything that she might tell him about the cases the Paisley police were working on, and that she was to ignore anything that he might say that could be on the wrong side of the law. Two weeks later they had their first fight. She came home late one cold night, bubbling with excitement and blabbering about a major marijuana bust that she and Josh had made on the outskirts of Paisley. As she was babbling, Steve was writing the story in his mind. When she had finished, he asked her to take him to where the bust had occurred; when she refused, he got angry and they had a short, ferocious argument that saw him spend the night on the sofa. In the morning he was cold, sniffling and remorseful. He climbed into bed and snuggled into Sandi's back, whispering his apologies. He'd hated their first fight, but their first make-up sex more than compensated.

The increase in truck movements around Tura began early on Monday morning and was hardly noticeable, unless you were Dean Prezky, who watched the big rigs like a hawk. Convoys of huge tip trucks carrying gravel dawdled through the town. Then there would be a lull before another convoy came through, carrying portable huts, generators, light poles and mechanical equipment. These were followed by Filliburton semitrailers bearing drill rig components.

These convoys normally travelled as fast as they could, often exceeding the speed limit. However, they were now crawling and this piqued Dean's interest. The materials and the equipment they were carrying told him that Filliburton was about to drill fresh wells and he wasted no time following them at a distance that he hoped would not alert the drivers. Once on the open road, they increased their speed to the legal limit, but no more, and he had no difficulty keeping them in sight. After thirty-five minutes, the trucks turned into the property that the spiv, Norris Scott-Tempy, had 'stolen' from Bill Morrisey. Dean cursed, because he had known about the CEGL eight-well program and there was little that could be done to thwart it. On the way back to town he paid little attention to the buses, normally used to ferry workers to sites, travelling towards him; if he had, he would have seen that they were empty.

That night, as he pulled beers behind the bar, he heard the continuous drone of truck engines. His gut told him that something was going on and ten minutes after he knocked off he was on the trail of another convoy. Again there was no excessive speed and the drivers made no attempt to lose him. Just like earlier that day, the trucks entered the Scott-Tempy property and Dean let out a barrage of expletives at his own foolishness.

Driving into Paisley the following day, he was held up by trucks in front of, and coming towards him, all travelling at, or less than, the speed limit. It was as if they were trying to fly under the radar and, had they not normally travelled at high speeds, it would not have been so noticeable. He felt in his water that something wasn't right, but he couldn't fathom what it was. That night, in the bar he could hear the sound of truck engines idling through the town, but he was dog tired. Rather than go on another wild goose chase, he drove home, frustrated and annoyed.

Dean wasn't the only one frustrated. Jack Thomas worked late into the night at the offices of the Fisher Valley Protective Alliance. Maps of the Tura *estates* were strewn all over his desk and on the floor beside his chair. His spy at CEGL had tipped him off that something big was about to happen, but he had no idea what or where; only the most senior executives knew the details. The 'spy' added that it was rumoured that the project had been named 'Genesis' and that he had used every combination of that name with the words 'Fisher Valley', 'Tura' and 'Paisley' to try to breach the company's computer systems, but had drawn a blank and was worried that he might have blown his cover. Thomas had told him to keep his ear to the ground but to desist from further attempts to penetrate the computer systems – he was far too valuable to run the risk of losing.

Thomas knew CEGL would target what they saw as the weakest link, which meant that it had to be the Tura *estates.* He deduced that to maximise the number of wells, they would aim their attack at one of the larger properties, so any that were fifty acres or less or that were not covered by arbitrated or coerced access agreements, had been crossed out on his maps. He was still left with eight properties spread across the whole *estate.* The spies he had positioned outside the Filliburton base had told him that there had been little activity, other than two drill rigs being despatched to the Scott-Tempy property.

Thomas remembered being driven to desperation the last time Filliburton had been about to launch an attack on the *estates,* not knowing which property to defend. Filliburton's intentions had been obvious then and their main base had been crammed with trucks and trailers carrying drill rigs, huts and equipment. It was then that the Tura resident known as the General, Mick Petheridge, had come up with the idea of blockading Filliburton's gates, effectively stopping their trucks and equipment from being moved. Hundreds of cars, pickups, four-wheel-drives and semitrailers converged on the road outside the base and five days later Filliburton gave an undertaking not to proceed if the blockade was removed. This time was different; there was no build-up of trucks and equipment to blockade and yet Thomas knew that Project Genesis was about to be launched. If need be, he could blockade one T-intersection and defend six properties, but he hoped he would not have to take that gamble. It was just after midnight when he turned the lights off and headed home to a fitful night's sleep.

Other than Frank Beck, no-one at Filliburton knew anything about Project Genesis and, while a few of his bosses had pumped him for details, he had, much to their annoyance, refused to even hint at what was occurring. The first move he made after completing his plan was to phone Moira to outline it and ask for unrestricted access to the Scott-Tempy property. She liked what she heard and, with her support, he immediately stopped the work gangs clearing the heavily-treed area on the property.

He also issued instructions to the supervisors to lay gravel tracks, but not install gates, to two more places at either end of the front of the property. On the night he planned to move, he had no intention of being blockaded and, if need be, he'd have the fence torn down so the convoy of the trucks that he would hide in the trees would not be impeded.

The transport company had been well paid and sworn to secrecy and their drivers, not knowing what was going on, had been bussed to Scott-Tempy's flea-ridden motels and told that they could be required at any time. Beck would be in the lead truck with his best team, to make sure nothing went wrong and to allow him to supervise the unloading. His plan was perfect and, by the time the Greens and other radicals found out what had happened, it would be too late.

Chapter 30

Steve Forrest had also heard the rumours about CEGL making a move on the *estates*. He phoned all of his contacts, trying to ferret out more details, only to come up blank. He even phoned old Mrs Elliot, but she didn't know anything. By Friday the rumours were growing stronger, but there was still nothing concrete to support them.

When Sandi arrived home just after 10pm, she was white and shaking like a leaf. Steve jumped up from watching the telly and took her in his arms. She was normally happy and bubbly and he'd never seen her like this before. 'What's wrong? What happened? Sit down and I'll get you a drink.'

'Hold me,' she sniffled. 'I nearly got bashed by a mob of angry truckies tonight. We got called out to a disturbance at one of those motel dives on the outskirts of Tura and, when we got there, two guys, surrounded by their mates egging them on, were belting the hell out of each other.' She paused. 'You can't print any of this.'

'I won't.'

'When we got out of the van, the truckies turned ugly and called us pigs and to piss off back to Paisley and for a minute it got scary. Even when Josh pulled his pistol out, they kept pushing closer. It was only when he fired a shot into the air that they backed off. He told me later that in all the years he's been in the force that was the closest he'd ever been to losing control and the first time he'd used his pistol.'

'No wonder you're shaking.' Steve held her even tighter.

'We tossed the two brawlers in the back of the divvy van and Josh told the mob to clear out or he'd call for backup. When we got back to the station, they'd calmed down and said they'd been sharing one of those tiny, dirty rooms for four days, and a fight broke out over what to watch on television.'

'Truckies waiting for a load. It's a tough way to make a dollar.'

'That's what we thought, but it turns out that they parked their rigs fully loaded. They've been on stand-by, waiting for a call telling them that they're about to be bussed to their trucks.'

'What? That's not how trucking companies operate.'

'Maybe not, but there are two truckies in every one of the thirty rooms at that dive.'

'What? That's crazy. Did you ask them what they were carrying?'

'Of course. The two guys we hauled in were driving tippers carrying gravel, but they said there were other trucks loaded with light poles, generators, huts and mechanical equipment.'

'Oh shit, so that's what they're doing. Where are these trucks? I need to know.' He dived for his mobile phone.

'You promised you wouldn't print anything. You promised you wouldn't use anything I told you.'

'Honey, listen to me,' he pleaded. 'This is different. Those trucks are being hidden by the gas companies so that when the time is right they'll be driven onto some poor sap's land in the middle of the night without his knowledge. If you tell me where they are and where they're going, I can stop them. Please, I'm begging you.'

'I shouldn't have said anything.'

'No, no, that's not right; I promise I won't publish one word of what you tell me. Think of the poor landowner, his wife, his kids and their gates being smashed off their hinges in the dark of the night. You can't let it happen.'

'They're at your old girlfriend's father's place and the drivers haven't been told where the destination is. I hope I won't live to regret this.'

'You won't,' he said, giving her a cuddle before punching Jack Thomas's number into his mobile.

The Tura Hotel stayed open to midnight on Fridays and, after Dean Prezky knocked off, he stood on the verandah, pulling his jacket up around his neck to ward off the biting wind. Two buses, carrying shiftworkers out to one of the drill sites, trundled past him but he paid little attention to them. When his mobile buzzed, he wondered who could be phoning him at this late hour. Jack Thomas took less than a minute to tell him what was going on at the Scott-Tempy property and Dean cursed himself for not twigging to it when he'd tracked those convoys earlier in the week.

'I'm about to alert the troops to blockade that prick's property. I'll make sure those trucks never get out,' Thomas said.

As Dean was about to respond, another three buses loaded with men drove past him. 'It's too late Jack, the drivers are already on the way to the property. The trucks will be gone before you can get enough strength out there to stop 'em.'

The phone went quiet and all Dean could here was laboured breathing. 'Jack are you there?'

'I'm about to text everyone to blockade the Old Farm Road T-intersection; you know, the junction with Matlock Row. God, I pray I've chosen the right location. Dean, I'm staying here and the others from Paisley probably won't make it in time, so you and your neighbours in Tura are going to have to hold them off. Good luck.'

Dean made two phone calls. The first was to the General, who already had the text message and had assumed control and the second to tell Vicki what had occurred and not to expect him home anytime soon.

Tom Morgan buzzed his manager's residence and a sleepy Andrew Brown answered, only to be told to throw a pair of jeans and a jacket on and be at the helipad in ten minutes. This was Morgan's way of helping Andrew gain redemption with the good folk of the valley, but he didn't say so. Charles Paxton, with Cosmos next to him, was already on his way to join Morgan. This was a fight he wasn't going to miss.

The track to the Tura *estates* was normally desolate after midnight but, as Dean sped along the red dirt tracks, he saw tail-lights in front of him and headlights behind him and vehicles moving down long driveways to the right and left. The troops were rallying and racing to take up positions at the end of Old Farm Road; it wasn't really a road but just a wider red dirt track.

A bit further along, Dean could see the lights of a double line of trucks, pick-ups, utilities, cars and four-wheel-drives lined up across the road, with only a small break in the middle for 'friendly' vehicles to pass through. About a hundred metres in front of the line, a group of men were building a bonfire to the left of the road which, when ignited, would make the road impassable. As more vehicles joined the barricade, the General shouted instructions and, by the time the enemy was in sight, the vehicles would be in tightly spaced rows and the passageway would be closed. As Dean climbed out of the Toyota, he shook Mick's hand and said, 'I sure hope we've got the right location.'

'Won't make any difference,' the older man said, a thin roll-your-own smoke hanging out of the side of his mouth. 'I've despatched two groups of men to cover the other properties. I've spoken to Tom Morgan and he's going to track the convoy in his chopper, so we'll know their destination early enough to reposition ourselves. Don't worry; I've got everything under control.'

Dean grinned and breathed a little easier. It was little wonder that this man was nicknamed the 'General' and was so highly thought of by everyone, from the Tura landowners to rich graziers and vineyard owners. It wouldn't be without hardship but, for the first time since he'd left the hotel, Dean knew that the gas companies would not be breaching any landowner's property tonight. 'Well done, Mick.'

Mick ignored the compliment, spitting on the ground and shouting at a newcomer to go and help build another bonfire a further fifty metres along the road, but on the other side. Nearly a kilometre from the front line, twenty men were in the bushes hiding long planks of wood with nails driven through them, ready to be laid on the road as soon they received Mick's orders.

Morgan had paid fifteen million dollars for the Sikorsky and its sophisticated navigation and tracking systems were state of the art. He flew high above the convoy, as it commenced its journey from the Scott-Tempy property. 'There must be more than a hundred trucks,' he said.

'You're not wrong,' Paxton responded, while patting Cosmos as the big dog pressed into him. 'Look at the cars pouring out of Paisley. They're not going to make it in time to be of any help though.'

'Yeah, that's what I thought, but the General wants them to form a blockade behind the last truck and trap them in what he said is a classic pincer movement.'

'Hmmph, sounds like he's been reading too many war stories to me.'

'Maybe, but he's a good man and a great organiser. If he wasn't such a bloody recluse, I'd get him to reorganise my warehouses. What do you think, Andrew?'

'I don't know him.'

'No, about the blockade?'

'I hope we don't end up in jail.'

'Andrew, you and your family are very unpopular in the valley through no fault of your own. You can change that in the next few hours, and when we land I want you to do everything the General tells you to do without question.'

'How will I know him?'

Paxton laughed. 'You won't have to worry about that.'

'They're heading to the Tura *estates* all right,' Morgan cut in. 'Look at that stream of lights below us. In ten minutes they'll be at the five-ways intersection and we'll know exactly where they're going, but my money's on Jack Thomas being right.'

Billy McGregor and his gang didn't want to miss any of the action and had taken only a few minutes to stock up on booze before speeding out of town. An hour later, their three cars were sitting behind the last truck. Although his mates egged him on to pass and get in front of the convoy, he knew it would be suicide to try.

Tom Morgan, having established that the convoy could only be heading to Old Farm Road, set the Sikorsky down behind the last row of cars, to the rousing cheers of nearly 200 men and a few brave women. The General, who had been worded up by Morgan, handed Andrew Brown two small petrol cans. It was 3.35 when he told him to prime the bonfires and then to wait for the vehicles in the front row to flash their lights, before lighting them.

Andrew wanted to refuse. He'd never been brave, never been a dissident, always accepted authority; and he was sure he was about to participate in a dangerous criminal act. Reluctantly he trudged down the road towards the bonfires, wondering what Tom Morgan had got him into. He heard the raspy shout of the General telling him to get a move on and ordering all vehicle lights turned off and smokes stubbed out. When Andrew reached the second bonfire, he looked back at the barricade, but couldn't see anything. However, in the opposite direction he saw a glimmer of light, which soon flared into powerful beams racing towards him. He felt sick, his gut was knotted and he was shaking, as the lights charged towards him. He fought the urge to throw a lighted match on the bonfire and run back to sanctuary. He felt certain that he was going to be run over and driven into the dirt like an insect, when the vehicles in the front row finally flashed their lights in unison. He hurled a match into the first bonfire, but didn't wait to watch it erupt in flames before sprinting towards the second one. He was sweating heavily when he reached the barricade, to applause and shouts of 'good onya, Andrew!' Tom Morgan stood in the shadows smiling; the resurrection of Andrew Brown had begun.

The lead trucks braked abruptly on seeing the flashing lights and huge fires on the road, but not quickly enough to avoid the planks and their vicious spikes, which tore through their tyres. As Frank Beck jumped to the ground in a blind fury the General gave the command and every vehicle in the barricade turned their lights on high beam, blinding him. He hadn't breathed a word to anyone at Filliburton and knew that someone at CEGL had leaked; he cursed Moira Raymond. Had he still been in the marines, he would have ordered the largest B-double to the front of the convoy to smash the barricade apart, but in the civilised world you went to jail for actions like that. Instead, he dialled 000 and screamed at the operator, telling her that it was a matter of life and death and to get a team of police out to Old Farm Road as a matter of extreme urgency. The next call he made was to Moira Raymond.

It was 5.17am when Josh Gibson was awoken from a deep sleep by a fractious superintendent in Sydney, who quickly briefed him and finished by telling him to get out to Tura and fix the problem. Steve had been awake most of the night and had wanted to race out to Tura as soon as he'd received the text message from Jack Thomas, but the truckies had terrified Sandi and he couldn't bring himself to leave her by herself. He knew the call would come early in the morning and the phone rang only once before he picked it up. 'Sure, Josh,' he said, 'I'll wake her.'

When Sandi put the phone down, she looked totally distraught. 'There's over two kilometres of trucks and trailers blockaded on the Tura *estates.*' She hurriedly threw her uniform on. 'Did I do that?'

'No, of course not.'

'What am I going to say if Josh asks me whether I told you anything?'

'He probably won't ask, because I'm still here. If he thought I knew anything, he'd expect me to be out there, but, if he asks, just say no.'

'I don't like lying.'

'Sometimes you have to lie when it's for a good cause,' Steve said, feeling like a hypocrite after what he'd thought about his parents' lies. 'Honey, you did the right thing.'

She was pensive and not her normal, bright self as they sat in the kitchen, picking at fruit and muesli. Ten minutes later they heard Josh beeping out the front and she brushed his lips. 'Are you going out there?'

'Yes.'

'I might see you; I don't know what time I'll be home.'

'Nor me.' He gave her a quick cuddle. Josh beeped impatiently.

She was barely out the door before he flicked the telly on. He saw the first aerial shots of this massive convoy of trucks wedged between barricades of smaller vehicles. It was election day, but the political battle hardly rated a mention and every channel was carrying the blockade. It was being portrayed as the little man bloodying the big corporate bully's nose. If coal seam gas and the Fisher Valley hadn't been national news before this morning, they certainly were now. It was 6am when Steve tuned the Cherokee's radio to 2ZL so he could listen to Aaron James on the drive to Tura.

Moira Raymond hated broken sleeps, but when the phone rang early in the morning she had a sense of foreboding. Frank Beck's attitude hadn't helped when he virtually accused her of being the source of the leak that had ruined his carefully-mapped-out plan. She had been short with him and, after hanging up, knew it was pointless going back to bed. Instead, she made a cup of coffee, before phoning the Chief Commissioner who, while abrupt, promised that he'd immediately organise to despatch a squad of his finest to Tura. She knew she should phone Spencer Harbrow, but the thought of his vengeful face sent a shiver down her spine.

It was 7.45am when the alarm went off on Harbrow's clock radio and the theme music for the ABC's national news resonated around his grossly-oversized bedroom. An excited young female reporter described the scene below her as utter chaos, with more than a hundred heavy transport rigs caught between two well-organised groups of protestors protecting landowners from the coal seam gas companies. He reached for the TV remote.

His face creased in a thin smile at the pandemonium he was witnessing. Truckies were congregating in groups around fires they'd built on the road to keep warm; placard-carrying protestors at either end of the convoy were hurling abuse at them; and the sky was thick with television and news helicopters. Three police cars, with lights flashing and sirens screaming, threw up a red dust storm as they sped towards the convoy. He'd known that Moira would fail, but this was more spectacular than he had dared hope for, and the unwanted publicity she had drawn to the industry would be extremely damaging. He would have no choice but to demand her resignation. While showering, he thought about what he was going to say when he phoned his co-directors. He would be sympathetic, but would ensure that they were not left in any doubt as to where the responsibility for this fiasco lay.

Josh was tired and testy and, other than *good morning,* hardly spoke to a relieved Sandi as they sped towards Tura. By the time they reached the rear of the convoy, there were seven rows of vehicles, mainly cars, four-wheel-drives and a few pick-ups, parked nose to bumper, five across the road, with stragglers starting an eighth row. Father Michael O'Rourke was in earnest conversation with Simon Breckenridge and Don Carmody while, on the other side of the road, about twenty men and women stood around a cut-down forty-four-gallon drum which Len Forrest had converted into a makeshift barbecue. The aroma of sausages and chops wafted through the air and Maggie Forrest stood next to her husband, buttering thick slices of bread. Billy McGregor, with a can of beer in hand, was sitting on the bonnet of his hot yellow Ford, which was parked in the middle of the front row; on either side were souped-up Holdens belonging to his mates. They were shouting at an overweight truckie dressed in an undersized blue singlet and black shorts, giving him hell about the size of his gut. Josh, still angry from the bollocking he'd received from the pompous superintendent, strode over to three of the pillars of Paisley's society, with Sandi in close tow. 'What do you think you're playing at, Simon? You should know better. I want you to …'

'Calm down laddie,' the old priest interrupted. 'We're doing the Lord's work. Do you object to that?'

Josh groaned, knowing there was no way he could win an argument against Father Michael. 'You're blocking the road, Father. What if there's an emergency and someone needs to get out or an ambulance or a doctor needs to get in? Have you thought about that?'

'If that was to occur, the cars would part like the Red Sea, my boy.'

'Jeez, Josh, this is a peaceful demonstration against what would have been a violent land seizure.' Simon Breckenridge said. 'If you protected landowners, we wouldn't need to be here.'

'You can't block the roads, Simon. I want you to tell everyone to move their cars or I'm going to have to arrest them. And, while you're at it, why don't you tell them the penalties they're looking at.'

'They know they could end up behind bars, Josh. Simple fact is that they're sick of getting trampled on by the gas companies and they no longer care what happens to them. Anyhow, what makes you think they're going to listen to me? I'm not their leader.'

'Nor me,' said Don Carmody. 'I'm just a simple merchant banker and vineyard owner, here to support my neighbours.'

'That leaves me,' laughed Father Michael. 'Sadly, I think there are a lot of heathens out here, so they're hardly likely to heed anything I say.'

Jack Thomas's decision to supervise operations out of Paisley had proved enlightened, because he would have found it hard to deny that he was their leader.

Josh felt less sure of himself. 'You know you can't win.'

'Maybe not, Josh. But before this is over, all of Australia will know of our plight,' Breckenridge replied.

'Josh,' Len Forrest shouted from behind the barbecue. 'Can I get you a sausage? Hi, Sandi. What about you?'

'No thanks,' Josh yelled back and then he heard the sound of sirens in the distance. He turned to Breckenridge. 'There's backup on the way and they're not going to be as nice as me, so you better move before it's too late.'

Breckenridge looked up at the Channel Six helicopter hovering above and laughed. 'So long as the media's around, they're not going to do anything, and by tonight this place will be swarming with reporters. Why don't you go and get something to eat, because you're going to be here for a long time?'

At the front of the convoy, Frank Beck was fuming and led a small group of his best men to confront the blockaders. 'You're no better than criminals,' he shouted. 'And someone's gonna pay for vandalising those trucks. Someone could have been killed.'

'After what you've done, don't you talk to us about killing,' Charles Paxton snapped, pushing Beck in the chest.

'Get your hands off me.' Beck cocked his right fist, but there was a bloodcurdling growl and he looked down to see Cosmos, with fangs bared, at Paxton's side. 'Get that mongrel away from me.'

'You know this dog loves everyone except those who've got a rotten streak,' Paxton said, patting Cosmos. 'After what you've done, I ought to let him go.'

'Take him back behind the line, Charles,' the General urged. 'We don't want any violence.'

'Yeah, do that,' Beck said, regaining his earlier bluster. 'I warn you, little man, you're going to be moved on. So why don't you save yourself a lot of trouble and just get out of the way?'

'Why don't you piss off back to your trucks, Frank, and take your scabs with you?' Dean Prezky butted in, and half-a-dozen men fell in behind him.

'If ya know what's good for you, you'll clear out,' the General added. 'We're not looking for trouble.'

Frank Beck had been in a similar position on countless occasions and could smell a change in mob mood, and his nose told him that Prezky and his followers were spoiling for a fight. 'We'll go, but we'll be back.'

After they'd gone, the General ambled over to Tom Morgan. 'I need your help.'

'Anything you want, Mick, just name it.'

'I don't know how long we're going to be here, but we're going to need food and you're the only means we have to get in and out.'

'That won't be a problem.'

'Hold on, you haven't heard all I have to say. You'll need to bring enough for the truckies too. I'm also guessing some of them will have young families and old parents to look after and they might be desperate to get out. It'd be great if we could say that we're prepared to fly 'em out, and don't forget every truck without a driver is another obstacle in the way of *big gas*. I'm not saying that you'd need them, but you could take Charles and Cosmos along as bodyguards.'

'You're a smart man, Mick. That'll give us the high moral ground in the media and with the public. I'll take Andrew back to the stud with me and he can be our quartermaster. After this is over, I have a job for you in logistics, if you're interested.'

'Thanks but no thanks. Tom, this is going to cost you a pretty penny before it's over. Are you okay with that?'

'So long as you don't tell anyone. I'd hate to lose my reputation as a tight-fisted bastard. What are you going to say when the press asks you what it will take to remove the blockade?'

'I was going to ask for a moratorium on coal seam gas in the valley, then I thought, why not New South Wales, and that led to the whole of Australia, but I'm still undecided. Fair compensation for landowners who've already been fleeced and damages for those afflicted with ill-health. That's just for starters.'

'They'll never agree to a moratorium, even if it's only limited to the valley. The international gas companies are just too big and powerful.'

'I think you're underestimating the voice of the public, Tom.'

'I hope you're right.'

By the time Steve arrived at the start of the convoy, a dozen or so police reinforcements were trying to take control, without success. A thickset, plain-clothes policeman was on his megaphone, threatening anyone who didn't immediately remove their vehicle with a night in the lockup. Even as he was shouting, more cars, containing groups of greenies rolled in, ignoring Josh and Sandi, who'd been relegated to stopping them completing the eighth row. Billy McGregor and his mates turned their radios on full blast, drowning out the copper's voice, to rousing cheers. Father Michael positioned himself in a central spot at the rear of the vehicles and was keeping a close eye on the police. Steve wondered what they might be doing if the priest wasn't there.

At eight o'clock that night, the first results of the election flashed across television screens. They revealed an amazing comeback by Labor, which had won forty-five seats out of a possible ninety-three, with eight undecided. It would be days before a final result was known, but winning two more seats would see Nick Gould re-elected for a record-breaking sixth term.

Chapter 31

Father Michael was an inspiration. It was a bitterly cold Saturday night. He sat near one of many camp fires, railing against the coal seam gas companies. The following morning, his voice was hoarse and his face a shade of white that almost matched his hair. He had not slept for nearly forty-eight hours. The years were catching up with him and his friends and parishioners were concerned for his health.

Don Carmody had been careful not to park his car in the blocking formation, choosing instead to park where it was easily accessible. He had flown the flag, but roughing it was not for him and the thought of spending another night in near-artic conditions was too much. Besides, supporters of the cause had streamed in overnight and ten rows of vehicles now blocked access to the road. Carmody was quick to volunteer to take Father Michael back to town; despite the priest's protests, he was bundled into the front seat and they were soon on their way. As they drove, they passed two caravans coming towards them, as well as a bus and countless cars.

The General had been in constant touch, urging those whom he termed as 'defending the rear' not to resort to violence. He expressed concern about controlling the professional protestors who were joining the cause. He also told them that it wasn't the drivers' fault and that they should be offered a share of the available food.

One of the newcomers had brought a diesel generator and a television, which he set up near the central camp fire, and they could soon see themselves on the screen. When Dean Prezky's face appeared, being interviewed by a Channel Six reporter, there was shouting and applause. Dean had been designated to provide the passion, while the calm and controlled reason was provided by the General.

Then there were boos and hissing as Frank Beck's arrogant face looked out at them; he pilloried the protestors for placing his drivers' lives at risk. The pretty young reporter asked him what property they had been going to enter and why it was necessary to sneak around in the early hours of the morning. Like a good politician who hates probing questions, he ignored her and ranted on about the planks with nails in them, the fires on the road and the illegality of the blockade. The reporter wouldn't be sidetracked, though. She brought the question back to why the convoy was stealing around in the middle of the night and had it been because it was going to forcibly enter some luckless landowner's property and, if so, whose property. Beck shook his head and rolled his eyes as if she were an imbecile, saying, 'Didn't you listen to what I just said?'

Steve had folded the rear seats of the Cherokee forward and slept in a thick, padded sleeping bag in the back. While uncomfortable, it was far better than most of the protestors were enduring. He had barely five minutes with Sandi before the heavies from Sydney had her and Josh foraging for pieces of wood to build a fire, after which they were sent back to town to fetch food and drink for their superiors. Steve was annoyed that he was stuck at the rear, knowing the big stories were unfolding at the front. Two television crews, complete with trucks and caravans, had joined a dozen or so reporters and had been interviewing the likes of Simon Breckenridge and Len Forrest, and even Billy McGregor had managed to get his fifteen seconds of fame. But this was nothing compared with the television and news helicopters that were continually landing and taking off behind the front line.

Three more police cars arrived overnight and more than twenty officers milled around, but they appeared directionless. Perhaps it was because their bosses were too scared or uncertain to provide them with definitive orders while the election hung in the balance. At around midday on Sunday, two police cars were despatched five kilometres down the road, where they set up a roadblock. The police had been unable to move the protestors, but they could make sure that no more were added to their ranks. Josh and Sandi had been treated like second-class citizens by the plain-clothed police and sent back to Paisley; as the officious senior detective had said, 'To look after local matters.'

~

Most of the protestors had had no time to throw food and drink into their vehicles and had not only spent a cold night but a hungry one as well. Much to Andrew Brown's relief, he was going home and would not be back; he allowed himself a soft whistle when Tom Morgan turned on the ignition of the copter. 'When we get back, I want you to take the truck into town and load it to capacity, and then get back as fast as you can. Buy meat, bread, vegetables, soup, tea, coffee, sugar, milk, mineral water and anything else you can think of. There are a lot of hungry people here to feed. Tell Ross at the supermarket to increase the size of his orders, because we'll be taking the same every day, and, Andrew, tell him we're not paying retail prices. Hell, I nearly forget, buy all the spades and toilet rolls that he's got.'

The Sikorsky could carry twenty passengers, but Morgan had had it customised for only nine, so that he could carry more gear for the stud. This would come in useful now. 'I'll make the first drop-off to those at the rear of the convoy, before heading back behind the front line.'

'How long is this going to go on for?'

'As long as it takes,' Morgan responded grimly.

That night *Your Nation* hastily put together a program titled *Gas Wars*. It opened with aerial shots of the massive convoy of trucks and trailers locked between, what Libby Hanover described as, 'Two immovable barriers.'

Harbrow had at first been reluctant to appear but, after a little thought, saw it as a golden opportunity. He sat in front of Libby, poised, reasoned and confident.

'Mr Harbrow, do your company and its contractors normally skulk around in the middle of the night before crashing through the gates of some unsuspecting landowner?'

'Libby, your words are colourful but they do not provide an accurate portrayal of how CEGL operates. We are good corporate citizens and, while we don't like to boast about it, we are possibly the largest donor in Australia to hospitals, charities and other worthwhile causes.'

'You didn't answer my question.'

'I was coming to it.' He smiled, displaying no angst or impatience. 'And the answer is "no". I have no idea why our contractor, Filliburton, thought that it was necessary to move their equipment at night.'

'In the wee hours of the morning,' Libby corrected. 'So, are you saying that your contractor is to blame for this blockade that has captured the nation's imagination?'

'Certainly not. We have worked with Filliburton for many years and they are a company of undoubted integrity, but that is not to say that they don't have loose cannons in their midst. Today I've asked them to launch a full investigation into this matter and to provide me with answers without delay.'

'This was an operation of enormous proportions and if, as you say, there are loose cannons, they must hold very senior positions.'

'Well, we won't know that until we get the results of the investigation.'

'What if I told you that I have information that a senior executive in your own organisation sanctioned what was known as Project Genesis?'

Viewers watched as Harbrow's bottom lip dropped and his confidence appeared momentarily shaken. No-one knew that he was the one who had ensured this information was leaked to *Your Nation* just before the program went to air. 'Libby, I don't know the source of your information, but I would be very surprised if what you said is true.'

'Hypothetically speaking, what would you do if it was? Would you dismiss the person?'

'Sorry, I don't deal in hypotheticals. Our executives are professional and ethical so, with respect, I have reservations about the accuracy and source of your information.' Harbrow's face appeared serious and sincere. 'Libby, can I say that I think the coal seam gas industry has been unfairly maligned by the media over the past few days. This industry provides cheap gas and electricity to millions of consumers, along with jobs for tens of thousands, and it pays its taxes. By any measure, the industry is comprised of good corporate citizens. And further I ...'

'Thank you Mr Harbrow, but this is not a forum for policy speeches. I think your investigation will reveal that someone very close to you authorised this clandestine operation, which has virtually closed down a community. Would you like to come back on *Your Nation* when you know the results?'

'I doubt your assertions but, yes, I'd welcome that.' He was content in the knowledge that he could finally rid himself of Moira Raymond.

Dennis Fulton had been torn between joining the blockade and staying in Queensland to block any attempt that *big gas* might launch against farmers on the Spurling Downs. He determined that the immediate evil was in Tura and made his way down to Tom Morgan's stud, from where he caught a ride with him out to the front line. When he alighted from the copter, he was greeted with cheers and shouts. 'Onya, Dennis!' Leaping up on the back of a utility, he gave a rousing, morale-lifting speech.

Five days had now elapsed and the nation was entranced by the battle that raged in the red dirt, spinifex and eucalypts on the Tura *estates*. CEGL and Filliburton had point-blank refused to negotiate until, what they described as an illegal blockade, was lifted. Reporters from all over the land worked behind the lines and with the truckies, and every night human hardship stories dominated the news and current affairs programs. Steve had hitched a ride with Tom Morgan in his helicopter and was firmly entrenched behind the front line, phoning or emailing articles into Buffy every day. He was dirty, unshaven and missing Sandi terribly, but he had a reporter's gut instinct for a story and knew that something big was about to break. The *National Advocate* had their own reporters behind the lines, but was also carrying Steve's stories every day. The *Chronicle* had never been more profitable.

The stand-off entered its sixth day on Thursday and Harbrow convened an emergency meeting of directors that afternoon, but did not extend an invitation to Moira Raymond. The whinges were to be expected and Phillip Bancroft was like a broken record. 'My clients aren't happy Spencer,' he snapped. 'Christ, the stock's off another twenty percent this week. You've gotta break that blockade before it breaks us.'

'It's not good,' Harold Llewellyn muttered, thinking of the battering his superannuation was taking.

'The publicity's killing us,' Clem Aspley added. 'That little prick they call the General has the media eating out of his hand, and Tom Morgan flying the truckies out looks like Mother Teresa.'

Harbrow had resolved not to rub them up the wrong way, but couldn't help himself. 'That's your area isn't it, Clem?'

'Don't hang this on me. Every television station and newspaper in the land is siding with the landowners, and it's getting worse. There was an article in yesterday's *Wall Street Journal* titled *Big bad gas*. Phillip's right, you've gotta get rid of the blockade.'

'So, you think we should enter into a moratorium with these thugs, Clem?'

No-one spoke and, as he watched their sorry, hangdog faces, he knew they had worked out how much a moratorium would personally cost them and that it wasn't an option.

'Let's get to the business of the meeting.'

'Aren't we going to wait for Moira?' Vic Bezzina asked.

'Given that I intend to ask for her resignation after the close of this meeting, I did not extend an invitation to her.'

'What?' Sir Richard scowled. 'Why?'

'She's directly responsible for the dilemma in which we find ourselves.'

'On your instructions,' Bezzina snapped. 'I'm not happy with this.'

'Vic, that's simply not true. I asked her to get four wells drilled on the Tura *Estates* but I had no idea that she was going to launch a commando operation in the middle of the night.'

'But it was Filliburton,' Llewellyn added. 'It wasn't us. Why can't we stick *them* with it? We've got grounds for damages?'

'Didn't you watch that bitch from *Your Nation* interview me? She knows we authorised it and, if we don't give her a head, she's not going to let up on us. She wants blood.'

'I watched the interview and wondered how she found out so many details about the operation,' Clem Aspley said, as he eyed Harbrow suspiciously.

'Why can't we give the media someone else?' Sir Richard interjected.

'We can; the last thing I want to do is lose Moira. But the risk is that we don't know how much Libby Hanover knows and, if we sack a scapegoat and she already knows it was Moira ... Well,' he said extending his palms upward. 'I don't need to tell you where that'd leave us.'

'Can't we send her on a sabbatical for six months?' Bezzina asked.

'And have this thing hanging over us and the share price for that long? It's unfortunate, but she has to go,' Bancroft said.

Harbrow smiled to himself, Bancroft was so predictable.

'So, we throw her to the lions, fess up, beg for forgiveness and hope the protestors lift the blockade,' Aspley said.

Why had he ever thought that this guy, with his dyed blond hair and faded, torn jeans, was smart? 'Why would I beg for forgiveness? We have a legal right to explore those properties on the Tura *Estates* and that is exactly what I intend to do. I'll apologise for mounting a clandestine operation in the middle of the night and that's why Moira has to go.'

'What are you going to do to get the blockade removed?' Aspley asked.

'Before we move on, let's settle what we're going do about Moira,' Llewellyn said.

Harbrow looked at the long-silver-haired man with disdain. 'Harold, you mustn't have heard me. I'm not seeking the board's consent, my decision is made.'

Vic Bezzina started to say something and then thought better of it.

'The police have been mollycoddling those bloody tree huggers but now we finally have a government that's about to change.'

'There's no election result yet,' Bancroft butted in.

'Nick Gould got the barest majority and one of the independents has accepted the speaker's job,' Harbrow said confidently. 'I'll be speaking to Nick tonight and the first thing I'll tell him to do is to send the police in, in force. Let's see how those ferals feel about blockading us after a few of them have felt a baton across the back of their skulls.'

'There's been no announcement,' Bancroft persisted.

'He's right, Phillip,' Llewellyn said. 'The last absentee votes were counted this morning. Nick will claim victory on tonight's news.'

'I'm not sure the police will be successful,' Bezzina said.

'Not by themselves they won't, but, once the army gets involved, it'll all be over very quickly.'

'You can't be serious,' Aspley said.

'It's hardly like it's unprecedented. The Federal Labor Government made air force personnel and planes available to crush the Qantas pilots' strike in 1989. They will have no choice now.' Harbrow smiled smugly. 'We must look like Venezuela to the rest of the world, and international investors aren't going to keep pumping cash into the country, knowing that a group of ratbags can bring it to a standstill. There are mining companies all over Australia desperately in need of funds and, if international investors get a sniff of sovereign risk, they're dead. If it was to get totally out of hand, it might even drive housing loan interest rates up, and you can imagine the outcry if that was to occur. No government could survive that.'

'I hope this doesn't backfire,' Sir Richard said. 'And, for the record, I don't agree with dismissing Moira."

'It won't backfire, but it's not going to happen overnight,' Harbrow growled, ignoring the knight's comment about Moira. 'Once the government is involved, we'll hardly rate a mention. Harold, you'd better talk to your friends in Canberra, but it would surprise me if they weren't already looking at ways to smash this illegal blockade.'

'I will, Spencer. I also want to put on record my thanks for Moira's fine contribution to the success of this company over many years. It's a damn shame she won't be continuing with us.'

'Gentlemen, your concerns are misguided. The questions each one of you should be considering are whether you want to see the company's share price exceed its previous high and if I am the man to ensure it does.'

There was a smattering of half-hearted yesses. 'Well, do you?' Harbrow snarled.

'Of course we do,' Phillip Bancroft said. 'We have total confidence in you.'

'I hope so. Does anyone have any other matter they'd like to raise?' Harbrow said, pausing. 'No? Then I declare this meeting closed.' He felt in total control again.

'Janet, get me a macchiato, then get Moira Raymond for me and then, when I'm finished with her, Frank Beck and then Nick Gould.'

Ten minutes later, Harbrow pushed himself hard into his high-backed chair, flung his legs onto the desk and took a long sip of coffee. 'Moira, the business out in Tura is a complete debacle, we're getting terrible press and the share price is getting hammered. Moving in the middle of the night like grave robbers was an ill-thought out strategy.'

'We've done it before.'

'Quite so, but we've never been caught and that's what makes Tura different. The board is very unhappy.'

'I heard about the hastily-convened board meeting. Did you forget to tell me about it?'

'Given the circumstances, it wasn't appropriate for you to be there. Moira, I don't know how the media found out that you authorised this operation, but they did. They even know you called it Project Genesis.'

'I bet you don't.'

'We have to give them someone and, seeing they already know you were behind it, we have very little choice. I want your resignation as an executive and director of the company immediately.'

She had known from the minute she heard the convoy had been blockaded that she was living on borrowed time. 'And if I don't resign?'

'You'll be removed. There'll be locksmiths there within the hour and someone from this office will temporarily assume control in the morning. I'm sorry it had to come to this, but it will be far better for your brand if you resign and go quietly. You kick up a fuss and make it worse, and you'll never get another job in this industry. You're a wealthy woman, Moira. Take a year off, go around the world and come back in a year's time, and this fiasco will be yesterday's news.'

'I bet you're sorry! But you're right, I am wealthy and I don't need to work, so maybe I should hang around, litigate for harsh and unfair dismissal, and make your life hell.'

'I know you don't need to work, but you want to work. Without work you wouldn't know how to fill your days and, besides you're still craving a CEO's position. If you think you're going to hurt me, think again. You bring legal action against the company and I'll hand it to our lawyers and leave it totally in their hands. I won't even know what you're doing, Moira, and, as far as I'm concerned you will have ceased to exist.'

'I'll resign, but, mark my words Spencer, you'll live to regret this day.'

As he put the phone down, he was disappointed. There had been no tears, histrionics or anger and he had hoped that she might beg to save herself, but she'd been cold and businesslike, depriving him of the pleasure he'd so looked forward to.

'I have Mr Beck,' Janet said over the intercom.

'Frank, I want you to distance yourself from what's happened out there, so you need to get out just as soon as you can organise it.'

'And how am I supposed to do that? Hitch a ride with Tom Morgan?'

'Don't be bloody silly. What's to stop you walking back down the line, cutting through the bush and finishing up behind those fools at the rear of the convoy? Frank, don't make me do your thinking for you.'

'What's Moira think?'

'She's no longer with the company.'

Beck paused; at least he no longer had to worry about where his allegiance lay. 'That was sudden.'

'It's the price of failure, Frank. The good thing is that, without the blockade, the police and army would've never helped us but now they have no choice. However, I want you out before they move. I don't know if it'll get violent but, if it does, it's critical that you're not involved.'

'I understand. I'll organise for someone to pick me up tonight.'

'Good man, and, when you get back, don't do any interviews. Lie low and in a few weeks this thing will blow over and you can take up your new position with us.'

'I was as much to blame as Moira.'

'I know that but, luckily for you, the buck stopped with her. Think about that when you're sitting in her chair and make sure you never approve any half-arsed plans from your subordinates.'

'It wasn't a half ...'

'We'll talk again soon Frank.'

A few minutes later, Harbrow was saying, 'Congratulations, Nick, I always knew you could do it.'

'Is that why you left your campaign contribution so late?'

'I don't know what you're talking about. Was the cheque late? You know I don't actually do the mailing myself.'

'Yeah, yeah. What is it I can help you with, as if I don't already know?'

'Nick, we have to smash that blockade. Christ, we must look like some type of South American anarchy to international investors, and don't forget this is costing taxpayers plenty.'

'Yeah, but sending the army in is going to be unpopular with the media and the public. I've already spoken to the PM and she's not happy.'

'Our investment is going to total twenty billion and we've already got long-term supply contracts with India and China aggregating fifty billion dollars. Are you and her going to let 300 ratbags jeopardise this deal and send a message to the rest of the world that Australia's a country with a high degree of sovereign risk? Can you imagine what that'll do to interest rates?'

'I don't need a lecture in basic economics, Spencer. We were hoping that the blockade might die a natural death.'

'Well, it's not going to; those bloody fanatics are trying to shut the whole industry down.'

'No they're not, they're just trying to save the land they live on, and I can understand exactly where they're coming from.'

'You sound like you're sympathetic to their cause.'

'I am, but don't worry, I can also see the bigger picture and know that if the blockade's not lifted it'll virtually shut down investment in the industry. Don't worry, Spencer, the PM knows she has to remove the protestors and between us we will, but neither of us like what we're going to have to do.'

Chapter 32

By the fifteenth day of the blockade some of the protestors were starting to lose their enthusiasm. The nights were growing colder and they'd gone from being dirty to filthy and were on edge from lack of sleep. Their families had no wages coming in, they were missing their kids and their kids were missing them and the days were long and boring. Vicki Prezky wanted to know why Dean had to stay when there were so many other protestors manning the barricades. Nearly a third of the truckies had chosen to fly out on Tom Morgan's helicopter and Charles Paxton was returning every second day clean and refreshed. Steve Forrest was red-eyed and sporting thick, black facial growth. He was certain something big was about to break and he wanted to be there when it did. The last thing he had expected was a phone call from Dr George Bingham, and he was astonished when he wanted to talk about one of his patients.

'His name's Jake Martin, he's forty-five years old and his body's riddled with cancer. The poor bugger's got a couple of school-age kids and a huge mortgage.'

'Sounds terrible, George; but I don't understand; you never discuss patients or their problems.'

'He's a driller with Filliburton and he's had a lifetime getting drenched with wastewater.'

'Oh, now I see. Go on.'

'He put a claim in under WorkCover but Filliburton's insurers are saying that it's not work-related and he's stressing about what's going to happen to his family after he goes. I doubt he'll last more than three months.'

'That's really sad. What's the union doing?'

'Nothing! They've paid negligible attention to safety, rarely if ever visit drill sites and have been less than half-hearted in their attempts to help this poor fellow with his WorkCover claim. I think the union officials are probably on Filliburton's payroll.'

'That's a serious accusation, George, and I'd be careful where I voiced it, if I was you.'

'I'm not a fool. This man needs help and I thought, if you interviewed him and then ran his story, it might bring pressure to bear on Filliburton.'

'I gathered that and it's just the type of story I'd love to run, but I'm not sure the *Chronicle's* as influential as you think it is. Besides, I can't leave here and I've got no idea how long this blockade is going to last.'

'You're too modest Steven. You and I both know that the *National Advocate* is running all your stories from the blockade and, after they've published, the likes of Aaron James and the other talkback presenters will pick his story up and pour pressure on Filliburton. If I can get Tom Morgan to bring Jake out to see you tomorrow, will you interview him?'

'You know I will, but I can't be certain that the editors at the *Advocate* will publish what I write. George, it's bitterly cold out here at night and not something you want to put your patient through.'

'Don't worry; I'll see to it that Tom returns him as soon as the interview is over. Steven, write with your usual passion and the *Advocate* will have no choice but to publish. I'm expecting to see your article on the front page.'

'I'll be in touch, but don't get your hopes up.'

At ten o'clock that night, Frank Beck called his leading hand over. 'The bosses at head office want me to report back to them in person. They've sent an SUV, which is waiting for me on the other side of the line.'

'Are you coming back?'

'Of course, just as soon as I can,' Beck lied. As he walked down the dirt road, the fires were dying and men were climbing into the cabins of their trucks for another uncomfortable night. It was a cold, moonless night and the wind bit into his chest. He passed a group of five men with their coats buttoned up around their necks, standing around some embers, drinking cans of beer that had been flown in by Tom Morgan. Their voices were harsh and one man said that he'd had enough and he'd be on the helicopter tomorrow, while his mates warned him that, if he was, he'd never get another job in the industry.

As Beck neared the last of the trucks, he left the road and trudged through the thick bush. A few minutes later, he stopped adjacent to the protestors and saw the headlights of moving cars and listened to two men fighting about whether they should stay or not. The blockade was starting to take its toll and, as he watched, three cars reversed from their rows to let a four-wheel-drive out, which immediately took off towards town. A kilometre on the other side of the line the SUV was waiting. As he got in, he savoured the warmth from its heater.

The man Tom Morgan helped out of the helicopter was gaunt, with a sallow complexion and his hair was a stark shade of grey. Had Steve not known otherwise, he would have put him in his mid-sixties. 'Take it easy with the handshake,' the man said, extending a bony, almost skinless hand. 'I'm Jake Martin.'

'G'day, Jake. Let's get you a seat.'

For the next fifteen minutes, Jake recounted his story, from the time he first started coughing up blood to the time Dr George had made his dreadful diagnosis. Even talking for such a short time took its toll and Steve watched on, helpless, as Jake gasped for air. He was stressed about what would happen to his thirteen-year-old daughter and his mildly autistic eleven-year-old son after he was gone.

'Can I get you a cup of tea or coffee, or a bottle of water?'

'I've got no appetite and I can't taste anything. Thanks, but can we just get on with it, because I can't last long without a rest.'

'Sure, Jake. How long have you been employed by Filliburton?'

'Nearly twelve years.'

'And what happened when you put your WorkCover claim in?'

'I dropped it into one of the girls in Human Resources and she read it and asked me to wait. I saw her go into another office and talk to a guy who I later found out was the Human Resources manager. Anyhow,' Jake stopped to take a deep breath, 'this guy started flapping his hands and shaking his head and you didn't need to be a Rhodes Scholar to work out what he was saying. When the girl came back, she told me that my illness had to be work-related before I could file a claim and that there's nothing to suggest that's the case.

While all this is going on, I noticed the lump of lard who calls himself the Human Resources manager watching us, trying to listen to what's going on, so I beckoned him over.' Jake had just the trace of a grin. 'Anyhow, the weak bastard put his head down like he didn't see me. Then the girl tried to hand me back the claim form but, luckily for me, I'd read every union newsletter and I knew that once I'd lodged the claim the company had no choice but to submit it to its insurers. She went back into her boss's office and then he waddled out and told me that the insurance company will almost certainly reject my claim, so it's hardly worth submitting.'

'Did he display any compassion?'

'You're joking. He asks me to take a seat while he spoke with his director and after a few minutes, returns with a face like the cat that swallowed the canary and says that there's no point in lodging a claim as it will definitely be rejected.'

'What'd you do?'

'Like I said, I knew my rights, so I left it with them and went home.'

'And?'

'A few weeks later I got a letter from their insurers rejecting my claim, stating that my illness is not work-related and that I have sixty days to refer it to some disputes conciliation body, but I ain't got time for that. I gotta know whether my family's gonna be taken care of and I gotta know now.' Tears trickled from Jake's cavernous, black eyes.

'Did you talk to your union?'

'Yeah, they said that it'd be hard to prove my affliction was work related. They're in Filliburton's pocket and they're not about to rock the boat.'

'Have you seen a lawyer?'

'I told ya, I ain't got time.'

'When you get back to Paisley, I want you and your wife to go and see this lawyer.' Steve wrote down Simon Breckenridge's details. He reached over and put his hand on Jake's knee. 'This fight might have to go on after you have gone.'

'It's hard to come to grips with. I'm not going to get to spend another Christmas with my kids and it's because of the poison those heartless bastards have been pumping into the ground. If only I'd been told what it was and what it could do all those years ago. Do you think you can help me?'

'I'm going to try, Jake. Now, we'd best be getting you back to town.'

As the helicopter took off, Steve opened his laptop and began typing. He had been deeply moved by Jake Martin's plight and the fire burning in his brain flowed to his rapidly moving fingers, as the article he had titled *Shame* took on a life of its own. He checked it once, but made no alterations before emailing it to Buffy, instructing her to run it on the front page tomorrow. Little did he know that, the following day, it would appear on the front page of a national daily; the *Advocate* printed it unedited, except for the title, which they amended to *Shame Bloody Shame.* Talkback presenters were quick to pick up on the story and Aaron James conducted a heart-wrenching phone interview with Jake Martin, after which he and his legions of listeners unmercifully lambasted Filliburton.

The generals in Canberra had spoken against suggestions by their bosses in government to involve the army in a civil dispute and many in the Labor Party were of the same view, but the fear of Australia being tainted as a country with a high degree of sovereign risk tipped the scales. On the eighteenth day of the blockade, a police car, a black truck, and six divvy vans, accompanied by an equal number of motorbikes, sped through Tura, followed by forty army vehicles carrying cranes, forklifts and other lifting equipment. Bringing up the rear was another convoy of Filliburton trucks loaded with gravel, huts, drill rig components and light poles.

Those manning the rear of the blockade were quickly informed and Len Forrest and his mates told a reluctant and scruffy-looking Simon Breckenridge that he had to get out before the confrontation took place, because it wouldn't help anyone if he was in jail. Fifteen minutes later, Breckenridge pulled to the side of the road as a red cloud of dust and a cacophony of blaring sirens raced towards him.

As the motorbikes pulled in behind the rows of vehicles and a crowd of about a hundred protestors, a police inspector jumped out of his car and shouted into a megaphone. 'This is an illegal blockade, so I am asking you to move your vehicles immediately. If you refuse, the army is following five minutes behind and they will move them for you. I urge you to act peacefully.'

'We're staying right where we are,' Len Forrest shouted. 'And if you try and …' Before he could get another word out, two policemen flanked him and led him away to one of the vans, his protests drowned out by the yelling of his supporters.

'Leave him alone,' Billy McGregor screamed, charging at the police, only to be brought down by a baton and unceremoniously hurled into the back of a divvy van.

'We are not messing around and we intend to remove this blockade with or without your help,' the policeman on the megaphone shouted, as the first army truck came into sight. 'We will not accept any responsibility for damage done to your vehicles and this is your last chance to voluntarily move them.'

Maggie Forrest threw herself in front of the first army truck, which had to brake hard to miss her, before she was picked up and thrown into the van with her husband. Anyone who resisted was locked away and soon two of the divvy vans, with a dozen noisy protestors in the back, roared away. The police brooked no interference, were not concerned about the television cameras and were ruthlessly efficient. Some of the protestors with cars in the back row moved them. This was followed by others and soon there was a flood of people all trying to get out at the same time. The rear barricade was broken and the army cranes and tow trucks had only to move the remaining, locked cars to the side of the road.

The motorbikes then moved slowly down the right-hand side of the road past the convoy of stationary trucks, followed by the police car – in which the overbearing inspector was a passenger – and the remaining four divvy vans. Following immediately behind the last van was an army truck carrying a huge crane, and three flatbed trailers. The inspector shouted the same message into his megaphone, but this time there were over 300 protestors who already knew what had just occurred, and no-one said a word. The General had warned them that shouting or retaliating would only identify their leaders, so the police were met with stony silence. Undeterred, an army sergeant and a group of privates connected a harness to one of the two cars in the middle of the front row and the crane lifted it onto the rear-most flatbed trailer. The process was repeated, until three vehicles were loaded and the first flatbed was heading for Paisley.

'You've seen how easy this is for us,' the inspector yelled. 'I'll give you one last opportunity to move your vehicles.'

'Stuff this,' said Dean Prezky, pulling out a pair of handcuffs from the pocket of his jacket and chaining himself to the next car to be moved. Two minutes later an army private cut through the chain with boltcutters and Dean was frogmarched, hurling abuse at the police, and thrown into the back of a divvy van.

'Let him go, he's done nothing wrong,' Charles Paxton shouted; as two police strode towards him, Cosmos snarled.

'Control your dog mister or I'll put a bullet in its head,' one of the policemen said, drawing his pistol, his face masked in fear.

'Cosmos, Cosmos heel,' Paxton yelled, grabbing the dog by its collar. 'Tom, grab him and lock him in the copter.'

As Morgan dragged the growling dog away, the police seized Paxton and the protestors surged towards them. 'No violence,' the General shouted above the growing din. 'No violence.'

Another half-a-dozen vociferous protestors were manhandled into the waiting vans before Dennis Fulton yelled, 'Stand your ground. They can't lock 300 of us up.' The words had barely escaped his lips before he was manhandled by three policemen, who tried to force his arms up his back so they could handcuff him. He was surprisingly strong and aggressively resisted their attempts, while assailing them with obscenities, but in the end they dragged him, kicking and shouting, to one of the divvy vans.

Meanwhile, the army trucks continued to move down the middle of the rows of vehicles, lifting them out of the way and onto the following flatbeds. Some of the protestors, with their cars parked at the rear, moved them, but most remained steadfast. The passage that the army trucks had cleared was quickly filled with dissenters lying or sitting down. The police inspector in charge of the operation had been advised that, once the leaders and troublemakers were locked up, the remaining protestors would fall away but, if anything, they seemed more determined. Frustrated, he grabbed the megaphone and shouted, 'I warn you, do not make me use force.'

This was greeted by jeers and catcalls as the protestors filled the area from which the vehicles had been carted away. Meanwhile, the inspector barked instructions into his two-way and soon the large black police truck, followed by the Filliburton convoy, rumbled into sight; the protestors steeled themselves, many locking arms. A large tank was mounted on the body of the black truck. 'Do not make me use the water cannon,' the inspector shouted. 'I implore you, clear out of the way and make it easy for yourselves.'

This was met with more booing and defiant hand gestures, but some of the bravado of a few minutes earlier had been replaced by looks of anger and resignation. Steve Forrest stood amongst the television crews who were filming the drama unfolding in front of them, not believing that the police would actually use the water cannon.

'They're bluffing,' he said to one of the cameramen. 'He who blinks first loses.'

At the back of the crowd, Tom Morgan made his way to the helicopter, asking those nearby if they wanted to join him on the trip back to Paisley, but he was met with stony silence. They had not washed or shaved for nearly three weeks, their eyes were red from lack of sleep, but their resolve was undiminished. Morgan had not the slightest doubt that the police would use the water cannon and, when they did, the blockade would be smashed. He also knew they might impound the helicopter and possibly arrest him, and he reasoned that he could do far more to help if he remained out of jail.

'You have one minute to move,' the inspector yelled, as the ominous black truck edged to within twenty-five metres of the protestors, its cannon swivelling and focusing on its targets.

Some at the front started to pull back ever so slightly and a woman screamed, 'Hold your line. Don't move.'

'They won't fire. They can't,' Steve whispered to himself. And then the first jet of water blew the protestors who were standing, off their feet, and those lying on the ground were rolled over like tumbleweed. The black truck moved slowly through the passage, sporadically firing its cannon, while the police arrested dissenters who were throwing rocks at them.

'No violence,' the General shouted, but those who were saturated, crushed and angry continued to hurl rocks. No-one could stand against the force of the water cannon and within minutes the motorbikes and convoy were on the other side of the barricade, roaring towards Shawn Rosen's property. The protestors quickly reassembled, clambered into their vehicles and gave chase, but the damage had been done. By the time they arrived at Shawn's property, the police were manning the front gates and the trucks were being unloaded.

Television stations across the nation broke into their regular programs to show graphic close-ups of the police hurling protestors into the back of divvy vans, the army removing vehicles with their heavy equipment and the water cannon pounding all those in its way. Some presenters described it as bastardy, while others said it was un-Australian. Newsroom switchboards went into meltdown as they fielded calls from irate viewers.

Spencer Harbrow sat in his office, rubbing his hands together in glee as he watched the coverage. There were those in government who had fought to keep his convoy of trucks from following the police and army, but his plans had prevailed and, with one decisive blow, he'd opened up the Tura *estates*. He glanced at another screen with stock quotes running across the bottom; CEGL's share price was up over six percent for the day on heavy volume. The public might hate what he had done but the stockmarket loved it and that was all he cared about.

Nick Gould viewed the television footage with disgust. He'd had no choice but to send the police in, but he'd been ostracised in the media and held up to ridicule by the cartoonists in a way that he'd never experienced before. He had talked about 'the national interest' and 'protecting sovereign rights' but this had been ignored. Instead, he was attacked for siding with big business to crush the little man. He was glad this was his last term in office, as the folk hero status he had enjoyed for so long had been badly tarnished; his popularity was unlikely to ever return to the heights of his halcyon days. One small saving grace was that the PM was copping even more flak than he was and she was the subject of scorn on the nightly current affairs programs. She had had no choice, and the press drew comparisons with the great Labor PM of the mid-twentieth century, Ben Chifley, who'd sent the troops in to reopen the coal mines and crush the miners' strike, only to be destroyed at the next election.

By the time Steve Forrest reached the Rosen property, workers operating heavy machinery had started digging out the earth and tippers were dumping their loads of gravel. Trucks were being unloaded on the track to Shawn's house and access to it was completely blocked. An angry group of fifty diehard protestors, mainly Tura landowners, screamed abuse at the police, but they knew they had been defeated and that it was only a matter of time before drilling on *their* properties would begin. Steve quickly typed up an article headed *No Justice* and emailed it off to Buffy. He then hitched a ride to his car with one of the disillusioned protestors.

He had talked to Sandi many times every day, but had not seen her for over two weeks. When he barged into the apartment unannounced, she threw herself at him, hugging him and telling him how much she'd missed him, before gently pushing him away. 'Phew, you stink.' His clothes were filthy and he had a full beard, his hair was greasy and his teeth had not seen a brush since the day he had driven out of town. 'You need a shower, badly.'

'Don't go away,' he said, throwing off his shirt. 'I'll be back in five minutes, smelling like a flower.'

Although he felt sorry for the landowners, he was glad the strike was finally over. He had stressed terribly about being away from Sandi, something he'd never felt with Bianca.

The shower door opened and Sandi hopped in, a playful grin on her face. 'Can I wash your back, Sir?'

'How about something a little more personal,' he said, pulling her close to him and kissing her passionately, as the warm spray splashed over them.

'You smell so good,' she said, nestling into his chest as she gently ran her fingers up and down his hardness, barely touching, knowing that it drove him crazy.

His breathing was shallow as he dropped his hands from her breasts and manoeuvred her up against the shower wall, his hands massaging and lifting her taut bottom ever so slightly as he guided himself into her. They were soon in rhythm and then he went faster and harder as the water beat down on them, and Sandi responded, gasping, her breath intensifying. Her release was fantastic and she screamed while he simultaneously exploded inside her.

As they swayed under the hot water, she giggled, 'How good was that and why have you got that dopey smile on your face?'

'God, I missed you.'

Chapter 33

Norris Scott-Tempy had never been popular with the good folk of the Fisher Valley but, once they found out that he had aided and abetted Filliburton by letting them hide their vehicles on his property, he became the most despised man in the valley. In the aftermath, someone took to his pristine, black Rolls Silver Cloud and painted the word *scab* all over it in fluorescent, white paint.

After the demise of Moira Raymond, Donny Drayton soon found himself demoted back to being a land access consultant and Bianca, facing diminished financial prospects, was quick to cool their romance.

The cell at the Paisley police station was capable of housing six prisoners in cramped conditions if absolutely necessary, so there had been no choice but to process the paperwork on the forty-six arrested at the Tura blockade and release them back into the community. Paisley Court was overflowing with reporters and gawking spectators on Monday morning. The defendants, who in the main were represented by Simon Breckenridge, faced a total of ninety-seven charges, ranging from obstruction, which carried a $440 fine, to assaulting a police officer in the execution of his duty, for which the maximum penalty was seven years imprisonment. The magistrate, an angry, middle-aged, balding man with bifocals sitting on the end of his hawk-like nose, was no fan of *big gas* and did not record convictions against those charged with minor offences, including Charles Paxton. Instead, he ordered each of them to pay fifty-five dollars in costs and to get out of his court and make sure they were not brought up before him again.

Serious charges against twelve of the thirteen remaining defendants, including Billy McGregor, for obstruction, intimidation and assault, were adjourned for two months and they were released on their own recognisance. Dennis Fulton was the only defendant committed to appear before a District Court Judge on the serious charges of inciting a riot, assault, obscene language, offensive behaviour and resisting arrest.

Dean Prezky bounced out of court wearing his *gas man* attire and was immediately assailed by television cameramen and reporters, all looking for a twenty-second grab that would lead into the nightly news. He was soon railing against the prime minister for sending in the army to stop ordinary law-abiding citizens from protecting their properties from what he described as 'rapacious foreign investors'.

Charles Paxton looked like a defeated man as he slumped out of court supported by his good friend Tom Morgan. 'They killed Charlie and now they're going to destroy the valley, Tom, and there's not a goddamn thing we can do about it.'

'It's too early to give up, Charles,' Morgan said unconvincingly, knowing that the value of coal seam gas projects across Australia ran into the hundreds of billions of dollars and that Queensland had already been described as the Saudi Arabia of coal seam gas which, by his reckoning, made New South Wales the next Kuwait.

Steve Forrest had been in court to support his parents who, after incurring $110 in costs, were free to go without a conviction, leaving their records unblemished. As they stood on the footpath, Steve looked around him and was hit by a sense of failure. The protagonists were quiet and the bluster of the past few months seemed to have died. He knew that they would bounce back and fight again, but that they would do so aware that there was no prospect of winning. Someone suggested going to the pub, but this was met with little enthusiasm and, instead, those who had fought the good fight drifted off to their cars. They knew that in the not-too-distant future there would be thousands of gas wells sunk in the valley.

On the walk back to the *Chronicle's* offices, Steve phoned Jake Martin. The phone was answered by a softly-spoken woman who, upon hearing who was calling, sounded concerned. 'He can't talk to you, Mr Forrest.'

'Is he all right? Who am I talking to?'

'I'm Jake's wife, Helen. Look, we can't talk to you. Please don't phone again.'

'I don't understand.' Steve could hear agitated voices in the background.

'Steve,' a raspy, familiar voice said. 'We can't talk to the media and you in particular.'

'G'day, Jake. You did a deal and Filliburton made you sign a non-disclosure agreement, didn't they? They're bluffing, Jake. There's no way they'll go back on any deal they've done with you. Jeez, if that document ever got out in the public and Filliburton reneged, they'd be crucified.'

'I dunno what ya talking about. I'm tired and I've had enough of being interviewed. I just want some quiet time with my family before ...'

'Did they look after your family, Jake? I sure hope they did.'

'Sorry, Steve, I can't say anything.'

'Did they tell you that, if details of the agreement ever leaked out, they'd cancel it and your family would get nothing? I promise I won't print anything. This is off the record.'

There was a long pause and Steve could hear the dying man breathing, as he fought to take in air. 'I don't know what you're talking about.'

'Okay, have it your way. I'm sorry we had to meet in such rotten circumstances. You're a brave man. If there's anything I can do to help you or your family, don't hesitate to phone. Good-bye, Jake.'

There was an even longer pause. 'Please don't think that I'm ungrateful. Without Dr George and you, I don't know where I'd be. I can go peacefully now, knowing that my family will never want for anything. Thanks, Steve, and God bless you.'

Steve felt sad but relieved. He knew that Filliburton or its insurers must have confidentially settled with Jake Martin, while at the same time frightening the bejesus out of him and his family. It was probably a drip-feed settlement with a lump sum and then annual or monthly payments that they could terminate in the event of a breach. Whatever had been said to frighten them, had worked perfectly.

CEGL's share price put on another three percent and Spencer Harbrow basked in the congratulations of his fellow directors. The pressing urgency to remove his three dissident directors had passed and, in his mind, he forgave them for having the sheer audacity to stand up to him; he was confident it would never occur again. He had done what no-one else could have in the circumstances and had fattened their wallets once again. They had become compliant and fawning. Besides, if he retained them, he would have no need to grease Joe Biederman's greedy palm. *Serves him right*, he thought. *If he'd done what he'd been asked, he'd be twenty-five million dollars richer, but he'd been too cute by half.* Biederman might try and cause him trouble, but the ownership of the Margaret Hills tenements was hidden beneath a labyrinth of companies and trusts that would take a lifetime and millions of dollars to unravel.

Jack Thomas had wanted to convene a meeting of the Fisher Valley Protective Alliance straight after the blockade had been smashed, but then had second thoughts and postponed it. The good folks of the valley had given their all and needed time to lick their wounds and recover, before embarking on another campaign.

Thirty days after the fateful day when two Labor governments had turned on their own people and supported a foreign-owned gas company, the Paisley Town Hall was again packed. Josh Gibson, who was manning the door, felt an underlying current of anger, but it was different from the last time the Alliance had met. Then it had been aggressive anger but now it was resigned. The *estatees* had stuck together through thick and thin and had resisted the temptation to put their properties on the market, fearing that once *big gas* got a foothold, values over the whole estate would fall dramatically. Now their spirit had been broken and two properties in close proximity to Shawn Rosen's had been offered for sale at rock bottom prices; the slum lord had swooped on them, after chiselling the owners out of a few more dollars.

Jack Thomas was still as passionate and fiery as ever but, as he stood up to speak, he could sense futility and see defeat on the faces in front of him. He said a few encouraging words and passed the microphone to Dennis Fulton. The Queenslander spoke about the thousands of gas wells on the Spurling Downs and said that he and his followers were still determined to oppose and block *big gas* from entering any property without the owner's consent, and that those in the audience should do the same in the Fisher Valley. Someone muttered, 'And with all your fighting, you've still got nearly 4000 wells up there.'

Billy McGregor wanted to shout his support for the cause, but all he could think of was the seven-year jail term hanging over his head and what he'd heard happened to young males in prison.

Tom Morgan, Don Carmody and Charles Paxton were rich, powerful and, in normal circumstances, influential but, up against the might of *big gas*, their power paled into insignificance. They had decided that they would pay the legal fees of those up on serious charges and had briefed senior counsel in Sydney on their behalf. Morgan and Carmody knew that eventually they would have to share their land with *big gas* and, like the good businessmen they were, they were already thinking of ways they might mitigate the damage and the number of wells.

Charles Paxton was unshakeable. His hate for those at CEGL who had killed little Charlie and caused Gentle Lady to throw a deformed foal knew no bounds, and he resolved to defend his properties with guns if necessary.

Father Michael O'Rourke remained silent, having been severely censured by his bishop and warned not to upset large donors to the church.

The meeting never really gained momentum and, while there were those who would still fight, they would never again see the numbers that had rallied to the cause at Old Farm Road.

At the back of the hall, Steve Forrest reflected that they had failed because they had been unable to get those in the cities, who were largely unaffected, involved in the cause. In years to come, those blissfully unconcerned city dwellers would question why there were food shortages and why prices were so high, but by then it would be too late to do anything.

Epilogue

In 2011 the French Parliament banned the process of hydraulic fracturing. The gas companies claimed the decision was political and not scientific. New Jersey is considering similar legislation.

In 2012 the federal government introduced a highly-unpopular carbon tax designed, among other things, to force a reduction in the burning of coal to produce energy. CEGL and its competitors ran a huge advertising campaign, branding themselves as highly responsible corporate citizens in support of the tax and, at the same time, promoted 'clean' gas. No-one talked about the methane leakage at the well-heads, the methane loss in the compressor stations, the methane loss in the pipelines, the poisons pumped into the earth and the energy used in converting it into a liquid for shipping. The campaign bolstered the erroneous public notion that clean gas was cleaner than coal. It was little wonder that the gas companies supported the tax; there was no way the methane loss could be accurately gauged or taxed and they could pass every cent levied against them on to their domestic customers; they also received export rebates for their international shipments. Better still, their unprofitable solar panels and wind farms, erected for public relations purposes and which would never be capable of producing base load power, became profitable overnight as a result of the higher prices passed onto consumers.

A District Court judge found Dennis Fulton guilty on all charges. The prosecutor made the judge aware of Dennis's record and that he had not paid one cent of the thousands of dollars of fines that he'd chalked up over the years. When the Judge asked him if he would like to say anything before she passed sentence, Dennis unleashed a tirade of abuse on the coal seam gas companies and what they were doing to his country. He refused to obey her when she angrily demanded silence and she added contempt of court to the other charges. She said this was one penalty he would pay and then sentenced him to two years hard labour in Long Bay. His many supporters were outraged and hurled insults at the judge, who was quick to clear the court.

Many in the media hinted that the sentence had been politically influenced.

By 2016 there were more than 2000 gas wells in the Fisher Valley, with more being drilled every day. Paisley and the other townships had doubled in size and thousands of workers, enticed by the big money, flocked from all over Australia to join the gas companies. Those lucky enough to own properties in the towns saw prices explode, while their neighbours on the land suffered huge decreases in the value of their properties. Gas wells, gravel tracks and pipeline easements littered the grazing and farming properties, reducing the arable land available for primary production. Yields on milk production decreased, cattle breeding fell away, while there was an increase in stillborn and deformed calves, and thousands of hectares of grapes were trashed when the fruit, for some unknown reason, became bitter and unusable. The beauty of the valley was gone forever, with man's network of gas wells resembling a graffiti patchwork overlaying the once-beautiful masterpiece created by the world's greatest Artist.

Tourism was drying up and the three million visitors, who once visited the valley, had fallen to less than two million and numbers were continuing to decline. Wineries, restaurants and bed-and-breakfasts closed down and their owners, unable to find buyers, packed up their belongings and headed for greener pastures, often leaving more than thirty years' goodwill behind them. Despite the fall in tourist numbers, the predominantly two-lane tracks and roads were clogged – with trucks and drill rig gangs.

Courtesy of some very large donations by CEGL, Paisley Memorial Hospital had trebled in size, which was just as well, as the Valley's incidence of dermatological diseases and lung, liver and kidney cancer exceeded thirty times the national norm. The water in the aquifers had been severely depleted, and methane, formerly contained by the pressure of the water, escaped to the surface. Many of the farmers, graziers and vineyard owners who remained had installed water tanks and were buying tanker water rather than run the risk of suffering methane or chemical poisoning.

With the decline in farm yields, prices for grains, fruit, vegetables and meat exploded and many in the cities ignorantly accused their country cousins and the supermarkets of ripping them off. The ranks of Jack Thomas's Fisher Valley Protective Alliance swelled to over 20,000, as the more astute consumers in the big cities twigged to what was going on and rushed to join the firebrand's organisation.

Norris Scott-Tempy was a seriously wealthy man and was described in the influential *Australian Financial Review* as one of Australia's new breed of gas barons.

Steve and Sandi had married and had a son and daughter and, while Steve had wanted to stay in the valley, Sandi had insisted that the environment was far too dangerous to bring children up in, so they had shifted to the 'safer', smog-ridden Sydney, where Steve became a star reporter with the *National Advocate.*

Teachers from Paisley Primary School took a group of students to the koala-inhabited forest in the south of the valley, only to find that the koalas had completely vanished. There was no sign of where they had gone but the good folk of the valley had no doubts about what had driven them away.

Almost unnoticed, a large law firm from Melbourne, *Stayner & Garside,* which was famous for bringing class actions against large corporations, moved into Paisley and opened a small office. A few months later, its counterpart from Sydney also discreetly set up shop in the town.

Charles Paxton never got over the loss of little Charlie and, while he and Faye remained under the same roof, they might as well have been divorced. Her life revolved around God and the church while he withdrew from his friends and society, but was seen at all hours patrolling his properties, double-barrelled shot gun under his arm. Drilling rigs went up all over the valley, but CEGL's employees, in fear of their lives, point-blank refused to enter what they called, 'That madman's properties.' One morning, while showering, Charles felt an intense pain in his chest and knew exactly what it was. Faye was at the church and he could have tried to crawl to the phone, but he didn't. Lying hunched over on the floor in agony, with the water beating down upon him, he wasn't scared – he was happy – he would soon be with little Charlie. The last sound he ever heard was old Cosmos scraping and crying to get in at the front door.

In 2019 two young boys were fishing in a small stream, a tributary of the Blaxland River, which trickled through a property on which wheat and maize were grown. They noticed a dead kookaburra at the stream's edge and, a little further on, a magpie, but had paid little heed to the bodies. After three hours, neither had had a nibble and they were packing up their fishing gear, when a fully-grown wild boar tentatively worked its way down to the water's edge only fifty metres from them. They knelt down, barely breathing, watching it looking around, before it started to drink. After it had drunk its fill, it backed away. It appeared to stumble and then, as it tried to run, its legs went from under it and it fell to the ground, struggling to get up again. In the few seconds it took the boys to get to the edge of the stream, the boar was dead.

Fortunately, the tributary was short and environment authorities were quick to shut off access and to warn farmers along its boundaries not to drink or let their livestock drink the water from it. They soon discovered they could set the stream on fire – somehow deadly methane gas was seeping into it. Two weeks later, they tracked the cause to a gas well four hundred metres away, which had been encased by cement that turned out to be faulty. Millions of cubic feet of methane had bubbled into the stream. The boys and their parents were sworn to secrecy by the environment authorities, who did everything they could to hush up news of the seep, knowing that it would provoke panic and community outrage. There were seven properties abutting the stream and Donny Drayton was told to buy them for CEGL, no matter what price he had to pay.

The legal firms acting for the parents of some of the children who had come down with cancer, and the landowners who had been shafted by the gas companies, found that getting a judgment was nearly impossible and that, every time they got close to mounting a major class action, it fell over. CEGL, through its lawyers, *Braithwaite Ogilvie and Llewellyn*, proved adroit at buying off the strongest members of the class actions, promising others they would settle if they dropped out of the legal action and threatening the rest.

Two young lawyers, who had been particularly aggressive in persuading parents to join a class action, were having a quiet drink in the Paisley Hotel one night. When they went out to the car park, without any provocation, they were set upon and given a terrible hiding and told they weren't welcome in Paisley. The legal firms trying to bring some justice, quickly learnt that *big gas* did not fight fair.

In 2021 the Fisher Valley experienced a one-in-a-thousand-year flood. It swept away houses, barns and fences, and thousands of animals perished. Forty-seven people died and the storm wreaked billions of dollars of damage. The huge wastewater pits, some as large as five hundred acres, which had been designed to cope with more common floods, failed to contain the toxic wastewater that they were holding. Such was the magnitude of the tragedy, that the overflowing toxic wastewater hardly rated a mention in the media, but waterways became polluted and tens of thousands of lush acres of farming land would never again produce crops.

By 2025, the first of the low-pressure gas wells had outlived their economic lives and the gas companies moved back onto properties in a futile attempt to meet their environmental undertaking to return the land to the condition it was in before the wells were drilled. How could they replace the vegetation they had removed twenty years earlier? Worse, the native animals had long since died or had found new habitats. Most of the wells were easily plugged with concrete, but there were stubborn ones that refused to be blocked and the ground around them moved in waves, as the methane fought to find a way to the surface. In some instances, the methane worked its way under water bores and streams, before eventually bubbling into the atmosphere. These 'rogue' wells were nearly impossible to plug and *big gas's* solution was to attempt to bribe the landowners of the properties on which they were sunk with confidential offers to assume the company's liability to restore and reinstate.

In 2030 a small herd of twenty cattle were found dead by a water bore and, when it was analysed, it was found to contain deadly amounts of toluene and benzene. Nearly one hundred kilometres away, a herd of goats suffered the same fate and alarm bells rang in the farming community of the Fisher Valley. Not even the most experienced hydrologists had been able to determine whether the aquifers were linked, but when identical poisons were found in adjoining aquifers, fears about pollution of the Great Artesian Basin and the mighty Murray River swept through the community. The once-great food bowls on the east coast had already been severely depleted and, while environment authorities said that the traces of contaminants found in the Great Artesian Basin were within acceptable levels, no-one believed that this would remain the case. The first of the poisons that had been pumped into the ground thirty years earlier were starting to seep through the earth and sub-structures and into the precious underground water.

The Health Department was quick to stop the slaughter and sale of meat from large tracts of the valley and the already-exorbitant prices of meat soared, but not for long. Consumers, frightened by what they were reading and watching on their televisions, stopped eating meat and farmers from all over Australia suffered; many went to the wall.

Spencer Harbrow had retired as a billionaire many years earlier, but CEGL had gone from strength to strength, taking over many of its smaller competitors, to achieve an undisputed position of market leadership. The share register remained dominated by overseas institutions, which received a stream of huge dividends from the destruction of Australia's farmlands and the sale of the gas extracted from under them to China and India. Ironically, the standard of living in those countries had taken a quantum leap forward, almost in inverse proportion to those living in rural Australia.

In 2035 Steve and Sandi Forrest returned to Paisley to celebrate the full and long life of his father, Len. The old Paisley cemetery had been extended to allow for more plots but otherwise had not changed. After the burial was over, Steve stopped for a few seconds in front of the tombstone of Charlie Paxton and contemplated that bleak day over twenty years earlier and the damage that *big gas* had wreaked on his valley. He was now one of Australia's pre-eminent journalists, but he had always known that he would one day, after his children attained adulthood, return to Paisley as the owner of the *Chronicle*. With his father's passing, that time had arrived.

Dean Prezky was sixty-two and had never stopped fighting the gas companies and, while not expecting to win, he ran for the Federal Senate as an independent; against all the odds he won. His slogan, *Big Gas is a Dirty Fracking Business* captured the public's imagination and the city dwellers, the savvy sons and daughters of parents who'd gone to sleep at the wheel thirty years earlier, overwhelmingly cast their votes for him.

Although Dean knew it was too late to reverse the disastrous decisions made by earlier goverments, he was determined to ensure such mistakes were not repeated.

Acknowledgements

Many thanks to David Tenenbaum of Melbourne Books for supporting *Dirty Fracking Business* and for his creative input. My editor, Daan Spijer, made an invaluable contribution to the work through his insightful comments and finetuning the manuscript. My good friends, Paul Burn and Dave Kendall, read the manuscript prior to the completion of edit and both suggested meaningful changes that I was happy to adopt. I have already mentioned John Thomson of the Hunter Valley Protection Alliance in the Foreword but it would be remiss of me not to thank him again. John is a fine wordsmith in his own right and acted as my unofficial and unpaid editor in respect of content and how best to express it.

The Author

Peter Ralph was a CEO of a large private company that he took public in the early 90s before becoming a successful share and derivatives trader. He now spends much of his time writing and the breadth of his business career has provided him with a background and insights well suited to writing suspenseful business and topical novels. He is the author of *Collins Street Whores* and *The CEO* and co-authored *Pass the Sugar* with Joe Hachem.